I0825142

The Lustrous Dark

The Lustrous Dark

LORETTA CHEFCHAOUNI

PEACHTREE
Teen

Peachtree Teen
An imprint of Peachtree Publishing Company Inc.

Printed and bound in January 2026 at RRD, Dongguan, China.
Edited by Ashley Hearn
Book design by Lily Steele
PeachtreeBooks.com
First Edition
1 3 5 7 9 10 8 6 4 2
ISBN: 978-1-68263-837-8 (hardcover)

Library of Congress Cataloging-in-Publication Data is available.

EU Authorized Representative: HackettFlynn Ltd, 36 Cloch Choirneal, Balrothery, Co. Dublin, K32 C942, Ireland. EU@walkerpublishinggroup.com

For Zaid, being your mother is the honor of my lifetime, and for Hakim, because we are so much alike, you showed me I was always deserving of love.

Letter from the Author

The first time I read the Moroccan folktale "The Jealous Mother," I knew I wanted to use it as inspiration for a retelling. But it was during a peer discussion with my writers' group about how the fictional mothers in our books reflected, or in my case up until then *didn't reflect,* our real-life mother/daughter relationships that I discovered what angle I wanted to approach it from. Writing has always been a sort of therapy for me, a way to make something beautiful out of traumatic experiences, but with this book, I decided I was ready to explore the pain of having a parent who struggles with addiction.

While life doesn't usually give us a choice about who our family is or how they treat us, you *can* decide what you are in the right headspace to read. This story includes depictions of drug abuse, abandonment, toxic mothers, childbirth complications, human trafficking, anxiety and depression, parental death, government-sanctioned violence against civilians, and grief. Please care for yourself if these topics bring up an emotional reaction and know it is more than okay to put this book aside for however long you need to.

My greatest hope is that the magical world inside these pages will feel like someone's safe space. When you're stuck in a situation you have little control over, it can seem like the whole world has forgotten you. If you've ever felt this way, this book is for you. Because though you may have been told otherwise, you deserve a family who loves you, even if it has to be one you make for yourself. And just because you love someone, doesn't mean you have to carry the weight of their battles. One of the things I love about Shay is her capacity to look for the best in people despite having her trust betrayed time and again. Some call that weakness, but I think it's her greatest strength. Hope is the ability to imagine more.

There are people who say magic no longer exists, or that it never did. I think our imagination proves otherwise. Through fantasy and stories, we imagine a better world, and by doing so, we are empowered to make positive changes and impact the future. Tomorrow is as much a magical place as Narnia or Wonderland, or Mekchaouen.

Reader, I can't wait to see what you fill those pages with!

Love,

Loretta

1

Tidings of peace, little traveler. May your journey be sweet and filled with remembrance of the One.

—a blessing whispered into the ears of a newborn child

The woman cries out, the kind of cry that once set every muscle in Shay's body on edge. The kind she's long grown accustomed to. The guttural intonation reverberates off the smooth tadelakt walls, keeping tempo with the flicker of candle shadows. Heavy swathed curtains fail to dull its urgent tenor.

The contraction recedes. Shay dips a cloth into the wooden bowl beside her and brushes rose water across the laboring woman's sweat-slick brow. The mother-to-be sinks back into the nest of pillows stacked behind her, gathering strength.

Shay kneels by her shoulders while Ghita occupies the more intimate position, tucked between the woman's quivering thighs. The apprentice doesn't need to share the midwife's vantage point to know the infant's arrival is imminent; she feels it stirring in the air like the chant of angels, as if the gates of paradise have slipped open. Though, in fairness, the look on the woman's face would be better described as someone staring down the leagues of hell.

The next contraction hits—after no more than two beakers' rest—and she squeezes Shay's hand like a tourniquet, reopening one of her newer scabs. Shay winces. She earned the cut on her last foraging trip, the results of which are now tucked inside a small satchel at her waist. She meets eyes with Ghita, who understands the unspoken question and nods. With her free hand, Shay fishes out the potent leaves.

"Here," she murmurs, and pushes a pinch past the woman's lips, depositing it in the gap between her gums and cheek. "It's sepaweed."

The woman stops moaning long enough to begrudge Shay a smile and loosens her grip. Shay sucks the spot of blood from her forefinger, a spark of iron on her tongue.

The herb wasn't easily obtained. It grows farther beyond the umbrageous boundary of Al-Ghaba Mayita than most dare to venture, and it is encased with the most vicious of thorns. *Thorn*, *chawka* in the Old Tongue, is a variation of *Shuika*. Shay's given name literally means *little thorn*. Having resolved to never be the burden the word implies, she goes instead by the shorter sobriquet.

Aided by the sepaweed, the guest of honor soon appears. Shay is always amazed by how little newborns are, and how perfect—their alien purple-gray skin and heads shaped like bunya nuts notwithstanding. The baby's eyes are open and bright, drinking in their surroundings with quiet wonder.

Too quiet, Shay thinks, as Ghita bends to their ear with a whispered blessing. The congeries of women—sisters, khalat, friends, and neighbors—who hovered all night in patient stasis now spring to life, gathering warm towels and distributing glasses of celebratory tea.

They haven't noticed something isn't right. And why would they when Ghita's undisputed skill and intuition warrant their deepest trust?

But the mother is still and silent, her worried gaze fixed on the small being wrapped in Ghita's arms. She appears to be waiting—like Shay—for the infant to pick up the wailing chorus where she left off. To cry, to squawk, to mewl. To . . . something, anything.

Shay imagines the mother refusing to take a breath until her child does. She has a mind to confer with Ghita, but she restrains herself. No need to cause the mother undue distress. A delayed cry isn't always a sign of trouble. As the moment drags from hopeful pause to concern to alarm, Shay feels the adrenaline of being trapped in a nightmare, the kind where she can't stop falling.

She sees the moment Ghita decides to act, reads the tautening of skin around the midwife's eyes. Shay's relief is so strong, it leaves a taste like tonic in her throat.

"Everything will be fine," she whispers to the mother, though she's not sure the words penetrate the woman's shock.

Ghita places the baby on a dry sheepskin rug. She rubs garlic oil onto their chest, their tiny hands and feet. The child's limbs are loose and limp. The massage should stimulate the sluggish baby, but they show no sign of being roused. Instead, their eyes slide intractably closed.

"What is the next step?" The midwife's demanding stare traps Shay like a pinned butterfly.

Shay knows to be prepared for Ghita's quizzes. Tests like this are expected as part of her training. But this is an emergency.

Time drips like water. Every thought, every fact the apprentice has studied evaporates, her mind as dried up as her throat suddenly feels. An invisible bell tolls, *Answer, answer, answer.*

"I . . ." Shay's tongue stalls. She peers into Ghita's eyes while their steady calm is overshadowed by a disappointment that makes Shay want to disappear.

The midwife pushes past the apprentice. A choked sound rasps from the mother, harsh and dry and more haunting than any other she's made. Shay's mind clears. Ghita reaches into her bulging medical bag, and when she hands Shay a stack of clover bean leaves and shoves her toward the baby, the apprentice snaps into motion.

Turn the child's head. Clean the mucus from their nose and mouth. The commands, while issued inside her own head, are delivered in the midwife's voice. Shay uses the leaves to clear the baby's airways, then looks to Ghita.

"Push on the baby's chest." Ghita grasps Shay's hands and positions them, aligning her thumbs. "Like this."

Shay carefully follows the midwife's instructions to apply chest compressions, then blows two gentle breaths into the infant's mouth. Only when the baby releases a hearty cry does she feel the terror she's held back. She shakes, crying and smiling at once. Ghita brings the now-wailing baby to the mother's chest and declares her sex to be female.

The new mother and daughter become the rightful center of the room's attention. As women stop, offering thanks to Ghita, Shay steps into the background—mostly.

She feels the brush of eyes on her and turns to see a lone male servant across the room of female bodies, his dark gaze as welcoming as the shade of a palm tree in the Mourian Desert. He nods at Shay in admiration.

She looks down. It's not like *she* did anything. A blush, more itchy than warm, crawls between her collarbones. By the time it climbs her neck to her cheeks and she looks back up, the boy is speaking quietly with Ghita. His posture suggests he is relaying a message. When he leaves, Shay blames the inexplicable twinge in her chest on indigestion.

She busies herself attending to the afterbirth, tidying the room, and encouraging the lingering entourage to depart so the new mother and baby can rest. She looks away as the baby suckles. She pays no mind to the sounds of sweet contentment, the adoration in the new mother's eyes, pretending it doesn't tug at something in her chest, a space reserved for all the things she missed, the cycles of memories she doesn't have.

But Shay holds all those lost moments inside her like a million ghosts.

A hand lands on her shoulder, and she jumps.

Ghita studies her, every line of her rosy-brown face assessing. "Are you well?"

Shay punches her lips into a smile like she's fluffing saggy cushions ahead of arriving guests. "Of course, I'm fine, khalti."

Ghita continues to study her, long enough that her cheeks threaten to cramp under the prolonged strain of her extended lips . Long enough that she becomes certain the midwife has deciphered not only what's bothering her, but exactly why this particular day is harder for her than most. "A servant boy has brought word that Mukhtar Asim is on his way to document the birth. Why don't you take leave for the morning prayer? I hear there's a corner in the servant's gardens where apple grass grows in profusion. Pick some while you're there for the sayeda's steam bath."

It hasn't escaped Shay's notice that the mistress's home, with its lofty ceilings and expansive second floor, is fancier than most of Nezjar's residences. But a separate garden designated for servants? That's a new level of luxury. Regardless, all Nezjarian women are equal when it comes to giving birth, and those who've carried children are accorded a higher level of respect than those with dozens of rings adorning their fingers. At least, it used to be that way, but times are changing—as Ghita often laments.

Shay turns to leave. She's stopped by an urgent tap upon her shoulder and swings back to find Ghita holding out her shawl.

"Remember to keep warm," the midwife chides. "Resting season will soon be upon us."

Shay accepts the garment with a quick nod. Though Ghita's vigilance can feel excessive, it's not unwarranted. Shay has a weak constitution, and the moon pepper leaves she grinds into her daily tea are the culprit. Regardless of how many vitamins she takes to offset the side effects, she often struggles with fatigue, always suffers from some cold or an upset stomach, and is beset with slow-healing wounds that sometimes linger for weeks. But all this is a price she willingly pays to keep her true nature suppressed.

She collects her scarf and steps into the bright light of a dome-shaped chandelier, only to realize that in her eagerness to flee the cloying scene of maternal bonding, she's neglected to obtain directions to this purported garden. How will she get there? The passage is empty at this late—correction: early—time of day, with a few doors left open and more closed. Left or right, either direction ends in another hallway.

"Quite a labyrinth, isn't it?" A boy emerges from the inner shadows of a nearby door. "Can I offer my assistance, Lalla?"

Not any boy—he's the messenger who spoke with Ghita. He has earthy-brown skin, languid eyes, and dark curly hair trimmed in straight lines that make his ears stick out. His nose is long and wide, and his impossibly full lips remind Shay of rose petals, bringing her thoughts back around to thorns. She twists the scarf in her hands before remembering to answer his question.

"Yes, khoya." She clears her throat of a flutter, which annoyingly migrates to her belly. "I wish for a quiet place to perform the dawn prayer. Could you direct me to the servant's gardens?"

"I shall take you," he offers with more enthusiasm than necessary.

"Oh . . . I would hate to be a bother." Shay shakes her head with an equally excessive amount of . . . whatever the opposite of enthusiasm is.

"No bother. I'm on my way to do the same." The boy smiles, showing the small gap between his teeth. Though Shay is positive they've never met, his smile has the strangely familiar quality of a place she remembers, if only from a dream. "Follow me."

Shay returns his smile with a tight grin. It seems a moment alone to calm her nerves is too much to hope for, and if some part of her finds the idea of his company less than disagreeable, that makes him all the more frustrating. "Thank you, khoya."

The boy walks left, slowly at first before falling into pace with Shay. The clack of their wooden soles meld into a singular rhythm against the smooth marble of the gleaming floor. "My name is Shadi."

"I'm Shuika," Shay responds automatically. Her regret is immediate. She waits for the quizzical look she's come to expect.

To her surprise, he merely repeats it. "Shuika."

Her name sounds more beautiful from his lips than it has any right to. *A thorn*, indeed. After all, wasn't her first act in life that of drawing blood? She drained the last bits of her addicted mother's magic into her infant body, ensuring her own survival and her mother's untimely demise.

"Call me *Shay*," she mutters, the flutter that previously occupied her throat replaced with a jagged lump.

"Look at that!" Shadi claps his hands excitedly. "We alliterate. Why, we're practically name twins!"

"Hmm." Shay focuses on counting the number of wall lanterns between each turn. She commits them to memory so as to find her way back later—alone.

Shadi leads her downstairs, through a kitchen where women are working wrist-deep in dough and fires glow from not one but four ovens, and out a set of wooden doors into the crisp of late harvest season. They cross a wide terrace made of bright zellij tiles placed in geometric patterns and arrive at a stretch of low grass. Between fragrant shrubs and succulents that grow from clay pots and raised beds and ceramic benches thoughtfully arranged beneath the shade of wide-leafed laurels, Shay can hardly imagine how grand the sidi and sayeda's private gardens must be.

The sky holds a cobalt glow Shay would describe as the color of magic, but not the kind forbidden by Al-Mukhtar. Not a magic drawn from Snow or passed through tainted blood. Just a stroke of good fortune that comes to those who have wished for something for a very long time.

She inhales the brisk air, not yet cold enough to irritate her delicate lungs, and notices the thin shift and loose trousers that identify Shadi as a servant. Her own woolen shawl feels suddenly heavy.

"Thank you for assisting me, khoya." Shay presses her hand to her chest and dips her head. "But now that I know the way, you are free to offer your prayers indoors."

"Do you see me shiver?" Amusement tweaks Shadi's lips at the corners. "My ancestors hail from Umm Chanala, home of the eternal resting season, which basically makes me part mountain goat and immune to the most extreme temperatures. Besides, nothing is better for the spirit than praying in nature. Come, you'll see." Over his shoulder, he adds, "And call me *Shadi.*"

He disappears behind a screen of pink-flowered oleander, leaving her no choice but to follow.

Shay finds him bent over an ovular fountain made of shiny brass, washing his feet and hands. She removes her leather slippers and does the same. The cool water makes her skin pop out in goose bumps. After, she wraps her scarf over her hair and begins to untie her shawl to use as a mat. Shadi holds up a hand to stop her. From a straw basket tucked against the base of a tamarisk tree, he shakes out two soft-worn rugs and lays them facing the holy city of Kiddah.

Shadi's voice falls easily into the Old Tongue. The sacred words ring musically in Shay's ears, lulling her into a trancelike space where she's temporarily freed from life's pressures. The constant weight of earning Ghita's approval. The deeper undefined ache that permeates her existence. She finds she agrees with Shadi's sentiment; praying on the ground feels better than a floor. As though the grass and trees and even the breeze that gently tugs her skirt are joining them in worship.

She's still kneeling in supplication when the rise and fall of laughter filters through the shrubbery. The volley of chatter continues as she and Shadi fold and put away their rugs. The meaningless hum of words slide past her ears like wind until the familiar sound of her name makes her jolt.

If her name were less uncommon, she might brush it off. It's not her habit to listen in on other people's conversations. She has never been one to partake in idle gossip. And she certainly has never done anything so noteworthy as to be the subject of it.

Shay's frequent illnesses prohibit her from most social events, and her dedication to her apprenticeship leaves her little time for leisure. If her lack of friends ever bothers her, she consoles herself that it makes her damning secret easier to conceal.

Shay's curiosity tumbles toward mortification as the topic of discussion becomes clear. Someone who was at the birth is recounting to the others how the baby's outcome had teetered in the balance, the way Shay faltered in those critical moments, freezing up.

"It borders on incompetence if you ask me," the tale-teller huffs. "And as someone who plans to have a large family, I find it concerning."

"A large family?" A new voice interjects. "You can't even keep a houseplant alive."

"Rude," the original speaker grunts. "And entirely beside my point."

"Well, I feel bad for her," another voice says. "I imagine her studies are rigorous. The few times our paths have crossed, she always looks exhausted, like she's been up all night. And I heard she was orphaned as a baby. So sad."

"Also, beside the point. Now, you all know I'm not a harsh judge of character"—the first person pauses when someone snickers in response to this assertion, likely to glare at them—"but it's enough to make me seriously consider binding my own stomach and birthing my future children with my legs propped to the wall."

Shay's gut twists, heat scorching the tips of her ears. She might lack Ghita's wealth of experience, but she's not *incompetent*. It's this day that has her turned inside out. Every cycle, she thinks she's moved past this vortex of emotions, and every cycle, she's wrong.

She turns to Shadi to inquire whether the garden has some rear exit, but he's already pushing through the shrubs, oblivious to both Shay's distress and the conversation causing it. Shay has little choice but to follow him, through a cloud of cloying floral that induces a surge of nausea, and back out to the terrace.

A group of servants, previously engaged in the hanging of newly washed birth linens from a rope stretched across the tiles, stops and stares at them. Most wear guilty looks, but the face of one girl burns with something unsettlingly close to glee.

"What were the two of you doing back there?" She wiggles her eyebrows, undoubtedly fishing for a new scandal to fuel her gossip.

"We were praying . . ." Shadi supplies, confusion thick in his voice and his blank face a testament of innocence.

"Praying?" The girl scoffs. She hides her face partially behind a sheet, more suggestive than shy. "Or having a frolic in the grass?"

She turns her hungry gaze on Shay, who feels compelled to run a hand over her head, thus liberating a stray leaf from the clutches of her hair and sending it fluttering downward as if to prove the girl's point. Shay's face simmers.

"You misunderstand, Lalla. I'm the midwife's apprentice," she says, which seems to her an airtight defense. It's common knowledge that midwives seldom marry, a fact that, Shay realizes when her words fail to have their intended impact, is *beside the point*.

"I know who you are." The girl throws the sheet back into the basket on the ground and steps around it. "But perhaps you should reconsider your vocation."

"C'mon, leave her alone," another servant mutters weakly. "I told you she's an orphan."

"That's not what I heard." The girl's lips sharpen to a scythe of a smile, and she takes another step toward Shay that carries the weight of an invisible strike. She casts a wide glance like a net, ensuring she's caught the attention of the other servants. "I have it on good authority there's more to the story."

Shay shifts nervously, wrapping her arms around her torso. Stirrings of dread flutter through her. But there's no way anyone could know about the hidden parts of her identity. The girl is bluffing; Shay just can't work out her motive, other than enjoying the spectacle.

Some people are like that. They thrive off others' discomfort the way the monsters beyond Al-Ghaba Mayita feast upon the bones of the buried, the blood of the wayward traveler.

"Whose authority is that?" Shadi steps close enough to create a barrier between Shay and the other girl. "And please don't say it's your khala who barkeeps at the brewery."

"What if it is?" the girl answers him, her eyes never leaving Shay. "Everyone has a story to tell, or a secret to hide, and the offerings at Dounia's Delights have a way of loosening the stiffest of tongues."

"They also have a way of loosening minds." Shadi chuckles dismissively, and the servant finally looks at him and frowns. "I hardly think the ramblings of those who are drunk or blitzed are worth repeating. Does anyone disagree?"

He looks sternly at each of the servants in turn. One by one they go back to their work, seemingly shamed by the stark beam of his gaze. Shay has to admit she's impressed. Even more so when, after he turns to face the girl again, she, too, succumbs to his influence, giving Shay the slightest nod by way of apology and backing off.

Who is this boy who by all reason bears little authority yet wields the power of a withering glare with an effectiveness to rival Ghita's?

He takes Shay's hand. His fingers brush the raised lines of her scars before settling firmly against hers. His skin is warm, yet she shivers as if it were cold. She's unaccustomed to having strangers—or anyone for that matter—touch her so unexpectedly, but too stunned to pull away. He tugs her back through the kitchen to a small alcove that serves as a pantry and turns to her.

"Are you well?" He releases her hand, and cool air fills the now-empty space in her palm. Whatever force his stare held outside is gone, replaced with timidness. He looks at Shay like a person watching a glass tipping toward the edge of a table, about to shatter.

But Shay doesn't need someone to catch her. She needs to know what *that* was all about. How did Shadi know that whatever tale the girl had heard originated from the brewery? Shay peers deeper into his face, and perhaps her own scrutiny holds more power than she realizes because his eyes flutter open and closed. His throat flexes.

"Do you know what she was going to tell them?" Shay asks, not sure until he averts his gaze.

"I-it's nonsense," he stammers.

Unease squeezes the pit of her stomach like a fist. "Tell me, please."

"I'm not certain it's the same rumor, but I did hear something while picking up a delivery from the brewery recently. It was about the midwife." He looks down before adding, "About your mother."

Shay swallows, fear scraping her throat like broken eggshells. As far as anyone knows, her mother was a nomad. That's the story Ghita invented. The one Shay has carefully adhered to. A lie her safety—*her existence*—depends upon.

"No one knows anything about my mother," she whispers, reciting a quick blessing for the dead inside her mind. Shay herself has been able to pry only the barest facts out of Ghita over all these solar cycles. Her chest squeezes with new longing and the desperate notion that she might grasp some flash of memory, a whiff of scent, or the notes of a song her mother sang while carrying her in the womb, but her mind comes up empty, a well from which she draws only shadows.

"That's the thing. A woman who frequents the brewery has apparently claimed to *be* your mother."

The shock that grips her is so jarring, she takes a physical step back. Her shoulders clatter against the jars of preserves on the shelf behind her. *That* is not what she expected him to say. "What?"

"As I hear it, a touched one—who I think it is important to note was blitzed off her kettle at the time—told the barkeep a story, and the barkeep repeated that story to her uncle and cousins, who repeated it to more people after that. So, you can imagine, in addition to the suspect nature of the original story, there have probably been some embellishments added along the way." He speaks with such a deeply apologetic tone, it's almost as if he's confessing some grave sin he himself has committed.

"Anyway, this touched one claimed that nearly eight and ten cycles back, she gave birth, but that the midwife stole her daughter and left a puppy in her place."

"*A puppy?*" Shay asks, not sure on what basis her brain has determined that this is the part of the story that needs interrogating. She tries to think over the strange noise inside her head, like her ears are covered by trumpet shells or her brain is stuffed with poof flowers.

Of course, it's ridiculous to suggest that Ghita could be capable of such a thing. More ridiculous, as Shadi has rightly pointed out, to entertain the ramblings of someone addicted to Snow—a drug that puts women in touch with ancient magic at devastating cost to their bodies and minds. Most ridiculous of all, the touched one he's talking about can't be Shay's mother.

Snow often renders women infertile. In the rare cases where a touched one manages to conceive, it is rarer still that they carry to term. When they do, the babies are unlikely to be viable. In Shay's case, it was her mother who died so she could be born, a fact she is constantly reminded of in her line of work.

Especially today.

On the anniversary of her mother's death.

Shay's birthday.

"My mother is dead," Shay says, the words clawing out of her like a revenant from the grave. She tries to elaborate, but the details Ghita drilled into her until she sometimes forgot they were fabricated now fizzle upon her lips.

"I'm not saying I think the story was about *you*, or that it's true at all." His voice gentles, lowering until it reminds Shay of softly rustling waves. "But if there were any chance, would you *want it* to be?"

Shadi is giving her a funny look again. Despite the skepticism he voiced, she's not entirely sure he disbelieves the touched one's story. She wants to say something to convince him it's false—all of it—but she doesn't trust herself to speak. Afraid she might slip up and somehow admit that, strangely enough, her mother *was* a touched one.

The shelved walls of the pantry seem to slant closer, tightening in. The air grows thin. Shay rushes out, leaving the question he had no right asking her unanswered.

"Lalla!" Shadi strides after her. "Please, allow me to escort you."

"I can find my own way back," Shay says without turning to look at him, startled by the bitterness in her voice. "I'm sure you have more messages to deliver, *hopefully ones that are true*."

She hurries across the kitchen, not stopping when her hip knocks into a table stacked high with rounds of fresh-baked khobz. Somehow, she takes all the right turns and makes her way to the birthing room as the mukhtar is leaving it. A reedy boy accompanies him, struggling to carry the heavy book wherein records of the medina's lineage are stored.

Shay respectfully inclines her head without slowing, but the mukhtar stops her with a sharp clearing of his throat. He is not the one she remembers Ghita telling her would come, Shay realizes. Not . . . *Asim*.

No, he has the same long robes, white beard, and red cap as every mukhtar she's ever seen, but his weathered face is unfamiliar. That in itself is less than surprising. Al-Mukhtar consists of twelve leaders who periodically trade positions between the four regions of Mekchaouen—excluding the fifth region of the Mourian Desert, ruled by Hazmaggi nomads.

What's peculiar is the look he's giving Shay. Does he recognize her? She stands straighter, holding her breath. This time, the rehearsed answers to questions of her heritage form faithfully in her throat. "Labas, Sidi?"

The man blinks. He shakes his head, smiling gently. "I'm sorry, Lalla. You look very much like someone I know. Are you close to the mother?"

It takes Shay a moment to understand he's referring to the mistress of the house. "No, Sidi, I'm the midwife's apprentice."

"The midwife." His smile slackens. "Hmm. I expect I should introduce myself. I'm Mukhtar Jawad. It's been some years since I presided over Nezjar. Why, you would have been a baby yourself last time I was here."

"Welcome, Sidi." Shay inches imperceptibly toward the door. The mukhtars all make her anxious, with good reason. If anyone cared to search for her name in that massive book the young page is bowing beneath the weight of, they would find that Shuika Fulan does not officially exist. "We are most pleased to host you in our beautiful medina."

"Yes, yes. It feels good to be back." He nods a few times. "I suppose we will be seeing each other again soon enough. A healthy specimen we were graced with this day. Keep up the good work."

He shuffles off, to Shay's relief, his page scurrying behind him. Who calls a baby a *specimen*? She rests her head against the solid plane of the door, closing her eyes for a moment. Her exertion catches up with her like a wolf drooling over felled prey. The toxic herbs in her bloodstream drag against her bones.

Her hand drifts to her depleted satchel, and her heart plummets. After everything, she's forgotten to fetch Ghita's apple grass.

2

If you have irises of unmatched color,
hurry to your mother.
If your hair is light like the sun,
You'd best know how to run.
If your palms have lines that cross or your tongue splits down the middle,
If one eye wanders thither or your skin by spots is riddled,
The hunters will detect you by the signs,
They'll spill your blood, hidden treasure to find,
They'll snatch you when you least expect.
Your poor parents will never see you again.
They'll bleed you to conjure spirit guides.
Oh, hizoura children, you must hide.
Pray you get home safe,
Pray they leave you be,
Pray your death is quick,
And then you will be free.

—a schoolyard rhyme

This is Shay's favorite time of day, right before sunset, when she slips through the back of the apartment she shares with Ghita and into the narrow alley behind it. Fading light makes ripples on the blue-textured walls, giving the illusion of being submerged below the Cerabbi Sea's cool waters.

The strays hear her coming before she's fully closed the door. Shay lifts a finger to her lips in a vain attempt to deter the shuffle of paw steps, the litany of meows as cats of all shapes and sizes leak out from under bushes, within shadowed nooks, and behind pails of garbage, spilling over one another in a bid to be the first to rub against her legs.

"Salaams, Mishmish, Beesoo, Louloua." She crouches to greet a tomcat with a faded orange coat, a tabby missing half an ear, and a white female with a crooked tail, distributing an abundance of pats, strokes, and ear scritches among them. A gray cat with a small white crescent marking his forehead, whom she hadn't caught sight of in a moon quarter, head bonks her for attention. "Oh, Qamar! Good to see you're back, kbida! You had me worried."

Qamar paws the straw tote looped around her elbow. Shay withdraws a thin cloth tied in a bundle and stuffed with a mix of fish bones, chicken skins, and crusts of khobz gone stale. Ghita would be appalled to see Shay "wasting" these leftovers instead of saving them for broth or sausage. She'd further maintain that the cats are better left to fend for themselves, saying Shay is doing more harm than good by conditioning them to rely on humans, abandon their hunter instincts, and become vulnerable to people with inclinations less tender than hers.

Shay tells herself—because there's no arguing with Ghita—that the affection she gives the strays has value. It enhances their well-being rather than makes them weak. In her core, she believes being loved feeds the hunger of the soul. And every creature has a soul.

So, each night after cleaning up from dinner, she waits for Ghita to settle into her corner chair with a book in hand—typically a collection of mystic poetry or scholarly essays—lest anyone accuse her of indulging in something as unproductive as a nap. She won't awaken until Shay goes back in and brews a pot of tea, and then she will uphold the pretense that she was reading all along, an accomplishment for anyone with their eyes firmly closed.

"The offerings are slim tonight," Shay whispers. Delayed by the birth, she missed stopping at the nearest sandwich shop, the one whose kindhearted owner often sets aside a medley of meat bits and trimmings.

As she portions out the scant treats along with more snuggles, she's sure to include those who linger back. Like Lawz, a brown cat with a limp; Sukkar, an older cat who's timid and sweet; and Mushaakes, a small but energetic kitten who relentlessly wiggles to the front of the crowd only to be buffeted to the rear. Fluffy Ghaymah, black Layl, grumpy Absii—Shay has named them all.

She relaxes, soothed by the gentle rumble of purrs, the warm nap of fur between her fingers. By God's blessing, the leavings stretch, her bag running empty long after she imagined it would. She lowers herself to the cobblestones and leans against the wall. Mushaakes spares no time springing into her lap. "Aww, I love you, too. I wish I could take you to sleep in my cozy pallet with me, zine diali, but Ghita would never allow it."

It would also wreak havoc on my allergies, she doesn't say. Already she feels the familiar prickle in her nasal passages, moisture pooling in her eyes. Yet, ironically, being around animals is one of the few things that eases her discomfort in the throes of a flare.

A rainbow of fabrics flap from laundry lines strung across balconies overhead, turning Shay's thoughts to the servants from this morning, their gossip. The messenger, who she supposes was less than deserving of her rebuke.

Would you want it to be?

Her heart pangs. Despite the threat of being discovered as a hizoura—a person who inherited magical tendencies from an addicted mother—Shay can't help wishing her mother *were* alive. She sighs.

The fact is, Ghita took pity on Shay when she was as desolate as this lot of strays. The midwife gave her a home and an honest trade. *A purpose*. She offered protection, both from those who fear magic and those who would exploit it. The least Shay can do is complete her apprenticeship and make sure Ghita's investment was worthwhile. No idle chatter is going to stand in her way.

With a low *snick*, the apartment door swings open, catching Shay off guard. Ghita fills its frame, if not in height, then in presence. She's unquestionably awake, the soft shadows of dusk failing to smooth the hard set of her face. The felines clear out, fleeing to their respective crannies well before Shay blunders to her feet. They seem to sense Ghita's disapproval like a charge in the air, as clearly as the sound of thunder, the scent of danger.

Shay scrambles for a reasonable excuse, still upset with herself for forgetting the apple grass. Meanwhile, the midwife's judicious eye has already clocked the tufts of multicolored hair clinging to Shay's skirt, the tang of meat hanging over the alley, and—perhaps the most incriminating evidence—the guilt Shay suspects maps her face as clearly as a guiding star.

"I came to call you to open your birthday present," the midwife says, the last words Shay expects to hear. Current situation aside, birthdays are not something Ghita is given to acknowledging, much less celebrating. She raises a shrewd eyebrow. "Though it seems I missed my invitation to your private party."

Stunned silent, Shay watches the midwife's lips twitch into a playful smile. Even then, it takes a moment for the joke to register. She sputters a delayed laugh, or something laugh adjacent—as close as she dares in case she has misread Ghita's undertone.

Ghita turns, and Shay follows her inside, where a pot of tea is already set to brew over a hot tray lined with coal. Their small dining room has been dressed for two with dainty glasses trimmed in silver, the decorative ceramic plates normally reserved for guests, and a broad platter laden with dates and figs and an array of Shay's favorite cookies. There's triangular briouat pastries stuffed with almond paste, chebakia—thin dough-strips fried in flower shapes and sprinkled with sesame seeds, and ghriba—short cakes flavored with orange blossom and drizzled in warm honey.

Shay hastens to gather mint and sugar from the pantry when Ghita sidesteps her. "Go and sit, Lalla Shay. Please, just relax."

Relax. Shay turns the word over in her mind. She can't get a grip on how foreign it sounds uttered from the lips of someone with a severe intolerance to inactivity.

Dazed, she obeys, sitting on a chair and watching as Ghita grabs a second pot to aerate the tea. The midwife lifts the first pot high, silver twinkling from the dimples of its surface, and pours the beverage from one pot to the other. She repeats the process back and forth and back and forth between two glasses.

Finally, Ghita hands Shay a glass of amber tea topped with delicate froth and recites the first portion of the old saying: "The first glass is bitter like life."

Shay sips. The sharp flavor and the heat in her throat cut through her sense of confusion. Ghita continues preparing the tea, adding ample mint leaves and an alarming amount of sugar cubes. Meanwhile, Shay can't decide whether she's touched or suspicious.

Ghita has always provided for her needs, and Shay is grateful to enjoy a comfortable life. Not everyone in Nezjar is so lucky. No more than a few blocks from their apartment building lies a shantytown, a makeshift string of shelters hobbled together with metal slabs and loose bed linens, inhabited by displaced citizens no longer able to afford Al-Mukhtar's ever-steepening taxes.

Clothing, food, and education are things Shay has never lacked, but this—whatever this is—she stopped dreaming of back when her only toys were the pinecones she collected on foraging trips and her only entertainment, the games she invented for herself. Ghita has never been unkind, but neither has the midwife been disposed to unnecessary kindness. Shay understood early on that what most families call affection, the midwife would classify as spoiling.

By the time Ghita sits across from her, Shay has drained her first glass of tea.

"The second glass is strong, like love," Shay recites the second part of the saying as Ghita refills her glass, pouring the elixir from such a height that the steaming cascade forms an even thicker layer of foam.

She can't say with any confidence that Ghita loves her. Their bond may not go deeper than that of a teacher and her student, but it provides Shay the security of knowing her place in the world. And in a realm on the brink of rebellion, being someone's apprentice is of greater value than being someone's beloved daughter.

Or so Shay tells herself.

"You haven't eaten any cookies," Ghita scolds, before biting into a piece of chebakia shaped like an elongated rose.

Shay smiles. She likes to think of scolding as the midwife's version of endearment and her bestowal of it as proof that she does, in fact, have some capacity of fondness for Shay. "I was waiting for you, khalti."

The midwife stops chewing until Shay picks a cookie. She chooses a ghoriba, the soft fluff and fruity zest thrilling her tongue, and follows the morsel with a happy slurp of tea so sweet, her toes curl.

Ghita stares expectantly, waiting for an appropriate compliment.

"May God keep you in good health, khalti. The cookies are melting in my mouth," Shay says obligingly, though she herself helped bake the treats, which, like the special plates, rarely appear in the absence of visitors. "And the tea is zwin. Thank you so much for doing all this for me." She stops short of asking, *And by the way, why are you doing this?*

The question sits heavy in Shay's chest, disturbing the airy warmth of her sugar-induced buzz. And beneath it, like a rock she dares not overturn, squirms a tangle of fears, the top contender being that Ghita is buttering her up to deliver bad news.

Is the midwife unwell? Have rebels begun harassing her?

Did these awful rumors reach any of her clients? Has it affected their trust in her?

"Are you ready?" Ghita presents a slim box tied with a glossy ribbon. Shay's hands shake so much, she nearly drops it. She's sure this can't be the first time she's received a gift, but she fails to recall a specific occasion that confirms otherwise. "Open it."

The midwife smiles warmly, her eyes sparkling with an excitement that's contagious. Shay's worries don't ease so much as they sail out the window. Grinning, she tugs the bow, unraveling the ribbon, and whisks the lid aside to reveal the most perfect pair of new leather gloves.

She lifts them gently, inhaling a scent like burning oak, and slips her hands inside. The fleece lining kisses her skin like a delicate cloud. They feel *expensive*. Unlike the common cow hide of her slippers, this feels like skin from the underside of a sheep or a young lamb, sanded to a soft buff and waxed to a subtle sheen.

On occasion, the husbands of Ghita's clients—be they bakers, butchers, or carpenters—offer her discounts out of gratitude for her services. Many consider her family. And that is the only conclusion Shay can draw as to how the midwife afforded such a luxury.

They fit perfectly. Shay blinks back tears, her throat closing, chest aching, like she's coming down with a case of sweats, only less unpleasant. Is this what it feels like to be loved?

"They're for foraging," Ghita explains, perhaps sensing the apprentice's bewilderment. "To protect your hands from thorns. After all, a midwife needs smooth hands; they're the first touch a newborn receives coming into the world."

"Khalti." Shay stares at her hands, riddled with scabs and rough patches that even liberal amounts of Ghita's homemade argan oil haven't managed to soften. She fights the impulse to leap up and embrace the midwife. "You're going to make me cry."

"Bah," Ghita grumbles. "What good will that do but turn our tea salty?"

Shay's laughter is thick and strained. "Can't have that."

"Certainly not." The midwife winks, throws back a hefty swallow of tea, and plunks her glass on the table in front of her. "You did well last night."

"This morning." Shay shoves a date into her mouth to stop herself from speaking further. Part of her starves for the praise; another part insists it was Ghita's knowledge that saved the baby. Shay barely managed to follow directions she should have known from memory. Even the servants who were present came to that conclusion.

Incompetent.

Shay shrinks into her shoulders.

A look from Ghita alerts her to right her hunched posture, a bad habit—and a sign of sloth and subservience, according to Ghita's medical books.

"But today you are eight and ten cycles, Shuika Fulan," Ghita continues. *Fulan.* A common placeholder name assigned to people whose identity is unknown. A name for the lost, the forgotten. "It is time to stop overthinking. Stop getting in your own way. You must be more confident. That's why I've decided you will catch the next baby on your own."

Shay chokes, then guzzles tea until the half-chewed date stuck in her throat finally shuffles down. She knew this was leading to something. Her mind, so vacuous at the birth, now readily conjures a thousand scenarios to demonstrate the ways she could fail.

Shay carefully arranges the gloves back in the box and slides the lid on top, buying time to compose herself before looking at Ghita. "When is our next mother due?"

"Before the next lunar cycle." Ghita refills Shay's glass with more tea.

Two moon quarters. Barely time to prepare.

The midwife folds her hands, resting them atop the mound of her belly. "The third glass is gentle. Like death."

Shay wonders, not for the first time, if death was gentle to her mother. This is her chance to redeem herself. She already failed her mother; she cannot fail Ghita, too.

She sets her glass down and taps a nail to the side of it, considering whether she should inform Ghita of the servants' gossip. Even if no one can prove she's a hizoura, the suspicion alone could stick to her like the smell of cooking grease on clothing. She'd have to work twice as hard to prove herself to the women of her medina. But really, the rumors should be easy enough to disprove. "Khalti, another benefit the gloves will provide is a barrier against germs . . ." Shay runs her fingertip around the rim of her glass and waits until the midwife hums in agreement, hesitant of ruining her good mood. Although, by all rights, this should be a day of mourning. "Perhaps I could wear them to visit my mother's grave?"

Anytime Shay has asked to pay her respects properly, Ghita has insisted that cemeteries are breeding grounds for disease. She watches the midwife's face, hopeful this time will be different, but when Ghita's expression darkens, Shay wishes she could retract the suggestion. It's a look she's seen once before and hoped to never see again.

She was nine. Ghita allowed her to play with a girl her age, the daughter of a laboring woman. Despite Ghita's instructions not to swim in the lake behind their home, the other girl convinced Shay it was safe. She didn't know Shay couldn't swim.

They only made it waist-deep before Ghita appeared at the shoreline, screaming for Shay to get out, tromping into the shallows, heedless of her long skirts, the same fear on her face then as now. As brief as her exploit was, Shay must have swallowed some of the water as she and the other girl exchanged playful splashes. She was sick the next moon quarter with severe diarrhea.

"I'm sorry, Lalla Shay." Ghita looks down in a most un-Ghita-like fashion. "Your mother was buried in the part of the cemetery reserved for criminals. The part closest to Al-Ghaba Mayita and most vulnerable to bone-eater raids. Last I checked, her grave'd been dug up."

"You mean . . ." Shay can't speak it aloud, but she understands. There is no body, nothing left for Shay to visit. Even this small connection to her mother has been denied her. And the lack of a proper grave site won't make the gossip any easier to refute.

The midwife goes stiff and sucks in a breath all at once, another look overtaking her face, more alarming than the one it replaces. Ghita has an extra sense, though nothing significant enough to be considered illegal. At least, not yet. She says midwives, as ushers of souls, have a special connection to the spirit world. Their ability—a sort of mental alarm that sounds when a laboring woman needs assistance—is one of the few remaining echoes of women's natural magic.

Under normal circumstances, Shay would eventually develop this echo herself, but the moon pepper will likely inhibit that, too. She realizes, belatedly, that in her excitement over the surprise festivities, she didn't add her daily portion of the herb to her tea. Her stomach twists, and she practically tastes the bitter residue on her tongue. She'll double up on her next dosage. She's already tired, and there's little time.

Before the midwife jumps up and rushes to fill her bag with tools, Shay knows the situation has changed. She no longer has two moon quarters to prepare herself to be tested, because the next birth, the one that is to be her initiation into midwifery—is happening now.

3

Official Decree on Magic
Quarter Two of the Second Moon of Tending Season
Sun Cycle Five and Fifty, TOM

It is apparent through the natural decline of Shawafa that the gift of magic, hereby defined as the use of powers beyond the ordinary physical and intellectual capacity to influence the natural order of the world, has been revoked by the Creator Himself. Therefore, the use of Shawafa either induced by the mind-altering substance known as Snow or occurring in those born of hizoura blood—or accessed by any other means—is declared illegal in all four regions of Mekchaouen and beyond.

The creation, distribution, and usage of Snow and any equivalent substances is also declared illegal. Any woman or mutahawil with dormant Shawafa found guilty of engaging in such activities shall be sentenced to a minimum of five years in the dungeons or may opt to transfer their sentence to a male child or relative who will serve five years as a Moulay in service to the realm.

It must be clarified that miracles, hereby defined as extraordinary events that cannot be explained by natural laws and are thereby attributed to the divine hand, do not fall into the category of magic, but are rather to be considered proof of God's blessing and affirmation of His approval of the realm's current leadership.

THE ARM OF GOD HAS MIRACLES IN ITS FIST!

A cat's distant screech raises the fine hairs on Shay's neck as she waits before the arched blue door of the stable for someone to answer.

An unknown woman is in labor. Ghita's sense typically reveals both where her service is needed and who needs it, but this time the mother's identity was unclear. None of her current clients are due. It would be unusual for a mother to carry a pregnancy to term without seeking preventive care, and Shay fears another scenario: one where the baby has come too soon.

She shivers, her thoughts taking a darker turn. Three times in as many solar cycles, they'd been called, not to a birth, but to an empty alley, a field, a barn—to discover the still body of a newborn delivered in secrecy, compromised by drug exposure and abandoned to die. The grim findings came as a blow to the midwife, who had never lost a baby and rarely a mother.

Rarely, as in *once*. But notably, that once altered the course of Shay's life.

After a few rounds of knocking and waiting, Shay has resigned herself to seeking a different stable, when the door opens. A bleary man blinks out, the narrow hall behind him lost in a smear of shadow.

"Labas, Sidi." Shay scoops a handful of luneers from the satchel at her waist. The man's tired eyes brighten. "I require your fastest donkey."

"You have come to the right place, Lalla." The man smiles crookedly, scratching his scruffy cheek. Shay follows him down the hall, where she's immersed in the reek of animal sweat and dung, like being dunked under foul water. "But renting Jarjeer will cost a tenner."

Shay wants to rail against the price hike, but amusement wins her over. "Do you give all your donkey's names, Sidi?"

The central area is divided by rows and into stalls that hold either a sleeping donkey, a few goats, or some chickens. The man lights a lantern from the coals of a low fire burning in a corner hearth and beckons Shay toward a bigger stall, set apart from the others at the end of another short hallway.

"No, Lalla. I named this donkey, because he's special." The donkey pushes to his feet at the stable master's voice. The man tilts his lantern toward the stall. Its light limns Jarjeer's coat, revealing it as smooth and shining with health. "Jarjeer is fed only the finest hay and vegetables and has never been whipped in his life."

"But is he fast?" One look into Jarjeer's big, dewy eyes melts Shay's heart. But where most births occur within walking distance, tonight's destination lies outside the medina walls, and cuteness won't get them there in time.

"I guarantee it." The man affectionately pats Jarjeer's rump.

Shay reluctantly hands him a leather note in place of the coins. Pushing back her shoulders, she hopes for the best. "Alright, Jarjeer. I'm counting on you."

She rides the donkey home to a waiting Ghita. Together, they hook him to their small riding cart, stopping to exchange greetings with the lantern lighter as he makes his rounds. The streaming afternoon crowds of Sultan's Alley have tapered to a thin trickle with the settling of night. Jarjeer deftly swerves around sellers lugging home their carts, men and women on evening strolls, and boys sent by their mothers to grab a jar of honey, a jug of oil, or a tooth-cleaning stick from a late-night replenishments shop.

A few winding turns, and the street they're traveling is suddenly blocked by armed Moulays.

As early as one and ten cycles of age, Nezjar's boys are recruited as pages or soldiers, the latter dressed in red uniforms and given muskets twice their height to carry upon their backs. To Shay's exasperation, the roadblock forces them to seek an alternate route. They turn around, but not quickly enough to avoid seeing an older Moulay kick in someone's door.

Apprehension flashes over her. Ghita huffs, the shape of a scowl visible on her shadowed face. It's happening more frequently: citizens reporting neighbors for being members or supporters of the Citizens' Naturalist Movement, Nezjar's arm of the resistance.

These raids on private residences, always taking place under the cloak of night, used to coincide with the spread of a new sickness or the onset of a failing crop, a sure symptom of insurrection. Once the rebels were rooted out, the problem quickly disappeared. But there have been no such crises in recent times. To Shay's memory, even the weather has remained consistently fair. Loyalty, it seems, protects the realm from ill fortune.

But several moons ago, Al-Mukhtar ruled that any citizen who reports a rebel will be relieved of their next round of quarterly taxes. A preventative measure, according to the decree posted in the square and marked with an official seal. Tonight's raid means that tomorrow there will be a hanging in the same square. A practice Ghita, too outspoken for her own good, is unafraid to label as true evil.

Shay agrees, if more quietly. She has as much to fear from the CNM as she does from Al-Mukhtar. If the latter deem her suppressed magic a legal offense, the rebels' view is no kinder. They accuse Al-Mukhtar of employing touched ones for magical favors and believe Snow and all other forms of magic must be eradicated along with the current leadership.

Shay understands how their ideology appeals to those who have lost sisters or daughters to addiction, but it's not her fault she was born with tainted blood. So extreme is their zeal that if they ever gained power, even those with small echoes of magic like Ghita would be in jeopardy. She isn't sure what eradication looks like in practice, but it sure sounds like something that involves killing off a whole lot of people.

She's heard the tales of children disappearing, of course. They're the biggest reason Ghita began administering the moon pepper to Shay when she was so young. Though, in most of those cases, the culprits aren't rebels, but rather treasure hunters or practitioners of witchcraft. Men and women who steal the children off to the desert, believing the magic in their blood will aid their search for buried riches. And the children—who are later found dead, if at all—are often not even true hizouras. Just normal children bearing some unfortunate physical feature that makes them a target of the uneducated.

To bypass the congested detour, Ghita rings a large bell at the head of the cart, identifying herself as a health practitioner. True to the groom's words, Jarjeer carries them swiftly to the medina's outer walls. The midwife recites a blessing under her breath as they pass the soaring minaret of the worship house, where up until a few solar cycles back, citizens gathered quarterly for congregational prayer. The callers' melodious invocations once echoed daily, reaching every corner of the medina.

That was before Al-Mukhtar commandeered the building to house Moulays in training, the best of whom will become mukhtars themselves. Ghita said she fears their next step will be taking away people's right to pray in their own homes. Shay used to doubt this could happen, back when she believed

Al-Mukhtar's powers to be proof of God's anointing. But what if the CNM's accusations are true?

What if Al-Mukhtar really are employing touched ones?

Jarjeer clears the gates. A sudden expanse of land opens before them, spurring the donkey to an even faster pace. Its speed rivals that of a horse. To Shay's relief, their gravel path veers away from the looming silhouette of Al-Ghaba Mayita, a place where trees shoot from the earth like a mouth overcrowded with teeth, every one of them a canine. Even after hundreds of foraging trips, she breathes easier when its hulking border is put well behind her.

A smoke pillar rises over an open field to the west, likely a campfire of the Hazmaggi tribe she pretends to descend from, perhaps making their way to Lahat to visit the Cerabbi Sea while the weather is at its most pleasant. Chants and ululations carry across the hills. A switchback leads the cart through groves of stocky fig and olive trees.

They're passing a rocky pasture dotted with sheep when Shay spots the farmhouse, kindling her anxiety. Will Ghita insist she deliver the baby even if there are complications? Or will she decide the apprentice isn't ready? Shay isn't sure which option unsettles her more.

Stepping from the cart, she's taken aback by a thick earthy scent. It's not unusual for the country air to smell fresh and sweet, but this is more cloying. Something lush and wild and not entirely pleasant. The donkey brays. Shay slips him a small carrot and pats his nose while Ghita unloads the cart. "Good job, boy."

She helps Ghita carry her bags, raising a lantern in her free hand and absorbing the building's miserable state. Vines smother the rough walls. Rogue tree branches jut through cracks in the roof and the missing panes of broken windows. A cry, at once human and not, erupts from inside, starting as a deep bellow that rises to a scream.

Ghita quickens her steps, making Shay jog to keep up. At their approach, the front door flings wide. An old woman runs out, swatting a few insects that buzz around her head. Jagged scratches run the length of both her arms.

Her torn dress hangs loose off one shoulder. She glances back at the building fearfully before she notices Shay and Ghita.

"God is great," the woman shouts, barreling toward them. "Help has arrived."

"Are you well, Sayeda?" Ghita drops her bags and reaches toward the distressed woman.

"Don't worry about me." The woman shakes her head, not bothering to wipe her tearstained cheeks. "There's no time. You must save my niece's baby."

"Of course." Ghita peers nervously at the farmhouse. Through the lens of moonlight, dense moss in colors of mold seems to slither across its stones. "Go rest on the donkey's cart and wait. We'll return and assist you shortly, God willing."

The potent, overripe scent intensifies as Shay and Ghita pass through the door and search the dim room for the pregnant mother. Finding her, Shay releases her own startled scream.

The woman stands on a table, arms raised. Tendrils of green smoke swirl from her glowing fingertips. A wide bloodstain spreads like a red sash across her dress. Her feet are bare, more blood puddled around them. Her face bears so many wrinkles, its other features blend together. Her skin tinges gray to green. Her eyes run milky white, voiding her pupils, the hollows around them pitted black, like kohl smeared by weeping.

A touched one? This makes the situation profoundly worse. There's simply no possible good outcome. The baby is unlikely to survive, and if it does, it will be at the mother's expense, either case casting a black mark on Shay's reputation.

The woman moans harshly. Her gaze darts about, unseeing, as though she's lost in some hallucination. There's a muffled cry across the room, where an argan tree—*an actual full-size tree*—grows right through the floor and sprawls like a greedy guest trying to finger every object within reach.

In fact, the whole room is overrun with plants and bushes of all varieties. They hang long and loose from the ceiling and spill in waves out of cabinets. High in the leafy folds of the tree, Shay spots the source of the cry and gasps. She slaps a hand to her mouth.

Covered in creamy film, the newborn Shay was meant to deliver lies curled inside a large, round nest. A nest surrounded by branches hung with thorns. Thorns the size of butcher knives. And just above the baby, a floppy purple flower with yellow flecks dangles like a canopy. Shay doesn't recognize the flower, not from the fields around Nezjar, not from the bowels of Al-Ghaba Mayita, and not from any of Ghita's books.

She doesn't move. Her shock is too heady. Then the yellow flecks on the petals begin to vibrate. A low buzz reaches her ears, a sound so out of place in the shade of night that it takes Shay a beat longer than it should to place it.

"Bees!" she shouts in abject horror. "Devil be damned. The baby's surrounded by bees!"

The second she steps toward the tree, the touched one swings around with sudden focus. She thrusts one arm in Shay's direction, smoke pulsing in green flashes from her fingertips. The room shudders. The floor ripples, tiles splitting. A giant root shoots up. It whips around, and before Shay can react, it belts her in the stomach. She stumbles into the wall.

"The baby will die," the feral woman screeches. She leans forward and balls her fists, the table shaking beneath her. A glass frame clatters off the wall and breaks.

"Why, Sayeda?" Ghita sets down her bags and raises her palms beseechingly. "Is something wrong with the baby?"

The woman frowns. For a moment, she looks uncertain. "The moon tells me things. It says my baby is a monster."

"Sayeda." Ghita takes a hesitant step toward the woman. "Your baby is beautiful. You should be proud. Please, let us help."

Shay painfully pulls herself upright, ready to jump to Ghita's aid if it's required.

"Stop right there," the touched one warns, and Ghita freezes. "The moon is my friend. It wouldn't lie. I must kill the little monster."

She thrusts both hands out, and the tree shakes violently. The swinging thorns slice the air around the nest, barely missing the infant tucked inside. The buzzing pitches louder. The baby kicks into crying, every high, spasmodic sob twisting Shay's chest tighter. And tighter.

Suddenly, the woman bends over and grips her middle, her already more haunted than human face contorting further. The shaking stops. The baby's wails settle into a string of low whimpers. Shay breathes a sigh of partial relief, still fighting her urge to run to the helpless infant.

"Sayeda." Ghita moves forward again with careful steps. "You're hemorrhaging, you must let me help you." She convinces the woman to lie on the table and allow her to massage her stomach before turning back to Shay. "Bring me clover bean leaves to measure the sayeda's blood output."

As Shay passes Ghita the leaves, the midwife gives her a pointed look.

"Have you noticed the variety of plants growing around us, Lalla Shay? It's quite spectacular. There's even a patch of sepaweed by the back wall. Won't you fetch a pinch for me? To ease the sayeda's pains?"

Shay dons her gloves, almost missing the midwife's quick wink. She picks her way across the room through the rampant growth.

"Watch out for tater sponges," Ghita calls.

Shay pauses, reevaluating her path, and proceeds with new caution. She learned her lesson about tater sponges at the age of ten and two. While foraging in the early afternoon, she unwittingly stepped on one of the seeds and was rendered unconscious by its toxic fumes. It was to the pitch of night that she awoke, and while Al-Ghaba Mayita is best avoided altogether, this is even truer after dark.

Shay locates the sepaweed, and carefully avoiding its thorns, she harvests the potent leaves. She turns back and spots one of the poisoned pods in her path. It looks innocuous enough, like a small potato with a thin and crunchy outer shell. Only when crushed underfoot will it release its incapacitating cloud.

Understanding washes over her. If one person had need to incapacitate another, the tater sponge could ostensibly be made to release its toxins not so accidentally. Shay stores the sepaweed in her satchel. She bends down, gingerly nudges the seed pod into the cup of her hand, and proceeds with featherlight steps. Her heart beats so hard, she fears the vibration alone may cause the seed to burst.

The touched one has returned to a trancelike state, but Shay has no doubt she'd snap out of it if either woman advanced toward her baby.

"I brought you the sepaweed, Sayeda." Shay's nerves spark like struck flint. She notes the clover bean leaves held in each of Ghita's hands, and despite adrenaline tunneling her focus to a pinpoint, she has the presence to wonder at the midwife's cleverness. Sometimes called *puppy ears* for their softness, the leaves' tight-knit fibers make them perfect for filtering small airborne particles.

Shay breathes in deeply. She positions her fist with the seed held inside near the touched one's face and squeezes, dispersing a black cloud. On the touched one's next inhale, her whitened eyes widen. She quickly caps her nose and mouth, but it's too late. Ghita presses one clover bean leaf over her mouth and hands the other to Shay. The barrier will help only so much. They must hold their breath as long as possible.

"What did you . . . ?" The touched one attempts to push herself upright. She struggles to lift one arm, succeeding only in stretching her fingers. Their tips bleed green smoke. The skin of her palm bulges. A small stick flies from the woman's hand and zips toward Shay's head.

She ducks. Sharp pain bites into her shoulder blade. She waits for an onslaught to follow. When it fails to, she straightens.

The light in the touched one's fingers is dying out. Her eyes roll back in her head, and she slumps to the table, limp.

"Hold still, child," Ghita mumbles through the leaf. The apprentice winces as the midwife removes a thorny spike that she then shows Shay. It's equal in length to Ghita's longest finger.

The baby fusses, drawing both women's attention to the nest. Shay squints through the black haze at the tree. Its writhing branches have calmed. Fat bees crawl lazily around the flower petals. The midwife tries to speak, but she wobbles on her feet.

Shay quickly shepherds Ghita to the front door and guides her through. She sticks her own head far enough out to gulp a lungful of fresh air.

"Wait here," she tells the midwife. "I'll go back for the baby."

"Are you sure?" Ghita coughs. Even as she clears toxins from her throat, concern etches creases onto her face. "The effects of the tater sponge may not last. If the Snow in the touched one's system counteracts it, she could awaken sooner than expected."

"I'll be fast." Shay leaves Ghita no chance to argue. She fills her lungs once more and plunges back inside. Shielding her nose and mouth with the leaf, she stumbles over rife foliage and mows her way to the tree. Her joints will suffer later, but she can't think of that now. She hugs the thick trunk and monkeys her way up as fast as she can with only one arm at her disposal.

At the tree's crest, she stretches her body across the long branch that holds the nest. The baby coos in a contented state of half sleep, all wiggly toes and dimpled arms. Praises to God, the toxic spores haven't floated up this close to the ceiling. Shay steadies her balance and reaches into the nest.

An angry buzz. A bee swoops down and lands on her gloved hand.

Shay halts, a stop so sudden and complete, her bones feel fused.

At this vantage point, what hangs behind the flower is exposed: a hive that doesn't belong to any ordinary bee. It's dented by two hollow sockets, the skull-like shape both fearsome and unmistakable. *Of course.* Unlike most common bees, ghost bees are nocturnal. And a single sting can prove fatal—even to someone not in the habit of regularly ingesting toxic leaves.

"Hello there, little friend," she whispers, willing her heart to settle lest her shaking hand provoke the insect. "I mean you no harm. I only wish to take the baby, and then I promise to leave without disturbing your hive or harming your colony."

While talking to a bee is not the most realistic strategy, Shay doesn't know what else to do. She waits for burning pain to pierce the leather of her glove, spreading numbness up her arm and through her body. Before she can shimmy back down the tree, she'll be completely paralyzed. Cold sweat seeps across her hairline.

The bee walks in a small, agonizing circle before it takes off and returns to the hive. Shay waits a bit longer, fearful the insect is simply seeking reinforcements. Once she's convinced she's been spared the wrath of a murderous bee army, she scoops the child to her chest.

A boy. One who looks quite healthy despite the drugs he's been exposed to. A true miracle.

He blinks at Shay and roots hungrily at the cotton of her dress. Cradling him close, she makes the nonsensical sounds people make when soothing restless babies. Though most of the black particles have dissipated, she continues taking shallow, sparing breaths until she clears the farmhouse. She pauses outside the door with a glance back at the kitchen table. The touched one remains there, still held dormant by the effects of the tater sponge. For now.

In the yard, Shay finds Ghita crouched over the body of the khala who was so frantic when they arrived. The midwife is softly reciting passages from the old scripture, while the khala, no longer frantic, lies still amid the grass, seemingly napping. Ghita looks up, her eyes damp and sorrowful, only smiling when she notices the baby. "Oh, thank our merciful God. The child is well."

Ghita stands, while the other woman remains unmoving on the ground. Even with the khala's eyes glazed in a vacant stare, it takes a stunned moment for Shay to register the absence of her breathing. "What happened?"

"She was stung by ghost bees." Ghita wraps her arms around herself and scans the quiet countryside as though fearing more of the dangerous insects will appear.

Shay looks closer at the dead woman, inspecting the multiple red welts that pattern her face and neck. She shudders, but quickly reins in her horror. It's not the worst death she's borne witness to. "Surely from God we come, and to Him we shall return."

The words bring her comfort, but . . . Shay can't help feeling guilty that the bee refrained from stinging *her*. The question is, why?

"Ameen." Ghita bends and strokes her fingers down the woman's eyelids to close them. "I hate to leave the body, but we must get away while we can."

"What will we do with the baby?" Shay wonders aloud, jiggling the fussing infant in her arms. Staring down at him, she scans the pink newness of his skin for some visible mark of the magic that must have saved him. By all odds, he should not have lived.

A loud crunch brings their focus back to the dead woman. Shay's stomach goes rubbery as the corpse withers before her eyes.

Her skin shrivels, hair and fingernails falling away, her insides melting with a sound like bubbling stew. Soon, nothing more than a desiccated mummy remains. Thin lines of honey dribble from her dried-up mouth and empty eye sockets.

Glory to heaven. The sheer number of stings must have intensified her body's reaction to the venom. It's still not the most gruesome death Shay has had the misfortune of seeing, although it ranks closer now.

"We'll worry about that later," Ghita says, answering the question Shay forgot she had asked. The midwife steers the apprentice by her elbow toward the waiting donkey. "Hurry now, Lalla Shay."

They've barely taken a seat when the silhouette of the touched one pops into the farmhouse's doorframe. Swaying unsteadily, she leans her forearm on the wooden jamb. "What are you doing? You fools! Don't you see that the baby has to die? Give it back to me this instant!"

"Calm down, Sayeda!" Ghita shouts from the cart. "The baby is already dead. We only wish to give the child a proper burial."

Shay tugs the baby closer. She gives him the pad of her finger to suckle, lest his cries disprove Ghita's words.

The touched one's age is difficult to place. There's something youthful in her voice, in how she carries herself. While her sagging skin and wiry hair, the bend of her body under its weight, suggest a woman advancing in age, and not gracefully. Yet she not only survived the rigor of childbirth, but she has strength enough left to stand there, issuing her bloody demands. Shay cannot understand it.

"Dead? Are you sure?" The woman wobbles her head and pauses. She looks back at Ghita, her white eyes gleaming with deadly intention. "The moon says you're a liar, khalti."

The touched one's fingertips kindle green.

Shay clucks her tongue twice. "Go, Jarjeer. Faster than you've ever gone."

The cart jolts forward. Shay shoots a backward glance at the touched one. She looks as thin as the moonlight surrounding her, her glowing hands thrown toward the sky.

4

The truest lover is a friend.

The truest gift is trust.

The truest misfortune is false belief.

The truest leader is a seeker.

—the poet Rimkin

Jarjeer rockets down the path, hooves clacking, gravel popping. The ride starts smooth, but soon the ground rumbles. Quakes cant the cart side to side in steepening arcs. Shay's stomach sloshes. More rumbling. A louder sound, like fabric ripping.

She peers fearfully over the side rail, feeling the prickle of cool night air against her cheeks. Vines as thick as snakes shoot from the ground and curl like hooks around the spokes of the wheels, thwarting their spin. Shay looks back to the farmhouse.

The touched one has moved from the door to the lawn. She reaches after them with outstretched arms, fingers a distant firefly glow. The earth hums with malice.

The mother shouldn't be able to access her Shawafa. The baby should have siphoned it. There's no other way to explain his survival. Glory to heaven, how much Snow did the woman take?

The midwife digs into her bag and hands Shay the one tool the apprentice has never seen put to use. The knife—carried in case a mother passes and the baby requires emergency delivery—summons a visceral chill, but it's the sharpest instrument they have.

Shay carefully trades the baby off to Ghita. She hangs precariously over the cart as it bumps up and down, lurching forward in bursts. Despite her valiant hacking, three new vines sprout up for every one she chops down. Sweat puddles at the small of her back, gluing her tunic to her skin.

The donkey stumbles as a vine climbs up his leg. The animal bucks free, dipping their bodies low enough to sniff the leafy grass and nearly overturning them. Shay clings to the railing until the cart rights itself.

She stretches forward and caresses Jarjeer's back. "Please, Jarjeer, you must run harder."

At her words, the animal takes off again, building to an impossible speed that blows Shay's hair to tangles. Jarjeer flies them away from the farmhouse, away from the touched one. Away from the reach of the magic she impossibly continues to wield. Only once they safely clear the gates of their medina does the animal slow to a soothing clomp. Shay and Ghita are shell-shocked, unable to utter a single word between them.

Back at their apartment, Shay waters Jarjeer before walking him back to the stables. She wonders how anything, even the influence of a powerful drug, could warp a mother's natural instinct to the point that she'd attempt to murder her child. Would her own mother have turned on her the same way if she had lived? This thought, held to the light of the worrisome rumors, hints to something Shay's loyalty to Ghita won't allow her to probe.

Although they weren't paid for tonight's birth, Shay dishes out extra coin to the stable master in compensation for the limp the bewitched vines inflicted on poor Jarjeer. She then borrows a pail of milk from the lactating goat of a neighbor who regularly borrows tomatoes from their rooftop garden. Shay hopes her foresight will please Ghita, never imagining she'll find the midwife seated by the hearth, sleeping robe draped open, with the baby happily latched upon her swollen breast.

Shay gasps. "Are you with milk, khalti?"

"Oh yes." Ghita blinks at her sleepily. "It's another echo passed to midwives for the unlucky cases when a baby is rendered an orphan. Surely you remember this information from your studies of maternal mortality."

She doesn't phrase it as a question, causing Shay to doubt her own surprise. Such an important fact would not be easily forgotten, but this is their first time caring for an endangered infant.

Shay removes her leather slippers, opting to leave off her bamboo house shoes in preference of the bare feel of clay flooring under her feet. She makes her way around the uneven and loose tiles she knows by heart, unhooks a latch in the floor, and stores the goat milk inside a small cellar space to keep it cool.

But . . . Ghita called the child an *orphan*, which isn't exactly correct.

His mother seemed very much alive when they departed. Shay almost asks if the midwife also nursed her, but thinks better of it. It doesn't really matter whether she did or didn't. Shay isn't her daughter either way. She's only an apprentice. And thankful, of course, to be provided such an opportunity.

"Can I get you anything, khalti?"

"Yes, Lalla Shay, thank you," Ghita murmurs, gently rocking the baby, his eyes drifting contentedly closed. "Some tea would be wonderful. Add a bit of morning thistle. It will aid the flow of milk."

Shay sets a pot to boil and grabs first the jar of morning thistle and then the moon pepper she forgot to take earlier. She sniffs the nearly empty jar, the bitter scent almost comforting in its familiarity, and for the briefest moment, she wonders what would happen if she stopped taking it.

Not how it would feel to access magic, but how it would feel if the poison holding her body in its grip were to loosen its hateful fingers. If she no longer existed on the brink of exhaustion.

If she were *well.*

Dismissing such foolish thoughts, she shakes the last of the leaves into her glass, enough to make up for the dose she missed. She drafts a mental reminder to forage more tomorrow.

"How did the baby survive?" Shay asks Ghita. For reasons she can't explain, it suddenly seems important she understand the answer.

"It's rare, but not unheard of," Ghita answers distractedly. "You're proof of that."

While that is true, it's not the same. Her throat tightens. "But my mother . . ."

"Touched ones don't usually give birth to boys. Did you know that?" Ghita says more decisively, then continues without waiting for a response. "I bet that has something to do with it."

It seems a very loose correlation. It would make more sense to Shay that the mother may yet be in danger once the drugs clear her system and she inevitably crashes. "Are you sure she'll be well? The mother?"

"Not as long as she keeps using." With a tired sigh, Ghita carries the sleeping baby to a basket lined with sheepskin, a makeshift bassinet. "But her bleeding was under control when we left her."

They sit by the hearth, cotton-weave blankets snugged over their laps, knees tipped close together, not quite touching. Most times, the apprentice cherishes such moments, the calm quiet between them an approximation to tenderness. But tonight her mind is neither calm nor quiet. Shay doesn't understand how Ghita can be so cavalier about all this.

Shay sips her tea, the sugar and mint unable to mask the sour tang of the moon pepper on her tongue. "What kind of Shawafa did she have?"

Every woman has one, a unique magical gift buried deep inside, almost beyond reach. There was a time, known as the Time of Women, when Shawafa was considered as natural as any other aspect of life. But now is the Time of Miracles. Or, as Shay secretly thinks of it, the Time of Men, for there are noticeably no female rulers. Of course, nothing in any history book Shay has read suggests there ever were, but sometimes she thinks, with all that power, there must have been.

Nowadays, only Snow activates women's Shawafa, and it does so temporarily. The classification of magic types isn't readily available information, but Shay has gathered some details from secondhand accounts, whispers of the ancient magic it awakened, the cycles it stole away. If the moon pepper that suppresses magic is a poison, then the Snow that awakens it is a plague.

"Hadiqmin." Ghita peers at the steam rising from her glass as if she might scry the future in its unfurling tendrils.

"The ability to control plants?"

Ghita nods. "Quite amazing when you think about it."

The overgrown farmhouse surfaces in Shay's mind, the remembered smell of overripe vegetation. She hears the frantic buzz of ghost bees, the bubbling flesh of a stranger's corpse—impressions sure to darken her dreams tonight and for many nights to come.

"Should we . . . ?" Shay shifts nervously in her seat. She swallows hard. Unlike harmless echoes, Shawafa is the illegal form of magic. If they report the incident, the mother could be arrested. Whereas, if they don't tell, perhaps the baby could be returned when it's safer. Maybe they could help the mother purge from Snow. "Should we do something?"

"Us?" Ghita shakes her head and chuckles dryly. "Every passing day sees more touched ones on the street. It's become an epidemic. Meanwhile, our esteemed leaders are preoccupied with taxes and rebels. Unfortunately, if they keep ignoring the problem, I see it only getting worse."

Which problem? The spread of addiction? Or the children being born to addicts? Before tonight, Shay didn't think the latter was possible, not without the resulting death of either the mother or the child. "Then what *will* we do with the baby?"

"I suppose I'll care for him."

The same way she cared for Shay? But . . . the child's mother is still alive. That makes it more complicated. The things the messenger told her the touched one had said about her baby being stolen suddenly seem less far-fetched.

"Someone told me my mother could be alive." Shay realizes she's spoken out loud only when Ghita's eyes widen. Does Shay imagine the sharp intake of her breath?

"You stuck to our story, I hope," the midwife admonishes. "That your mother was a nomad who was left behind by her tribe because she was too sick to travel."

"And she died during my delivery," Shay recites to appease her. If the first part of the story is a lie, could the second part also be? Doubting Ghita, even in the confines of her thoughts, feels like a betrayal, but the parallels between this child and herself are too striking to ignore.

"Congratulations are in order." The midwife abruptly changes the subject, her face and posture shifting to a businesslike formality with her tone. "A midwife in Kiddah has unexpectedly passed away without an apprentice to appoint as her successor. I recommended you as a replacement and received word you've been accepted."

Shay's head spins. How long ago did Ghita recommend her? "You . . . want me to move to Kiddah?"

"The next caravan leaves in three days." Ghita swallows the last of her tea and rises. She opens a nearby drawer, and the next thing Shay knows, the midwife is handing her a crisp caravan ticket that smells of fresh ink and unceremonious dismissal.

"I . . ." Shay stares at the parchment for a moment, the sharply penned details of her departure blurring as her vision quakes. She looks up at Ghita, unmoored. "My training . . ."

"Is complete." The midwife doesn't meet Shay's eyes, seeming to address some invisible entity perched upon her shoulder. "You are competent and caring. I'm confident you will be successful in your new post."

They are words Shay has longed to hear, has striven for with all her being, but they feel hollow. Only earlier today, the midwife informed her she had two moon quarters to prove herself. Things seemed more imminent once the birthing call came, but . . . the child was delivered without Shay's assistance. Why, she wasn't even there.

"You saved him," Ghita says, as though Shay's thoughts were wholly transparent. "Very brave, if you ask me."

A sound rises from Shay's throat, one that could signify agreement or dispute, and she's completely unsure which expression she intends. Even if she were convinced she deserved this, she finds herself aching for *more*. For something she can't quite translate into words.

"I must get some sleep before Sami wakes again. He'll likely be extra fussy until he acclimates to no longer receiving Snow from his mother's bloodstream." Ghita turns, effectively buttoning up the conversation.

Shay cups her cheek like someone on the receiving end of a strike. *The baby already has a name.* Her heart pangs for the child, sure to grow up as she did, without a mother. When he's older, will Ghita tell him the truth about how his mother tried to kill him? Or will she lie to save his feelings?

"Wait," Shay calls out. This is all too sudden. It feels so final. And it is impossible for her to imagine her future when so much of her past remains shrouded in mystery. She will always be looking over her shoulder for it, like a shadow without a shape. "What was her name?"

Shay doesn't specify whom. She's asked the question a million times and never gotten a straight response.

Ghita stops, keeping her back to the apprentice. This time, she answers, "Hind."

With that, the midwife shuffles off to bed.

5

The Creation Myth of Mekchaouen

It is maintained that God created the world, an endless sprawling valley of the lushest greenery and most vibrant gardens. That He created humans to live off the land and rule over the animals. The first people had no language and communicated using a primitive system of pointing and grunting that lacked any nuance or depth. It is said that one of the angels took pity on humankind and taught people to speak in the language of paradise itself.

This had undesired consequences. For the language was so beautiful, it distracted people from engaging in the activities necessary for their survival, like hunting, gathering, and mating. All humans wanted to do was talk and listen to others talk. To sing, and listen to others sing.

Spellbound women were so touched, their tears fell in an unceasing flow that accumulated and grew into the Cerabbi Sea, covering one third of the world in water. Men were moved to levels of faith so zealous, their hearts would burst into flames, their bodies combusting. Thus, the ashes of their bones became the sands of the Mourian Desert and covered another third of the world.

With the livable land reduced to one third its original size and the population dwindling, God spoke to the people. He ordered humans to create a new language and reserve the Old Tongue for prayers and celebratory songs alone. The Marabouts were ordained as keepers of the Old Tongue and tasked with building the sacred prayer house in the center of Kiddah.

God is then said to have separated Nezjar from Kiddah by creating the Umm Chanala Mountains. He prescribed that those who are able should make a pilgrimage at least once in their lifetime, traveling to the frigid mountains and spending a quarter there with the

Marabouts at the holy institute. Seven days devoted to spiritual learning and drawing close to their Creator.

Time passed, and people were sent to explore the desert and determine if it had any end, and though no end was found, some preferred the desert life. And so, the first Hazmaggi tribe was born. Likewise, more people set out on boats to explore the Cerabbi, and these became a tribe of sea nomads, the B'hamu. And so, the realm of Mekchaouen was divided into five unique regions, its people connected as one human family.

As daylight crowns the horizon with a white lip of promise, Shay dresses in a comfortable djellaba, evaded by sleep. She brings along the caravan ticket, her pocketknife, and a burning need for answers as she slips through the narrow bends of Sultan's Alley. Three days is no time at all to prepare for her life to be upheaved, and the foraging landscape in Kiddah is foreign to her. It is crucial she harvest enough moon pepper to last until she's able to grow her own.

In the twilight shadows that hang between the blue facades of buildings, stall owners roll ware-laden carts over the cobblestones. The rich aroma of woodsmoke billows from the communal ovens warming up. Steam infused with eucalyptus drifts from the bathhouse. Passing the tannery, Shay crushes a handful of mint. She presses the fragrant leaves to her nose, veiling the noxious odor of curing hides.

Will she carry the imprint of these sights and sounds with her to Kiddah? Or will they be replaced by the new wonders awaiting her in the holy city? The air grows tight as she approaches Al-Ghaba Mayita. Dipping into the tree line of tall pines, Shay feels the scrape of hungry eyes. She whispers a blessing to ward off whatever might be watching through the thin skin of morning mist.

Hind. In the quiet of the woodland, she meditates on the name that has possessed her thoughts since it was issued from the midwife's lips. She cradles it in her mind like a fragile egg, tracing each letter as though she could stitch them into the fabric of her soul.

For the first time in her life, Shay allows herself to indulge in a waking dream, inventing an alternate set of circumstances. One where her mother lived, where instead of being a midwife's apprentice, she learned some other trade. Perhaps she'd be whipping up delicious treats in a confectionary or sewing fine garments in a boutique.

The moon pepper patch is easier to reach than most of the spots Shay frequents, and at this season of earth's cycle, the plants should yield a sufficient amount of the suppressant for her needs. At least, that's what she expects.

Instead, she finds that the stems of the entire patch have been stripped bare of leaves down to their roots. Shay gapes at the ravaged plot, unable to make sense of it. A sinking dread, mixed with the smallest touch of relief, creeps over her.

The culprits could be rabbits or deer, and yet, for her life, Shay can't remember the last time she saw a rabbit or a deer in the forest. At times she's heard *something* moving through the underbrush, and she once spotted a creature that could have been a monkey or a goat munching bean fruits in the branches of a rune tree. But she's certainly never crossed paths with another human, and what would anyone else want with moon pepper? It tastes like the devil's piss and has only one redeemable value.

Panic makes it hard to breathe. Shay doesn't know how long it would take for her latent powers to manifest, what those powers would look like, or how difficult they'd make it for her to continue hiding her hizoura status. She stares at her hands in the splintery light through the thatched branches as if they might start glowing any moment. When they fail to do so, she scours the patch, double-checking that no leaves were left behind.

"Ouch!"

Shay's gaze snaps to the empty thicket. Her heart blooms into her throat, beating slow and heavy. "Who's there?"

Shrubs rustle and shake. Fingers come twisting through vines, and the hands attached to them part the heavy stalks. Shay tenses, her spine wooden. A body emerges from the shadows and brambles, stumbling out as though the forest has birthed him. The familiar boy swats frantically at the legs and sleeves of his servant uniform.

This production goes on for a few moments before he looks up sheepishly and grins. Shay exhales in delayed relief. Then her eyebrows tug together. She doesn't grin back, her lips leveling into a severe line. Why is *he* here?

He walks toward her, thrusting one arm out ahead of him as he shoves his sleeve up to his elbow. "I've been bitten. By a fiddler ant, I think."

The white blister ringed in angry red that protrudes from his wrist would suggest his hypothesis is correct. It does not explain why he's here, but the green stain tinging the skin around his fingernails is a big enough clue that Shay's mouth goes dry when she sees it. She knows that stain well. Knows that even with frequent scrubbing, it takes several days after harvesting moon pepper for it to fully wash away.

"What are you doing out in these woods in the first place"—she pauses, swallowing past a nest of nerves as she rummages through her recent memory for his name—"Shadi?"

She smiles now, if only to cover for the fear she hears in her own voice, and quickly looks away from his hands. Her mind has already dismissed the idea that he might be a hizoura, might be here for the same reason as her. The whole patch is gone. Shadi carries no satchel, and his pockets are certainly not deep enough to hold such a large number of leaves.

No, Shay has already formed her own explanation. If the rebels have realized moon pepper suppresses hizoura magic, they might have destroyed the patch to prevent those who wish to hide their identity from doing so. Hizouras would then be easier to pick out and "eradicate." What better way to determine who to keep a closer eye on than spying on this location and keeping track of who comes around?

"I . . . umm . . ." Shadi peers into the darkness that furls like drapes in the hollows between the trees. "I like to slip away in nature sometimes. To clear my head."

Shay scoffs, though inwardly. There isn't a citizen in Nezjar who slips away to the forest for leisure. Besides, Shadi doesn't seem to have a thought in his head to clear it from. For a Naturalist, he doesn't come across as very cunning. Unless it's an act to lower her guard, which would be cunning indeed.

She nods toward his swelling wrist. "Well, my advice is to find a banana peel to rub on that. And the next time you feel the urge to spend time in the woods, chew on a raw clove of garlic first. It won't taste great, but the fiddler ants will go out of their way to avoid you."

"Really?" Shadi smiles gratefully as he folds his sleeve carefully down over the bite. "Thanks!"

Shay shakes her head, finding it difficult to see Shadi as any kind of threat. Perhaps she is simply a poor judge of character.

"Can I walk you home?" he asks.

Shay stiffens. Notably, he hasn't asked her why *she's* here in the forest. A normal person would ask. But, if her theory is correct, he would *already know*. The rumors must have put him on her scent. In fact, he probably only told her about them so he could assess her reaction. And now he's trying to find out where she lives. Oh, he's *good*.

"I'm not going home." She has somewhere else she needs to go. Something else she absolutely must do before she can leave her medina behind. "Besides, you really should get that bite taken care of before the swelling gets worse. You wouldn't want to lose a finger."

Panic flashes in his eyes, and Shay has to restrain a laugh. *Did he really fall for that?*

"It was nice running into you again, Shay," he calls out as she rushes away, provoking her to glance back. He's rolled his sleeve up again. His gaze shifts from looking down at the insect bite with comical concern to looking up at Shay with an expression she can't read. Is it worry? Embarrassment?

Filtered sunlight through the dense wood washes his face in an umber glow. In the contours of Shadi's guileless smile, she fails to find any trace of the hate she would expect from a Naturalist.

✧ ✧ ✧

Nearing the medina square, Shay sights armed guards. They mill the perimeter, looking as formidable as small boys toting large guns can. As if the fact that the herb she relies upon has been plundered weren't making her nervous enough, hammers ring in the distance, the shouts of men at work, no doubt erecting gallows.

Shay shudders, remembering last night's raid and the glimmer of another scene from the more distant past. She ducks her head and flees the hulking shadow of the wooden apparatus, as if she could outrun the sharp teeth of memory.

She soon makes her way to the seedier side of the medina, its abandoned buildings rendered soft in the pink haze of early light, and tucked amid them, her destination. Morning breeze teases the fabric of an elaborate tent, sewn in patchwork design and bedecked with glittery sequins.

Shay's heart pulses like a living thing inside her throat.

Dounia's Delights.

She doesn't believe—*can't believe*—Ghita would lie, yet the vagueness of the midwife's narrative certainly suggests she's hiding something. Shay thought she would stay in Nezjar forever. She'd care for Ghita as she grew old, and only after the midwife had squeezed out every last drop of a long and satisfying life would Shay have taken over her position.

The brewery stands as quiet as a secret. The thick exterior rugs used to deter nighttime intruders have been rolled up. The heavy stones that hold them down are pushed aside. The door flap hangs open and untied. It's early. Shay thought she might have to wait around a while, but is the barkeep who heard and proceeded to spread the touched one's claims about her stolen baby already here? And what will Shay say to her if she is?

She has no idea what form the answers she seeks will take. She only knows with sudden conviction that not being a burden isn't enough after all. Shay wants to be loved, to fill the mother-shaped emptiness inside her.

Stiff corners press between her shoulder blades. The ticket wedges in the hood of her djellaba, a practical feature of the garment that does double duty as a head covering in harsh weather and a spacious storage compartment when needed. She brought the parchment with her as though it might otherwise disappear. To Shay, it is a symbol that she has achieved success in the eyes of her teacher—and, in so doing, lost her position in the only place she's ever called home.

If there's any possibility, however small, that the claims have merit, Shay owes it to herself to investigate the matter. Before she's shipped off on a caravan to Kiddah, where she'll have to start all over, having forfeited any chance at understanding where she's from. Heart wild, she nudges the flap wider and steps into the establishment proper.

Thick sugary clouds swirl above a handful of dinged-up tables. A couple of middle-aged men smoke shisha and play a game of tuti in the back. Shay isn't sure what she expected, but the reality is less than exciting, although the atmosphere would presumably enliven after dark.

Shay sidles up to a long bar counter. She quietly takes in the strange and colorful bottles that line the shelving unit behind it. The barkeep is balanced atop a wooden stool, inspecting the bottles and replacing those found empty. Shiny locks smoothly drape her shoulders, their straight press no doubt achieved by wielding a comb dipped into a jar of lava procured by B'hamu divers—rumored to be part merfolk—from volcanic caves under the Cerabbi Sea.

"Labas?" Shay tempers the volume of her greeting but still manages to startle the woman, who wobbles unsteadily before climbing down from the stool.

"Labas, Lalla. I didn't hear you come in." The woman slaps a hand to the bodice of the stylish blue takchita she wears cinched with a thick belt. She has richly dark skin, lushly flared curves, and her wide eyes are rimmed in kohl. Idly, she massages the palm of one hand with the other and flexes her elegant fingers. "I'm afraid the brewery is not yet open for business."

"But you have customers . . ." Shay glances uncertainly toward the back table.

"My uncle and brother," the barkeep says dismissively.

When Shay doesn't move, the woman produces a prettily embroidered handkerchief from below the counter and uses it to dab invisible sweat from her hairline. "You're welcome to come back at midday."

Shay swallows her nerves. They squirm in her stomach. "I . . . actually wanted to talk to you."

The barkeep's brown eyes soften. She shakes her head. "We're not hiring right now."

"Not about that." Shay shakes her own head, groping for words. "About a customer. A woman . . . a touched one."

"You'll have to give me more to go on." The barkeep slings the cloth over her shoulder and crosses her arms.

"Her name might be Hind?"

Frown lines etch across the woman's forehead. She grunts. "Hind is a common name."

Something sours in her tone, and her lip twitches in repugnance, making Shay suspect she knows more. She looks closer at the cloth flung over the woman's shoulder, woven in the style of the blankets Nezjar is known for. "May I see your handkerchief?"

The barkeep grabs the cloth and looks at it, her nose wrinkling. "It's soiled. I can get you something clean . . ."

"I want to see the embroidery."

Nodding, the barkeep relinquishes the cloth, which Shay unfolds. Many washings have left the cotton fabric rough, but the threads have retained their vibrance. The rich patterns in which they are arranged attest to the artistry of a talented seamstress. "Did you make this?"

"Do you like it?" The barkeep smiles, a smile so thin that it may as well be a clover bean leaf slapped over a musket wound. Sadness seeps through like blood.

"It's beautiful." Shay scans the mostly empty tent. She imagines how busy it must get, filled with rowdy customers and individuals of ill repute. "Why work here when you possess such talent?"

The woman's smile retreats.

"I *was* talented." She gives her hands another brisk rub as though warming them. "That was before I injured my hands. And now I work here. Where I'm forced to deal with the likes of Hind Hibachi."

Shay gulps, anticipation straightening her spine. "So, you do know her?"

"If I did," the barkeep says, snatching back the cloth and returning it below the counter, "I would have barred her from my establishment for distributing Snow. Not to mention her outstanding tab."

Nibbling her lip, Shay contemplates the woman's words. "You mean she was selling it?"

The barkeep pauses, her voice laced with warning when she speaks again. "Not selling. She offered it for free to young women. Women who quickly become dependent on the drug and go live in the kasbah for as long as Al-Mukhtar can use them. When they eventually get cast out, they'll spend the rest of their miserable lives in the Bib. And that's if they're among the lucky ones." She turns back and grabs a bottle from the wall, uncorks the neck, and sniffs it before returning it to its place. "But you didn't hear such treasonous talk from me, eh?"

Shay settles onto a stool with a seat of woven leather, allowing herself a moment for the words to filter through her mind. Her thoughts shift like desert sands. She's heard the rebels' accusations of touched ones being employed at the kasbah before, but the claim of Al-Mukhtar discarding them after Snow has drained their vitality is a new one.

The barkeep glances over her shoulder and raises her eyebrow as if questioning what Shay is still doing there.

"Did she ever mention having a child?" Shay's voice stretches as thin as pastry dough, but it gets the woman to turn around and fully face her.

She looks Shay up and down the way a market goer might examine goods, searching for some flaw they can leverage for a lower price. "Touched ones say a lot of things when they're blitzed."

It's all the confirmation Shay needs, and the only person who can tell her more than that is the woman herself. It's unlikely this Hind Hibachi is one of the touched ones who reside at the kasbah—she wouldn't have been patronizing the brewery if she did. If she is, instead, one of the castoffs the barkeep speaks of, that means . . .

Shay knows where to look for her: the shantytown, colloquially called the Bib. "Thank you, khalti."

The woman tilts her head as Shay rises to go. Understanding passes over her face, then sharpens to alarm. "I wouldn't go there if I were you."

Shay hesitates. The Bib is hardly a place anyone would go for enjoyment, but the woman's tone suggests a more sinister meaning. "Why not?"

She huffs. "The Bib isn't just where poor people live anymore. It's a hideout for criminals. A place where rebels are free to take cover because no mukhtar would soil his spotless white robe by venturing in. The Moulays don't even conduct raids there."

Shay believes this; the midwife herself refuses to enter the slum, its women forced to come to her or deliver their babies alone. As a hizoura, Shay has more reason than most to avoid the rebels, especially when she may have already attracted one's attention. But, instead of the trepidation she should feel, a lightness floats like soap bubbles in her chest. If she had to give name to the feeling, she'd call it hope.

Seeming to sense her words have not had their intended impact, the barkeep continues: "You'll need a guide to get through all the rigged traps, and no one there will trust you unless you know the secret hand signal."

Shay grips the counter, dizzy with the implications. She strums her fingers over the years' accumulation of dents and scrapes that have been worn into the wood grain, her leather gloves a barrier that dampens their sensation. "Do you know the secret hand signal?"

"Why would I?" The woman kneads her hands again. She grimaces. "Now, if you'll excuse me, I have work to do."

Shay's shoulders sink. If the barkeep seemed the type to be swayed by dramatics, she'd drop to her knees then and there to beg. One of the men offers her a sympathetic shrug, then returns to his game, which, judging by the fan of cards held in his hand, he's losing.

She whips her face back to the barkeep. "Did you say the touched one owed you coin?"

The woman sighs wearily. "Are you offering to pay it?"

Shay reaches through the slit in the side of her djellaba. She cups the small satchel hidden beneath, worn around her waist. In her gloved palm, she weighs its lightness. Her heart goes as still as the moment before a storm breaks. After her extra payment to the stable master, she has little coin left to her name, but the gloves . . .

The gloves were a gift, and so much more. A symbol of the care Ghita poured into her training and the midwife's expectations for her future. Shay cherishes them, both for their utility and their sentimental value.

"Does it hurt?" she asks softly. When the barkeep looks confused, she explains, "You told me you injured your hands."

"A little," the woman admits, but Shay has spent enough time around women in pain to recognize when one is downplaying the severity. "They tingle sometimes. And feel cold."

With a strike of regret, Shay peels off her still-new and much-loved gloves. She squeezes the leather between her palms, soaking up its softness. The barkeep's hands look similar in size to her own. She squares her shoulders. "These might provide you comfort. I'll give them to you if you'll help me."

6

Our Lallat are waiting to be restored.
The keepers of magic, the fairest four.
Rabia tends the earth, and Rasha draws the tide.
With the sun, Noor dances, and on the wind, Iman rides.
Earth, flame, water, air.
We remember their names, our Lallat fair.

—a Hazmaggi chant

Shay hates coming to the slum. It breaks her heart to see small children playing in dirty puddles and napping next to fly-covered piles of debris. Yet, she can't help noticing how the women talk and smile brightly among themselves as they hang clothes and carry water. They seem happy despite their lack of what others deem necessities.

It doesn't take long for a young boy to come running up to Shay. With unmatched slippers on his feet and his tiny frame swallowed beneath an adult-sized tunic, he's hardly the fearsome rebel the barkeep led Shay to believe she'd be greeted by.

He stretches his open hand up and out. "Labas, Lalla. Something for me? Please?"

Shay fishes the last luneers from her satchel. God knows it isn't much, but when she presses the coin into his palm, the child's face brightens into a heart-melting grin.

"God protect you," she offers hoarsely.

The child tucks the luneers into his pocket. He grabs her hand and sprinkles the top of it with kisses. "May He bless you and your parents."

Tears prickle Shay's eyes at the innocent blessing. Ghita is the closest thing to a parent she has known, and the midwife surely deserves God's rewards. But what of the mother she hopes to find, the one the barkeep accused of luring young women into a life of addiction? Is such a woman eligible for redemption?

Shay takes a step forward, when the boy springs in front of her.

He glances first to one side then the other, fidgeting in place. "Are you going the right way, Lalla?"

Shay peers into the distance, trying to determine what the boy is looking at. Finding nothing amiss along the uneven belt of makeshift shelters, she squats at eye level with the child and lowers her voice. "Is someone watching us?"

The boy scratches his dirty arm and nods nervously.

Telling herself the worst that can happen is she'll be turned away, Shay holds her palm up in a khamsa sign, her three middle fingers touching, pinky and thumb separated out to the sides. She lifts her hand high enough to be seen by whoever is hiding. To complete the signal, she rolls her fingers into a fist that represents the all-seeing eye of protection and taps it to her forehead.

The boy's shoulders relax, but he tips his chin higher. "That's the secret signal. But do you know the *secret* secret signal?"

Shay frowns, her throat tightening. The barkeep didn't mention a *secret* secret signal. She gazes up at the bright white of the noonday sun. It floats in a pool of soft yellow like a reverse egg. But there are no clues written among the clouds. Sweat gathers in her palms.

"Just kidding!" The boy chuckles and winks at her. "There is no secret secret signal."

"M'zein." Shay stands, her panic dissolving into laughter. "You fooled me that time. But I have a serious question. Do you think one of your friends out there would be willing to help me find someone?"

"It's your lucky day, Lalla." The child puffs his small chest. "Badar knows *everyone* in the Bib."

"I see." Shay swallows uneasily. She assesses the boy's tender frame. Is it even safe for him to be running about unsupervised here? "What about the traps?"

The boy looks at her askance. He pats his arms and legs, grinning widely. "I still have all my limbs, don't I?"

✧ ✧ ✧

Badar scampers over stone blocks and wood beams. Shay's heart hammers with exertion and the fear that a misstep will trigger a trap and she'll be sliced by a swinging knife or crushed under an avalanche of rocks. The child races, his stride never breaking, down the narrow rows that run between crowded shelters. Many residents have hung torn sheets for privacy where their walls are lacking, half the stones having crumbled away.

Some dwellings, Shay notices with more than a little unease, openly display the checkered flag of the Naturalists. The offense would be unthinkable elsewhere in Nezjar. One building even has their slogan painted on its side: A COMMON GOAL FOR A COMMON PEOPLE!

The deeper into the Bib they plunge, the clearer it becomes that not everyone here is happy. Touched ones linger in dark corners. The emaciated women alternately pick at their scabbed skin and yank what little is left of their thinning hair. Each twitch is like a move in a compulsive dance they've been cursed to perform.

Their backs are hunched, their hands curled into claws. Warts bubble on their faces. One dried husk of a woman sits right out in the open on a palm leaf mat, appearing at risk of being bowled over by the faintest of breezes. She pulls a dropper of amber liquid from a glass vial and squeezes a glistening drop onto her tongue.

Shock ripples through Shay's body. The touched one throws her head back, her papery eyelids fluttering. A white film spreads over her irises and blots her pupils. Her black lips melt into a sloppy grin, exposing teeth in the early stages of decline. Red wisps of light pulse at her fingertips.

Shay's skin turns cold. After all these cycles of believing her mother is dead, will she now find her to be alive but trapped in same thrall of addiction as these women?

"Come," the boy urges, tugging Shay's sleeve. "My memma always tells me to keep my eyes on pretty things. She says that which you look upon, you become."

"Your memma is a wise one." Shaking off the chill, Shay quickly pursues the child. They swerve around a small herd of goats in their path and finally stop before one of the few shelters with a door, albeit one resting crookedly in its frame.

Could her mother have been here all along? Surely, Shay would have felt some invisible thread pulling her by the heart, the same way the sea must feel the inexorable tug of the moon. But isn't it true that she's always carried an unnamed longing inside her? She attributed it to her constant contact with expectant mothers, but what if it was more? If she had any inkling her mother could be eking out an existence in the medina's slum, she would have found a way to help her.

But maybe she still can.

Panting, and more winded than a girl her age should be, Shay turns to Badar as he stretches on his toes and beckons her to bend her ear.

"Wanna know a secret?" he asks, whispering mischievously. "There are no traps."

Giggling, the boy darts away, leaving Shay to question everything she's heard about the resistance. Al-Mukhtar would have citizens believing the rebels were heartless brutes who wouldn't think twice about putting their own children in harm's way. But what if they're just the brave few willing to stand up in the face of tyranny? What if they actually protect the realms' most vulnerable?

The door is shaped like a giant keyhole and painted the indigo of night. Once upon a time, it might have been called fancy. Now it's rusted and peeling and doesn't look at all out of place amid the surrounding clutter where nothing matches.

Hesitantly, she knocks. A warm breeze carries distant chatter, the squawk and bray of livestock, fumes of garbage rotting nearby. What if the woman isn't home? Shay knocks a few more times.

Her thoughts skip back to the touched ones who huddled in the shadows. One of the women was slumped against a wall, seemingly unconscious. This Hind may be inside her dwelling right now, suffering an overdose that has left her unable to answer.

"Hind?" Shay knocks again, louder.

The misaligned door gives beneath her efforts. It cracks open to reveal a slice of mud-brick wall. Shay looks back over her shoulder, half hoping no one is watching and half seeking someone who might give her permission to enter. No one is close by or paying attention. Telling herself it's not intruding if someone needs help, Shay steps inside, the door falling shut behind her.

The room, for there is only one, looks almost homey. A single small window draws Shay to the back. She pushes the curtains apart, releasing a cloud of dust and letting in enough light to distinguish that the lumps on the sleeping pallet are merely blankets and pillows. In a corner sits a folded prayer mat, a book of scriptures held aloft by a wooden stand, and a clay bowl cradling a string of glass remembrance beads.

With a heavy sigh, Shay turns back toward the door. It seems the woman is out, after all. The skid of her sole over something wet stops her just before she steps on a fancy-looking bottle. It's tipped upon its side, its contents dribbling out onto the layer of unfinished boards that serve as a floor. She squats and picks it up, sniffing the neck as she reinserts the stopper.

Peach blossom. A sweet warmth spreads across the pathways of her mind, coaxing a smile to her lips. The scent, somehow achingly familiar, echoes of infantile memories. At least, that's what Shay chooses to believe. She closes her eyes and basks in the feeling.

Only when she opens them does the shape that lies twisted across the room come into focus. Gasping, Shay tosses the bottle aside. She lunges toward the woman whose form the shadows previously concealed.

Her pale skin looks bleached, shading the dark circles beneath her eyes all the blacker. Sparse fluffs dust her head like a light layer of snow, patches of pink scalp peeking through. Her arms stick from her sleeves, her neck from her collar, thin as twigs, the knobs of her elbows, knuckles, and chin seeming enormous in comparison.

"Hind?" Shay gives the woman's shoulders a gentle shake, making her head loll limply from side to side. "Are you well?"

Something dark trickles from the side of her mouth. Shay's mind flashes to the khala's corpse back at the farmhouse. With flaring panic, she dives into action, but as she gently uncurls the woman's stiff body, the crisp crackle of bones suggests she's too late. Nevertheless, Shay delivers compressions to her frail chest. She breathes air against her chilling lips.

"What in the seven hells are you doing?" The woman pushes Shay off her with sudden strength. Wheezing, she wipes her mouth with the back of her hand and glares at Shay.

Their eyes are the same shade of smoky brown. Faded Hazmaggi tattoos scrawl across her cheeks and forehead. Odd, given that Ghita said the detail about Shay's nomadic heritage was fabricated.

"That's funny. You don't exactly look like the sort to break into women's homes and assault them in their sleep."

She's obviously alive, but no less a thing of horror, and Shay's first impulse is to deny that such a creature could be her mother. Yet, even in the meager light from the shelter's grime-streaked window, the resemblance is notable. As her adrenaline dies down, Shay's fingers trace her own slightly crooked nose, her tapered chin. With a strange sense of detachment, she wonders if everything she thought true is a lie and all the lies are true.

"Devil got yer tongue?" the woman derides. She leaves Shay lumped on the floor and shuffles to the middle of the room. There, she dumps a bucket of hot coals into a pit dug into the ground where it has been left uncovered. Shay watches her hang a dented teapot of water over the fire.

Recovering her voice, she sputters, "Wh-what are you doing?"

"Never seen someone make tea?" the woman grumbles. Despite her mockery, a hint of kindness touches her face, turning pit marks into dimples. She pats a large, round starmia made of tattered leather beside her. "Come sit."

Shay's tongue adheres to the bottom of her mouth as she crosses the room obediently. All the cycles she carried this wish inside her, this unspoken yearning for maternal love, she never once stopped to think of what she would say to her mother if given the chance. Her heart pumps hard under the cotton of her djellaba, gushing all the words she cannot find.

For her part, the woman says nothing more. She goes about preparing tea, her method similar to Ghita's but different in a way that takes Shay a few moments to pin. It isn't so much her process as the way she holds herself as she moves. So unlike Ghita's confident posture. The touched one, old as she looks, has the body language of an unsteady but eager toddler.

She finally hands Shay a glass, accompanied by a tight smile. Shay holds the warm tea in her hands as though she can't recall what to do with it. When she opens her mouth, she has no idea what she means to say until the words tumble out. "Khalti, do you know who I am?"

The touched one taps her dirty nail on her glass and looks at Shay as if she insulted her. Something like pain glistens briefly in her eyes before she blinks it away. "Do you imagine I can't recognize my own flesh and blood?"

Shay's voice freezes in her throat. Time stops, the question hanging between them like a breath cloud on a cold day. Her mind slowly whirs, repeating the barkeep's revelations. She doesn't know whether to jump up and scream for joy that her mother is alive or break down and weep for the condition she's in. Maybe she'd know the correct reaction if she could get past the feeling that none of this seems real.

"It's true, then," she finally whispers, but inside her ears, her voice is a shout. Could Ghita have made a mistake? Did the midwife leave her mother for dead by accident? No, Ghita is much too thorough. She'd never be so negligent. Besides, she told Shay there was a grave . . .

"Drink some tea, habibti," the woman murmurs. "We have a lot to talk about."

Shay's hand seems to lift the glass to her lips by itself. The tea is good, though the mint is not as fresh as that which she's used to. The warmth of the beverage steadies her. It clears her head a bit.

"Khalti," she starts, then sips more tea to avoid continuing.

"La," the touched one corrects her. "Mmi."

If a heart had ears, Shay's would perk like a cat hearing the lid peeled back on a tin of preserved fish. But the word, and all it implies, is sacred. If she never bestowed such a title upon the midwife, whom she lived and worked with and learned from, how can she apply it to a stranger? Someone she knows nothing about other than that she's an addict? "It's a bit soon for that."

"Hind, then. You can call me *Hind*."

"Hind," Shay starts again. "I . . . I'm sorry."

Hind's forehead creases, adding about a hundred cycles to her age. "Why?"

"If I really am . . . If you really are . . ." Shay widens her eyes and clamps her teeth, not wishing to cry and embarrass herself more than she did by trying to resuscitate the woman. "I would have come sooner, if I'd known. I would have offered to help you."

"What makes you think I need help?" the touched one scoffs.

"I didn't mean to imply—"

"We both know what you meant." Hind waves a skeletal hand. "You can judge me if you want. I just . . ." She covers her mouth as she smiles, the gaps between her spindly fingers exposing the sorry state of her teeth. "You're real, aren't you? You're not a ghost . . ."

Shay raises her arm and inspects it as though she herself isn't sure whether it's made of flesh or spirit. "I could ask you the same question. Ghita told me you died."

"Ghita!" The touched one scowls, her lips pulling so tight that they almost disappear. She takes a long sip of tea before she speaks again. "She told me the same about you."

Shay shakes her head as stubborn loyalty rears inside her. There must be more to the story. There has to be. "Why would she do that?"

"S'pose she wanted you for herself." Hind shrugs one pointy shoulder, her sullen expression burnished in an orange palette by the light of the small fire. "The way I hear it, her own daughter died tragically."

Shock falls over Shay's mind like a blanket, making shapeless lumps of every thought. "Ghita had a daughter?"

"So they say." The touched one chews her bottom lip. "But they say a lot of things."

The idea of Ghita's betrayal doesn't provoke the anger Shay would expect. Neither does she feel hurt, at least not yet. Either of those emotions would be something concrete, a thread she could hold on to and make sense of. All she feels is confusion, her equilibrium thrown headlong into a senseless rift. More than anything, she wants to understand. "Tell me what happened."

The touched one arches a thin white eyebrow. "Everything?"

Shay takes a bracing sip of tea. "Everything."

7

The Legend of Illi and Udad

Once upon a time, two tribes lived on mountain villages that faced each other, separated by a lake. A shepherd named Udad would always spy a maiden named Illi from across the water when he'd bring his flock to drink and she'd come to the opposite shoreline to do her family's washing. Smiles and glances turned to waves and gestures and soon they developed a secret code that allowed them to communicate daily across the distance. They fell in love. Alas, they were to forbidden to marry outside of their tribes. As they pined for each other, their sadness grew, until one day Illi signed a most heartbreaking message to her beloved. Her father had promised her hand in a marriage set to be performed after the passing of one moon. The pair began to cry.

So great were their tears, they fell into the lake and the waters rose and rose and overflowed. The ensuing flood wiped away both their mountains. As the waters kept rising, Illi and Udad swam toward each other. They are said to have drowned in each other's arms. To this day, claims persist of their benevolent spirits being sighted, and locals believe that if a new bride and groom swim the waters of Barhira Kabira, their marriage will be blessed.

Hind sighs, a low, hollow sound. Her brown eyes glisten with a faraway cast. "When I was about your age, a Hazmaggi caravan was passing through Nezjar during Jou Boulka. I was at the festival, and well, do you believe in love at first sight, Shuika?"

Shay is taken aback by the use of her given name, by how different it feels coming from her mother. She considers the question and foolishly thinks of Shadi. Is it possible to meet the person you're meant to be with, only to find they may belong to the very group that wants you dead? "I don't know, khalti—Hind."

"Well, I fell in love with a Hazmaggi man."

Shay studies Hind's tattoos, the delicate symmetry of the designs against the crumbling planes of her face. "So, you're not Hazmaggi, then?"

"Not technically." Hind shakes her head, her white hair swaying around her shoulders. "When my family wouldn't accept my lover, I ran away to live with the nomads. I married into their tribe, took their markings onto my skin. Even when my husband was taken by sudden illness and died, the tribe still considered me one of their own."

"Was your husband . . . my father?"

"No." Hind holds up a finger as she drinks from her glass. "I got depressed after my husband died. The tribe tried convincing me to remarry, but I couldn't bear the idea of replacing my first love. The next time we passed through the festival, I tried Snow for the first time. I did it to fill the empty hole that felt like it was consuming me from the inside out. I just wanted to feel something, and at the same time, I didn't want to feel anything."

Shay always assumed women tried Snow out of curiosity about their Shawafa. Out of a desire to access magic, despite it being forbidden. It never occurred to her that someone might use the drug as a means of escaping their pain.

"It didn't take long for me to become an addict. I tried hiding it from the tribe. But when a little boy fell off a camel and was injured, I couldn't stop myself from using Shawafa to heal him. And still, the tribe tried to help me get purged. Then valuables began to go missing, and they rightly suspected me of stealing them to sell for drug money. I was banished." Hind's voice dips low with either shame or remorse, or a combination of the two.

In Hind's story, the Hazmaggi did all they could for her, showing her the same grace and care as their own people, until she crossed a line. While in the cover story Shay has so often repeated, the tribe seems unsympathetic, willing to leave behind a woman whose only offense was being sick. It's a detail that never sat right with her, though she couldn't work out why until now.

"I returned to Nezjar, but my family didn't want me back. A widow and an addict. I used my Shawafa to earn what coin I could, but customers became scarce when the hangings started."

Shay notices that Hind hasn't mentioned anything about working for Al-Mukhtar, but that isn't her most burning question. "If it's alright, may I ask about my father?"

The touched one sets her empty tea glass on the makeshift floor and picks the grime under her nails. "I had to earn coin somehow, so I sold my body. Back then, I had a body worth selling. That's why I'm sorry to say I don't know who your father is."

Shay has seen women in similar situations come to Ghita for herbal solutions. She might consider it a brave thing, taking on the task of motherhood alone, except no child should be exposed to Snow.

"Once I knew I was pregnant, I stopped using," Hind says, as though Shay has been thinking her thoughts too loudly. "I swear I did."

Shay stares into the fire, afraid Hind's eyes may not lie as well as her tongue. Or is she afraid the words are true? That she has no real need of the moon pepper Ghita has been so insistent that she faithfully ingest? It just seems improbable to her that anyone could overcome such an addiction without help.

Her thoughts turn to Sami, whom Ghita took in for his own protection. She can't imagine any reason why the midwife would have taken Shay as a baby, other than the same. Even if she accepts the possibility that Ghita wasn't fully honest, she still believes her to be a good person.

"But after the midwife told me you died . . ." Hind's voice unravels. "I couldn't overcome another loss like that. I went straight back to Snow, and I've been using ever since."

Shay struggles to bring her thoughts into focus. She was shocked to learn touched ones can carry to term and sometimes even deliver healthy babies. But how could someone who used Snow for so many cycles survive despite its deadly side effects, the rapid aging it inflicts? "How old are you?"

Although it's a question one doesn't normally ask a woman, the touched one doesn't flinch. "I think what you really want to know is, how am I still alive?"

Shay silently nods.

"An understandable question. Most touched ones who start young as I did don't make it to the age of thirty," the touched one concedes. "It's the Shawafa of Shifamin. I'm able to apply my healing magic to myself, which mitigates some of the deterioration Snow causes. I may still die before reaching forty, though."

Not if I can help it, Shay thinks. Now that she has found her mother alive, she desperately wants her to stay that way. "All this time, all you've been through, you had no one. But you can get purged now, if that's something you want."

The touched one puckers her lips and shivers as though a cold draft has passed through the room. "I don't know if I'm strong enough."

"I can help." Shay grabs Hind's hand and startles at the paper-thin feel of her skin. She adjusts her grip for fear of snapping the woman's bony fingers. "You don't have to do it alone. We can be strong enough together."

"I . . ." Hind looks anxiously into Shay's eyes, as if their gaze might burn. The tide of her face turns from fear to hope to something Shay can't read. Guilt or . . . regret? "I can try."

"Yes!" Shay exclaims. She's been waiting all her life to feel the connection that only a mother and daughter can share. It hardly matters if she's the one doing the nurturing. But what about her new position in Kiddah? Shay's excitement fizzles.

She awoke this morning thinking a chapter of her life was closing, that she'd successfully completed the training she'd worked so long and hard for. She couldn't have imagined she'd find a new reason to stay in Nezjar.

The touched one gazes toward the fire, scratching a scab on her arm, her idle rhythm like that of the women from the alley. Shay's not naïve enough to think purging will be a magic carpet ride . . . Surely, Ghita will know which herbs are best suited to curbing cravings and lessening the symptoms of withdrawal. Shay should talk to her before she makes any decision. And the midwife must be getting worried. Shay has been gone half the day.

"Hind?"

The touched one turns to face her, and Shay immediately sees it. A cloud of want that gathers at the edges of her expression. Like a snake coiled in wait, it's only a matter of time before the hunger for more Snow unleashes its venomous bite.

"Is it safe for you to stay here alone for a time? I couldn't help but notice that some of your neighbors are affiliated with the Naturalists. Has anyone ever threatened you?"

"We don't bother our neighbors here. On the contrary, we look out for one another." The touched one wraps her arms around her torso, looking small. "Are you leaving? You just got here."

"I have to take care of some things." Shay scans the shelter, assessing the touched one's provisions. A frying pan hangs by a nail on the wall, but the shelves consisting of wooden planks stacked on bricks are empty with the exception of a handful of tea leaves and a quarter jug of olive oil. "You need food. Is there anything you'd like me to bring back?"

"You're going home to her," the touched one whines. "Aren't you?"

"I have to hear her side," Shay says calmly, as though explaining to a child the unfortunate necessity of some unpleasant task. "I owe her that."

"She'll poison you against me." Hind shakes her head slowly, then fast. "How do I know you'll return?"

Shay pauses, or more accurately, gets stuck. If the touched one doesn't believe she'll come back, she might be more inclined to give in to her urges, going out and using again. Shay remembers her body twisted on the floor, feels the same panic that coursed through her in that moment. So strong it makes her vision dim at the edges and the air feel like bricks bearing down on her. The touched one hadn't overdosed then, but what about next time?

There cannot *be* a next time. Shay must make sure of it.

"Why don't you lie down while I'm gone?" She fluffs the pillows and draws the bedding of the pallet. The touched one obliges, and Shay tucks the musty, moth-worn blankets around her thin shoulders.

The touched one hums a few notes of a common lullaby before she grabs Shay's hand, her grip unexpectedly tight. "You promise to help me, right?"

A familiar fear snaps between Shay's ribs. The fear of not being enough. While failing to meet Ghita's expectations always felt like something dire, it wasn't generally a matter of life and death. Not like this. "Of course I will."

The touched one grunts, but she doesn't release Shay's hand. The apprentice—or is she now the touched one's daughter?—exhales. "Let go. I . . . I have something to give you."

The touched one loosens her hold, and Shay reaches around to access the deep hood of her djellaba. She stares at the fateful ticket for a long moment in which she weighs the accumulation of her hard work against the gravity of her deepest longings. She finally holds it out to Hind.

"What is this?" The touched one snatches the ticket and holds it close to her face. She read the words inscribed upon it, her wrinkles scrunched into a labyrinth. "Is this yours?"

"Before you get the wrong impression, allow me to explain," Shay says gently. "The midwife wants me to start a new position in Kiddah. I'm meant to depart in three days' time. But see? I'm leaving the ticket with you as an assurance that I'll come back first."

Hind glares at the ticket like she wants to rip it in two. Then she grunts from somewhere deep in her chest, and relief flutters over her face. She meets Shay's eyes with a nod. "I believe you, then."

"But I need you to make me a promise in kind," Shay says carefully. "Promise me you'll stay lucid until I return."

Hind waits long enough for Shay's unease to grow, rising up her rib cage to the rapid beat of a hummingbird's wings, before the woman reluctantly answers, "Wakha."

8

If Al-Mukhtar work miracles, why do they need an army of Moulays?

Do God's anointed require protection from mere men?

A COMMON GOAL FOR A COMMON PEOPLE!

—seen painted on an administrative building in Nezjar's town square after vandalization by rebels

Shay stretches on her tiptoes and rotates in a circle, scanning the tops of the shelters for the tall needle of the prayer house's minaret. Once she locates that, she'll use it as a landmark to orient herself and map her way out the Bib and back home. There, she can sort through all this with Ghita and then seek her advice about the gutted moon pepper patch. The midwife may even know of an herbalist who grows their own or a temporary substitute Shay can use.

Unless . . . Hind was telling the truth about quitting during her pregnancy. The only way for Shay to test that claim would be to do nothing and see whether her magic surfaces. The thought scares Shay to her core, but she can't deny that the idea of feeling better has its appeal. She can scarcely imagine what it would be like.

"Muezza! Muuueeezza!"

Looking back toward Hind's shelter, Shay spots her next-door neighbor standing outside, a broom held in one hand while the other shields her eyes from the afternoon sun. A flour-splotched apron spreads around her generous midsection. And a scarf stitched with the same pattern of the Naturalists' flag is tied across her wide shoulders.

Shay gulps. She considers going back inside until the woman does the same, but the khala sees her and waves.

"Msaa el kher," the woman greets, resting the broom against her shelter and straightening her apron. "Labas?"

"Labas, thanks to God," Shay replies. "Were you . . . looking for someone?"

"My cat, Muezza." Worry flashes across her milky-brown face. "She didn't come home last night."

Shay nods sympathetically. "God willing, she'll come back soon. Probably off having a little adventure."

"I'm sure you're right." The khala sighs. She extends her hand. "I'm Bushra."

"I'm Shay." The woman's handshake is warm and firm and as friendly as any of Shay's neighbors in the medina. The ones who lend her sugar from time to time. The ones she regularly checks on, inquiring about their family's welfare. The ones whose children she knows by name. People she wouldn't hesitate to assist in whatever hardship may arise, who wouldn't hesitate to assist her in return.

She searches Shay's eyes, frowning slightly. "And what about you, habibti? I saw you turning around there. Were *you* looking for something?"

"Oh." Shay glances toward Hind's indigo door. "I was just visiting my . . . Well, I recently found out that your neighbor is . . . um . . . we're related. Sort of."

"I see." The woman nods; her lips relax slightly. Then she frowns again, deeper this time. "But do be careful with that one. She may not have your best interests at heart."

Shay blinks. How odd. A woman wearing a symbol of a group that wants people like her *eradicated* is advising her to *be careful* of her own mother. The thing is, she seems sincere. Shay shakes her head. "Of what should I be careful, khalti?"

The woman grunts. "I don't like to speak ill of anyone, but I feel I must warn you. What Hind Hibachi and others like her do to their own bodies is their business, but she shouldn't be enticing young girls to take a drug that will ruin their lives."

The barkeep's accusations ripple through Shay's mind. Her heart sinks. It seems the woman was right in her assertions. Shay meets the neighbor's eyes. Eyes that are clear and intelligent and no more clouded by hate than Shadi's were.

"Khalti," she says softly. "May I ask you about the scarf you're wearing?"

The woman notches her chin upward, her eyelids lowering to half-mast. Her gaze takes on a guarded sheen. "It is a pretty design, no? It doesn't mean anything. But if it did mean something, it's probably not what you've been conditioned to think."

Shay nibbles her lip. *What had she expected the woman to say?* She doesn't want to stir up trouble, but she also wants to make sure the touched one will be safe until her return.

"And you're fine with living here?" She waves her hand toward Hind's shelter. "Next door to . . ."

"I feel sorry for her." The woman shrugs, then sighs, a sound that's somehow both uncertain and resolved. "But at least I know she isn't going to turn me in."

Shay supposes that's fair. It makes sense for the Naturalists to form a temporary alliance with the outcast touched ones if they share a common threat. The idea of Hind enticing young girls to try Snow unsettles Shay. No, it disgusts her. Because *entice* isn't the right word. She's been *grooming* them for Al-Mukhtar. Maybe Khala Bushra is right—Shay does need to be careful.

She swallows, guiltily wishing she could go back to the moment before she knew her mother might be alive and stay there in her ignorance. How can getting what she's always wanted feel so wrong? If only Ghita had been more forthright from the beginning. "Khala, do you happen to know where I could find a young boy named Badar?"

The woman's chilled expression grows warm again. "You mean my grandson?"

Khala Bushra cups her hands around her mouth like the cone of a trumpet shell and bellows Badar's name. Unlike the elusive cat, the boy comes rambling out of a nearby alley almost immediately. He shows Shay the way back through the sprawling maze of the Bib, more slowly this time, pointing out landmarks she can use to find her way back to Hind again. It turns out there were no traps in the Bib, so why does Shay feel like she's traversed an emotional battlefield and barely made it out with her sanity intact?

✧ ✧ ✧

Shay finds Ghita seated on the floor, cracking argan nuts open with a heavy stone. The force of the midwife's pounding suggests that either the shells are excessively thick, or she's excessively agitated, and in either case, it seems wiser to quietly help than to interrupt. They work in tense silence until the basket of nuts runs empty, by which time Sami is hungry again and the events of the day feel more like something Shay dreamed than real occurrences.

"I saved you a bowl of loubia from lunch," Ghita says, when Shay has tidied the floor and stored the precious argan kernels in glass jars to be crushed and pressed into oil later.

"Thank you, khalti." Shay gathers the cold dish of white beans and spicy tomato sauce that Ghita knows to be her favorite. As she sits near the midwife and baby, she wonders if Hind has eaten today. The flavorful stew in her mouth suddenly has all the taste of dry ashes. She sets the bowl aside, struggling to swallow. "There is something I wish to discuss."

A twitch passes over the midwife's face, but her voice comes soft, drifting on the air as though her lips never moved. "Speak your mind, child."

"I need you to tell me more about my mother, about my birth," Shay hedges, attempting to broach the topic without making outright accusations.

"We've been through it all before." Ghita huffs dismissively. "What does it matter now? When you have a bright future straight ahead of you?"

They had not, in fact, been through it at all. It would be much more accurate to say they had tiptoed around it, pushed it aside, and at the very most, skimmed the surface of it. Shay draws a grounding breath. "I know, and I'm so thankful for the training you have accorded me. For this wonderful new opportunity."

those cast out. Shay peers down the narrow street, her heart still pounding, half expecting him to return.

"Did he see you?" the touched one asks with alarm.

"Only in passing." Shay's attention snaps back to Hind. "Why?"

Hind releases a shaky breath. "Let's just talk about this when we get home, shall we?"

Home. She would say that's the place she just left, but it's not anymore, is it? Not in two days' time, anyway. Seeing her mother like this, Shay feels all her hopes for a new life swing on an emotional pendulum toward despair.

"I can't believe this," she says, stepping back. "I cannot believe you're blitzed right now. I told you to stay in bed. Not to leave. I said I'd be back. You promised you'd stay lucid."

Hind waves a bony hand in a shooing motion. "I said I'd try."

The man—whoever he was—is gone. Shay's adrenaline ebbs, and fatigue rushes in like scavengers descending on a kill. It's been a long, confusing couple of days. Did she misunderstand the touched one's intention? Does it matter? "Is this what you call *trying*?"

Hind looks away. Absently, she reaches between the folds of the desert-style robe that swathes her hair and body and produces an apple. She bites it and pulls a face. "Skin's thick," she says around the morsel, juice dribbling from the corner of her lips. "A sign this resting season will be harsh."

Shay exhales. Hope drains from her body with her breath. The slant of sky above the alley has grown heavy with rain clouds. They dip low, the gray of giant swollen ticks. "Coming here was a mistake."

The touched one straightens to attention, looking almost comical, like a child playing soldier. "No, no, no. Don't say that. I can explain everything."

"Why?" Shay asks so loudly, the touched one winces. "I wanted to help you. Why would you go right back out and use again? You couldn't even go one day. You couldn't"—Shay chokes on the words—"do it for me."

"I meant to go to the market," the touched one whines, and nibbles the fruit. "But all I managed to get was an apple before they closed off the square."

The midwife wrinkles her nose. "I sense a qualifying statement."

Shay tries to laugh, but her effort devolves into a weary sigh. "It's just . . . Don't you always say that knowledge of the past provides tools that help us navigate the future? I've memorized all the technical aspects of midwifery, I've practiced applying the skills, but the bond between mothers and babies still perplexes me. Maybe if I knew more . . ."

"What more is there to know? A mother's love is written in her blood. It's dormant, like Shawafa, until awakened by the act of giving birth, and when a new mother holds her baby, the infant feels her warmth, hears her heartbeat, and recognizes her scent. Simple, really." The midwife's eyes are falling shut as she speaks, a mirror to the baby she's rocking in her arms.

Frustration mounts in Shay's chest. "Khalti, I talked to someone today. Someone who knew my mother. They told me things that were . . . confusing. That didn't match up with what I remember you telling me."

"Is that where you were all day?" Ghita's eyes fly wide, her gentle motions coming to a halt. The baby whimpers in his sleep, and Ghita lowers her voice, returning to rocking him once more. "It's normal to have doubts about any new endeavor, but I wouldn't have staked my reputation on your success if I didn't believe in you."

Shay shoves another spoon of loubia into her mouth, if only to keep herself from saying something she might regret. She's all too aware that any future she may have is still dependent upon the midwife's endorsement of her. But if she doesn't address this now, when will she have another opportunity to do so?

"There *is* something I've never told you," the midwife says, and something in her tone, a rawness Shay is sure she's never heard before, makes her drop her spoon back in the bowl and swallow what's in her mouth, unchewed. "But now that you are older, I think you should know."

Shay holds her breath, and it feels like everything around her has moved closer, like the room has become smaller. Or she's underwater. Is Ghita about to confirm Hind's story?

"I wasn't always a midwife. I was once married. My husband was a fisherman, and we had a beautiful daughter named Sofia. She hated it when her father would leave on his fishing trips. And one night when she was nine, she secretly followed him to the sea. I didn't notice her absence as quickly as I should have.

"On that fateful night, I happened to be hosting a book club meeting in my home with some lady friends. It was raining lightly, and I was able to follow her footsteps, along with the trail left she left by dragging along the wooden bucket I used for bathing her. I suppose in her child's mind she thought it would work as a boat she could use to go sailing after him.

"But the trail disappeared at the water's edge. And there was no trace of Sofia. Not until the next morning, when the empty bucket washed ashore. Not until a moon quarter later, when B'hamu divers finally found her body."

The midwife's voice is calm and steady despite the tragic story she has relayed. Her body remains still and composed. But Shay knows her well enough to see what no one else would be likely to notice:

The subtle change in her breathing pattern, as if each breath requires careful thought rather than being an automatic process.

The dull pain that haunts her eyes.

"Why am I telling you this now, you may ask? Well, I'm telling you so that you will understand that everything happens for a reason. My marriage could not withstand the loss of my daughter. I found myself single and learned midwifery to support myself. A calling I now understand I was meant for and one that I may never have otherwise discovered. And then you came into my life.

"I know all about the rumors, Lalla Shay. But you must let go of them, of all these questions, and look forward to what lies ahead. You ought to be preparing for your fast-approaching journey."

Shay's mind whirls. Ghita knows about the rumors? Shay almost wonders whether they had anything to do with her premature referral to a new position, but the thought is quickly overridden by both a sudden sympathy for Ghita and a renewed sense of obligation to her.

She remembers why she left this morning and her pressing predicament. "It was my intention to prepare, khalti. I went to the forest to harvest moon pepper, and the patch was gone."

The midwife's eyebrows spring up. "Gone?"

"Yes, gone. I planned to harvest enough to last until I settled in Kiddah and could plant my own seeds, but someone else picked the whole patch clean. Who would need that much moon pepper? And moreover, what should I do?"

Ghita takes a deep breath and purses her lips. "Well, what would you do if I were not available to seek advice from and you had to find your own solution?"

"What?" The word comes out with the gasping softness of an embrace-turned-knife-between-the-ribs. But Ghita's question is not asked out of meanness. It's simply true that in Kiddah, Shay will, for the first time ever, be completely on her own. "I'm not going to make it very far if someone discovers what I am."

"You'll be fine," the midwife says, more reassuringly. "Kiddah is bigger than our medina. More people makes it easier for those who are a bit different to blend in and escape scrutiny. Plus, you're no longer a child. If your powers do emerge, you're more likely to be able to control them now than when you were younger."

Shay nods, the words like scraps of meat fed to the attack dogs of her anxiety, more a distraction than a remedy. A little voice in the back of her mind whispers that if Hind was telling the truth about the midwife's daughter, her claims of not using during her pregnancy may also be true. It's a thought Shay hardly takes comfort in, since it suggests she spent her childhood being sick for no reason.

The midwife looks like she's about to say more, when her gaze homes in on Shay's hands. "You said you went out to forage, but you weren't wearing your gloves when you returned."

Any bravado, any anger Shay has allowed to take up space inside her disintegrates. She closes her fingers and splays them open again as if the gloves will magically reappear. She forgot, or didn't think Ghita would notice, or just didn't think. Try as she may, she cannot meet the midwife's eyes.

"I must have dropped them," she whispers hoarsely.

"What's that?"

Shay stands abruptly. "I'll go back out and find them, while there is still light," she vows with such earnestness, she nearly convinces herself.

"You haven't finished eating," the midwife scolds.

Shay quickly empties the bowl, forcing herself to push every bite past the dry ache in her throat. Because the midwife is wrong. So wrong. She's not ready to stand on her own. She may have grown into the form of a woman on the outside, but on the inside, she's still a little girl. Needy and desperate for approval.

✧ ✧ ✧

In the absence of an intention to actually look for the gloves, Shay climbs to the rooftop garden, where she can think. The sun is fading, the sky slipping into the amber robes of early evening. The sounds of bustling on the streets below are winding down to a slow hum. The herbs and flowers in the garden grow more fragrant as dusk nears, as if by releasing their sweet scents, they might entice the sun to linger a little longer.

Shay lowers herself to a sitting position and leans back against the parapet. She gazes upward across the horizon and spots the distant glow of Najmat Al-Maghrib. It's the first star to appear in the night sky and is often visible to the naked eye in late afternoons during this season of earth's cycle. There is small comfort in the thought that even in a new medina, the same constellations will always spread above her.

The stairwell that runs up the side of the building creaks and clangs. Shay cranes her head, anticipating the appearance of her neighbor Zaytuna, who often tends to her goat around this time. But an altogether different face pops into view, followed by a body dressed not in a servant uniform this time, but a classic—if simple—gandoura.

She's too stunned, and honestly too tired, to muster a reaction.

"Salaams," Shadi greets her, making his voice timid and soft, as though to avoid startling her. Which would make more sense were she not staring directly at him.

"Let me guess." She tilts her head thoughtfully. "You sometimes like to slip away to other people's rooftops. To clear your head?"

He chuckles, and Shay dislikes her inability to detest the sound. "No, believe it or not, I knocked on the door downstairs first. But the midwife told me I'd find you up here."

The confusion that passes over her is brief, like a cloud momentarily blocking the sun. Of course, the midwife knows exactly where she is. Shay has never been as good at hiding things as the midwife is at sniffing them out. Given the circumstances, it might have behooved her to work harder at developing the skill of deceit.

She narrows her eyes at Shadi. "Did you follow me home?"

"Oh." Shadi blinks a few times in rapid succession before flashing his palms in innocence. "Oh no. I wasn't . . . It wasn't hard to find you. I merely asked for directions to the midwife's home."

Shay takes a calming breath. That makes sense. And he's changed clothes since she saw him last, so . . . yeah. She just really, really needs to be alone and think right now. "Wakha, so why are you looking for me?"

"Do you mind . . . ?" He gestures toward the empty space beside her. "Can I sit down for a minute?"

No. "Um, sure." Shay scoots far to one side, even though there's ample room already.

"Thanks." Shadi eases down next to her, and Shay notices the edges of his hair are damp, dribbling droplets of water down the smooth skin of his tanned neck. He smells like soap blended with essential oils. Sandalwood, maybe? And he somehow managed to scrub the green stain from his fingers, which reminds her of all the reasons she should not be noticing *what* he smells like. "I came because I want to give you something. To thank you for your advice earlier. The banana peel really helped."

Shay nods as he holds out his wrist for her to inspect. Indeed, the blister is smaller and much less painful-looking. Still, it's not the kind of thing that warrants a house call to thank someone, much less a gift. He reaches into his pocket and pulls out a small sachet.

Shay knows what it is before he hands it to her. Before she catches a whiff of the pungent odor. Before she tugs loose the drawstring to reveal the vibrant green leaves tucked inside.

Moon pepper.

"What is this?" She asks angrily, her fist clenching around the cloth and crunching the herbs inside. "I don't know what you think I am, but . . ."

"Please, let me explain," he says gently, his voice soft as an evening breeze. "I took it for my sisters. They live far away, and moon pepper doesn't grow there, so I picked it all to take to them. I needed to make sure they had a supply that can last for quite a while, because I don't get to visit them often. They require it, especially in the region where they reside, for their safety."

Shay is not certain he is telling the truth. Between the midwife and the touched one, she's not sure if anything anyone says is true anymore. But all she really hears him saying is that there are others like her. She's not the only one.

Of course, she knew there must be other hizouras, but she's never known one personally. Or even met someone who has. Too bad Shadi said his sisters don't live nearby. Shay thinks she'd like to meet them.

"It didn't occur to me that anyone else would need it," he continues. "Not until I saw you in the woods today. If that's not enough, I can bring you more."

"No, that's fine. It's . . . Thank you." The amount is enough to get her out of Nezjar, at least. And Shay is grateful, or she wants to be. Would be, if she everything weren't as confusing as it is right now. She laughs, suddenly feeling foolish. "I guess you're not a Naturalist, then?"

He stiffens, inhaling sharply. "Is that what you thought?"

"Well, it made sense at the time," Shay blunders, now worried she's insulted him. "I thought you picked the moon pepper so that any hizoura in the area would have to come out of hiding and you could . . . you know."

He blanches. "I could . . . what?"

She runs a finger across her throat, clicks her teeth. "Kill me?"

He winces. "First off, I'm so sorry that you thought that. I—wow, I have never been pegged as a murderer before. That is certainly not the impression I intended to give."

Shay shakes her head remorsefully. "You didn't. That's not how I meant it. But do you see the logic in my thinking?"

"I'm not sure the Naturalists would kill you either, but it is probably best to avoid their notice."

"Oh." Shay tilts her head. "What do you think their plan is, then? My understanding is they want to eradicate magic in all forms."

"Yeah, sure, but for now they have no power. They have as much reason to stay hidden as you do. The main thing they want is to overthrow Al-Mukhtar, destroy Snow, and stop its production, right? I don't think you have to worry about them hunting down hizouras, at least not until after those goals are achieved."

"How would they accomplish those goals?"

Shadi shrugs, then squints thoughtfully. "I guess they'd have to find the source of Snow, and destroy that."

Shay has never met someone willing to talk to openly about the rebels. Most people are afraid to even discuss the topic, lest they be accused of insurrection. "And after? What do you think would be the fate of those with tainted blood?"

"If it were up to the Naturalists?" He speaks carefully, as if the words are tipped with burrs. "I don't think even they are in agreement. They'd probably have to take the matter to their council for a vote."

"They have a council?"

He waves his hand in uncertainty. "I would assume."

"Shadi, please be honest," Shay says, trying not to sound like she's desperate for someone, anyone to be honest with her. "How do you know so much about the Naturalists if you aren't one?"

He gives her a look that feels as though he's truly *seeing* her. Shay isn't sure what that even means, just that it's not unwelcome. "I went to one of their meetings," he breaks eye contact, glancing off to the side when he speaks. His throat flexes. "I hung in the back and observed. I figured I needed to learn as much as I could about them. Know thine adversary and all that. For my sisters' sakes."

Shay frowns. *He's lying!* Or at the very least, there's something he's not telling her. And, at this moment, she's irrationally thankful that she can tell. That's comforting. In some strange way, it makes her trust him. Since she can't discern when or if Ghita or Hind are telling the truth, it feels good to at least know where she stands with Shadi.

Her standards have hit rock bottom.

"Shadi?"

He gazes at her with the same intensity as before. Not just seeing her, she realizes now, but a look that says he wants to *know* her. "Yes?"

She's not sure what she wants to ask until the words spill from her lips. "What would you do if you had to choose between someone related to you by blood or someone with whom you shared a history?"

"That's tough." He sighs in understanding and nods as if it were a yes or no question. "But you don't have to be related to someone to develop a bond that's as strong, if not stronger than, blood. It's all about how well you know them."

Shay's not sure that's the answer she wanted to hear. But maybe it's the one she needed to. Before she can thank him, he continues: "Then again, there is something to be said for familial loyalty. Like, your family will always be your family, right?"

Shay's shoulders slump. She shouldn't have asked.

"That's not very helpful, is it?" Shadi smiles apologetically. "I guess the more important question is, why do you have to choose? Why can't you maintain ties with both?"

His words have an unexpectedly soothing effect. She's still not sure who to believe or what course of action to take, but she feels like the answer is within reach. Like maybe if she rests on it, it will come to her. "Thanks, Shadi."

He stands, perhaps picking up on her weariness, and dusts off the back of his gandoura before offering his hand and helping her to her feet.

"And thank you again, for the moon pepper," she adds.

"Of course." He gives her a serious look, and the world below suddenly feels much farther away, as if the rooftop, the two of them, have been cut off from all that exists. "You know your secret is safe with me."

She can't explain why she believes him, but she does. "Likewise."

He turns around at the head of the stairwell and gives her an awkward wave. "Until we see each other again, God willing."

Shay starts to frown but quickly hides it behind a smile. She hasn't told him she may be leaving and doesn't wish to bring it up now, so she waves in return. "God willing."

He starts to leave again but turns around once more. "Just to be clear, I think you deserve to have people in your life who *choose you*, instead of making you choose."

Shay's cheeks warm, and she's not sure why. Most likely, he means that's what people in general deserve, not her specifically. After all, he doesn't know her well enough to make such an assertion. She thinks back to what Hind said about love at first sight, but Shay has never had time for romance before, and she certainly doesn't have time for it *now*.

"Yeah, I mean, there's only one me, right?" she asks, trying to cover her embarrassment. No—discomfort. Self-consciousness? Whatever one would call this irritating and *fuzzy* and inconvenient feeling.

"Exactly," he says, as though that were the message he intended to convey all along.

9

Sleep, little baby,
Until dinner is cooked,
And if it isn't, the neighbor's will be.
Sleep, little baby,
Until the house is cleaned,
And if it isn't, the maid will come.
Sleep, little baby,
Until the laundry is washed,
And if it isn't, we will bathe in our clothes and lie side by side in the sun.
Sleep, little baby,
But don't sleep too long.
The food will be eaten, the house will be dirtied, the clothes will be worn,
But my baby, oh, my baby, won't always be a baby, you see.

—a mother's lullaby

After fumbling through the dawn prayers and neglecting to eat a proper breakfast, Shay gathers together a couple of rounds of khobz, a half dozen eggs, and some assorted vegetables from the garden. She swipes her foraging knife, remembering how Ghita allowed her to buy it when she was old enough to understand it wasn't a toy. Not a gift, really. *Not like the gloves.*

Swallowing a pang of guilt, she arranges it all in a knapsack she fits into the wide hood of her djellaba. She doesn't take the moon pepper Shadi gave her, not yet. She hasn't felt any stirring of magic inside herself, not that she knows what it would feel like. For now, she brings the sachet of leaves along, keeping it handy in case, and heads back through the winding streets of Nezjar toward the Bib.

Time will tell if she needs it. Whether Hind lied.

Shay failed to obtain solid answers from the midwife, but she must keep her word and check on Hind. Besides, the loss of the gloves is bad enough; Shay cannot lose her ticket, which is currently in the touched one's possession.

If she lets the midwife down, she'll be out of a career, and if she lets Hind down, well, the unthinkable could happen. But what if Shadi is right? What if she doesn't have to choose? Hind could come with her to Kiddah. Shay could help her mother there.

Two days is not much time to raise money for a second ticket, but if Shay is willing to delve farther into Al-Ghaba Mayita than normal, who knows what rare flowers or precious herbs she may locate? If it's a long shot, so was finding her mother alive. That their paths have crossed is all the proof she needs that there must be a way for them to make a life together.

And if Hind has made mistakes, done terrible things, at least she's willing to turn over a new leaf. In a way, Shay will be saving not just Hind but any girls she would have gone on to influence. The cycle can end. With every step, her confidence grows, and her conviction soars. Helping Hind is not just the *right* thing to do, Shay feels, with sudden certainty—it is the *only* thing that matters.

Shay raises her hand in signal as she enters the Bib a second time, though if any rebels are looking out, she doesn't catch so much as a glimmer of them. There's an aura to everything now, light reflecting off the structures around her in that kind of sharp intensity that early morning brings, with all its promises of *newness* and *possibilities.*

She's close to Hind's shelter when voices rise from a nearby alley like angry flares.

Logic dictates, or at least strongly recommends, that it's best to avoid trouble and continue on. But one of the voices sounds masculine and the other feminine, which alone might override her logic, even if the latter voice weren't Hind's.

Shay has hardly been reacquainted with her mother long enough to recognize her voice, and yet, by some soul-deep recognition, she does. A charge vibrates over her skin like a glass rod rubbed with silk. It's a feeling that's difficult to ignore.

"You know what you must do," the male voice barks out as Shay draws closer. "That is, if you hope to be spared a ride on the blood-wagons."

The woman whimpers, a low and desperate sound, and Shay rushes forward, colliding with the man as he exits the alley. She stumbles back and looks up, immobilized. Half his face bears deep burn scars, while the other half appears younger than she expects. Young, and what any girl her age—herself not excluded—would consider comely. Shay averts her eyes, not wishing to stare, but not before she notices that the man's eyes hold a strange quality that makes them the oldest-looking part on his body.

"Watch where you're going," the man growls, proceeding to call Shay a name that makes her flinch. As his gaze lands squarely on her face, he stops, squints, and lurches forward. Just then, a group of women carrying kindling on their backs comes by. Seeing them, the man pushes roughly past Shay and slinks away, melting into the shadows.

Shay races forward to where the touched one hunches against a wall, her body curling inward in as close to a ball as one can manage and still be standing. She scans Hind up and down, and finding no gross injury, she gently cups her shoulders. "Hind, are you well?"

The touched one allows herself to be unfolded. Seems disoriented as Shay's eyes roam her face.

A reddish welt, the beginning of a bruise, blooms over her left cheekbone. Guided by Shay's stare, the touched one cradles her own cheek, her fingertips sparking green. She removes her hand, and the mark has vanished. That's when Shay sees—really sees—her eyes. Gone are the smoke-brown irises she gazed into only yesterday as they made plans for a new start, erased in a vacuum of white.

"Who was that man? Is he your supplier?" If Al-Mukhtar provides Snow to the touched ones who reside at the kasbah, someone else must supply it to

Shay shakes her head, not sure how that's relevant until a gallows-shaped shadow falls over her mind. She shakes her head harder to dismiss the memory. "Another hanging?"

"Two days in a row." Hind nods, swallowing. "Since I couldn't buy food . . ."

Shay finishes for her: "You bought Snow instead?"

"When you say it like that . . ."

"And to think I wanted to take you with me." Shay feels like someone waking from a warm, cozy dream into the harsh cold of morning in the peak of resting season. "I needed this, though, to know more about my past, the things Ghita kept from me, so I could put it to rest before starting out on a new venture. But I think it's best we part ways now. So, if you can give me the ticket . . ."

"What ticket?" the touched one asks in the most innocent tone, the white blots of her eyes unable to hide the guilt flicking over them.

"The one I gave you when I promised to come back." Shay's thoughts tumble around her head, a cruel realization forming. Nothing about the state of the touched one's provisions suggested someone with a reliable source of coin. And while Shay isn't sure exactly how hard Snow is to come by, she knows it isn't free. "What did you do?"

Hind strangles out a dry sob and starts blabbering: "I just wanted one last blitz before quitting for good. That's all. I wasn't ready. I couldn't help it. I'm sorry. Please, don't be mad. Don't leave. This will be the last time. Try to understand. Snow ain't cheap."

"You sold the ticket?" Shay's voice comes out a wisp. She shakes her head, still hoping it isn't true. "And you used the coin to buy more Snow?"

Hind's whited eyes go milky with tears. She nods.

"How could you?" The knapsack Shay packed hangs heavy between her shoulders. How foolish she was to worry about someone who gave so little thought to her in return.

At first, she thinks the wail she hears is coming from inside her head, her brain creating a reenactment of her frustrations, but it draws out and raises in volume. An animal of some sort, she thinks. Perhaps warning other animals of danger.

A little late, my friend.

"I'll escort you home," she tells Hind, beginning to walk back toward her shelter. "And leave you the provisions I gathered before I go."

"You brought me food?" the touched one says in soft surprise, allowing herself to be pulled along. "That was thoughtful. Got anything sweet in there?"

Shay shakes her head, rubbing her ears as the cries continue, the likes of which no living creature should ever make. Not a warning. No, these are sounds of pain. Torment, even.

"What about bread?" Hind stumbles slightly, eyeing Shay's bulging hood as though imagining what untold treasures it holds. "A sandwich sounds divine."

Shay grits her teeth. "Do you hear that?"

The touched one smiles loosely as though pretending to understand a joke. "Hear what?"

"My question exactly." Shay veers off the gravel path, away from the rows of dilapidated shelters. The touched one follows at rapid sprint as she skirts around discarded furniture, a small chicken pen, and the sapling fruit trees of a burgeoning community garden.

"What are we looking for?" Hind pants, gazing around in confusion.

"This way."

The animal's protestations bleed into a baleful moan. Shay parts a patch of tangled shrubs to reveal a shivering cat. The poor thing is missing half its fur, the entirety of its face an open wound.

The touched one gasps, appearing at her shoulder. "How did you know it was there?"

Shay blinks at her. "It was making enough racket to alert the whole Bib."

"No," Hind says quietly. Her eyes dart from Shay to the wounded animal and back. "Just look at it. Why, it barely has the strength to muster a whimper."

Ignoring her, Shay kneels in the dry grass. She stares into the one good eye the cat has left. Pain, deep and crushing, reflects in its opalescent depths. A burning sensation sears across her skin, and Shay gasps. *Too hot. Too hot. Help me.*

"Good thing the Snow hasn't worn off," Hind grumbles, squatting beside Shay. A blush of green flows to her fingertips. With both trepidation and awe, Shay understands the touched one's intention.

"It's alright. We're going to help," she says gently to the animal. The feline lays its head down and quiets. Hind positions her hands over the animal's exposed skin. The green glow spreads from her fingertips until her whole hand illuminates. Thin tendrils drift over the cat's body.

"She was burned by hot oil that a drunk poured from their window," Hind declares. Shay measures her breath as, follicle by follicle, new fur appears beneath the green ripples. The light flows over the cat's head. Mangled flesh reforms, its ruined eye restored.

When the touched one withdraws her hands, the cat pushes to its feet. It bounds to Shay and rubs against her thighs, purring loudly. Shay runs her hand across its silky coat of fur, then buries her fingers in the thick ruff of its neck, amazed at the transformation. She smiles at Hind. No matter what she's been conditioned to think about magic, she can't help feeling the touched one has done a good thing. Nothing short of a miracle, really.

"You sure care about animals, don't you?" The touched one hobbles to her feet, the light in her hands now subdued.

"Of course." Shay doesn't see how anyone couldn't. Animals feel things just like people, and most of the time, they're easier to be around. "God created humans and appointed them stewards of the earth, including the plants and animals that grow and live here."

"It's like you have a special connection to them, though," Hind says, more musing to herself than inviting further commentary. "Like they understand you."

✧ ✧ ✧

As Shay unloads the meager provisions onto Hind's shelves, the touched one prepares tea and pours *two* glasses. She seems to have recovered from her confrontation with the man, perhaps soothed by the cat's rescue, but then, she's not the one with reason to continue being upset. No, that's too small a word. Shay is *angry*. But even she couldn't help being glad when Khala Bushra confirmed that the feline was the missing Muezza. The neighbor was so happy to have her pet returned, she offered Hind coin as a reward. Coin that Hind adamantly refused, a noble if ironic gesture.

Shay is starting to see that, despite outside appearances, there is an underlying current of community in the shantytown. Although she wonders how Bushra would feel if she knew her feline companion was healed by the very magic the Naturalists object to.

"I really mustn't stay," Shay says, though, in truth, she's not eager to return and explain to Ghita why she no longer has the caravan ticket in her possession. Light rain patters against the window. It's not falling hard enough to prevent her from walking home, but she worries whether Hind's shelter will leak if it picks up later.

"About the man you saw . . ." Hind holds out Shay's glass, inviting her to hear more. The white screen over her eyes is fading, smoky brown seeping back into her irises.

Shay accepts the tea, telling herself it's only because she's thirsty. "Did you buy Snow from him?"

"What?" Hind waves Shay into the sitting area, taking a moment to mull over the question, like there's more than one possible answer. "Not exactly."

The warm tea glass in Shay's hands is grounding. She does her best to project the composure Ghita taught her to have in the many unexpected situations a midwife can face, although this particular situation is somewhat out of her purview. "Explain."

"I'm in debt, habibti." Hind speaks softly, as though it will cushion the reality of her admission. "For Snow I was given on credit."

Shay sighs. A not-small part of her still wants to help her mother, but her idea of taking foraging to the extreme seems silly in light of this new information. "How much coin?"

"Not coin." Hind shifts uncomfortably. "I owe the man from the alley magical favors."

"Magic?" Shay set her glass down on a wobbly side table. She needs her hands free to brace the sides of her head in case her brain erupts, a phenomenon Shay imagines is extremely rare but that nonetheless feels imminent. "You can't use magic without taking more Snow."

"Exactly." Hind shrugs helplessly. "I want to quit. You know I meant everything I said today. It's this place, these debts that are holding me back. I'd be different if I could start over. If I went somewhere new."

"How will you ever get purged if you keep using?" Shay's mind churns, and through the layers of confusion, a startling answer comes to her: When Hind said she couldn't hear the cat, Shay dismissed it as the touched one's lack of lucidity, but that doesn't explain what Shay *felt*. It was as though the animal's pain had been inside her. Or she had somehow been in its mind.

Like magic . . .

She should put the moon pepper leaves in her tea right now. She's gone too long without them already. And if what happened *was* magic, if her powers *are* emerging, that means Hind definitely lied about using Snow during her pregnancy.

Shay stands and shakes her djellaba's hood until the sachet of herbs tumbles out onto the floor. She scoops it up and fumbles with the drawstring, her fingers trembling.

Hind watches her with an uneasy expression.

Shay pauses. "What?"

"Did you know my Shawafa has two functions?"

Shay blinks as though the touched one has spoken in another language. Without answering, she goes back to the drawstring, which appears to have gotten worked into a knot.

"Primarily to heal, but also to diagnose," Hind continues, unperturbed. "It's how I knew what happened to the cat. I see wellness like waves of harmony and disease like disruptions in those waves. These disruptions, they don't all look the same. Different ailments have their own signature. With experience, I've learned to read them. And that is how I know you've been taking something that's making you sick."

"Moon pepper," Shay admits, her fingers stilling. Her heart stills with them. "But I missed my last dose."

The stench of the leaves seeps through the cloth, and her stomach sours in response.

What if she could use her magic for good, the way Hind did with the cat? What if *she* could pay Hind's debts for her? No Snow involved?

Shay stares at her hands and tries to feel something, to connect with whatever came over her back in the ally. A tingle, a shiver. A spreading warmth. Some spark of magic under her skin, a thrum within her veins.

To her disappointment, nothing happens.

"It doesn't work like that," Hind explains, seeming to understand what Shay is attempting. "The powers of a hizoura don't manifest all at once. You have to learn how to use them, like learning to swim."

Shay shakes her hands in frustration. "We don't have time for that."

"There is a faster way," Hind says, drawing the words out like they taste delicious. "But before I show you, I want you to give me whatever toxin you have that the midwife has been pumping into your body for God knows how long."

Shay is surprised by how easy it is to hand over the sachet, how liberating it feels. She never realized—or more accurately, never admitted to herself—that she has always *hated* taking the herbs.

Smiling, Hind digs into the front of her robe. She pulls out a pouch hung on a cord and empties its contents onto her palm. Her fingers quickly close, and she makes a show of unfurling them one by one . . .

"A ring," Shay says, confused. Admittedly, it is the most stunning piece of jewelry she's ever seen. The band of polished dark wood melds into a large chunk of silver crystal, a gem Shay can't identify.

"La." Hind clicks her tongue, delight sparkling in her eyes. She twists the ring back and forth in her fingers, pinging thin prisms around the room. "This is a hjabat. A rare talisman that imbues any woman who wears it with access to her Shawafa."

Shay's not sure which is more unbelievable: that such an object exists or that Hind would continue using Snow while possessing such a ready solution.

Unless there's something the touched one isn't saying. Her shoulders tense. "Does it have side effects?"

"None. It doesn't make the wearer blitzed. It isn't addictive. And it won't accelerate the aging process." Hind holds up a finger. "The only problem is it doesn't work for me."

Shay frowns. "Why not?"

"Touched ones have conditioned their Shawafa to respond to Snow." Hind slides the ring onto her bony finger. "See? Nothing. But *you* . . . your powers are unsoiled. Pure. And the hjabat will make the process of mastering them . . ." She snaps her fingers, her smile growing so wide, it almost looks too big for her face. "Instantaneous."

Something feels wrong. Shay knows magic is unpredictable. Take, for instance, Sami's mother and her Shawafa. Hadiqmin, Ghita called it. The midwife described it as amazing, but it nearly killed Sami. And it *did* kill the khala at the farmhouse.

In the times before natural magic disappeared, Sami's mother might have been a gardener and used her Shawafa to nudge her plants and vegetables to flourish. She might have grown herbs so powerful that meals enhanced with them would leave a person full for days. Foods with such high nutrients, they could save the realm's poorest from starving. And flowers with scents so lush and lasting, their perfumes could raise the lowest spirits. But with Snow, that same Shawafa manifested as killer thorns, snaking vines, and ghost bees.

Which would be the case with the hjabat?

"You're overthinking this." Hind scrutinizes Shay's face like someone combing the ground for a dropped coin. She holds out the ring. "This is the only way for me to avoid using more Snow. We can easily earn enough to pay my debts and to cover the price of two caravan tickets to Kiddah. Or you can leave me here, but I'd certainly hate to up and die after finally being reunited with my daughter."

A million protests wither in Shay's throat. Despite a rocky start, she wants to believe she and Hind can be a family of two. Sure, the touched one has lied to her, effectively stolen from her, but there's still hope for her to change. She just needs to be *alive* to do so. And maybe this way, Ghita will never even know about the missing ticket.

No sooner does she slip the hjabat on, feel its snug squeeze around her finger, the drag of its heft on her delicate hand, than the crystal emits a silver glow. Shay stares, mesmerized by the sparkling light, unable to look away. Even as she breaks into shivers. Even as she cracks into sweat. A dark speck appears at the crystal's center. It pulses, a shadow sun chasing light to the edges until the gem smooths into a flat well of black.

Shay tries to ask Hind what it means, her query lost amid the sickness rolling through her stomach. Everything tilts sideways, the way the world must look to a newborn. Then she's falling, the darkness pulling her down.

And down.

And down.

She croaks out one word before the gloaming takes her: "Mmi?"

10

Every new road is a choice, and every choice, a new road.

—Hazmaggi proverb

Shay isn't in her body. Or at least she can't feel it.

She can't feel anything. Her mind sifts through a fog of silver light. She catches the scents of blood and sweat and something deep and earthy—smells she associates with the act of birth. Soft voices murmur, coming from an unknown location, from every direction, and none.

Shay can't move. She'd say she's floating, but even that requires being attached to a body. Distantly, she thinks she should panic, knows something has gone wrong with the hjabat, can conceptualize what an appropriate level of concern should look like even if she's unable to rally it.

The silver cloud that holds her feels neither threatening nor peaceful. Neither warm nor cold. She is lost and found. Alive and dead. Everything and nothing. How strange. And how perfectly natural.

The murmurs grow louder. Women. Shay picks out four distinct voices, each honeyed and smooth in its own right, before their words start making sense.

"This one is yours, Iman. She belongs to the silver pantheon."

"I can see that, but I don't think she's ready."

"Find a way to make her ready. I can't bear these conditions much longer."

"You've endured this for a hundred solar cycles already," a fourth voice chimes in. "A little longer won't hurt. Think of it as an extended vacation."

"I'd never willingly choose to vacation in a dank and dusty cave," the third one argues back. "These conditions are wreaking havoc on my complexion."

"Seriously, Noor?" the first voice asks. "You do realize you're made of glowing minerals?"

"This isn't about our comfort," says the second voice, the one belonging to Iman. "We all know things have taken a dark turn in our absence."

"Is she the one we have been waiting for? Where are her companions?" questions the third voice, the one called Noor.

"Alas, she is alone." This, Shay is mostly sure, comes from the first voice. "And it doesn't look like she will awaken anytime soon."

"Metaphorically speaking?" Noor asks.

"No, physically," the first voice answers. "Glory to heavens, the rocks aren't the only dense things in this cave."

"Stop that," Iman scolds, clucking. "It's because of the hjabat. She can't move as long as it's on her finger. It seems she hasn't crossed the veil using her own powers, probably doesn't understand that she could. She's only here because the talisman has been spelled."

"How tragic," the fourth voice declares. "If only we were there to help her."

"Why are you all looking at me?" Noor asks, sounding exasperated.

"It is your moon season," Iman says dryly.

"Oh, fine. *Wake up.*"

The last words are spoken into Shay's ear followed by two quick snaps. As though riding a shock wave, she becomes aware of the hjabat's heavy pull on her finger. Then a sensation of greater heaviness, like wet sand filling her bones. She blinks, and her vision clicks into focus.

Ashen branches make fractal patterns above her like the network of arteries in Ghita's anatomy books. Beyond, a red moon casts the night sky in a sheen the color of fresh-spilled blood.

That can't mean anything good.

Pine needles poke into her arms and legs. Cold seeps through the fabric of her djellaba, moist soil clinging to her back. The air smells less metallic now, more like rot. The voices grow softer and move farther away, blending into a slippery blur.

A crisp rustle alerts her to the movement of something nearby. The smell grows so strong, Shay would gag if everything other than her eyelids weren't paralyzed. In fact, she's not entirely sure she's breathing, although she must be. She isn't dead—at least, she doesn't think so.

More rustling, indicating more than one something. Shay tries to remember how she came to be here. Here in . . . Warped wilderness swirls into focus. She's in Al-Ghaba Mayita. Deeper than she's ever been. But how did she get here? The last thing she remembers is sliding Hind's ring onto her finger. It was supposed to lend her magic, not knock her out.

What did her mother do?

Even now, Shay's panic stays a subtle buzz below her skin, as if her emotions are wrapped in the fluff of poof flowers. The rustling moves closer. Pads of small feet press against her skin, followed by the heft of a plump animal, the skitter of tiny nails up her arm. A flash of fur comes into view. A squirrel. Except, like the forest itself, the creature is all wrong.

For one thing, it outweighs most cats she's encountered. Its beady eyes glow red, patches of dried pus mat its red-brown fur, and it smells awful, which solves one mystery. The creature sits on her chest and stares at her, its mouth so overrun with pointy teeth that its jaws can't neatly close.

Louder movement, from bigger things that ramble and smash around the forest. Before Shay can ponder their nature, the squirrel unleashes a high-pitched squeal.

Shay closes her eyes as if that will mute the horrid sound. When it doesn't, she wills her body to roll, her arm to lift, any part of her to engage in some motion with the capacity to shake the squirrel off. Something about the animal's sickly appearance reminds her of her connection with the wounded cat, how Hind said it understood her. Unable to talk, she makes desperate eye contact with the squealing creature.

Please stop.

The animal quiets, and Shay breathes a sigh of relief, pleased to discover she *can* breathe. But her mind quickly races again, fueled by thoughts of being attacked, if not by the squirrel, then the other animals she heard. Their lingering presence prickles her periphery. Lacking options, she doesn't take time to dwell on how little she knows about the way her hizoura powers work.

She maintains eye contact with the squirrel and envisions the animal using its dexterous paws and little thumbs to remove the ring. The squirrel flicks its mangy tail, then scrabbles off her chest. She feels the ring wiggle back and forth on her finger a few times before the creature slips it off.

Pain hits her like a landslide. Her limbs are sore, her ribs feel bruised, and her back is stiff, as if she's been run down by a herd of donkeys. The squirrel squeaks and chirps, and the timbre of these sounds is blessedly softer and less offensive than its previous vocalizations.

Shay slowly raises her body upright. Her headache makes her dizzy, which makes her nauseous, but she takes it as more evidence that she's alive. She draws a few deep breaths. The squirrel holds the ring out in its strangely handlike paws, waiting. She accepts it and hopes the creature will leave her be.

The crystal's surface has returned to smooth-faced silver, leaving no trace of the primordial darkness she glimpsed. With her attention on the hjabat, it takes a few moments for Shay to realize the other animals—if you can call them that—have formed a circle around her.

There are deer with eyes clouded white. Chunks of their flesh have fallen away, exposing warped bone and broken ribs. Bony spikes line the backs of wolves with empty eye sockets. Foxes, rabbits, and one large bear are covered in seeping lesions, half-healed scabs, and bulbous tumors. What may be an owl peers down from the branch of a nearby tree, half its feathers stripped away and a fat worm dangling from its cheek.

Shay wobbles to her feet and fans her arm in a wide shooing motion. "What are you all staring at? I don't want any trouble. Go on now! Leave me be."

The monstrosities slowly back away, slinking into the leafy folds of the forest undergrowth.

"Hello? Hind?

"Are you there? Is anyone there?"

When no one answers, Shay gazes at the ring. She wonders if the strange voices she heard are somehow trapped inside it, but that makes no sense. In any case, she's not willing to risk deathlike paralysis by putting it back on her finger to find out.

Shay secures the hjabat in her waist satchel and hugs herself. She can't be alone. Not when she's finally found her mother. Their situation may not be ideal, but they can work on things . . .

Or so she thought.

The panic that's hung back rushes in like an angry mob.

No. No. No.

Tears sting the bottom of her throat. She turns a circle, tall cedars spinning with her, a majestic sprawl of shaggy fronds. Ghastly faces seem to peer from their fat scales of bark, with gnarls for eyes, mouths twisted in hollow screams. There are plants she's never seen: mushrooms that look like spindly fingers clawing up from the ground and vines of white flowers in the shape of tiny skulls.

How did she even get here?

On her second spin, the shallow ruts of wheel marks jump out at her.

They stretch out to form a long path through the grass. One that looks fresh.

Her heart wrenches.

There's no break in the line, no sign that whoever dropped her here turned around and went back the way they came. What business would Hind have this far inside the forest? Or in the land of Ard Al-Ghul that lies beyond?

She peers as far as her eyes can see in one direction and then the other, tracking the grooves to where they disappear in the thick of the woods. The stars might provide a point of reference to orient her, but the dense forest canopy blots any bright enough to cut through the moon's red veil. Shay squats to study the dirt trail. She dips her finger into a crescent-shaped imprint, the kind a horse pulling a carriage would leave behind.

Did her mother—no, she doesn't deserve that title—did *Hind* haul Shay's unconscious body out here and dump her? Her aching bones support that theory while also suggesting the deed was done ungently. But she couldn't have done it alone. It has the man in the alley's suspicious scent all over it, except Shay can't imagine what part of leaving her stranded could possibly decrease the touched one's debts.

Shay could try to find her and ask her to explain it all, but Hind lies as easily as birds break into song. Here's what she knows: The direction opposite of where the hoofmarks are pointing will take her back to Ghita's condemnation and certain disgrace, while following them will lead her straight into her mother's web of lies and betrayal.

There may still be some way for Shay to salvage her apprenticeship. Failing that, Ghita at least deserves an explanation. After all she's invested in Shay.

But the midwife did suggest it's time for Shay to find her own solutions.

After waffling longer than she cares to admit, Shay makes the only choice she was ever going to.

✧ ✧ ✧

Shay jumps at each shuffle in the brush, every distant wail. Crickets warble and insects trill, their pitch so high, her teeth lock. Having been unconscious for the journey, she has no idea how deeply into the forest she was carted, and the more she walks, the surer she becomes that Hind played her for a fool.

By the red glow of a not-right moon, she painstakingly follows the wheel tracks. The darkness is unhelpful enough without a trail that behaves wonkily to slow her down. It often disappears into the base of a large trunk or a tight stand of trees, only to mysteriously emerge on the other side.

She steps over a root poking up from the ground and avoids a sneaky pothole, but stumbles smack into a sticky web moments later. A spider the size of a dinner plate scuttles over her foot. Her nerves get so frazzled, she spends twenty beakers in one place, unable to determine whether it's a boulder up ahead or a hungry bear ready to pounce.

Shay knows waiting for sunrise would be wiser. The problem is, if she stops moving, she could fall asleep here. That isn't an option. Since she was young, Ghita and the other khalat have warned her and every other child in Mekchaouen about the dangers of the forest. Their young minds were filled with tales of children who played too close to the edge and disappeared, never to be seen again.

They say there's a tree that produces only rotten apples. That whoever eats one will see their own death. Spirits, appearing as dead loved ones, lure people into lakes to be drowned or onto rocky outcroppings from which they plunge to their demise. It's even possible the voices she heard, or thought she heard, belonged to such forest spirits—another reason not to attempt further contact.

Teetering on the edge of exhaustion, Shay stops to rest on a fallen log. That's when she first smells it.

A delicious sweetness infiltrates her senses. A scent so sugary and rich, so fruity and mouthwatering, she can't help but follow it to the edge of the forest. She's so enchanted as she stumbles through the clearing that the scene before her doesn't register right away. In fact, for the briefest moment, she imagines she took the other route after all and has arrived safely in Nezjar.

But no. *No.*

This is not her medina with its neat blue buildings and alleys awash with life.

This is someplace else entirely.

A place where abandoned-looking buildings crouch as though afraid, their crumbling facades caked with grime. Where thuja trees line the streets, bared of all but their prized wood. Their shorn branches rise like arms begging mercy from God, sharp-beaked vultures nesting in their crooks.

A sleek carriage coasts along a cracked red clay road, drawn by ghastly skeleton horses. Unlike the forest creatures, which seemed only half dead, these horses are entirely composed of gleaming, fleshless bone. Bright, floating orbs occupy the sockets where their eyes should rest.

Shay gasps, but the sound comes out more like a death wheeze.

She closes her eyes. Opens them. The vision before her remains unaltered.

This can only be Ard Al-Ghul, a place where the monsters are hungry and humans are the bill of fare. Whatever reason Hind has for coming here, Shay sees no sign of her now, and the trail she left behind goes no farther.

But that *smell* still hangs in the air. Even stronger than before.

Glory to heaven, what is *that*?

Shay knows better than to step one toe into Ard Al-Ghul. At least, her brain does. Her stomach, however, protests quite loudly. More of the syrupy scent carries to her on a breeze. She licks her lips, thinking it won't hurt just to see where it's coming from.

11

I know what I saw. It was a large wagon attached to a team of six horses, but they weren't normal horses. These were skeletons with glowing eyes. I'd have thought they were ghosts if I didn't hear them whinny and nicker with my own ears. It was like something out of Ard Al-Ghul, but sitting right there on the street behind the kasbah, near the back entrance where deliveries are made. And before you ask, no, I haven't touched a lick of pomroot ale in moons.

—overheard at the local bathhouse

A thick mist rolls and ebbs through the air, pulsing like a heart. Shay stands before the curves and spires of an iron gate, scrolled out like the prettiest of cages. Behind it hulks a building comprised of multiple towers with domes shaped like onions, the whole structure clad in dark wood shingles of mismatched size and formation. If a place can be said to stare, this one does so with a level of malice that makes her skin crawl, her skin *swarm*.

She kneads her arms, whispering a blessing of protection. Beyond the gate, the mist is dotted with bushes. Upon them dangle clusters of bright, round wanderberries, their red skin luminous in the rose-tinted moonlight. Were they any closer, she could reach between the iron slats and grab one. She'd rub it inside her wrist to double-check that they're really wanderberries and not the near look-alike but extremely poisonous widowberries.

Shay steps closer. The tip of her nose meets the smooth iron, her stomach panging with hunger. A shadow flutters through the shrubbery, feathers and leaves shivering in a dark green blur. When they still, Shay beholds the form of a beautiful bird.

Its feathers shine a deep, iridescent purple. Its eyes glint a dark jade green. The massive bird wastes no time perching on top of a bush with thin branches that should bow under its weight. It snatches berries in its beak and swallows them one after another.

An involuntary moan escapes Shay's lips.

The bird pauses its feasting. Slowly turns. And looks directly at her.

Unlike the squirrel, the bird speaks to her, reaching out first.

Why, hello there. She hears the slick voice inside her head, which feels strangely intrusive. But then, Shay doesn't have enough experience with her developing powers to say how it should feel. *A pleasant surprise at an hour so late. What brings you to stand here at my gate?*

Shay isn't sure why the bird is speaking in rhyme. Or why it claims ownership of the gate. But she knows she's starving, and if it's possible for a squirrel to remove a ring from her finger, it stands to reason a bird could deliver a few berries to her. If she can just eat enough to quiet the gnawing of her stomach, to regain some of her equilibrium, she can consider how to go about looking for Hind. Preferably without running into any monsters.

"I seem to find myself far from home, and in need of sustenance." Shay doesn't feel particularly awkward talking to a bird. She talks to animals often enough. She's even been inclined to think they understand her, though perhaps not to this degree. "Would you be so kind as to carry some berries to me in your beak, seeing as I can't reach them on my own?"

The bird tilts its head. *These berries? These would be poisonous to your kind. They're widowberries, you see. But I'm sure there's another way I can help you.*

Shay doesn't understand how the bird, the sharp hook of its beak stained wine red, is apparently immune to the poison. She shakes her head. This is *Ard Al-Ghul*, a place she knows little about other than to fear it. Mainly because not many people who make the journey ever return to Mekchaouen to tell the tale.

Surely, it can't be much longer until sunrise. Perhaps she should be asking the bird to help her find Hind, but her stomach is panging, and poisonous or not, those berries still smell *delicious*. "What other way did you have in mind?"

I'm so glad you asked.

The bird rises from its perch. Its broad wings flap, slowly at first, then faster and faster, beating into a violet shimmer. Shadows elongate, mist mingles with feather, and the bird fades in and out of focus. Shay's eyes can't seem to linger on any single detail long enough to make sense of it. When the movement slows, the bird is gone, and a very different shape has solidified: a man standing next to the bush.

Shay doesn't know what to make of him. He's tall, dressed in a pressed navy tunic and matching trousers. A black scarf wraps around his head and loops loosely around his neck, an accessory more suited for desert sands, where protection from the elements is vital. His skin is pale and gray, and his eyes are as black as a touched one's are white. The hard lines and smooth contours of his face align with unnatural symmetry, as though carved upon his flesh with a chisel.

Bloodsucker.

The word floats into Shay's mind, but she's still not sure until the man—creature—walks up to the gate and smiles at her. His teeth gleam the ivory of snow, and his eyes dance with wickedness. He inhales like someone entering a kitchen where a fine meal has been left to simmer.

"As I was saying..." The bloodsucker chuckles, low and dangerous. The gate creaks open, though his hands never move from his sides. He steps onto the red clay. Shay rocks back on her heels. "If you come inside, I'm sure we can find some more suitable victuals for you to partake of. Tea, perhaps?"

He reaches a gloved hand toward Shay, who stumbles back. The fear that comes over her is less of a feeling at all and more of an extra sense, as acid as any taste. More thundering than any sound.

"I think . . ." She swallows, her throat aching with the effort of keeping her voice even. "I shall have to decline."

"Come now," the bloodsucker croons. His voice has a dull ring. A once-living thing, hollowed out, stuffed with feathers, and overlaid with silk. "Don't be shy, zine diali. Why, a moment ago, you were more than happy to ask what you assumed was a mere bird to steal the berries off my bushes for you. Now we can do this the pleasant way or the not-so-pleasant way, but I do hate to wrinkle a good ensemble."

Shay scans the empty street with its rows of crooked buildings. Unlit alleys branch off at intervals. The mist blurs all the edges, making everything less than real. That red moon still radiates its eerie glow across the sky. The world below it, a mirror haze where shadows jump to life and the material seems to be an illusion.

Her heart taps an alarm, warning that her life depends on getting away. Unfortunately, even if she achieves that, there's nowhere to run except right back to Al-Ghaba Mayita. The stories she grew up hearing omitted one critical detail: what to do upon actually encountering a bloodsucker.

"I won't ask twice." The bloodsucker's voice grows stern.

Shay has spent much of her life following directions. Avoiding conflict. Being undemanding. Her first instinct is always to please, but something tells her that if she accepts this invitation, it will be the last tea she ever drinks. Daring to meet the bloodsucker's eyes, she whispers, "What are you going to do to me, Sidi?"

The creature frowns, a gesture isolated to his lips. They tug down at the corners as if snared by hooks in a flat parody of emotion. "I don't want to hurt you, Lalla. No more than a bee wishes harm upon a flower."

Though Shay doesn't believe him in the slightest, she suddenly cannot tear her gaze away. His eyes are a lightless beacon, drawing her deep into a center of stillness. A sweet nothing that promises eternal peace.

She nods, her neck behaving of its own volition. The bloodsucker takes her hand, and she flinches at the cold that bleeds through his gloves. But she doesn't pull back, even as he leads her toward the still-opened gate.

The bloodsucker pauses. He lays his other hand on her shoulder. "Glory to heaven, you're shaking like a leaf. Are you frightened of me?"

Shay's mind scrambles for a thread of conversation to delay their passage. She fears—knows—once this threshold is crossed, her fate will be sealed. "No,

Sidi. I'm only worried about my mother. I lost her in the woods, and I don't know where she is."

"That's terrible," the bloodsucker says indulgently. "Perhaps you should leave your shoes in front of the gate. If your mother comes by and sees them, she will know where to find you. Would that make you feel better?" The gate rasps in sinister greeting as it swings farther inward, widening its arms so two can pass inside.

"It may be better to wait here a little longer?" Shay chatters nervously. She assesses the bloodsucker's grip on her wrist and wonders how much force it would take to break free. "I'm sure she'll be along soon. And *she* would want some tea as well. She loves tea. I mean, we both do. You know what they say about us Nezjarians: Tea runs in our veins."

"Yes." The bloodsucker's eyes zero in on her throat, and the tips of his incisors peek from between his thin lips. Keeping one hand on the gate, he yanks Shay close. She gags on the copper tang of his breath. "Speaking of your veins . . ."

Shay's survival instincts rush back. She stomps on the bloodsucker's foot and twists her wrist from his grasp, only for him to hook her waist and bind her tightly against his tall frame. Her skin tightens, a frigid chill pouring over her. Shay bucks her shoulders, pounds her fists against his hips and thighs, but her protests are of little use against his iron grip.

His frozen fingers squeeze her jaw. He whispers in her ear, soft and menacing: "Still yourself, Lalla. Or I'll snap your neck right now. And that would spoil the fun for both of us." With a whimper, Shay deflates. A sob bubbles up her chest. "That's better."

The bloodsucker flips her around. Her back scrapes the gate as he looms over her. The creature places one arm to either side of her head, gloved fingers curling around the iron rails. His heavy body presses into hers in a manner that's grotesque in its intimacy. His bloodless lips smack, a string of drool glistening from his protruding incisors.

He smells, not like a dead body but like death itself, all the cloyingness of overripe melons mixed with the musk of sodden earth. His nose is perfect.

Jawline sharp. Each feature is attractive on its own, but wrapped together in waxen skin, their sum becomes something uncanny. "It has been a long time since I've tasted someone so pure of heart. Your pristine blood will do wonders for me. I might even feel the smallest bit human again—can you imagine?"

Shay shakes her head. A slew of pleas cements inside her throat. Without realizing why she's doing so, she reaches into the satchel beneath her djellaba. With clumsy fingers, she unfastens it. It's only when she makes contact with the cool metal spine of her pocketknife, the one she uses for trimming branches and tough stems, that her intention crystalizes.

The bloodsucker smiles wider, the tips of his incisors lengthening to impossible points before Shay's widening eyes. "I know I should wait until we get inside where we can enjoy our privacy, but you are so tempting. I think I'll have a sip to tide me over."

"No, please, no." Shay's voice breaks free, her words the only shield she can throw up in her swelling terror. She flicks her wrist, but the knife doesn't open. She flicks it again and again and again, until she hears the blessed *click* of the blade. With her range of motion limited, she struggles to angle her hand as she continues talking. "My blood is no good. It's tainted, you see." Her best bet is to jab the blade between his ribs. Ideally, she'll rupture an organ, and failing that, she can use his surprise to get away. "I . . . I'm the daughter of an addict."

"Even better." The bloodsucker dives for her neck. Vicious teeth plunge into Shay's throat where the flesh is soft as a kitten's underbelly. Her fingers flex in surprise, the knife slipping from her grip. Blood howls like wind in her ears. The thump of her heart grows loud and slow, almost soothing as it drowns the pain.

Shay hears voices. She thinks she's lost consciousness and reconnected with Iman and the others until the murmurs rise into shouts that sound distinctly masculine.

The bloodsucker peels his lips from her neck with a *squelch*. She's weak and limp, and her body would collapse on the grassy verge if his were not pinning her to the gate. She can open her eyes to narrow slits, but no farther.

The creature growls, whipping his head around. He lifts his hand and swipes the blood dribbling from his chin. "Hello, neighbors."

"Neighbor?" questions a gruff voice. "What kind of neighbor commits such barbaric acts right out in public? Have you no shame, Tarik?"

"Shame?" The bloodsucker turns, dragging Shay with him. Her head flops against his hard chest. He pets her hair and shushes her, and it's only then that she becomes aware of her own crying. Tarik scoffs. "You have some nerve speaking that word as you crawl back from your nightly excursions with the innards of rotting corpses clumped between your teeth."

Shay blinks. The sight that comes into focus is so frightening, she actually clings tighter to the bloodsucker. A group of monsters surrounds them on the clay road. They have skin so thin and translucent, every bone is put on display. Their pale eyes glow like lanterns, some set within sunken pits and others bulging from their heads. Their arms stretch to their knees. Greasy hair hangs past their ears in strings, and their faces are something cut from the fabric of nightmares and sewn by a drunken seamstress.

Bone-eaters.

"At least we aren't killers." Absurdly, the bone-eater who speaks wears a wide-rimmed reed hat topped with colorful pom-poms. He leans upon a cane, its handle fashioned in the shape of a small and realistic-looking skull. Perhaps too realistic. He runs a hand down his scraggy white beard, disturbing a trio of flies from their rest.

Tarik narrows his eyes, gripping Shay tighter. "I'd mind my business if I were you, Aidi. Go on home." The bloodsucker gestures to a building one yard over. The squat two-story cottage boasts a thatched roof, a bent chimney, and a small yard overrun by tangled weeds and bulbous mushrooms. "Unless you want dibs on the leftovers?"

"You're disgusting." A bone-eater swathed in a hooded black cape steps forward.

"Stand down," Tarik hisses, baring his teeth. "You're on my property. And you're scaring my guest."

"We're on a public street, actually," another bone-eater with a hunched back and long, thin antlers branching above his head chimes in. "And I'd ask your guest to tell us herself whom she fears."

"I'd say that chivalry isn't dead, but, well, look at you." The bloodsucker tosses his head back with a droll laugh. "As to your complaint about public spaces, worry not, my guest and I will be going inside now."

Tarik moves to pass through the gate. Shay moans. In her weakened state, the only objection she manages is that of stretching her arm over the bloodsucker's shoulder. She reaches out toward the distant forest that separates her from home and safety. Through pooling tears, she meets eyes with Aidi.

"I think not." The bone-eater steps forward. "The girl is hardly more than a child."

He lifts his skull cane high, and the jaw of the handle drops. With a dry wheezing sound, it gathers the mist around them in a trail that recedes into the gaping maw. The thinning mist makes room for moonlight to beam down in red gashes.

"I'm not wearing my night cream," Tarik screeches, throwing his arms up against the intrusion. "You miserable grave robbers!"

"At least we don't sleep in coffins," a short, chubby bone-eater with wide, upward-curving horns barks out.

"Now you're just being cliché," the bloodsucker says indignantly. "How about you go scare some sleeping toddlers and cause them to soil their bedsheets?"

In slow wobbling steps, Shay backs away while the creatures exchange barbs. She's unsure whether the bone-eaters are the saviors they appear or simply present a new, perhaps less immediate, threat. She counts seven of them in total. One, with fat horns that curve downward to either side of his head, smiles at her through a mouth full of jagged teeth.

She retreats one man's length before Tarik realizes what she's doing. He lunges after her, only to immediately trip over the cane Aidi flings across his path. Without further hesitation, Shay runs for it. She steadies her feet by sheer will. Her vision blurs. Unsure of her way, she heads in the general direction of the forest's twisted silhouette. At the end of the block, while she's deciding which turn to take, a pitiful cry rings out.

She glances back to where Aidi swings the cane. He whacks the bloodsucker repeatedly as the creature lies on the ground. The other bone-eaters circle around and take their turns punching, kicking, and stomping on him.

Shay fumbles. A stabbing pain runs from the ball of her shoulder to the base of her skull. Her hand seeks the two round punctures on her throat, and when she draws her fingers back, they're slicked with a shocking amount of blood.

Her gaze swings from the forest, with its creatures so ruined, they shouldn't even be alive, and back to the monsters of Ard Al-Ghul. A silver flash winks from the ground, a stone's throw from the ongoing fight—if you call seven-on-one a fight. *The ring!* It must have fallen from her satchel when she dug through it for the knife.

As much as Shay wishes she never laid eyes on the talisman, she perceives that it is an item of great power. Power that can be misused in the wrong hands. Power she may find herself in need of. Ignoring everything Ghita taught her about survival, Shay follows her instinct and runs right back to the fire she should be escaping.

She sneaks up to the fray and darts in to retrieve the ring. But, as she bends down, the mist from Tarik's yard comes rushing back. It settles around her shoulders, dimming the world.

"Look," one of the bone-eaters shouts, pointing at her crouched form. "I think the human girl has fallen."

All at once, the seven of them are crowding around her. Her throat dries up. She frantically paws the ground until her fist closes around the ring. She stands. Or tries to. Her legs sway beneath her like stalks of grass.

"Are you well?" the shortest bone-eater asks, appearing at her side.

"I should go now," Shay mumbles, but her feet defy her command. She looks down to see what's wrong with them, and then the clay road comes rushing toward her.

"Whoa, easy now." Someone catches her. Someone who smells, most atrociously, like unwashed bodies and flatulence. Still, it was nice of them to catch her. They hand her a wad of moss, and she presses it against her bleeding wound.

"Thank you."

"Come inside with us," the caped bone-eater says. "Allow me to clean your neck and properly bandage it."

Shay nods, equally horrified and amazed that she's talking to an actual bone-eater. She never imagined they might be intelligent. Or live in *homes* and have *neighbors*. Did someone mention medical supplies?

They lead her past the bloodsucker, lying limp and spread-eagle on the ground. His lips—the same ones guilty of slurping down her blood—are split and bruised. His face, in contrast, looks less pale than she remembers. More supple and, despite some swelling, more . . . human.

"Lalla?" Tarik groans, his body shaking suddenly, as though racked with silent sobs.

Shay gasps. His wretched state evokes in her the smallest bit of sympathy, if not outright concern. "Sidi?"

A smile flickers on his mangled lips. "You tasted delicious."

Not crying, she realizes. No, the bloodsucker is convulsing with laughter.

12

If you would not consume the flesh of your neighbor, neither let yourself speak of them unkindly. For those who partake in gossip and relish rumor have no more decency than ghouls. If you could see their souls in the spiritual plane, their faces would be dripped in red from that which they gorge upon.

—Meditations from the Marabouts, *Volume 7*

The bone-eater's salon is messy by the standards Shay was raised with. Sure, some measure of uncleanliness can be expected with seven males living under one roof, but how much effort does it take to clear the floor of dirty socks, ale bottles, and—wait, is that a pile of bones? Shay shudders.

A sage-green seddari frames the room in a U shape. When one of the bone-eaters offers her a seat, she's careful to choose a spot free of the dirt stains she assures herself are not from someone's grave. A lantern sits on a low round table in the room's center. Its thin glow flickers over walls the yellowed color of phlegm.

The caped bone-eater, who identifies himself as Kabeer, retrieves a basket containing small surgical tools and various herbs typically used for making poultices. He kneels beside her. Though he removes the moss as gently as he possibly can, Shay hisses when drying blood rips from her tender skin. With a closer glance, she identifies the moss as sourshade, known for its antiseptic properties.

"Do you have medical training?" Shay inquires, watching the creature dab something that smells strongly of alcohol from a vial onto a clover bean leaf.

The other brothers, now positioned in various stages of recline around the room—at least one is already snoring—snicker.

Kabeer silences them with a bruising look. "You could say that."

Shay stops his gnarled hand as he reaches for her neck. His skin feels tough as tree bark beneath her fingers. "Or?"

Kabeer runs his free hand down his scabrous face. "*Or* you could say I am a devourer of knowledge." He gives his brothers a warning glare before they can make a sound and proceeds to clean Shay's wound.

"Do you mean you read?" Shay asks a beat later.

"I *can* read," the bone-eater gruffly asserts.

"I wasn't suggesting—"

"Deebi." Kabeer finishes affixing a wide bandage to Shay's neck, pointedly ignoring her. "Would you go find our guest some clean blankets and a pillow?"

"And see what you can muster for her to eat," Aidi adds. Shay has pegged him as the elder, and she wonders if it is his habit to assert his authority.

"I don't think any of that will be necessary," Shay says, though she can't deny her need for sustenance. It is, after all, what drew her from the forest in the first place. The last substantial thing she ate was Ghita's loubia, and by her estimation, a full day has passed since. What she wouldn't do for a heaping bowl of the midwife's spicy beans right now. Why, she'd climb the Umm Chanala mountains barefoot for a spoonful.

The brothers all stare at her, dismay cast across their distorted faces.

Aidi leans forward on the cane propped between his legs. He sighs. "You can't seriously be thinking of going anywhere in your condition."

"Do you intend to keep me prisoner, Sidi?"

"You have lost a significant amount of blood, Lalla." His voice, for all its gruffness, sounds sincere. "But we are not like our neighbor. We will not impede upon your free will."

"Well, then, I do thank you for your assistance." Shay nods gratefully at Kabeer, busy arranging his supplies back in the basket, and to the rest of the bone-eaters. "All of you. But it would be improper for me to stay."

In truth, Shay is thinking less about propriety and more about the tenuous nature of her safety. The lump in her throat has sharp edges, and the knots in her stomach have teeth. She's unable to say with any certainty whether the greater danger lurks within the cottage or without it. Therefore, despite the immense effort standing unassisted requires, she forces herself to walk across the room. She opens the door and peers out upon the thick landscape of dawn.

"You really should wait until morning proper," the bone-eater with downward curving horns advises. *Deebi.* Unless Shay is misreading it, the look on Deebi's face suggests he is applying a wealth of restraint by not jumping from the couch and shutting the door himself. Shay would not have imagined a bone-eater's expression could *be* so . . . well, expressive. "You need to rest. And once the sun comes up, it will be safer for you to cross back through the forest to your home."

Home. The word pokes between Shay's ribs. Beyond the door, twilit shadows hover like a floating wall of invisible ink. Diaphanous mist coats the domed towers and darkened windows next door like a skin of algae on a pond. A breeze rustles the tall grass before sweeping over her like a spray of frost.

You tasted delicious.

"Not safer by much," one brother scoffs.

Shay turns back around, considering. It's obviously dangerous for her to wander alone around Ard Al-Ghul in search of Hind. Memories—of her mother's promises, their future plans, the warm, familiar scent of peach blossom—strike like stray arrows. She shoves them from her mind. Whatever Shay felt on her side, Hind was only biding her time for the chance to discard Shay like spoiled milk.

With this realization, she feels the last bit of strength go out of her, as surely as if the bloodsucker had drained her dry. "Are you sure it will not be an inconvenience?"

Before Aidi answers, a bone-eater with crescent-shaped horns on his forehead—the scoffer—yawns loudly. "Since it appears the human girl will live,

I'm going off to bed." He ambles from the room, initiating a chain reaction from the other brothers, until only Aidi and Deebi remain.

"Deebi will get you settled," the elder says, offering Shay a shallow bow.

"Thank you, Sidi," Shay says, not wishing to question too deeply whether the scoffer sounded relieved at her favorable prognosis, or disappointed.

"I'm Deebi." The remaining bone-eater tips his horned head low. "And who do I have the pleasure of hosting?"

"I . . ." Shay swallows. She perches on the seddari, brushing distractedly at the nearest stain. "I'm Shay."

"Shay. It's nice to meet you."

"Deebi." She says the bone-eater's name, still finding it odd that they all have such normal-sounding ones. Shay squeezes herself and realizes she's shivering. The cottage was chilly to begin with, and she's made it worse by letting in the colder air from outside. "I hate to be a bother, but would you mind starting a fire?"

"A fire?" Deebi stares at the empty hearth as if noticing its existence for the first time. He smacks his wide forehead. "Right. Humans get cold easily. Not to worry. I'll fetch coals from the kitchen stove."

The bone-eater darts off. He returns quickly, armed with a metal bucket of hot coals and an armful of blankets, the latter of which he piles on top of Shay. The fabric is coarse. Its rough fibers scratch through her djellaba. But their bulk is blessedly warm. She huddles beneath them, dozing as Deebi fans the coals with a blowing tool. Once he gets the fire started, he scurries away again, chattering on about food as he goes.

Hungry as Shay is, her tiredness prevails. Before the bone-eater returns, she's already drifted into a deep, if troubled, sleep.

✧ ✧ ✧

Shay dreams of the bloodsucker. A dream in which he disguises himself as her mother to lure her within his iron gates. There, he tells her all the things she'd want her mother to say. That she's proud of her. She loves her. And she'll never abandon her again. Words so sweet, Shay can almost pretend the scent of peaches she's come to associate with Hind hasn't been replaced by the reek of blood, lingering on her skin and clothes. Her breath.

He carries her into that awful house. Serves her bitter tea that coats her tongue with the taste of copper. It makes the room spin around her like she's a Marabout performing a sacred dance.

But this feels the opposite of sacred.

It feels like being peeled open, her every emotion, every thought exposed like the pulp of a fruit. Her nerve endings are on fire. And Tarik hangs over her, smiling down with her mother's lips, her Snow-ravaged teeth bathed red with Shay's blood.

She jolts awake, choking on a scream.

Thick shadows paint her surroundings in dark lumps and gray puddles. Her head feels doubled in size. Her skull feels black and blue. She listens and detects no sound. None loud enough to rise over her ragged heartbeat.

The pillow her head rests upon feels hard and lumpy. The stiff bandage pasted to her neck itches. She attempts to scratch it, but her hands are—*bound at her sides*? She yanks her wrists, and the scrape of thick rope gnaws into her flesh. The terror of her dream floods back, and with it, the alarming realization that it may not have been a dream.

Every part of Shay runs cold like her body is sliding into hibernation. She cannot stop shivering. All she can think is how disappointed Ghita would be in the choices she's made. How Hind would likely be disappointed she's still alive. And how that may not be a problem much longer.

She should scream or kick or do something to keep her wits about her.

Uselessly, piteously, Shay sobs.

Through a blur of tears, her eyes track the rope. It runs from her wrists to the legs of the tables on either side of the sleeping pallet. And there, to her left, like a boon from a benevolent spirit, winks the silver handle of her pocketknife. The one she dropped when Tarik bit her. If she pulls hard enough, she might just topple the heavy table. Might be able to reach the knife and cut through the ropes.

In the grip of swelling hope, she doesn't stop to ponder why she's been left bound with a means of escape placed so temptingly within her grasp. She readies herself to heave. Then come footsteps, slow and steady. *Thud. Thud. Thud.* Gritting her teeth, Shay strains against the ropes, using her body as leverage. The table doesn't topple, but it shakes so that the knife bounces and skips. She rocks herself back and forth in thrashing movements. Advancing bit by bit, the knife nears the table's edge.

Closer. Closer. *Almost there.*

The footsteps quicken. Too close. *Thud-thud-thud.*

The door creaks, and Shay freezes, her forehead slick with sweat.

A lantern enters first. Its brightness practically blinds her to her captor's identity, but the shadows of horns bulge on either side of their head, curving downward. "Are you well, lallati?"

"Deebi!" Shay's relief is only partial. She is not in the bloodsucker's home as she feared. But that does not explain what is going on. "I am tied like a horse hitched to a post. No, I'm not well! But thank you so much for asking."

The bone-eater sets the lantern, along with a tray of food, onto one of the side tables. He loosens Shay's bonds, babbling nervously as he works at the knots. "I truly apologize about this, but I assure you, there is a good explanation."

Once her hands are free, Shay scrubs the tears from her face. She's overcome by the unsettling feeling that something has been done to her. She pats herself, searching for clues. At least her satchel, with the hjabat tucked back inside, is still tied around her waist.

"No one hurt you." Deebi stoops low as he sits carefully on the edge of the pallet. He gives her a narrow glance that seems to ask her for permission to elaborate.

Shay scuttles back. She cowers against the mound of pillows behind her. Her eyes land again on the pocketknife, and she wonders how effective such a paltry tool would be against the monster who restrained her. Or did he free her?

She's confused about which. "What happened?"

Deebi pinches the tip of one horn nervously. "You were sleepwalking," he tells her, then cocks his head to one side. "If I may ask something, have you ever experienced a brush with death?"

"I don't think so." Shay rubs her tender wrists, perplexed. "Why?"

"Sometimes, survivors of bloodsucker bites develop a psychic link with their attacker. This is more likely to happen, and the bond tends to be stronger, if the human has had a previous experience with the spiritual realm."

Shay immediately thinks of Ghita's echo. "Like a midwife? Or maybe her apprentice?"

"Yes, yes." The bone-eater nods, his weighty horns slicing through the air. "Midwives are very close to the other world. Which is generally a good thing, I suppose, but not in this case. We found you en route to the bloodsucker's home, and after we wrangled you back here, you immediately attempted to leave again. Our only option was tying you down. For your own safety, you see."

Sickness spreads through Shay's stomach. She believes the bone-eater because she feels the truth of his words. The connection he speaks of quickens inside her like some unnatural conception. Some abomination. "How long does this condition last?"

"It should go away when your wounds heal," Deebi says, but his tone is less than reassuring. "Until then, whenever you sleep, you will be helpless to resist the urge that calls you to him."

Shay suddenly, desperately, wishes to be back home. Even if it means facing Ghita's recrimination. Even if it means never seeing Hind again. "And if I leave Ard Al-Ghul?"

"Unfortunately, you can't. The journey through Al-Ghaba Mayita takes well over a full day by foot. It would not be possible for a human to travel such a distance without stopping to rest."

Shay's shoulders dip. It seems she's even failing at being a proper failure. "At which point, I'd be compelled to walk back here—back to *him*—in my sleep?"

"Exactly." The bone-eater looks at her with something like pity, if creatures such as he bear the capacity for such feelings. "But I have some good news. My brothers promised to look for an antidote while on their nightly outing. They set out a while ago and should be back by morning."

"Wait." Shay knuckles her temples. *Nightly outing* is one way to phrase the act of plundering Nezjar's graves, but if the brothers have already left . . . For the first time since coming to, she notices the moonlight piercing the beams of the thatched roof in bloody needles. "How long was I asleep?"

"You slept through the whole day." The bone-eater gives her a lipless smile. Shay finds it oddly endearing, but not enough to soften the blow of realizing she's slept right through any chance of catching the caravan to Kiddah. Yet it's not the missed career opportunity that disappoints her. It's knowing she left Ghita with no explanation other than to assume Shay doesn't care.

But she *does* care. Now, more than ever, she knows how lucky she was that Ghita took her in. How lucky Sami is.

"I see." She draws a deep breath, focusing on the room around her to stay her tears. The simple wicker furnishings, stone walls, and ample linens are cozy, if sparse, with some plants and candles scattered about.

The food sitting on the tray, however, looks disappointingly unappetizing. There's a mug of dirty water. A bent crust of moldy khobz. Some slices of apple gone brown and mushy. And a slab of meat that looks horribly undercooked, which is to say, it's soaking in a fresh pool of blood.

Apparently, the bone-eaters were unprepared for a human guest. Her thoughts snare on an odd detail. "How are you and your brothers able to make the trip to Nezjar and back in one night, if it is, as you say, well over a full day's journey each way?"

"It is, for *humans*. Bone-eaters achieve greater speeds because we shape-shift," Deebi says, as if that should be obvious. In answer to Shay's unspoken question, he adds, "Into hyenas, most of the time."

Shay supposes that's no stranger than a bloodsucker taking the form of a bird. She has more questions but hesitates to speak them, fearing the answers may well send her running for the forest despite the risk. The bone-eaters don't seem to wish her harm, but then neither did Hind. At first.

"You should eat, lallati." The bone-eater lifts the tray and holds it toward her.

Shay tries her best to smile pleasantly. Refusing what's offered goes against the etiquette that's been deeply ingrained in her. She picks the safest-looking item, a dried fig, and bites in. Only to discover it's filled with tiny wriggling worms.

Coughing, she drops half the fig back on the plate and grabs the water to wash the other half down, politeness prohibiting her from spitting it out. The silty water burns her throat. She coughs harder.

The bone-eater remains quiet until Shay stops coughing and looks at him, his already-fragmented face split further in worry. "Is the food not to your liking?"

"No, it's fine," Shay says automatically, about to add that she's not really *that* hungry. But she's well and truly famished. "Alright, I'm lying. But please don't be upset. It's just . . . this isn't what humans like to eat."

"I'm sorry. I . . ." Deebi inhales and exhales, his chest rising and falling, as if physically working to collect himself. He wrings his mangled hands. "Tell me what kinds of food you like, and I'll get them for you. Just don't tell my brothers I messed up."

"I won't say a word. I promise." Shay can't help wanting to reassure him. If she understands anything, it's the feeling of being a disappointment. A warmth one might call fondness sparks inside her. The bone-eater seems *kind*. "And I'm happy to cook for myself. Well, for all of us, but where would you get the ingredients?"

"There are other humans in Ard Al-Ghul," the bone-eater whispers, as though imparting a highly guarded secret. "Rebels who live here in hiding."

Shay has heard about the lists. The ones that publicize the names of those rebels most wanted by Al-Mukhtar. Those whose capture would reap a sizable reward. It makes sense that such fugitives would come to Ard Al-Ghul as a last resort. If Naturalists with nowhere else to go hide themselves among the medina's poor and forsaken in the Bib, why not among the monsters here?

Shay can't help but wonder if she, a failed apprentice, the daughter of an addict, belongs here as much as they do. But no, she hasn't sunk that low. Yes, she made a bad decision—perhaps multiple bad decisions. But she can fix them.

She still has the ring, which she could sell, if only to repay Ghita for the cost of the stolen ticket. It will take time to earn back the midwife's trust, to find another position. One perhaps not quite so far. She needs only to take this antidote and convince the bone-eaters to escort her back through the forest.

But does she really want her old life back? To return to taking that wretched moon pepper and enduring constant sickness for the sake of safety?

Shay finds the question hard to answer. Something dark has hatched within her, a feeling that life will never be as simple as before. As sweet as it once was. She may tell herself it's only the bloodsucker venom, but deep down, she fears something irrevocable has been set in motion.

From the moment she put on the ring, she became lost.

Home has never felt so far away.

13

Ghita's Harira Recipe

Ingredients

3 tablespoons vegetable oil
6 large tomatoes, peeled, seeded, and pureed
1 stalk celery with leaves
1/4 cup finely chopped fresh parsley leaves
1 tablespoon salt
1 tablespoon smen
1 teaspoon ground cinnamon
11 cups water, divided
3 tablespoons tomato paste
1 cup flour
chopped fresh parsley, for garnish

1/2 pound lamb, beef, or chicken
1 large onion, grated
3/4 cup dried chickpeas, soaked overnight and peeled
1/4 cup finely chopped fresh cilantro leaves
1 tablespoon ground ginger
1 1/2 teaspoons freshly ground black pepper
1/2 teaspoon ground turmeric
3 tablespoons dried lentils
2 tablespoons vermicelli
2 cups water

Steps

Cut meat into tiny pieces. In a pressure pot, heat oil and sauté parsley, cilantro, celery, and onion together with the meat until the vegetables are soft and the meat is browned. Add three cups of water, tomatoes, smen, spices, and chickpeas. Cover and cook at high pressure for 30 beakers. Release pressure, and add eight cups of water, lentils, vermicelli, and tomato paste. Cook at high pressure for an additional 15 beakers. Release pressure. To thicken harira, start with two teaspoons of flour and add desired amount of water.

Mix well and add to soup, stirring until combined. Repeat as needed according to your preference for a thicker or thinner soup. Season with salt and pepper to taste, and garnish with additional parsley for serving.

Shay's harira isn't on par with Ghita's. She used the same ingredients: lamb, chickpeas, lentils, cilantro, parsley, tomato, and thin strips of pasta. But Shay wasn't able to replicate the thick and silky quality the midwife's always has. Hers came out light and zesty instead, which the brothers seem to find tasty enough, unaccustomed to human food as they are.

Despite her hunger, Shay herself is unable to get much down. Aidi tells her the queasiness and lack of appetite she's experiencing are consistent with the symptoms of a bloodsucker's bite. He brings her a mug filled with a thick, steaming beverage that looks like mud. Concerningly, he sets a wooden pail beside her chair. The brew smells worse than her moon pepper tea ever did. She'd almost prefer Deebi's previous offerings of raw meat and moldy bread.

She raises the mug halfway, and *nope*. Her stomach revolts, her body aching with the memory of the illness she bore for so long, the slow poisoning of her body. She sets it back down. "Do I have to drink it all?"

"It's best to get it over with," says Aidi—whom Shay has mentally dubbed Aidi the Aging. He refuses to remove his reed hat, even at the table, and that creepy cane rests across his lap. "Tarik is one of the oldest bloodsuckers in Ard Al-Ghul. His venom holds much power."

Shay's hand drifts unconsciously to her neck, which throbs as if in confirmation of the bone-eater's words. Last night's dream flashes through her, less the images and more the feelings. Of being invaded. Of having something private, something vital, torn away without consent.

She stares down at the bubbling liquid. A white shape bobs on the surface. It looks disturbingly like a tooth. With a shudder, she hoists the mug to her lips. She tilts her head back and chugs the antidote. It goes down smoother than she expects, coating her throat with the aftertaste of licorice.

Her stomach cramps almost immediately, which is a diplomatic way to say she doubles over, falls from her chair, and rolls around on the floor, blinded by pain. Someone sits her up, supporting her from behind the way Shay has supported many a laboring woman. Someone else shoves the bucket in front of her. And not a moment too soon.

Her stomach empties with a volume and force the tiny bucket is ill-equipped to receive. The substance that erupts from her in a geyser is dark and gelatinous. When she thinks she's empty, that there can't be anything else left in her body, she retches again and throws up bloody bits she doesn't want to think may be pieces of vital organs.

Finally, she slumps back against the bone-eater behind her . . . Dasri—the Deerlike, in tribute to his great antlers. She swipes a string of slime from her chin. It splats on the floor, where it proceeds to pulse and undulate, sliding across the tiles like a slug. Bono—the Bad-Tempered in Shay's mental index—stomps it underfoot. Shay hears what sounds like a small yelp.

"You're well now," Dasri assures her. He helps her stand and leads her to the salon, where Deebi hands her a glass of cool water. It's clean and drinkable this time, by God's mercy.

Aidi and his cane sit closest to her. She wonders if he sleeps with the thing, the way Al-Mukhtar force Moulays in training to sleep, and even bathe, with their muskets. He studies her as though deciding whether she has passed some test. That look reminds her so much of Ghita, she aches. "How do you feel?"

Shay considers the question. Her gullet is sore, like she overexerted herself but on the inside. Probing deeper, she identifies another feeling. One of being emptied out. Cleaned. Unlike the way the moon pepper seems to be clearing her system bit by bit since she stopped taking it, this is a sudden draining. Intense but, she hopes, complete. She never thought she'd be so grateful for vomiting. "Better, I think."

She slowly notices all the brothers have quietly gathered on the wraparound seddari, a development that is either touching or worrisome.

"That's good," the elder bone-eater says. Then he hesitates, as though he's about to say one thing but decides upon another. "Thank you. For that delicious meal you prepared. And sorry you didn't get to enjoy it."

"It was the least I could do." Shay shakes her head humbly, though she does appreciate the acknowledgment.

"Did you notice she also tidied up?" chimes in Beni—the youngest, or the Baby. "I never even knew our floor tiles are such a lovely shade of aqua blue. And I can see myself in these drinking glasses! It's like they're brand-new!"

"Is that supposed to be a good thing?" Bono snickers, the crescent-shaped horns on his forehead jiggling. "Be careful. Or you'll crack them."

Shay is surprised they noticed, although she hoped they would. Their gratitude may make them more amiable to the favor she must now request. "So, the antidote seems to have worked, and I wondered if I might convince one of you to be my escort back through the forest."

Aidi stiffens and gives a startled cough. "Who told you it would be safe to go back?"

"Well, Deebi . . ." Shay sputters. Deebi the Downcast, because *Disappointment* seems too cruel of an epithet even if unspoken.

Kabeer clucks his tongue. His face is half covered by the hood of his cape, which he also never removes, hence his designation as Kabeer the Cape-Wearer. "Deebi, Deebi, Deebi."

All the brothers turn expectantly toward Aidi. The elder bone-eater rubs the smooth cap of his skull cane, avoiding Shay's eyes. "I bear unfortunate tidings."

Dread pools in her stomach. "What do you mean?"

"You cannot return to Nezjar, I'm afraid."

"I thought the antidote was supposed to be enough." Shay looks frantically around at the bone-eaters, but none of them meets her gaze. "What's changed?"

"We saw something while passing through your medina." Aidi removes his hat and carefully places it on the center table, baring the receding hairline that explains his attachment to it. "Posters. Plastered everywhere. With information about a girl fitting your description, Lalla. Saying she's wanted for the crime of stealing and that any sighting of her should be reported to Al-Mukhtar."

Shay gasps, her dread turning to dismay. She flounders. "That makes no sense. I haven't stolen anything!"

"Are you sure?" Aidi plunks his hat back on, as if his momentary sympathy has run its course. He continues to rhythmically rub the skull. "They say a priceless magical talisman went missing around the same time you did."

Thinking of the hjabat, Shay quickly checks her waist satchel and finds it empty. Her stomach drops. She narrows her eyes, looking around the room from one brother to another. "Where is it? Did one of you take it?"

The tallest bone-eater, with antlers like lightning bolts zagging straight up from his head, timidly lifts his hand.

"Hammu?" Shay frowns. And to think she nicknamed him Hammu the Hushed. It's always the quiet ones. "How could you?"

"Sorry." He digs the ring from the chest pocket of his baggy, moth-eaten gandoura and hands it to Shay. "You forgot it by the washing basin. I found it there and thought it would make a pretty addition to my collection."

Shay shudders to think what other jewelry he might have in his collection and, more to the point, where he collected it from.

Aidi sighs and taps his cane against the floor. "The question is, how did the talisman come to be in your possession?"

"It's not what you think." Shay lowers her head and rubs the silver crystal, her action not unlike Aidi's stroking of the cane ornament. She was so eager and willing to go along with Hind, never questioning how she'd obtained the ring to begin with. More concerned with proving she could be of help, that she was worth choosing. That her love was better than some miserable drug. "I was tricked by someone I thought I could trust. Wanted to believe I could trust. Someone who was supposed to care about me."

Shay's chest tightens. All her foolish hopes bunch up inside her. She doesn't know what to think about the posters. How could Al-Mukhtar know about the hjabat unless Hind told them? Beyond the crime of stealing, she could be sent to the dungeon for possessing a magical talisman. And that's if they don't choose to make an example of her.

Somewhere in the back of her mind, she wonders exactly who the authorities think she could have stolen the ring *from*, but this detail gets lost in the tide of her despair. It's hard enough to reconcile that her mother never truly wanted her around, but does Hind hate her so much she wishes her dead?

"Wasn't there also something about a reward?" Bono asks, his too casual tone not quite hiding something eager.

"What?" Shay's head shoots up. Every muscle in her body coils. "I didn't do anything. You have to believe me."

"Of course we believe you," Deebi says earnestly.

Aidi gives her a rotten-lipped smile. Shay tries to concentrate on the compassion swelling in his lambent eyes rather than the sharp serration of his teeth. "You're sensitive, Shay, even for a human. Your heart is pure, and I say this as someone with intimate knowledge of human hearts."

Shay shivers, quite sure this time that the knowledge in question was *not* gained from books. The bone-eaters have been gracious since her appearance, perhaps because they perceived her to be an innocent victim. Would they now hand her over to be dealt with by her own kind? "What will you do with me?"

"I think we should take a vote," Kabeer says, earning severe looks from some brothers and nods from others. "To be fair."

Shay clenches her hands to keep them from shaking, the shape of the hjabat indenting on her palm. She cannot be arrested. But if she is unable to return to Nezjar, where will she go? It stands to reason that if the realm's leaders wish to apprehend her, nowhere in Mekchaouen would be a safe haven. She could surrender and present her side of the story to Al-Mukhtar, but what would that mean for Hind? Bearing false witness is also a crime. Despite her betrayal, Shay couldn't stand to see the touched one come to harm.

"Human leaders aren't known for being the most just," Dasri argues. "They're corrupted by power. And this current lot are the worst ones yet. For graves' sake, they run a horse-drawn catering service to the bloodsuckers!"

"True," Bono says, his voice now subdued. "But it is our way to stay out of human matters. Keep our interactions with them to those that serve our particular purpose."

Aidi sighs heavily. "Very well. All those in favor of relinquishing the human girl to the authorities of her realm, raise your hand."

Shay stares at the ring, afraid to breathe.

The memory of a dark spectacle comes to her once more, and this time she's helpless to suppress it. It closes around her like the crowds that pack the market roads, the kind of mob not looking to procure colorful spices or nuggets of incense—but to witness a horrific display.

She once had an elderly neighbor, a kind woman named Fatimazara who was thought to be the oldest woman in her medina. No one knew her exact age. Rumors placed her cycles somewhere between ninety and one hundred and twenty, not that her activity level was any indication.

Fatimazara made a habit of breaking into nearby dwellings when her neighbors were out, her clandestine mission a far cry from thievery or destruction. Rather, she left their floors and dishes cleaned, their dirty laundry washed and hung to dry. Fatimazara invited Shay and Ghita to her apartment every quarter for couscous. And she always brought them cakes and biscuits on holidays. What Shay remembers most are her twinkling eyes, her cheeky smile.

Fatimazara's twenty-cycles-old grandson was one of the first of Nezjar's citizens arrested for sedition. The night the Moulays took him, Fatimazara's heart gave out. The healers were busy at the time, dealing with an outbreak of the sweats, but Ghita possessed a rare sea bonnet flower, which the midwife used to whip up a sustaining tea.

Bedbound, the old woman asked Shay to attend the hanging in her place so the apprentice might offer a blessing for her grandson upon his final breath. After, Shay told Fatimazara the young man's death had been quick and painless. The old woman returned to God herself the following day.

In truth, his death had been anything but peaceful. Shay remembers every detail in brutal clarity. The awful crack of his neck when it snapped, a sharp but surprisingly wet sound, like crunching into an apple. The way his eyes bulged and his face contorted like he was being visited by some harrowing vision no one else could see. The stink of his bladder giving out, his limp body as it swayed over the spreading puddle, the rope still creaking when she had to look away.

Shay harbored doubts about the young man's guilt. Even when, after the hanging, the sweats ceased to spread, the stricken miraculously recovered, and everyone agreed it was a sign that rooting out the rebel had returned Nezjar to God's favor.

Would people draw the same conclusion about her? Imagining that rope around her own innocent neck, Shay sees her realm's injustices with newfound clarity: The gallows are a distraction from the truth. The Naturalists are right about Al-Mukhtar's miracles. They appear to be an act of God because no one ever sees who's really performing them.

But it *must* be touched ones.

The barkeep and Hind's neighbor both confirmed as much, hadn't they? And in a world where a mother can pretend to love her child while nurturing no such feeling, of course the men who portray themselves as above using magic would secretly rely upon it.

Slowly, Shay works up the nerve to look around the table.

Kabeer has his arms firmly crossed over his chest. Bono is picking his teeth with a knife. Only Deebi meets her eyes, giving a discreet nod, his hands shoved under the table as if to avoid any confusion regarding their position.

Shay exhales in relief. Not one of the brothers has raised his hand.

Aidi clears his throat. "All those in favor of giving the Lalla refuge here with us for as long as she needs, raise your hand."

One by one, the hand of each brother goes up, with Bono waiting until all the others have raised theirs as though he enjoys drawing out the suspense.

"You mean . . ." Shay shakes her head, processing Aidi's words. "You want me to stay?"

"The world is dangerous place for a human with a pure heart," Aidi says. "But we won't let any harm come to you. Will we, Brothers?"

A series of grunts echoes around the table.

"Thank you." Shay looks at each brother again, seeing past the mottled skin, eerily unblinking eyes, and horns of assorted variety. It seems she was wrong; her situation is no better than the fugitive rebels who hide here. But if the human world has no kindness to offer, then she'll dwell with monsters. At least they don't hide what they are. "Truly."

"I do think it's in your best interest to give me the ring." Aidi taps his clawed nails on the skull ornament. "To hold it safe for you, of course."

Shay is transported to the moment she accepted the ring from Hind, a choice she can never go back and undo. It makes no sense to hold on to it now. So why does she feel like she's betraying her mother, or maybe even betraying herself, when she places it into the bone-eater's waiting palm?

Shay glances over her shoulder, again, making sure she's alone. Whatever presence she imagined she felt vanishes upon threat of observation. She turns back to washing dishes, startling at each creak of wind through the cottage's joints. With the kitchen scrubbed, she goes around and checks the shutters and door bars, twice.

Mice rustle in the walls; eaves whisper overhead. Flickers move just out of her vision, teasing her as she climbs to the room the bone-eaters have afforded her upstairs. With the brothers on their nightly outing, the cottage feels hollow, like still-living heart with no beat.

Shay is unaccustomed to sleeping in an empty home.

She offers her prayers and is pulling down her blankets when a phantom itch creeps over her, like crawling ants set loose under her skin. Unable to shake the feeling, she finds herself standing in front of the window—it doesn't have shutters like the ones downstairs—watching downy snowflakes fall beyond the glass.

The solar cycle's first snow has arrived. Shay rarely recalls Nezjar's moon changing color, but with the shifting seasons, the moon over Ard Al-Ghul has shifted, too. Gone is the reddish tint of a human heart that heralded her arrival, replaced by an aura of icy blue.

The white fluffs change direction with the wind, gusting first one way and then another, like a troupe of tiny dancers, all in sync. The itch intensifies, and Shay peers past the snow to the dark dwelling next door.

A lantern flickers in an upstairs window. It throws momentary light over the shadowed figure that stands there, watching her. Even from this distance, she swears she sees the white gleam of Tarik's sharp incisors.

Shay leaps back from the window, her heart beating into a knot. She firmly yanks the curtains closed and dives beneath her blankets. The antidote severed the connection that drew her to the bloodsucker against her will, but that doesn't mean he can't come for her some other way.

Despite the thickness of her blankets, it takes a long time for Shay to stop shivering. Sleep does not find her easily this night, nor for many nights to come.

14

Greetings of peace, loyal soldier of the Sisterhood,

Our scholars have recently been in contact with a Marabout who supports our cause. The holy man has rare access to preserved historical documents that confirm what we have long suspected about the existence of four hjabats and their importance to our mission. As we have reason to believe one of these talismans may currently be located in Nezjar, you are to remain at your current post and await further instructions.

THE WAY BEFORE WILL BE ONCE MORE!

The Morchidat

P.S. When was the last time you trimmed your hair, Yassine?

—a letter, burned after being read but later gathered in ash and remade for posterity using the transformative Shawafa of Mutahawil

Tapping rouses Shay from her recurring dreams of running through Al-Ghaba Mayita. She never sees who's chasing her. Hind. Tarik. Al-Mukhtar. So many threats; such a dark and dangerous world.

The tapping grows louder and more insistent. Wincing, Shay opens her eyes to unexpected brightness. She assesses the length and angle of the midday shadows across the room and scrambles out of bed to open the door. Deebi stands on the other side.

His eyes, the green of fireflies, flash with worry. "Lallati, I was about to break down the door."

"I'm sorry, khoya." Shay rubs her eyes and yawns against the back of her hand. "I didn't realize the time."

His gaze remains concerned. "Are you well, lallati? Have you come down with something?"

In truth, the nightmares are not the worst part of her nights. It's the time she spends awake, in the company of her thoughts. She bounces between being angry at Hind and despairing over whether she's even still alive. She debates whether, if Hind suffers delusions similar to Sami's mother, she's even liable for her actions. But stealing the ring and pinning her crime on Shay? It feels too deliberate and cunning to blame on addiction.

Sometimes, Shay wishes there were an antidote to the unreciprocated love that burns inside her, as poisonous as any venom. From her newfound distance, it's easier to see that neither Hind nor Ghita told her the full truth—whatever that is. Only the version that served them best. Even Shadi, the boy Shay remembers with fondness, hid something important from her. Shay is sure of it.

Is everyone in all the world a liar? Or does Shay attract deceitful people to her like a lodestone? Is she destined to repeat the same scenario over and over?

"No, no." She smooths her hair over her shoulder to appear presentable. The question she always comes back to is why. Why did Hind do this to her? How did Shay manage to fail at something as basic as obtaining her own mother's love? Was she too needy? Overeager? As little as Shay actually sleeps, it's no wonder she can barely crawl from bed in the mornings. "I'm fine. Just a little tired."

The bone-eater appears unconvinced. "Is there anything I can do for you?"

"Oh, Deebi." Shay is taken aback by the question. The answer of no forms quickly on her lips, replaced when she has a sudden thought. "Actually, could you stay with me tonight? When your brothers go out? Just this once?"

"I would love to." Deebi frowns and shakes his head sadly. "But I don't think Aidi would like that."

Shay sighs. "Of course. You're right. I wouldn't want to get you in any trouble."

Deebi shifts from foot to foot. "Is there something I could bring back from the medina, perhaps? Sowing season is upon us. There are strawberries and roses in abundance. Or would you prefer something else?"

"That's nice of you." Shay works up a smile, hoping it doesn't look as fragile as it feels. As though it could slip from her face at any moment, and break. "Whatever you choose, I'm sure I'll be delighted."

"Wakha." Deebi gives a hesitant nod, then a firmer one. "I'll leave you to rest, then."

"Oh, I'm awake now," Shay assures him. "Just give me a few moments, and I'll be down."

Nodding more, the bone-eater turns and makes his way downstairs. He looks back over his shoulder several times until Shay closes the door. In truth, she would like nothing better than to return to bed and stay there indefinitely.

She has no fever or other symptoms of illness.

Physically, she's never been healthier. In the absence of the moon pepper, her skin is softer and brighter. Her hair, once thin and brittle, has become thick and luxuriously soft. She's even rounded out, muscles and fat blossoming in places where before she was all hollows and bone.

Yet it's more than being a little tired.

In truest truth, sometimes it hurts to breathe.

Her power, if it can be called such—thus far she's only used it for redirecting simple kitchen flies away from the food she's preparing—emits a soft light that glows around the edges of a drawer inside her mind. And still, she suffers from debilitating waves of an invisible pain she is neither able to explain nor understand.

She dresses, straightens her bedding, and kneels upon her small carpet. In these moments of supplication, she seeks divine guidance, searching for the meaning in it all.

She used to think she knew her purpose, had an identity, but she's no longer sure what she was created for. If her life could be undone so profoundly in a single stroke, she has to wonder which parts of it, if any, ever mattered to start with.

At least the brothers need her to take care of them.

Raised voices carry up the stairs. The brothers are always boisterous, but there's a tense undercurrent to their present exchange. They're arguing, or at least engaged in a loud and passionate discussion.

"We can't keep her locked up here like some slave," Kabeer contends.

"Slave?" Aidi echoes. "We're protecting her. She knows she's free to leave anytime she wants."

"I don't want her to go," Beni whines. "I love how good my clothes smell when they're clean. How good *she* smells. And she has a lovely smile."

"It's just that she hasn't been smiling lately," Hammu grumbles. "Surely, you've all noticed?"

"We all like having her here," Dasri chimes in. "But, it's true, she's unhappy. I thought she merely needed time, but resting season has passed, and her state is only declining."

"What more could we possibly do to make her happy?" Bono asks. "We already bring home everything she requests. I even started wiping my feet when I come in the door, for graves's sake."

"Maybe what she needs is something she hasn't asked for. Something she doesn't know she needs." Deebi drops his voice low. "I have an idea . . ."

The conversation fizzles to a bare hush, and Shay is unable to catch any more of it. Her curiosity unsated, she tries to slip downstairs unnoticed. The brothers fall silent at her approach, each one suspiciously engrossed in their activity of choice.

Aidi and Dasri busy themselves with cleaning and polishing a pile of bones. Kabeer and Hammu play a game of marbles, except . . . the marbles they're using appear to be glass eyeballs. Bono and Beni weave string figures between their fingers with what Shay strongly suspects are ligaments, and Deebi is teaching his pet scarab beetle, Aicha, to do tricks.

Shay announces herself with a greeting the brothers exuberantly return. She then sets about tidying the kitchen, unsure what to make of the partially overheard conversation. They all seemed so worried. She presses the tines of a fork she's washing into the center of her palm. Tiny pricks of pain flash like guiding stars, leading her out of her inner fog.

She must forget Hind. Forget her old life. She's no longer the midwife's apprentice. Neither is she the touched one's daughter. She's a girl in exile. A girl who should be thankful she has a place to hide.

Despite her self-admonishment, every bite of the big breakfast she prepares goes down by force and tastes like nothing. Before lunch, she finishes stringing the chain of remembrance beads she's been working on, fashioned from the shells of nuts and seeds. With seven bone-eaters producing dishes and laundry, there is no shortage of things to do. A sock always needs mending or a button needs fixing, but when afternoon rolls around and the brothers settle down for their daily naps, Shay finds herself unable to resist the siren call of her pillow and blankets.

Sleeping now will only make doing so at night more difficult, but the numbing void of sleep is her sole relief.

On her way to the kitchen the next morning, Shay is startled by the unlikely sound of humming. She stops cold. The melody itself is soothing, but bone-eaters don't *hum*. And the cadence is too high and lilting to be made by any of the brothers, anyway.

Instead of being concerned about a stranger's presence in the cottage, Shay finds her curiosity sparked. She reaches the kitchen entrance and lingers there in the doorframe, staring at the inscrutable sight of at a girl around her age. The girl stands in front of the sink, scrubbing dishes. Even from behind, Shay can tell she's pretty: tall, like Shay, and a fair bit curvier. Thick, perfectly round curls spiral down to the center of her back.

She stops humming. Her shoulders rise as though she senses Shay's nearness. Then she turns around, and Shay sees she was wrong. The girl is not pretty; she's exquisite.

Her skin glows, the golden brown of Mourian sands. With wide cheekbones, simmering brown eyes, and lips that pucker as though she just ate a lemon, the entirety of her face is a well-crafted poem. Whereas Shay has been endowed with a delicate appearance that seems to put those around her at ease, this girl possesses a wilder beauty, the sort that verges on intimidating.

"Well, aren't you a quiet one? Snuck right up on me." She dries her hands while walking over to Shay. Reaching her, she lightly presses her cool cheek to first one side of Shay's face and then the other. "I'm Khawla."

Shay's initial surprise is wearing off, and confusion kicks over her like dust clouds. "What are you doing here?"

"You must be Shay," she says, one hand lingering lightly on Shay's upper arm. "Is that short for something?"

"Shuika."

"I like that." Khawla leans back against the sink as though perfectly at home. "Well, Shuika, your benefactors have decided to hire me on as a maid."

"There must be some mistake." Shay frowns. She may have grown a bit sloppy of late, but surely the bone-eaters don't intend to replace her. "We don't need a maid. I already do the cooking and cleaning and look after the brothers."

"Of course you do." Khawla unties the apron from over her clothing and hangs it from a hook on the wall next to Shay's. "But who looks after you?"

Shay shakes her head. She grabs her own apron but twists the garment in her hands rather than puts it on. "Why would I need anyone to look after me?"

The maid laughs irreverently. "Why would a bunch of bone-eaters need someone to look after them? They're hardly children!"

Shay shakes out her apron with more rigor than required. She loops it around her waist and pulls the strings tight enough that the effort of breathing distracts her from the girl's words and what they might mean.

If the bone-eaters stop needing her, what else does she have? "I still don't understand why you're here."

"Think of it this way," Khawla says, and while speaking, she gently loosens Shay's apron before she can cut off the flow of blood to her legs entirely. "Everyone needs an occasional day of respite. I'm here so you can have yours."

Khawla returns Shay's apron to the hook.

Shay sighs in relief. A day to herself doesn't sound so bad. Perhaps she can finally sleep off whatever is ailing her. As she deliberates over what to call it, her memory supplies Hind's description of her grief when she lost her husband. She said it was like an empty hole consuming her from the inside out. Shay thinks that's how she feels, but how can someone grieve what they never had to begin with?

Khawla smiles. "How about I make us tea? Sowing season has brought fair weather. We could sit outside and chat. Get to know each other."

"But . . . there's much to do, Lalla." Shay is already thinking of the things she'll need to teach Khawla about each brother's particular likes and dislikes. Their temperaments and moods. Who is allergic to what and who takes which medicines. "And besides, we must never go outside."

Khawla's smile slips, stopping just short of a pout. "Why on earth not?"

"Ard Al-Ghul is dangerous." Shay glances at the window. Only now does she notice how sunny it really is. The fog that perpetually shrouds Tarik's property and spills over to their lawn is still intact, but scattered light has finally managed to seep in. It makes everything look soft and glowing. How did resting season pass so quickly? It's been moons since she's stepped outside the bone-eaters' dwelling.

"Everywhere is dangerous." The maid shrugs like someone who isn't afraid of anything. Shay considers what Deebi said about the other humans in Ard Al-Ghul and concludes that's likely accurate. "That's why it's safest to always travel with a friend."

Safe. Shay doesn't remember the last time she felt that way.

"There's a bloodsucker living next door," she blurts out, desperate to impress upon Khawla how close the danger is. "When I came here, he attacked me. I don't know what I would have done if the brothers hadn't come along."

The tang of Tarik's coppery breath, the black pulse of his hypnotic eyes, the helplessness of having her dreams invaded, rear up in her mind, as fresh as if the attack happened only yesterday. The rancid taste of the antidote going down, the burn of spewing venom coming up, are memories imprinted on her throat. She lowers her head to hide the tremble of her chin.

"That's awful." Khawla waits for Shay to lift her eyes. "I am sorry that happened to you."

Shay blinks, the threat of tears a sting in her eyes. Suddenly, Khawla leans forward and hugs her, surrounding her with warm skin and soft fabric and the strange sensation of being held. Shay's sure this can't be the first time she's been hugged. However, she can't recall a specific incident that proves otherwise. Ghita always limited her physical touches to the briefest pats on the back, a rare and hard earned form of recognition.

She thinks she should do something with her arms, if only she could muster the strength to lift them. Instead, she stands there, letting herself be held in a tender squeeze. Shay lets go. And somehow, she feels stronger. The memory of what the bloodsucker did and her fear of him don't go away, but they seem more bearable, like maybe she doesn't have to carry that weight alone.

"Do you think we could sit near the window?" Khawla asks at last. "Maybe open it a crack? If you're comfortable with that."

Shay nods. She proceeds to gather tea leaves and sugar while Khawla fills a kettle with water. But her head swims with questions. "Khawla?"

The maid hangs the pot over freshly lit coals, then turns to her. "Yes, Lalla?"

Shay means to inquire about her situation. She wonders what dire straits could have possibly left the maid with no alternative other than taking a position under the employment of bone-eaters. The pay can't possibly be adequate enticement.

Belatedly, it occurs to her that question might come across as rude. Moreover, the maid could ask Shay the same question in return. She'd have to explain why she's a wanted criminal. She'd have to talk about Hind. And how can she admit that she was rejected by her own mother?

"Um . . ." Shay stammers, her throat bricking. She's revealed enough—too much really—about herself so soon. She pivots. "Deebi mentioned that there's a mint bush growing out back."

The maid's eyes widen in delight. "I'll go right now and clip some."

Shay withdraws a pair of sheers from a drawer and silently hands them to Khawla. She swallows and, with a slight tremor in her hands, pushes the window pane a quarter of the way up. Cool air gentles her cheek. As her eyes drift partly closed, something moves in the grass outside, almost camouflaged, but not to Shay, who *senses* the snake as well as sees it.

She nudges the creature with her mind. Feels its ribs and lateral muscles contort and bend as it changes direction. Away from the path that leads to where Khawla is snipping mint leaves, blissfully oblivious. It seems to work. Though, later, Shay will tell herself that perhaps the snake altered course on its own and she only imagined having any part in it.

Deebi told her the other humans in Ard Al-Ghul are fugitives. In all likelihood, Khawla has ties to the Citizens' Naturalist movement. Shay must keep her hizoura magic a secret. Sure, Shadi may have downplayed the threat the rebels pose to her. But that doesn't mean her new acquaintance won't spurn her if she learns the truth.

The opinion of a stranger shouldn't matter, but despite the risks that come with trusting people, Shay would not mind if the maid stayed long enough for them to not be strangers anymore.

15

Quick overview of the four pantheons of Shawafa (plus a note about elementals):

Green: The pantheon of Rabia, associated with earth energies—nature, growth, restoration and fertility—most commonly manifests as Shifa (healer) or Hadaiq (gardener).

Silver: The pantheon of Iman, associated with air energy—communication, expression, transformation, and travel—most commonly manifests as Waswas (whisperer) or Mutahawil (shifter).

Red: The pantheon of Noor, associated with fire energy—strength, illumination, defense, and lust—most commonly manifests as Batal (champion) and Hamsa (shield).

Blue: The pantheon of Rasha, associated with water energy—calm, flexibility, wisdom, and balance—most commonly manifests as Ghaib (concealer) or Taqs (weather caster).

Note that element manipulators, known as Jinnamin, can manifest in any of the above pantheons and are able to create, shape, and control one of the four elements.

—*excerpt from* Harnessing the Flow: A Compendium of Feminine Magic

Shay can't find her remembrance beads. She's thoroughly searched her sleeping room, the kitchen, the salon, and the washroom. The cottage is not so large that there are copious places to look. If Hammu laid his sticky fingers on them . . .

Soft thumps and sounds of shuffling come from the bone-eaters' sleeping room. Since the brothers have left for the night, Shay surmises Khawla must be in there. She would assume the maid is cleaning, since that is what maids generally do, but in the first quarters of Khawla's employment, she has shown scant domestic proclivity, spending more time doodling in notebooks that leave her side of their shared room a bin of pencil shavings. With her penchant for conversation and a rather delightful ability to impersonate the brothers' speech and mannerisms, she's been more of a distraction for Shay than anything. Although by no means an unwanted one.

"Khawla, have you seen—"

A cast of silver shines from between Khawla's fingers as she holds up the hjabat, about to slip the heavy ring onto her other hand. She pauses, looking over at Shay, her face brightening. "Look what I found hidden away in Aidi's wardrobe!"

Thoughts of the missing beads fall away, and feelings of mistrust rise in their place. Shay swallows tightly, but experience has shown her not to ignore her suspicions. "Why would you open a box that doesn't belong to you?"

"It's not like I'm planning to keep it," Khawla says with an easy smile, as if that makes her actions permissible. "I just like being nosy."

"Well, don't put that on." Shay hastens closer and stops herself a breath away from snatching the ring. "Just—put it back where you found it."

Khawla lowers her hand. She tilts her head. "Why are you so upset? Is it yours?"

Shay almost says no—that would be safer. But the longer Khawla is here, the more accustomed to her presence Shay becomes. Her growing attachment will only make it harder when the maid inevitably learns the truth and consequently abandons her.

"Yes." Shay sighs with all her chest. She squats down on the closest sleeping pallet—Deebi's if the knotted blankets, scattered crumbs, and pillows puddled thick with drool are any indication. "Please don't ask me to explain. It will be so much better if you can just put the hjabat away."

"What did you call it?" Khawla stares at the ring with a new glint in her eyes, before turning that gaze and its ferocity on Shay. "You have to tell me now."

The maid plops down in front of Shay on the floor. A wiser seating choice, come to think of it. Shay scoots off the pallet and joins her there. She wrings her hands. "Alright. I'll tell you. But give me the ring first."

Khawla cradles the talisman in her palm and brings it level with her nose. She regards it with squinted eyes. "But it's not a ring, is it?"

"The hjabat," Shay reluctantly amends, holding out her upturned palm. Her heart sinks to the pit of her stomach. Somehow, her mother is still managing to ruin her life even while being completely absent from it. "Please, give me the hjabat."

"Wakha, wakha." Khawla relents, placing the ring in the cup of Shay's hand. The maid peers at her steadily. "I understand if you don't know me well enough to trust me. But I assure you, your secrets are safe with me. Should you choose to confide them."

She has no idea about the magnitude of what she's asking. And yet . . . Shay gets the impression that even though Khawla really wants to know, the maid won't continue pushing her if Shay denies her request. It softens her defenses.

"It was all a huge misunderstanding," Shay explains, picking her words with care. The ring sits heavy in her hand, as if it has accumulated the weight of all her sorrows. "And now I'm wanted for arrest, even though I didn't actually do anything. I'm almost sure I've been set up."

Understanding flashes over Khawla's face. The maid nods. "Someone betrayed you."

Shay tells her then, about being reunited with her birth mother only to discover the woman was in debt. As she speaks, a pressure she didn't know she held inside her deflates, like a cooking pot releasing steam. She talks about how she was tricked into wearing the hjabat, lost consciousness, and awakened in the forest. About how she stumbled upon the bloodsucker's house and was rescued by the bone-eaters. About the posters the brothers described to her after seeing them in the medina.

Everything but the fact that her mother is an addict, that her own blood is tainted with magic. That she has the ability to . . . what exactly? To form a mental connection with animals, she thinks.

Khawla touches Shay's shoulder. "You've been through a lot."

Shay prickles unexpectedly, though the words are kind. She wants Khawla to see her as an equal who could be her friend, not as someone she should pity. "I'm sure others have had it much worse."

"That's true. Many others, in fact." Khawla drops her hand to her lap. Hesitation flickers in eyes, and then they bloom with something more intense. "What if I told you there was a way to ease the pain of so many who suffer needlessly? And that the talisman you possess might be the key to returning the world to the state of peace and justice that once existed?"

"Didn't you hear anything I said?" Shay squeezes the ring in frustration, its sharp facets digging into her skin. "The ring is dangerous. Even if it did whatever it was supposed to do, I could still be hanged for having it. And all it did do was make me have a nonsensical dream about some strange women."

"Now *that* is interesting." Khawla taps a finger to her lips, which twitch with the promise of a smile. "How much do you remember about this dream, Shay? Can you describe the women?"

"I don't know." Shay opens her fist and peers at the hjabat, trying to remember. She convinced herself the vision was a hallucination brought on by hunger or disorientation or the forest itself, but Khawla's current expression causes her to question this conclusion. "There were four of them. I couldn't see them at all, but their voices were what I can only describe as . . . otherworldly."

Khawla releases the full breadth of her smile. "I know who they are, Shay, and they are our last and greatest hope."

As much as Shay wants to know what exactly Khawla knows that she doesn't, she's slightly more concerned with *how* she knows it. Bracing herself, she asks the question she's been dreading the answer to. "What are you really doing here, Khawla? And don't tell me you're a maid. I've watched you walk right over piles of dirty clothes on multiple occasions, and only yesterday I found unwashed glasses tucked inside the cupboard."

"That's fair." Khawla chews her lower lip. She runs her palms down her thighs. "I'm Khawla El Fessi, and I think you may already suspect this, but I'm part of the rebellion."

Shay's shoulders slump. But she knew this was coming. Knew how ridiculous it was to hope she was wrong. At least she had the foresight to be selective about which parts of her history she revealed. "You're a Naturalist."

"What?" Khawla blinks rapidly. "No. Not them. CNM see the truth about Al-Mukhtar and are more than justified in wanting to overthrow them, but their ideology is deeply misguided. They can't entirely be blamed for that. So much history has been rewritten, but my faction has preserved many original texts that would otherwise be lost."

Shay's brow pinches. She swallows, her throat dry. "Your faction?"

"Yes." Khawla puffs her chest, a gleam of pride evident in her eyes. "The Sisterhood of the Keepers."

Shay sets the ring on her thigh. She smooths her fingers over her cheeks, remembering to breathe. The world was already complicated, truth and lies hard enough to separate, five beakers ago when, to her knowledge, this conflict had only two sides. "Wakha. And what does this have to do with me? With the hjabat? The bone-eaters?"

"Everything," Khawla says, and the excitement on her face would surely be contagious if Shay weren't far too tired to engage in it. " The truth is, I've had dealings with the bone-eaters for a while. Mostly buying jewelry off Hammu. I usually clean and resell it, but it's also one way for me to keep my eye out for a talisman like this one. I did think it was strange when they first asked me to pretend to be their maid, but they told me about you, explained how they felt you needed a companion, and offered me some heirloom pieces that could feed my family for moons.

"Being we don't get many human newcomers this side of the forest, I'll admit I may also have wanted to meet you and make sure you weren't a spy for the establishment—just erring on the side of caution."

Shay should be offended at the insinuation, but the false pretense irks her more. "You were hired to *spend time with me*?"

Khawla winces. She shakes her head insistently. "It's not like that. The bone-eaters care for you, which is, honestly, a strange phenomenon for bone-eaters, but once I met you, I understood. You have a presence of light and warmth about you that is quite impossible to dislike."

Shay shrugs. She's too unused to such direct compliments to know how to accept one, and she's quite sure Khawla would be less generous if she knew everything there is to know about her. "I'm an outcast."

"Or maybe you simply haven't found your kindred people yet," Khawla says soothingly. "Shay, I think you connected with the spirits of the Lallat when you put on the hjabat, and the outrageous thing is you act like you don't even know how amazing that is."

"The Lallat?" Shay's chest stirs despite her staunch commitment to apathy.

"They were our rulers, back when all women had magic."

"Right." Shay shrinks at the mention of magic. She tugs her sleeves down, as if to cover her hands. As if they might start glowing the way the touched ones' do. "Before magic died out, which God allowed to happen because those with Shawafa failed to use it wisely."

"That's simply not true," Khawla insists. "The Lallat had a system of laws in place to ensure magic was used for the benefit of the community and never for personal gain or to inflict harm. Magic didn't die out. It was stolen by men who were jealous because they weren't gifted the same strengths."

Shay can't deny that it makes a certain sense. After all, if Al-Mukhtar were really against magic, they would take more definitive action to stop Snow from being produced. "The Naturalists think we should all be equal. As in no one being allowed to have magic at all, in any form."

A stillness comes over Khawla, her face a picture of neutrality. "What do you think?"

"Me?" Shay rubs the silver crystal. Even now she can sense the ants that crawl through the cracks of tile in the floor, leaving a scent trail to guide their colony to a new food source. The pregnant mouse in the wall that has just woken up and is collecting materials for her nest. And the hungry spider on the ceiling, gliding rung to rung across its web, descending upon its prey. It can be overwhelming, a constant buzz of awareness she's not sure what she's supposed to do with. "I think maybe prayer is the only magic we really need."

"So, let's say someone is born with a natural talent for painting: Should they use that gift and glorify their Lord by sharing the beautiful pieces of art they create? Or should they deem their gift forbidden, and deprive the world of their talent, believing God alone has the right to create objects of beauty?"

"Beauty?" Shay thinks of Hind, so desperate for a blitz that she'd forsake her own child, of Sami's infanticidal mother. The touched ones rotting away in the darkened alleys of the Bib. "Have you not seen the damage magic can wreak?"

"Not magic," Khawla says with gentle firmness. "Snow. And yes, I have. But it won't be like that when we return natural magic to the women of Mekchaouen."

She speaks with a passion that's unsettling. Or maybe Shay has become more cynical. If these Lallat are real, they certainly picked the wrong girl to reveal themselves to. "How does that work?"

Khawla squints. "How does what work?"

"How will the Sisterhood return women's natural magic? What's the plan?"

"I don't know," Khawla admits. "The details exceed my ranking. But I do have a friend who could be persuaded take the hjabat to our leader and ask what should be done with it. I was planning on meeting him tonight. Would you consider coming with me?"

Shay blanches, a new panic squeezing her throat. "You were planning on going out? Tonight?"

"Don't you know?" Khawla vibrates with barely contained excitement. "Tonight is Jou Boulka!"

Every sowing season, Mekchaouen's citizens dress up in animal skins and cook meat over large fires in the street. Ghita never allowed Shay to attend the festival, calling it a celebration of debauchery. Shay always thought it was more about the symbolic struggle between good and evil, but she never wanted to go badly enough to argue the point.

We can't just leave without telling the bone-eaters. I could be arrested if I'm recognized. Al-Ghaba Mayita is too dangerous at night. The whole world is too dangerous.

All these reservations play through Shay's mind, but she can see on Khawla's face how important this is to her. She either truly believes the realm can be saved, or she thinks the ring will earn her recognition from her faction's leadership. Shay can understand both desires, even if she isn't completely on board with the cause herself.

"I suppose it wouldn't hurt just to see if the ring really is important."

"Yes!" Khawla jumps up, yanking Shay with her by the hand. So great is her excitement, Shay wonders if Khawla intended to ask her to the festival all along. And despite her misgivings, she hopes that is the case. "This is going to be so much fun. And don't look so worried. I have a plan!"

Of course she does. As Khawla drags her from the bone-eaters' quarters, Shay remembers her reason for entering them in the first place. "Khawla, wait. I wanted to ask: Have you happened to see my prayer beads anywhere?"

"No . . ." Khawla halts. Her body freezes up, and her eyes flutter closed. After a brief moment, she opens them and marches straight to Aicha the scarab beetle's glass living enclosure. She removes the lid, dips her hand inside, and withdraws it with Shay's beads dangling from her fingers. "I wonder how those got in there . . ."

"I have no idea, but thank you." Shay takes the beads. She must have dropped in the enclosure while she was in the bone-eater's room yesterday.

After noticing Deebi's increasingly frustrated attempts to train his pet, Shay decided to use her abilities to secretly help him. But she doesn't tell Khawla that. She may not be involved with the Naturalists, but she's still a rebel. And instead of spurning magic, this new faction seems to revere it. All Shay wants is to lie low and keep her neck noose-free, and advertising her ability probably isn't the best way to accomplish that.

She does find it most peculiar that Khawla knew exactly where to look.

16

Jou Boulka, the night of skins: A festival with roots in Hazmaggi tradition that has been adopted over the years by the mainstream culture of Mekchaouen. Some say its rituals represent the cycle of birth and rebirth; others say it is a celebration of fertility. It is believed to be bad luck to light a fire in your home on this night, therefore meat is cooked outdoors on public fires instead. Citizens dress up in furs to honor the spirits of the animals that have been sacrificed to provide nourishment. Children are known to knock on doors and ask for money or wool or goat skins. It is believed that a child who manages to touch the skin of one of the costumed festivalgoers, who often thwart the children's attempts by hitting them playfully with a severed animal limb, will have good fortune in the coming solar cycle.

—Encyclopedia of Holidays and Celebrations

The first step of Khawla's plan is to dress them up in disguises. She clips small horns into their hair and loops bracelets adorned with the hooves of mini-goats around their wrists. She then lines up tubs of paint in the colors of red, white, black, and green, and proceeds to employ them with an artistry that makes Shay think her earlier comment about the gift of painting was something more than a random comparison.

Khawla stains Shay's skin in the deathly pallor of a wraith who hasn't glimpsed a drop of sunlight in ages. Black circles hang around her eyes. Tiny marks around her mouth create the illusion of threads stitched into her flesh. On her own face, Khawla draws black veins that wind around her eyes, appearing to twist under her skin and seeming to carry a substance much darker than blood. The maid paints another mouth over her own in sweeps of red and uses white to set rows of jagged teeth within it.

The results render them indistinguishable from the nonhuman inhabitants of Ard Al-Ghul. The girls creep down red clay streets up to the edge of Al-Ghaba Mayita. Here, Khawla walks to a poplar tree with a symbol carved upon its bark—the yaz—made of a straight line with an intersecting upward curve on the top half and an intersecting downward curve on the bottom half. It's a motif that symbolizes freedom, often seen in Hazmaggi tattoos. Khawla presses her hand to the symbol, her eyes fluttering closed again, her face bearing that look of concentration.

When she opens them, she reaches into the thick cloth sash tied around the waist of her skirt and pulls out a tapered candle. She holds it with two fists and cracks it, but instead of breaking in half, the stick illuminates with a fluorescent glow. A grin tugs the corners of Shay's mouth.

Not a candle—a jinn stick.

The same lava used to straighten hair can also be encased in beeswax to form a child's toy. Shay used to collect them from the ground on the mornings after festivals when Ghita wasn't watching. Once broken, the stick will stay aglow for about a day.

Her palms dampen right along with her sense of adventure when she recalls the gruesome animals from her last forest foray, the way red moonlight reflected in the eyes of those that had any. The shadows of night that seemed to conspire to hide the girls in their escape now sway like thick ropes ready to coil about her neck.

It may not be too late to convince the maid to turn around. In fact, if what Deebi told her is true, getting to the festival tonight shouldn't even be possible. "Khawla, I'm confused. Doesn't it take at least one whole day for humans to cross Al-Ghaba Mayita by foot?"

"Not if you know the right shortcuts." The maid's eyes sparkle with mischief and starlight. As though sensing Shay's growing apprehension, she grabs her hand and squeezes it lightly. "Listen to me. I want you take a deep breath. And then look up."

She does. A dark sky unfurls above her, bedecked with the flickers of a thousand candles, a star for every wish tightly held in someone's heart.

"Now, if we're to play the part," Khawla whispers, her voice suddenly near Shay's ear, "we have to summon our inner beasties."

Shay smiles nervously. "Our inner what?"

The glow of the jinn stick sharpens the effect of the maid's face paint, her smile transformed into a fang-toothed snarl. "Ready to show me how loud you can be?"

"I—" Before Shay responds, Khawla tosses her head back, releasing a roar. Laughing in turn, Shay musters a growl of her own.

"You can do better than that!" Khawla urges. "Think about someone who hurt you. Someone who deserves to be devoured."

Tarik rises in her mind. Shay again tilts her head toward the moon, silver and swollen and shimmering, thinking now of the hjabat's crystal face. How Hind lied to her. Ghita, too. A rage that feels both unfamiliar and strangely natural bubbles into her chest. She opens her mouth, and the sound that emerges is raw and howling. And full of power.

They plunge into the forest's depths, met with the cling of moist air. Each brisk step they take over the sodden earth releases the stench of rotten eggs. As they move from tree to tree, Shay spots more of the yaz symbols, and other symbols she can't identify. It hits her how little she knows about this Sisterhood she's agreed to confer with.

"Can you tell me more about this friend of yours we're meeting?" she asks. Khawla's arrival felt like nothing less than a life raft appearing at the critical moment when she needed one to stay afloat. Shay neglected to consider that the maid already had family and friends of her own, had a whole life before coming to live with the bone-eaters that Shay isn't privy to. "What's his profession? Well, besides being a rebel, I suppose."

Khawla laughs, the sound cut short by a far-off cry, the not-distant growling that closely follows it. "He's a bit of a yahyah of all trades. And speaking of professions, I'm curious, is it common practice for midwives to take on multiple apprentices at once?"

"They take one at a time usually." Shay points out the scarlet leaves of a patch of venomous vine, and they both step carefully around it. "Why do you ask?"

"Oh, you know me," Khawla answers coyly. "Just being nosy as usual."

Animals rustle, near enough to make their presence known without stepping into the girls' path.

"How do you do it?" Shay asks. It's obvious Khawla knows where she's going, a confidence born of well-trodden familiarity. Everything about the forest gives Shay the uncomfortable feeling of having one foot in the real world and the other in the world beyond, of being *between*. If it has any such effect on Khawla, she doesn't show it. "How do you spend so much time in the forest?"

"You get used to it." The maid ducks beneath a low-hanging branch fringed green in glowing moss. "It wasn't always a scary place, you know."

"It wasn't?" Shay asks as the girls join hands, crossing the slippery rocks of a stagnant creek. Fingers of blue mist clutch at their ankles.

"When magic thrived, so did the forest. This was a place of abundance. It provided plentiful shade and cover for prey animals. Grassy meadows for grazers. Everything had its balance. Mature trees and young saplings. Pristine lakes and flowing creeks." Khawla leads Shay inside the dark belly of a cave where they can only see as far as the small bubble of light thrown by the jinn stick. "When magic died, the forest died, too. Men used to hunt here, you know, when the birds didn't possess more legs than a spider and the bears didn't have fur as coarse as jabberfish spikes or bellies filled with maggots the size of salmon. Now, men who dare pass through are more likely to *be* hunted. If not lost for eons. What with landmarks known to rearrange themselves on a whim maps aren't useful here anymore."

Shay is quiet for a moment. She never thought about magic impacting the natural world the way it impacts human politics, but the last thing Khawla said seems significant. "Don't you ever get lost?"

"Me? Oh, I have a special affinity for directions and finding things. That's why the Sisterhood often sends me to relay messages or conduct reconnaissance missions," Khawla says, that edge of pride flushing back into her voice.

The jinn stick flickers then, and blinks out, resigning them to darkness.

"Devil be damned," she says, and though Shay can't see her shaking the stick to no avail, she guesses that's what's happening. "It must have been an old one."

A special affinity sounds an awful lot like an echo, or maybe even the fledgling gift of a hizoura. Never having called someone a friend, Shay can't be sure how much sharing is considered appropriate, but she doesn't want to keep secrets from Khawla. And if Khawla really sees their emerging friendship as more than a job, she won't pressure Shay to join the Sisterhood if she doesn't want to.

Shay always thought she had to be one thing or another, that her existence required a purpose, a label. *Apprentice. Daughter. Outcast.* But what if she could just *be*, and that was somehow enough? Maybe the answer she's been praying for has been right in front of her all along.

"I want to show you something," she whispers, brushing Khawla's arm in the inky darkness.

Shay takes a deep breath and reaches out with the part of her mind where her Shawafa resides. She directs her flow of consciousness to the kindle worms hidden deep within the crooks and crevices of the limestone ceiling. Nothing happens for long enough to make her think she's only going to embarrass herself, but then glowing dots of blue emerge one by one. They illuminate en masse, transforming the cave ceiling into a theater of cosmic lights.

"Glory to heaven." Khawla gasps in delight. "Wait—how did you do that?"

"I guess you could say I have an affinity with living creatures."

"Hmm . . ." Khawla bumps her shoulder into Shay's. "I knew there was something special about you the moment I laid eyes on you."

The caves make a kind of tunnel system that Khawla explains serves to shorten the distance to Nezjar. Shay continues to summon the kindle worms to light the caves they pass through, and in the alternating stretches of forest between them, she enlists the assistance of friendly fireflies.

They reach the parts of the forest recognizable to Shay from her foraging excursions more quickly than it seems possible. Soon, she's stepping from the trees into a clearing where the lights of Nezjar line the hilltops in greeting. Shay's first thought is it should feel like she's come home. But the notion is at odds with the hollow ache of her chest, as wistful as the notes of a half-forgotten song.

She wonders how Ghita has fared in her absence. And Sami. And her beloved crew of strays. The truth, she now perceives, is she always needed them more than they needed her.

A sigh slips from her throat like a ghost. She never really belonged here, did she? In a strange way, Hind has spared her. Prevented her from accepting a life she may not have chosen had more than one path ever been offered.

Her second thought is more of an observation. The moon hanging over Nezjar wears its natural face of gold-white marble. No glowing film of ominous red, icy blue, or mystical silver. It's as though within Al-Ghaba Mayita, and Ard Al-Ghul beyond, things appear differently. Perhaps, in some ways, they appear truer to the way they really are, the hidden made visible.

A whistle from the darkness interrupts her introspection. The boy who must be Khawla's friend steps from the shadows. Shay can only blink. A long headdress made of a goat's pelt frames the face of someone she hasn't thought about in some time but has also never quite forgotten.

He squints back at her for a long moment, and then he smiles.

17

Man of Skins

A wicked man once chased a maiden, who sought refuge in a sacred place.
And, oh, the things he did to her there,
the shame and the disgrace.
The spirits bore witness to his crimes, and though they did not intervene,
An animal departed that place, and the man never again was seen.
Gifted horns and a whip-thin tail and sprouting pelt where naked flesh should be,
He henceforth wore his deeds in outward form, for all the world to see.

—*from* Rhymes of Rage: A Poetry Collection

Shadi's hair has grown out, dark curls hugging tightly to his earlobes. But his gapped smile—the one making everything in Shay's stomach melt in what surely must be some allergic reaction—is as big and annoyingly irresistible as ever.

"Do you two know each other?" Khawla asks, her voice sounding unnaturally innocent.

"No," Shay says.

"Yes," Shadi says at the same time.

"Not well," Shay attempts to clarify. Her face feels heavy and stiff beneath her makeup. If Shadi knows who she is, so could anyone else. She frowns at him. "How did you recognize me?"

"Your eyes . . ." Shadi clears his throat. "They're, um, brown."

"Yes, I have brown eyes." Shay nods slowly as though speaking to an easily distracted child. "As does more than half the population."

"Right." Shadi gulps. With half his face bathed in moonlight, half secreted in shadow, Shay can't determine whether he's embarrassed or confused. "But yours have this touch of dusty gray. It's like there are these soft clouds floating in them."

"Shadi, explain what's going on," Khawla demands, but her barely suppressed smile suggests the question could just be an act.

"Do you remember the girl I told you about, the midwife's apprentice?" Shadi speaks from the side of his mouth, fiddling with his thumb.

Wait—why would he have told Khawla about her? And why does the idea of it fill Shay's chest with warm flutters instead of the irritation she would prefer?

Khawla rounds her mouth. "Oh right, I must have forgotten about that."

Shay chooses to ignore whatever Khawla is up to, turning her focus to the satisfying rush of vindication. She knew Shadi was hiding something. Now she just has to decide whether his being with the Sisterhood makes her trust him more or less. And she can't let any leaky stomachs or chests palpitations or other *conditions* cloud her judgement. She feels the weight of the hjabat along the groove of her clavicle, secured there by a cord hung around her neck and tucked beneath her kaftan's bodice.

Distant pops and bright flashes usurp their attention as festivalgoers burn bamboo bangers filled with gunpowder, steel dust, and iron shavings in the distance.

Shay plasters on a smile that threatens to crack the paint around her lips. "Let's go see what this festival is all about, shall we?"

"Yes!" Shadi and Khawla agree.

The hooves on the girls' bracelets clink softly as the trio makes its way up the central hill to the medina. Up top, the louder sounds of beating tbilat and trilling ghayyat take over, and then they descend into a sea of singing voices that usher them through the festival entrance. By the time they reach the main thoroughfare, the very air has turned charged.

The clamor of laughter and chanting and the aromas of spit-roasted meshwi and fried rings of sfenj swirl in a sensory stew. Colorful lanterns and bright torches abound. Children weave through the crowd, waving small rattle drums. Old men hand out bowls of snails in steaming broth, and women pour tea for passersby. Dancers form lines and circles and twirl colorful flags or clack handheld iron qraqeb as they take turns performing acrobatic kicks and mesmerizing spins to the hypnotic rhythm.

Elaborate sheepskin and cowhide costumes and wooden masks render anyone Shay might know unrecognizable, easing her fears that someone else may identify her with the same ease that Shadi had. She keeps a cautious eye out for Moulays, but even they seem to have been given the night off from their duties.

Shay holds both Shadi's and Khawla's hands to keep one of them from getting lost in the fray. The three move as a unit, like boats tied together on the ocean. They stop in front of a fire pit where Shadi grabs them a skewer of lamb each. The street food is a treat Ghita never allowed Shay due to her poor digestion. She digs her teeth into the meat, savory spices tingling over her taste buds. They devour the qotban and lick the grease from their fingers.

Still uneasy, Shay searches the shop windows and street signs, looking for the posters Aidi described. The fact that she doesn't find any gives her hope. Maybe her alleged crime has been forgotten, replaced by the passage of time with matters more current and of greater urgency.

Would she return to her old life if she discovered herself to be free? Or would she go somewhere new? *Become* something new? The thought is daunting. Shay wonders if a newly hatched butterfly ever wishes it could go back to the familiar confines of its cocoon.

Khawla pulls her toward one of the small bands scattered throughout the festival. The rebel girl lifts her arms high and dances with graceful swirls and shimmies. Her body moves the way water cascades from a precipice, like it's only natural. Shadi dances too, unencumbered by his heavy headdress, his enthusiasm making up for any lack of grace. He throws Shay a shy smile.

The steady pulse of music builds to a pounding in her core. The revelry around her tangles with her memories of the long-ago hanging, the rabid heckling of the crowd. Her chest squeezes. She recalls the bone-eaters' frequent warnings that she stay inside and not open the door. Perhaps she should not have come here, where everything feels too colorful, too loud, and too . . . much.

"Are you well, Lalla?" Shadi asks, concern creasing his brow. "Can I get you something to drink?"

His sudden nearness momentarily steadies her. She nods, managing to say, "Yes, please."

But as he rushes off, the crowd closes in again. Shay stumbles back. She bumps into woman draped in heavy furs. A mask that looks like a real animal skull covers her face. And behind the gaping socket holes, her eyes are sheets of white. The apology on Shay's lips evaporates as the woman grabs her arm for balance.

"Have a look at you," she slurs, crooning. "Your makeup looks amazing. Did you do that yourself?"

"N-no," Shay sputters, still overwhelmed, as Khawla steps up beside her. "My friend helped."

Despite her misgivings about the festival, the word *friend* tastes sweet on Shay's lips. It feels true. Or at least possible.

"Arbia, come see how utterly creepy this costume is," the first woman calls to a second woman wearing a purple feathered mask. Shay flinches at the sharp hook of its beak, too close in resemblance to the bird form the bloodsucker once wore.

"Look at those teeth," Arbia exclaims, approaching and admiring Khawla's makeup. "I'm so impressed. Come here so I can see you better."

The women draw Khawla apart from the crowd, fawning over her as they go. And Shay follows along, relieved to escape the jostling dancers.

"I think we should invite them to our private party," the first woman says, to which Khawla casts Shay a wary glance.

"Yes!" Arbia yells before noticing Khawla and Shay's mutual hesitation. She nudges her companion with her elbow.

"How rude of me," the first woman says. "We're Labiba and Arbia." In turn, they each lower their heads. "And who are you lovely beasties?"

"I'm Loubna, and this is Houda," Khawla supplies, thinking on the spot.

"So pleased to meet you," Arbia says. "Now that we've been properly introduced, it would be our great honor invite you to a private party we're hosting."

"It's very exclusive," Labiba interjects.

"What kind of party?" Khawla asks, her voice clipped. She retreats a step from the women. Alarmed, Shay wonders if Khawla's disguise may not be working after all.

"Tell me, Lalla, have you ever delved into the lustrous dark?" Labiba asks with all the warmth of melted sugar. She shifts her fur pelt to the side and runs a long fingernail across the belt that loops her narrow waist. Its straps hold a multitude of tiny bottles.

Shay knows as soon as she sees them—the woman aren't plotting to turn her in at all; they're touched ones peddling liquid magic. Bottled pleasure. And, for those whose hearts are broken beyond repair, those all out of wishes, a ready means of escape.

"Not interested," Khawla says, glowering at the bottles.

"What about you, Lalla?" The woman quirks her head at Shay.

She opens her mouth, certain her response will echo Khawla's, baffled when her throat falls sterile. Arbia slides her hand around Labiba's waist. She plucks a shiny bottle from the belt and holds it out. "The rush is like riding the biggest wave in the Cerabbi or floating upon the highest cloud over Umm Chanala."

Of course, being blitzed must feel amazing. Why else would a mother choose Snow over her own daughter? Shay glances at Khawla. The rebel girl raises her hand as if to deliver an objection, but only covers her mouth, the disapproval in her eyes speaking volumes.

All Shay can think is that if she knew how it felt for Hind, maybe she'd understand. Maybe her mother's betrayal would hurt a little less. Or maybe she just wouldn't care. "I haven't."

"Oooh, the first time is the best," Labiba gushes.

"I wonder what your Shawafa would be?" Arbia giggles. "Would you be a Jinnamin like me?" She extends one arm, and her hand lights with a red glow. A faint crackle, as a small flame blossoms from the center of her upturned palm and hovers in the air above it.

"Or, a Ghaibmin, like me?" Labiba squeals. "We're a rare type from the blue pantheon. I bet you've never seen a trick like this one." She twirls her arms in front of her, and her fingertips emit a blue glow. Shay isn't sure what the touched one is doing until the outline of her body blurs.

Shay's breathing stills. Labiba's form grows lighter and lighter until the crowd becomes visible behind her. For a beaker, she disappears, long enough for Shay to glance around, making sure she hasn't hidden herself behind a vendor's cart or passerby. Labiba reappears just as gradually, transparent at first and growing solid bit by bit.

"That's amazing." Shay turns wide-eyed to Khawla, but the rebel girl seems unimpressed. On any other night, such a public display would surely cause a scene, but on Jou Boulka, no one blinks an eye.

The woman shrugs one shoulder. "I get that a lot."

"I'd like to see you roast a chicken," her companion scoffs.

"I can't." The woman shakes her head, the heavy jaw of her mask jiggling. "But I can steal one right out of the coup."

"True." Arbia brings the bottle of Snow closer to Shay and twists it in her fingers.

The amber liquid inside glistens. Shay imagines what she could do if her animal bond multiplied, what great hordes she could summon, what wild beasts she could tame. Though, in all honesty, she'd be content to just hear the animals around her more clearly. To understand her own gift better.

She doesn't realize she's wrapped her fingers around the bottle until she hears Khawla's soft gasp beside her. Arbia smiles at Shay, her too-red lips curving up from either side of her beak.

A sudden clatter, and something cold splashes around Shay's ankles.

"What in the devil's armpit is going on?" Shadi stands there, a muscle razoring along his jaw. Glass shards gleam amid a foaming puddle of fizzy lemon drink spilled across the cobblestones. He snatches the bottle from Shay's hand and shoves it back toward Arbia. "Take this before I smash it on the street next."

The women promptly depart, presumably seeking some other young girls to corrupt. Shadi ushers Shay away from the broken glass, and then he rounds on Khawla. "What would have happened if I hadn't shown up?"

Khawla drops her gaze for only a moment. When she lifts her head, her eyes glint iron and fire. "I make it a practice not to determine other people's choices for them."

"Shay obviously isn't in the proper frame of mind to do so." Shadi runs an exasperated hand over his face and points a finger at her. "Of anyone, you should know that."

"Shay is standing right here." Shay's voice comes out more level than she feels. The strength of it grounds her in the present, bringing her fully into her body.

Shadi swallows. He pinches the bridge of his nose and slowly meets Shay's eyes with an unflinching gaze. "I won't apologize for stopping you."

Shay breathes in deep. The truth is, she's grateful. Her whole life might be different if someone had stepped in the first time Hind used. "No, I'm glad you did."

He nods, then narrows his eyes toward Khawla, who shrugs.

"I'm sorry," Shay says. The spirit of the night has been soured, and it's her fault. She covers her face, paint smearing beneath her fingertips—one more thing she's ruined. "I'm not comfortable here, honestly. I think perhaps festivals aren't suited to my tastes."

"Understandable," Khawla says, as they watch an inebriated man strut up to a nearby donkey. He loudly declares it to be the prettiest woman he's seen all night and proceeds to invite the beast to accompany him home. The trio breaks into laughter, and between their explosive bursts, Khawla tells Shadi, "I actually have something of importance to discuss. Can we move this to a more private location?"

Shadi grins, his eyes thoughtful. "I know just the place."

"Alright, but no breaking in or trespassing now," Khawla warns. "Shay needs to avoid drawing attention."

"When have I ever engaged in such reprobate behavior?" Shadi asks incredulously. He quickly amends, "Don't answer that. Just trust me. You're going to love this. Both of you."

The girls follow him away from the festivities to a quiet hilly area that borders the forest. Shay is beginning to think Shadi oversold the location, when from behind the scrubby ledge of a plateau, the toothless gap of a cave mouth appears. It's not so large that she would have noticed it on her own, and the dark cleft of its opening doesn't exactly welcome solo exploration.

"Khwati." Shadi bows toward the entrance. "Welcome to the best-kept secret in Nezjar."

They duck inside an obsidian abyss. A long tunnel stretches ahead, and the only light comes in the form of a strange flickering at the end of it. The closer they move toward the light, the brighter it glows. Ribbons of red, blue, silver, and green dance along the curving walls.

The tunnel leads to an archway so narrow, they must squeeze through it one at a time. Shadi goes first. Shay steps next onto a ledge, pressing close to him to leave room for Khawla to come through last.

A wide, open cavern unfolds before them in a panorama of radiant color. Glowing stalactites drip from the ceiling like melted jewels, reflecting off one another to kaleidoscopic effect. From deep below, four towering stalagmites rise, adding an infinite layer to the brilliance. One pillar is silver, the others blue, and red, and green.

Shadi sits on the ledge and lets his legs hang. Shay sits in the middle, Khawla beside her. Wresting her eyes from the display, Shay peeks at her companions, their peaceful faces flashing in a sequence of changing lights. For their musical enjoyment, drops of water plink like wind bells in the rain.

Shadi catches Shay staring, which should be awkward but somehow isn't. "I'm telling you. It never gets old."

"It's amazing," Shay whispers, as if anything louder might break the spell. "I can't believe more people don't know this is here. How did you find it?"

Something painful spikes behind Shadi's eyes. Cuts into his brow. "Do you believe in the Creator, Shay?"

"Of course," Shay answers reflexively. "How else would we be here?"

Shadi looks unsatisfied. "I mean, really believe, really understand that every time we stand and pray in the Old Tongue, He's right there, answering us back word for word. That it's more than worship. It's a conversation."

Shay gives a slow nod. She's never thought of her prayers exactly that way before, but she does feel connected when she performs them. Not just to the Creator, but to all creation. At the same time, she also feels as if the rest of the world falls away, all the worry about what her place is in it. Her past regrets and future concerns. Somehow, realizing how small you are in a vast universe can be the greatest form of freedom.

"Since when did you become a Marabout, Shadi?" Khawla quips.

Shadi rolls his eyes before going back to Shay's original question. "I used to have doubts myself, especially after my family endured a period of loss. I couldn't understand how God let terrible things happen. I thought about ending it all. One night, I prayed that God would give me a sign if I should keep living. Nothing happened. And so, I wandered out into the night, prepared to lose myself in Al-Ghaba Mayita."

Shay sucks back a gasp. She's heard the stories. Of people, overwhelmed with life's sorrows, venturing into the forest with no intention of coming out, whether that means being consumed by beasts or following a forest spirit off a cliff. It's said Al-Ghaba Mayita will not refuse a willing sacrifice.

"But somehow, I ended up here instead." Shadi waves his arm at the brilliance surrounding them. "I guess that was my sign, wouldn't you say?"

Shay stays quiet for a long moment. She's sure that story couldn't have been easy for Shadi to share, to live through, and she's glad he made it to the other side. Before she knows what she's doing, she lays her hand on top of his.

"What happened to your family?" In Shay's periphery, Khawla frantically shakes her head. Shay withdraws her hand. "I'm sorry . . . I understand if that's too personal."

Shadi takes a deep breath and musters a wan smile. "I don't speak about it often, but I don't mind that you asked. There was a night raid on our home. My younger brother was taken from us. My sisters are afflicted with nightmares to this day."

Shay's mind skips to Fatimazara and her grandson. The gallows rise in her mind once more, and with them, a tide of bile in her stomach. Even more than a distraction, the hangings are a fear tactic, a means by which Al-Mukhtar control the masses. "They arrested him?"

Shadi gives a dry laugh and jams his thumbs into the corner of his eyes. "Do you call it *arrest* when the 'rebel' is nine cycles old?"

This time, Shay can't restrain her gasp. The bitterness in her stomach boils over her ribs, submerging her heart in acid until every chamber burns. She doesn't know what to say, knows nothing she could say would make a difference. Then she remembers the day of Khawla's arrival at the bone-eaters, when Shay told the maid about Tarik's attack.

"I'm sorry that happened." Shay looks deep into Shadi's soulful brown eyes. Eyes that look bottomless in the most beautiful way. "There's nothing that could ever justify that." And she hugs him, the same way Khawla hugged her.

But it doesn't feel the same.

Shadi feels solid in all the places Khawla is soft. He relaxes in her embrace, his breath fanning her neck, his fingers fitting the notches of her spine like they're the keys of a flute. His warmth seeps into her, spreads through her body and sinks to her deepest core, a place that answers with a searing blaze.

In the corner of her eye, Shay sees Khawla again, this time with a small smile bowing her lips. Shay stiffens. She shouldn't be feeling this way after Shadi shared something so horrible. The only heat she should feel is anger on his behalf.

Anger for Fatimazara. For every citizen taken by soldiers in the night to be brutally hanged the following day with no explanation of their crimes. She pulls back abruptly, slamming her back into the jagged slab of cave wall behind her.

Shadi looks stunned, then concerned. "Are you well, qalbi?"

Qalbi. My heart. No one has ever called Shay that before. She winces. His look holds the same aching tenderness as the one he once gave her on the roof of her old apartment, as if he wanted to know her. But that was long ago. She was a different person. Who would want to know her now? "My mother is an addict."

She blurts the admission, the words too soft and small in the vast space around them to ring as loud and heavy as they do inside her head. Inside her chest. Khawla grabs Shay's hand at her side and squeezes, and Shadi's hand glides to rest upon her other shoulder.

"I suspected as much," he says gently, without judgement. "Between the gossip and the moon pepper. You look better now, by the way."

"It's a hard thing, loving someone who is destroying themselves," Khawla chimes in, giving Shay's hand another squeeze.

Between them, Shay feels almost safe, and though she knows the folly of hoping that such a feeling will be more than fleeting, she wants to try. She wants to give Shadi and Khawla the chance to prove to her that she can trust them.

Shay tugs the hjabat from her bodice and slips the cord over her head. As soon as she holds it up for Shadi to see, one of the four pillars, the silver one, flares even brighter, bursting with radiance. Shay shields her eyes as streaks like lightning reflect off its craters and contours. Everything is bathed in the gleam of stardust.

"Um . . ." Khawla gawps at the dazzling display. "Has that ever happened before, Shadi?"

Shadi shakes his head, speechless. He looks at Shay, questions brimming in his eyes. She tells him what she already told Khawla about her vision in the forest. He listens intently, his gaze drifting more than once to the ring cradled in Shay's hand with an expression of wonderment.

When she's finished, he hesitates, swallowing. "Shay, I think Khawla is right about the hjabat's importance. How would you feel about coming with me to meet my mother?"

Shay's eyes pop wide. "Wh-what?"

Shadi side-eyes Khawla. He sighs. "You didn't tell her?"

"Oh, right." Khawla grimaces, raising her palms by way of apology. "Shadi's mother is the Morchidat."

"The who?" Shay doesn't know why the title causes dread to pool in her stomach, but something tells her the reaction is not unwarranted.

"Don't mind the scary-sounding designation. She's the leader of the Sisterhood of the Keepers," Shadi clarifies. "And I'm sure she would be very interested in seeing the hjabat and hearing about your experience."

Shadi is the son of their faction's leader?

Shay takes a moment to absorb that news before she considers what he's asking of her. It seems to Shay too big a step, one that could entail more than a simple meeting. Once she gets entangled with the resistance, it may be hard or even impossible to walk away from them.

Her thoughts rattle around like noisy ghosts. Just look at what she almost did earlier tonight when offered Snow. Her behavior wasn't exactly a sign of stellar judgement.

She needs time to think this through. "When do you want me to go?"

Shadi ducks into his shoulders and looks up at Shay through his dark lashes. "Now-ish? Would be good."

Now.

If only there were somewhere Shay could go to seek good counsel. She needs the advice of someone with a level head, with wisdom. Someone without political loyalties. And the only person she can think of is the one she left behind without so much as a proper goodbye so she could chase some childish dream of a mother's love.

Ghita.

A sharp ache overtakes Shay's chest.

The midwife may not be perfect, but she is honorable.

"It's just that Mmi—*the Morchidat*—happens to be visiting Nezjar on business," Shadi elaborates, hinting that the timing is a rare stroke of good luck.

Shay looks from Shadi's earnest face to Khawla's careful expression and down at the ring, as if the Lallat might spontaneously reappear with words of wisdom to impart. She closes her eyes in a long blink before opening them. "Do we have time for another stop first? There is someone else in Nezjar I must see."

It's well past time she made things right.

18

That school in which you studied, I'm the one who built it.

—Ghita Bensultana

The route to Ghita's apartment draws them away from the crowds, down alleys where moonlight turns blue walls to glacial ice. The din of the revelry follows them, carried between buildings, testifying to a festival at its height with no sign of slowing.

Shay tries to internally prepare herself. She rehearses what she will say to the midwife, how she will explain herself, but as they near their destination, another, deeper, apprehension tugs at her. It hangs like a heavy cape around her shoulders, dragging behind her every step. She doesn't see or hear or smell anything she can point to as being out of the ordinary, but a foreboding disrupts her thoughts, insisting that something is deeply wrong.

Finally, Shay stands before the same door she walked through countless times, bearing fresh cuts on her fingers and a bundle of foraged herbs in her arms, or sporting the puffy eyes of a sleepless night and the smiling lips of a successful birth.

Black paint confirms that tragedy has struck. Illuminated by watery moonbeams, two crisscrossed slashes mar the door's wooden surface. A symbol that declares a building unsafe to enter, either due to structural collapse or because someone has been quarantined with infection.

Shay glances at Shadi and Khawla to find them glancing back and forth at each other, their wide eyes pearled by silver shadows. She knocks softly on the door and pauses, listening. Then she calls out, "Khalti, are you there?"

She knocks louder, calls out more urgently, "Ghita, it's me, Shay. Are you well?"

Their neighbor Zaytuna pokes her head out from the upstairs window. "It's late! What's this commotion about?"

"Khalti," Shay says with some relief. "I'm very sorry to disturb you, but I'm looking for the midwife."

"Are you with child?"

"No." Shay looks down, ridiculously, at the flat span of her stomach. "It's me . . . The apprentice."

"Bnti, is it really you?" Zaytuna disappears for a moment and returns with a pair of wire-framed spectacles perched on her nose. "Hold on, I'll be right down."

Shortly, the woman clatters down the stairwell on the side of the building. At the bottom, she draws a threadbare robe over her sleeping gown as she marches up to Shay. Zaytuna grabs both her hands and peers into her face like someone confronted by a ghost. "Where did you go, bnti? The midwife was quite distraught by your disappearance."

"I . . ." Guilt slithers between Shay's ribs. "I was lost, khalti." It's the only explanation Shay thinks of, and she reasons it to be accurate in more ways than one.

Zaytuna huffs, jamming a hand on the crest of one hip. "I told her not to let you keep foraging so close to that awful forest."

Shay's eyes drift back to the black smears across the door, shocked afresh by the sight. "Do you know where she is?"

"I'm so sorry." Zaytuna runs a nervous hand over the brightly colored scarf that covers her hair. "The midwife . . . she fell sick."

Shay sets her teeth. It can't be true. Ghita never got sick. And if she ever did feel the slightest symptom of approaching illness, she always knew what herbal tincture to take to nip it in the bud. Of all the times for her to succumb to illness, how could it happen when Shay wasn't there to help? She's reaching toward the door handle when Zaytuna stays her hand with her own.

"What are you doing?" Shay wails. A pang of panic fills her throat. "She needs me."

Zaytuna lowers her voice to a somber wisp. "She's not here, bnti."

Shay steps back from the door, and her hands are shaking. Her whole arms are shaking. She sniffles. Was the illness so dire, Ghita had to be admitted to a clinic for treatment? "Did she go to the maristan?"

Zaytuna shakes her head sadly as Shadi and Khawla take hold of Shay from either side as if she might fall. "I'm so sorry," the neighbor repeats, her mouth twisting like the words are bent into peculiar shapes that cause friction on her tongue. "It is a great loss to the community."

"What?" Shay manages to stutter. "Where is Sami?"

Zaytuna looks confused. "Who?"

"The baby . . ." Shay wipes her wet eyes, new tears rising more quickly than she can dry them.

"Why don't you come upstairs," Zaytuna offers, pushing the question aside before Shay can decide how much is prudent to say. "I can make some tea."

The shaking moves to Shay's legs, her body under the grip of denial, every bone joining her mind in its fight to reject the neighbor's words. Zaytuna has no reason to lie, yet it can't be true. Ghita can't be . . . gone. The midwife was a force of nature. Shay would sooner believe the moon itself had fallen, leaving behind a gaping hole in the fabric of the sky.

Wiggling free of her companions, Shay lunges for the door.

"I wouldn't go in there if I were you." Zaytuna's voice turns sharp with warning.

"Is it contaminated?" Khawla asks worriedly.

The woman's face clouds over. Her chin trembles. "It isn't safe."

Something is off about all this. Shay pivots back to the woman and speaks gently. "What really happened here?"

The neighbor straightens her face like a new bedsheet, but she can't smooth the edges of fear from her eyes. "Just come upstairs. You don't need to see what's in there."

Desperation mounts in Shay's chest. Whatever has happened, it's surely her fault for leaving. Why couldn't she have been content with what she had? Why was she so needy, so greedy, so hungry for a kind of love that was never meant to be hers?

Turning from Zaytuna, Shay pounds on the door, a scream ripping from her throat. "GHITA!"

Khawla's caring hands are on her upper arms, but Shay can't stop pounding.

A flurry of scratches from the other side of the door. The brass knob twists from inside. Whoever she expects to see when the door shudders open, it certainly isn't the bouncing ball of gray fur that quickly twines itself around her leg. "Qamar! How on earth did you get inside the house?"

"You should have listened to me," Zaytuna rasps, backing away. "Go turning over rocks, you're asking to uncover snakes." She scurries back upstairs, leaving Shay to stare inside the apartment, the familiar walls and furniture buried beneath a darkness that swims with shadows.

"Maybe we should go." Khawla releases Shay and wraps her arms around her own body.

Shay bends to shower Qamar with overdue affection in the form of pets and scritches. She glances up at Khawla. "I understand if you'd rather wait for me outside."

"If you go in, I'm coming with you," Shadi says.

"We may need this, then." Khawla pulls a jinn stick from her sash. "Found it on the ground on the way over."

They step inside as Khawla breaks the stick. She holds it out like a magician's wand to light the way ahead. Wind gusts through a shattered window, which explains how Qamar got in. As Khawla waves the glowing stick, its sweeping light reveals overturned chairs and broken decorations. They move to the kitchen, where cabinet doors hang from their hinges like broken wings and shards of plates and mugs crunch like packed snow beneath their slippers.

The horror is incomprehensible, but Shay can't look away from it. In a wordless daze, she stumbles to their sleeping room. The midwife's books are torn, reservoirs of wisdom and knowledge now piles of shredded pages, tossed like leaves and debris after a storm.

Shay kneels before the empty bassinet Ghita made for Sami. She splays her fingers over the plain wool blankets, half expecting to find them warm. Their utter coldness confirms that whatever took place here happened days ago at least.

She doesn't register the tears streaming down her face until Khawla and Shadi kneel quietly to either side of her. "Who could have done this?"

Their silence is answer enough. Shay thinks they know as well as she does. The soldiers came for Shay, just as they had come for Shadi's brother. But none of them, least of all the midwife, had done anything wrong. Things look so much clearer now that she's spent time away from her medina.

The people don't follow Al-Mukhtar for their good providence. They follow them because they're afraid. Like the neighbor upstairs, who'd rather invent a story about the midwife being sick than talk about what really happened here. Maybe she even made herself believe it. How could Shay have ever believed Mekchaouen's leaders' so-called miracles came from God? She prefers to believe in the God who led Shadi to that cave, a God of mercy and beauty and hope, not one who condones control through brutality and violence.

And if it wasn't a raid, if it was robbers or the type of deviants who prey on women living alone, what is the sense in this destruction? Whoever did this *wanted* someone to find the aftermath, to be reminded how thin the illusion of safety is and has always been. And what of Sami? Would he be raised to train as a Moulay? Or returned to a mother unfit to care for him?

Through her tears, Shay makes out the blurry shapes of parchment strips strewn among the rubble. Suspecting they are not made from the same thin paper that filled Ghita's books, she lifts one between her fingers. Yes, these are thicker, the kind of parchment reserved for official decrees. Each torn strip holds another fragment of an image. Is that . . . an eye?

A quick sweep of the room produces two mostly intact halves. She holds them flush, and her heart twists at the sum of her own face—depicted not on a wanted poster, but a sign for a missing person.

Ghita was trying to find her.

"Wow." Khawla stands next to her, appraising the handmade flyer. "The midwife could draw quite well. Her line variation and blending techniques really capture your nature," she says with the authority of someone speaking as an artist herself. "Do you think this could be the sign the bone-eaters saw in the medina? Is it possible they were in a hurry and mistook it for a wanted poster?"

Shay can't speak, busy adding and subtracting facts and lies. She distinctly remembers Kabeer's assertion that he could read, so a lack of literacy is not a viable excuse. Her mind quickly crafts another scenario, one where the bone-eaters knew the posters were one thing but told her they were another. But why? And how had Aidi known the ring was a *magical* talisman when Ghita's posters made no mention of it? Did he trick her into thinking he was helping her so he could keep the hjabat for himself?

Shay feels the effervescence of laughter bubbling deep inside her, jagged and bitter when it hits the back of her throat. It's a joke at this point, the way everyone keeps lying to her. She's a joke. Ghita didn't raise her to be *this* gullible. She feels so stupid. And angry, at herself mostly.

But then, if Shay's *not* a fugitive, why *was* Ghita's apartment raided?

"We should go," Khawla says, regarding Shay worriedly. "In case the building is under any kind of surveillance."

The words raise an alarm inside her, breaking through her shock. As desperately as Shay wants to know exactly what happened here, she won't learn anything more tonight. Besides, she still can't be certain she's not a wanted criminal. The neighbor saw her; would Zaytuna turn her in? That's what Al-Mukhtar brought the people of her realm to. They turned them against one another, making enemies of neighbors.

"You're right." Shay turns to the door as Khawla's jinn stick illuminates an oblong stain set beside it. A dark, shapeless splotch, blemishing the burnished wall. Blood—dry now, but cast in long ribbons where it once dripped toward the floor.

Her body collapses into Khawla's ready arms, and Shay sobs into her warm chest as loss renders her senseless. She thought she knew what grief was before, but this—this is true grief. It's cruel, and it's relentless, and it feels like being pummeled by a thousand hurled stones.

19

The Legend of Ard Al-Ghul

Once, two sisters traveled across the wide forest to visit a sacred shrine. They each packed food, but one sister ate all of hers as soon as she felt the first pang of hunger, while the other restricted herself, portioning out her servings to make them last over the course of a long journey.

They rested briefly after visiting the shrine, then headed homeward, but the first sister had saved no food for the return journey. Seeing that her sister had set aside half of what she packed for this purpose, she asked her to share. To teach her a lesson, her sister cruelly asked for payment in the form of one eye. Rather than starve, the first sister gave one eye, but before long, she became hungry again and gave her other eye for more food.

Now blind, she needed to be led along by her sister, slowing her down. Eventually, the second sister abandoned the first. She cried out so loudly that the spirits in the unseen world were drawn to her rage and despair. One was a ghoul who fell immediately in love with her. Because she could not see what he really looked like, she imagined him to be a handsome hero who had saved her and allowed him to take her to the land beyond the forest. There, he married her.

The ghoul would care for his bride by day and cross the forest to visit the medina where her sister lived by night, tormenting her for what she had done. The couple had monstrous children, and their children had children, who took up the task of terrorizing the human realm each night.

And these made up the original inhabitants of Ard Al-Ghul.

Shay shouldn't be able to take a breath in and let it out again when Ghita never will. But she does. She shouldn't be able to move, to command her legs and lift one foot in front of the other, but she does that, too.

It helps that Khawla and Shadi are with her. It's strange, this feeling that if she falls, one of them will catch her. If she cries, they won't accuse her of being weak. She tries to pull herself together for Ghita's sake. Breaking apart won't help her get to the bottom of what happened, but in her mind, the blood on the wall isn't dry. It keeps dripping, dripping, dripping, when the stuff that flowed within the veins of someone so formidable should never have been so easy to shed.

Khawla guides them back to the forest's edge, to another tree marked with the yaz. Shay turns to Shadi before they part ways, the hjabat's pull a heavy drag around her neck. Its cold weight is a reminder of the decision she must make.

"I think I shall have to postpone my meeting with your mother," she finds the wherewithal to say.

"Of course." Shadi folds his hands over his heart. "I understand how much you're hurting. And I wish I could go with you, if for no reason than to be present with you in your sorrow. Regrettably, duty obliges me to stay, and so, until we meet again, I leave you in the hands of our Creator. He is the best keeper of our trust."

"Ameen," Shay murmurs, touched even now by the kindness of this boy who has turned out to be funnier, cleverer, and more caring than she could have known when their paths first crossed.

Their surroundings make a dull impression as Khawla leads her back through Al-Ghaba Mayita. In a detached way, she notices the forest is quieter than before. No insects hum; no crickets chirp. The tree branches are unstirred by the flutter of wings, the undergrowth unburdened by the scamper of feet. Only a brittle wind rattles the dry leaves like a dying breath, as if the forest is expressing its condolences.

Her mind holds no thoughts beyond this until they reach the border of Ard Al-Ghul and morning light cracks the horizon. Its vivid glow is that of a slimy yolk seeping from a broken egg shell. The brothers will be home by now from their nightly activities and are apt to be displeased to learn she ignored their numerous warnings.

The kindling sun seems incompatible with the pall of darkness inside her, as if the sky itself should remain draped in black. The first thing Shay notices as they near the bloodsucker's imposing house isn't the rattle of wheels or the thud of hooves down the clay street. It's the way Khawla, who's paying better attention, has already adopted an alert stance.

She tugs Shay so deep into the nearest hedge that wild thorns maul their backs through their attire. An approaching carriage appears and grinds to a stop in front of Tarik's gate. Billows of red dust settle around a team of ghastly skeleton horses. A bone-eater sits in the driver's seat. Though Shay has grown used to the brothers' appearances, this slobbering, bug-eyed creature seems to belong in a different class. Behind him, a dome of dark fabric covers a long iron bed, hiding its cargo from view.

Shay shivers. She watches through a weave of thin branches as her neighbor's front door swings wide. Tarik ambles down the path to the gate, mist trailing after him in a vaporous cape. He nods in greeting to the bone-eater, the gesture wordlessly returned by the creature. Khawla tips two fingers to the side of Shay's chin, nudging her head gently away from whatever is about to occur, but Shay resists. She no longer wishes to hide from the truth of the world, no matter how ugly.

The bloodsucker whisks aside the canvas flap, allowing Shay a glimpse of the touched ones huddled inside. A dozen or so women, all bound and shackled. Their heads hang over bent knees, most beyond bothering to look up at the sudden influx of light. A brave few peek at Tarik through stripes of dirty hair. And their eyes quiver.

Fear sours the air. It leaves Shay choking. Tarik sighs loudly. A woeful, put-upon sigh. He climbs wearily into the carriage and draws the flap closed behind him. Whatever Shay expects to happen next does not prepare her for the ensuing litany of muffled moans or their rapid crescendo to screams of pain.

Cuffing her hands to Khawla's shoulder, she hiss-whispers, "What is going on?"

"Al-Mukhtar has a truce with the bloodsuckers," Khawla explains, disgust curdling her voice. "They don't come to Mekchaouen to prey on humans, and in return, our leaders provide them with an alternate source of sustenance."

"Touched ones?" Shay feels faint.

Khawla nods gravely. "The ones who are already near to death and no longer able to tap into their Shawafa. If the touched ones either refuse or are unable to recruit new addicts to live in the kasbah, this is how Al-Mukhtar disposes of them."

Nausea is a bonfire in Shay's stomach. How often does the carriage come? How did she live next door so long and never notice? No wonder Hind did the things Bushra accused her of. She had a choice, but not much of one. How much longer before this becomes her fate, too?

"We should go while he's occupied." Khawla tugs Shay's sleeve.

"No. We have to do something." Despite her brave words, Shay can only reel from the absolute horror. These women are being delivered like lambs to the slaughter, both aware of their fate and too weak from prolonged drug use to resist it. It wasn't enough for Al-Mukhtar to steal women's magic—the men have weaponized addiction. They use it to strip away the touched ones' freedom and dignity, and then, as a final insult, they rob them down to their last drops of blood.

She keeps thinking that surely the bloodsucker's thirst must be quenched, but the noises go on and on. The slurping magnifies until it sounds like he's right next to her ear. Her chest tightens like she's stuffed in a dress several sizes too small, and she wants to peel off her own skin just to breathe.

Just when Shay thinks Khawla is right and they should run to the bone-eaters for help, she meets the glowing eyes of a horse. She doesn't try to communicate with the creature, at least not consciously, but it seems to sense her distress and rears back, whinnying. In a ripple effect, the other horses start snorting. Steam furls from their nostrils, and their hooves stomp in agitation. The bed of the carriage rocks precariously, and Shay doesn't know whether she should attempt to calm the horses or spur them on.

"Whoa." The bone-eater heaves on the reins to no avail. "Easy now."

Tarik stumbles from the carriage just before the horses take off. He looks around drunkenly as they gallop down the clay road, the front of his white tunic bearded with blood. He catches sight of Shay, who—surprising no one more than herself—has stepped out from her hiding spot to glare at him.

He barrels toward her, but Khawla steps in front, shoving Shay behind her.

"What are you doing, loitering in front of my property? Looking for more berries?" the bloodsucker seethes. Over Khawla's shoulder, his lightless eyes find Shay's, probing them as though seeking an entry point to penetrate her mind. She makes hers hard like glass, reflecting whatever venom he throws. "Don't think because I've already eaten, I don't have room for dessert."

Khawla raises her chin. "We're merely walking home, Sidi. You're the one taking up the whole road with your revolting buffet on wheels."

The bloodsucker snarls, baring his fangs. Then, unexpectedly, he dials back his aggressive posture and tilts his head. "Since when is the little dove allowed out of her cage, anyway? Where have you two been this early? Or, should I say, late?"

"Why are you so obsessed with my friend?" Khawla pokes her finger into the bloodsucker's chest, but all Shay hears is the word *friend*. It rings like a silver chime. She grins as Khawla continues. "Do you think I don't see you out here night after night, your beady little eyes always watching our cottage? No one trims their shrubs that much."

"If you don't remove that finger, I'll gladly do it for you," Tarik says with chilling calm.

Khawla's eyes widen. She looks at her finger with dismay, as if just noticing where she poked it. She snatches it back.

"Good choice." The bloodsucker smiles slowly. "Because while I would gladly eat you out of principle, I'm sure you don't taste anywhere near as sweet as my little dove does."

Shay balls her fists to resist touching her neck, despising the visibility of her scars. The way they wave like a white flag on her skin. But, she corrects herself, she should think of them as war stripes. A badge to honor the women who don't have the privilege of surviving to wear them.

"Just like I said." Khawla shepherds Shay toward the bone-eaters' cottage at a speedy walk, calling back, "Obsessed. It would be disturbing if it weren't so pathetic."

The bloodsucker doesn't pursue them, but he laughs. "If you're not careful, you may find that sharp tongue of yours pickled in a jar. Lawn care isn't my only hobby, you know."

The second Khawla lays hand to the cottage doorknob, the door swings inward. Deebi fills its frame. His face, at first terribly grim, brightens upon seeing them.

"Khwati, you've returned," he says, his voice swelling with relief. "We thought something terrible had happened to you. I only barely stopped Kabeer from throttling Tarik; he was convinced the bloodsucker had snatched you for a midnight snack."

"I'm fine, khoya," Shay says, even if it's only true in the physical sense. Witnessing the horror of the blood-wagon on the heels of learning about Ghita's death has left her harrowed. "I didn't mean to cause you alarm."

"Come, let my brothers see that you are well." Deebi smiles, his mouth tight at the corners in what could either be a sign of anxiousness or his normal ghoulish face. He steps aside for them to enter.

With the eyes of all the bone-eaters on her, Shay lowers her head and stares at the muddy toes of her torn slippers. She hears Deebi close the door, the soft pulse of Khawla's breath beside her.

"What in the seven graves are you wearing?" Aidi asks, punctuating the question with emphatic taps of his skull cane against the floor. His voice is so very calm. "Lalla?"

She lifts her eyes. Not every bone-eater looks as happy to see her as Deebi did. "It's a costume for Jou Boulka." She fidgets with the goat hooves.

"Jou Boulka takes place in the human medina." Aidi sighs, a sound that for all its softness carries a heavy dose of condemnation. "We have told you, repeatedly if I'm not mistaken, not to leave the cottage."

"I—" Shay starts, but Khawla jumps in.

"Sidi, she was safe with me. We disguised ourselves in costumes, and it was a one-time occasion. Just to cheer her up. Which, if I recall correctly, is my primary purpose in being here."

"And did it?" The bone-eater studies Shay carefully. "Did it cheer her up?"

"Well . . . I'm afraid she ended up receiving some rather shocking news regarding the death of her prior benefactor," Khawla explains. "It has turned out to be a jarring night."

"Khawla, you were hired so that Shay would be happier *here*." Aidi leans forward, rubbing the skull ornament methodically. "Not to drag her out *there* where she risks exposure to all manner of danger and heartache."

"It's the companion's influence," Beni whines. "Shay would never have done such a thing on her own."

"As I see it," Bono contends, sucking his teeth, "if she thinks it's safe to go traipsing around the human medina, maybe she no longer needs our refuge."

Bristling, Shay remembers the posters and cocks an eyebrow. "Or maybe I never needed it in the first place."

"Beni is right." Khawla jumps in quickly. "I convinced the Lalla. I can be very persuasive, and although she was reluctant, my insistence wore her down. I think perhaps we should all get some rest and talk about this when we are clear-minded. As I said, the lalla has been dealt quite a blow."

Aidi's eyes widen. Given their tendency to bulge from their sockets at rest, the effect is disconcerting. "Do you take responsibility for this?"

Shay tries to object, but Khawla cuts her off with a curt head shake. "As I said, it was my suggestion, but respectfully, I think there is some discussion to be had about such things as independence and healthy boundaries."

"I'll take that as a yes." The bone-eater tugs his scraggly beard, only for it to fluff out like an angry cat the moment he releases it. "In light of your actions, I hereby order you to leave our home and to stay away from our charge. Effective immediately."

"I . . ." Khawla's jaw drops. "Again, I mean no disrespect, Sidi, but what makes you think you understand the needs of a human girl better than I do? Better than she understands herself? Do you think she would have preferred to continue being left in the dark about the loss of someone for whom she cared deeply?"

"Can you get your things, or do you require Deebi's assistance?" Aidi asks with forced politeness.

"No, Sidi." Khawla gives Shay a regretful glance. "I can manage on my own, thank you," she says, and turns toward the stairs.

Shay may feel tired to her bones. She may appreciate that the bone-eaters defended her when she was under threat and gave her some small purpose when she had no other reason to go on. And, though she's still not sure whether they had ulterior motives, she does have them to thank for her meeting Khawla.

But what matters at this moment is that Khawla called Shay her friend. And friends don't let friends take the fall alone.

Shay clears her throat. Something on her face makes Deebi frown in worry and Bono lean forward in interest. She looks straight at Aidi and juts her chin. "If Khawla leaves, I'm leaving, too."

Aidi blinks. Shay sees something in his eyes she might mistake for loneliness were he not one of seven siblings. He blinks again, and whatever it was is gone. He waves the cane dismissively, breaking eye contact. "Then I suppose this is goodbye."

The other bone-eaters stare in stunned silence as Shay and Khawla join hands and, together, make their way upstairs. Once Shay sees her bed, all she wants is to crawl beneath her covers and forget everything that happened tonight. But she knows from experience that no amount of sleep will reverse the hands of time, and reality will not tire of waiting for her to arise. Khawla hauls an empty rucksack from the closet and has just unbuckled it when a timid knock sounds at the door.

Shay pulls it open and takes in Deebi's pleading eyes, the pout that carves hollow gouges and long puddles onto his ruinous face. A face meant to scare little children. But the thought that she herself was once afraid of him seems silly now.

She squares her shoulders. "You can't change my mind."

"We need you." Deebi lets out a long breath, releasing a stench like rotten onions.

Shay won't be deterred. "I'm sure you and your brothers survived well enough before I arrived."

"Well, yes," Deebi admits. "But it wasn't the same. You bring a warmth to our dwelling, a brightness we didn't know before and have since become accustomed to."

"What I hear you saying is, if I leave, you'll have to cook your own meals and wash your own clothes."

Deebi coughs into his mangled hand. "Is that what you think matters to me?"

"Maybe not to you, specifically. But what about the rest of them?" She gestures toward the banister at the head of the stairs.

"We all care for you, even if not all of us know how to show it." He holds up his leathery palms, imploring. "Even Aidi."

"Just because someone's intentions are good, doesn't make their actions right," Shay says, her shoulders dipping. Even if she has her doubts about Aidi's intentions, she can't pretend any of this is Deebi's fault. She came here hoping to rest and process all this, but even if that had worked out, she could not have stayed for long. Not while the circumstances of Ghita's death remain a mystery. "Besides, something horrible happened to the midwife, and I can't find out what if I am here."

"What if we could help with that?" Deebi looks down as he asks the question, suddenly captivated by his blackened nails.

Shay glances at Khawla, who has paused shoving her clothes along with more notebooks than Shay was aware she owned into the sack—notebooks filled with sketches, Shay realizes. Putting aside her curiosity, she turns back to Deebi. "How?"

Deebi mumbles incoherently a few times, as though unsure how to word whatever he's trying to say. Twisting the tip of one horn, he sighs. "Are you aware of what my brothers and I do on our nightly haunts?"

Shay makes a stern face. "You frighten children and eat corpses. Neither of which are acceptable activities, I'll have you know."

Deebi straightens his spine. "I'm sure our lifestyle seems unconventional to you, but you must try to understand that humans need someone to fear, as surely as they need love. Better for them to vilify us, than turn on one another."

Shay thinks of how people needlessly fear hizouras, the songs children would sing in the schoolyard that gave her nightmares of being snatched off the streets for years. The way Hind's family refused to accept her Hazmaggi husband, and even Ghita, perhaps unknowingly, perpetuated misconceptions about the tribe. The way certain women take issue sharing spaces like the bathhouse with mutahawils. "We do that anyway."

"Trust me, it would be worse without us," Deebi says. "And, in order to be good at haunting, we need to understand as much as we can about how the human mind works. That's where our graveyard activities come in."

Shay is quite sure the bone-eaters have a very limited understanding of the human thought process, but then, she cannot claim to understand it any better. "What do you mean?"

"When we eat a corpse, we absorb that person's memories. We learn more about what people fear and use that knowledge to improve our scare tactics. But, believe me, lallati, humans are bigger monsters than bone-eaters could ever be. The things I see in those memories, things humans have done to one another, those are what keep me awake. The murders aren't even the worst of it."

Shay blinks. Then she blinks again, and a few times more as her mind skips from one thought to another across a river of logic. "Are you saying that when you eat a corpse, you gain knowledge of how that person died? And if someone killed them, you would know who it was?"

"Yes, that's right." Deebi wipes his forehead with his sleeve.

Shay glances again at Khawla. Her face, as usual, betrays no clue as to her opinion. Shay contemplates this most terrible of ideas, and in the end, her need to know the truth prevails. She smiles as sweetly as the thing she's about to ask is bitter and says, "And you would do that, for me?"

Deebi nods, then pauses. "Just to make sure there is no misunderstanding, do you wish for us to consume the midwife's corpse?"

Shay screws her eyes, shutting out the graphic description, although that is precisely what she means. "I'm asking you. It would mean a lot to me, to know the truth."

"I know you're asking me, but I'll have to convince my brothers. Grave foraging is not a solitary act, you understand."

"Oh." Shay swallows, the recent memory of Aidi's face when she said she was leaving turning the saliva in her mouth to dust. "Do you think they will agree?"

"I think they'll listen to me." Deebi peers back over his shoulder, his mottled tongue darting over his gray lips. It is awfully quiet down below, and

Shay suddenly imagines the brothers huddled at the bottom of the stairs, eavesdropping. "But if I'm able to convince them, will you stay with us? Forever?"

"Deebi," Shay says, taken aback, but also strangely touched. One thing's sure: Khawla was right about setting better boundaries. "It's sweet that my presence means so much to you. But I can't stay here forever. Surely you understand that?"

"Why not?" Deebi sulks. "As a bone-eater, I'm intimately aware of what horrors occur in the human world. If there's one certainty of human life, it's suffering. And you, lallati, you are too tender and soft to make it in that world. You do not deserve to suffer so."

Tender and soft. Isn't that what Shay has always tried to be? The opposite of a thorn. And yet, hearing herself described that way is just plain annoying.

"But we won't let anything bad happen to you if you're with us," Deebi continues. "You would be safe here."

"A bird in a cage is also safe," Shay gently insists. "But it can never put its wings to use and fly. Surely, some of the human memories you've seen have been good. Even beautiful?"

Deebi grumbles a begrudging concession.

"I cannot promise to stay forever." Shay reaches over and takes Deebi's gnarled hand in hers. "I won't lie to you. But I can tell you that when I leave, I'll always come back."

Deebi seems to ponder this, as though perhaps he didn't realize there could be a third option besides her staying forever or leaving forever. And Shay understands the tendency to think that way. Perhaps the minds of monsters and humans are not so different, after all.

Khawla comes up beside Shay, the sack strapped to her back. She clears her throat.

Deebi blinks, then focuses on Khawla. "I—um—I'll give you two a moment, then."

Shay turns to Khawla, gripped by the same sense of finality she just tried to assuage in Deebi. The fear that leaving means forever. Tears flash to her eyes, but if she expects the bone-eaters to be able to say goodbye, she supposes she must do the same. "Where will you go?"

"Don't worry. My parents will be more than glad to see me." Khawla squeezes Shay against her in a sideward hug to accommodate her heavy baggage. She lowers her voice to a whisper. "I'll come back, when the brothers are out."

"But Aidi—"

"Doesn't need to know." Her friend smiles gently. "Whatever truth you will learn from them, you will not be left to bear it alone for long."

"Thank you," Shay says, and in all her life, she has never felt so supported.

20

From the peaks of Umm Chanala, to the underwater caves of Chefrika,
How pleasant is this land we know.
From the winding alleys of our blue diamond to the shining palace of our capital,
How beautiful is this land we know.
Oh, sweeping sands of desert places, oh, glittering waves of the horizon,
There is no more beautiful place to be.
Mekchaouen, we love and pray for thee.

Rulers rise and fall, some are just and some are evil,
But the land remembers, the earth embodies the Creator's will.
When signs come from near and far,
When change is written in the stars,
The mountains will sing, the forest will rejoice,
People of faith will declare with one voice,
There is no more beautiful place to be!
Mekchaouen, we love and pray for thee!

—official anthem of the realm of Mekchaouen

Shay isn't sure what Deebi says to his brothers, but it he gets them to agree to her request. That night, she gives Aidi the address of Ghita's apartment. They'll go there first and familiarize themselves with her scent, to help with locating her grave in case it's unmarked.

"We will tell you what we have learned when we return," the elder brother says, as the bone-eaters don their coats in preparation for their journey.

Shay frowns. She supposes it makes sense for them to perform the act at the graveyard, or wherever it is they normally conduct that aspect of their affairs. But something about it feels wrong. "Do you think you could bring her back instead?"

Deebi looks up from his bootlaces in surprise. "You want us to consume the body here?"

"I just . . ." Shay thinks she may never be able to accept that Ghita is gone if she doesn't see her one last time. "Want a chance to say goodbye."

The brothers grunt their agreement, and Shay is left alone in the cottage. It is not the first time, but after meeting Khawla and being reintroduced to Shadi, alone feels so much lonelier than it did before. She wanders to the kitchen, surprised to discover the dishes cleaned, the floor swept. In fact, there is not a sock that needs mending or a button in need of fixing to be found in the entire cottage. Shay washes up and prays, and with nothing else to busy herself, she climbs upstairs and lies on her sleeping pallet.

For all her exhaustion, her eyes stay wide open, her mind stubbornly awake as the night drags on. Moonlight weeps through the thatched ceiling, suspending diamonds of dust in its cold fingers. In this deep quiet, her power slips from that mental drawer she keeps it in. Shay counts more than one hundred different species of flies, spiders, beetles, ants, and other bugs she doesn't know that currently inhabit the sinks, furniture, and walls of the cottage. Rest does not seem to be on the agenda.

Giving up, Shay stands and gravitates to the window. She peers out into a darkness so rich, it shimmers. Shay used to fear what lived in such darkness. But that was before she came to understand that a greater darkness lives in the hearts of men.

As if summoned by her thoughts, a pale face pops up in the window.

Contradicting her brave thoughts, Shay startles back from the sight of Tarik. When did he grow bold enough to approach the brothers' dwelling? And how did he climb to the second story? Shay's muscles go rigid, like she's an animal entering a paralyzed state to fake death.

Staring Shay straight in the eyes, Tarik taps a gloved finger against the window.

"I come in peace, little dove." He raises his voice to be heard through the glass.

"Go away." Shay wishes she sounded stronger. It hits her how alone she is. As defenseless as a fruit dangling from a tree branch, ripe for the picking. "The brothers won't be happy when they hear you were poking around here."

"Then I guess you don't want the gift I've brought? I do believe these are of great value to you." Moonlight catches on the blades of his cheekbones like they're silver knives. He reaches into the inner pocket of his vest and withdraws something small and flat and made of . . . leather? A pair of leather gloves.

Shay's leather gloves, the ones Ghita gave her for her birthday.

Shay is half convinced they're an illusion. If the bloodsucker can transform from a bird to a man in a state of full dress, perhaps he can also make any other pair of gloves appear to be the ones the midwife gifted her. Or maybe she fell asleep after all.

Shay leans closer, her breath misting the glass between them. "How did you know they were mine?"

"Open the window, little dove."

Even on the half chance the gloves are what they seem to be, Shay can't resist the lure. Because Tarik is right. They are of value to her. So much more so now that the midwife is gone. If she can only touch them, she's sure she'll be able to tell if they're real.

She unlatches the window and heaves it up. A cool breeze raises goosebumps on her arms as she extends her hand. "Let me see them."

Tarik passes the gloves to Shay. He rests his arms on the windowsill, looking smug. "I thought you'd like them."

Shay feels their concreteness in her hands, their familiar softness and stretch, their strength a tribute to the woman who gifted them. She brings them to her face and inhales deeply, as if she could glean the essence of Ghita's soul from their oaky scent and bottle it inside herself.

Tarik narrows the soulless pits of his eyes. "Aren't you going to say *thank you*? I went well out of my way to get them back, you know."

Shay lowers the gloves, understanding falling over her like a shroud. The bloodsucker shares more than a neighborhood with the bone-eaters. "You didn't just taste my blood. You drank my memories. Didn't you?"

"Only some." The bloodsucker smiles, baring his fangs. "But since that day, my craving for the taste of you is my soul's constant companion."

"What?" Shay steps back in horror, remembering Khawla accusing Tarik of being obsessed with her.

"Never mind." Tarik curls his lip over his fangs in a feeble attempt to conceal them. "As I said, this is a peace offering. Please, do try them on."

Shay imagines how Ghita would deride her lack of self-preservation. But the thought only increases her longing to hear that reproving voice she never thought she'd miss so dearly, only makes his suggestion that much harder to resist. She slips her hands into the gloves, their snugness a balm she hadn't know her heart needed.

As she flexes her fingers and admires the gloves, the moon's pale glow strikes some dark substance that flecks their sleek surface. A substance that, on closer inspection, looks an awful lot like blood. *Whose blood?*

Shay's stomach pitches at the thought of the last person known to have had the gloves in her possession. She can't peel them off her hands fast enough. She thrusts them at Tarik, who takes hold of them if only to keep them from tumbling to the ground below. "What did you do to her?"

"The barkeep?" Tarik asks innocently. "Don't be jealous, little dove. I promise she meant nothing."

Shay paces back and forth in front of the window, pinching the bridge of her nose. "What about the truce?"

"What do you know about the truce?" He chuckles.

She stops, facing him. "I know bloodsuckers aren't allowed to prey on humans within the medina's boundaries."

"Take that up with the Vampiiruh Presidium," Tarik says, his fingers constricting to a fist around the gloves. "But I would suggest ensuring you know the facts before making baseless accusations. How confident are you that this is even human blood, not that of an animal?"

"I think you should go now." Shay attempts to close the windowpane, but Tarik reaches out and effortlessly blocks it with the heel of his hand.

"Are you rejecting my gift?" He frowns, looking much closer to delighted than sad. "And here I thought there was still a chance for us to reconcile our differences."

"Differences?" Shay balks. "Such as your desire to kill me, you mean?"

"You take one little nibble of someone, and they hold it against you for eternity." Tarik clutches his free hand to his chest, feigning heartbreak. "If that were all I wanted, I could have already jumped through this window and eaten you."

Shay wraps her arms around herself, calculating how fast she could run to the kitchen and where to locate the biggest knife. Maybe if she shoves the dresser up against the window, it will buy her time. "And why haven't you?"

"Fair question." Tarik pins Shay with his dark gaze. "Would you believe me if I told you stress affects the quality of blood? It's so much tastier when given freely. And blood like yours deserves to be savored."

"That is never going to happen." Shay shudders, the pain of Tarik's bite all too readily remembered. "I am asking you, again, to please remove yourself from my window. How are you even there? Are you floating?" She raises on her toes to peer down, confirming that Tarik is indeed levitating.

He moves back, still hanging in midair, but now a foot away from the window. "Remember this moment, little dove—the moment you were offered peace and turned it down. But make no mistake, I am equally fond of enmity."

With that ominous proclamation, his slender torso sinks like a flagging kite below the window and disappears into the night. Shay quickly shuts the pane and latches it. She stands there for what feels like infinity, breathing heavily and not quite believing he's gone. Sure enough, untold beakers later, something slaps against the window with a force that shakes the glass in its frame.

Once her soul returns to her body, Shay braves a look down to the ground, knowing the gloves will be there before she sees them. She scans the yard for Tarik, not finding him until she looks across to his house. His silhouette looms in the upstairs window that faces hers, backlit by the halo of a candle.

It has the makings of a trap, but while Shay didn't want to accept the gloves from Tarik, it feels wrong to leave them discarded like refuse. Besides that, the blood on them is evidence of Tarik's crime.

She could wait for the brothers. *Should* wait for the brothers. But what if it rains or an animal finds them? What if, what if, what if?

Stop overthinking, she tells herself—and quails. Ghita's voice, she's used to hearing, but when did Hind take up a lectern in her head? Nevertheless, Shay darts downstairs and hurls herself into the night. She doesn't pause to check whether Tarik is still at the window. Doing so would only slow her down.

She retrieves the gloves as fast as she can, her heart a maelstrom in her ears. Only once she's safely back inside does Shay catch the tang of vinegar and see that the blood has been scrubbed away. Dropping the gloves in her lap, she collapses on the seddari and cries.

She cries for the beautiful woman who accepted the gloves, hoping they might resolve the pain in her hands, a mistake she paid for with her life. For all the women, reduced to what men can take from them, who have paid a similar price for daring to want more.

She's still there when the brothers return.

21

Whoever said women's magic has died has never attended a birth. For what is a womb but a magic portal? What is breastmilk but a life-giving elixir? And what is a midwife but an earth-bound angel? A shepherdess of souls?

—*from* The Womb is a Garden: Essays on Midwifery

Ghita's body has never looked so small. She's been laid on the huge dining room table, and her white funeral sheets wriggle with the movement of crawling beetles. At Shay's request, the brothers provided burning oud, assorted flowers, and beeswax candles, the pleasant scents of which almost mask the oddly cheese-like smell of decomposition.

Shay offers a special prayer for the dead. She supplicates for the soul of the woman who was, for all intents and purposes, her foster mother, asking she be forgiven for any wrongdoing, pleading she be spared any punishment in the life that follows, and that she's granted nothing but eternal happiness and peace.

Once finished, Shay stands beside the body. From a logical standpoint, she understands the midwife's spirit no longer resides in this world. But it isn't logic that compels her to speak.

"Ghita Bensultana." Shay's barely begun when the tears overwhelm her. "I should have listened to you. I should have been there. I should have thanked you while I had the chance. I should have told you . . . should have said . . . I love you. Even if I know you'd never have said it back. I'm sorry, khalti, for what I've done, and for what I'm about to do.

"I know it's wrong, allowing your remains to be desecrated, but I need to know what happened. Who did this. And if Sami is well. Nothing makes sense anymore. A world without you in it, God forgive me, is like a world with no gravity. Whoever killed you, they have killed me. But when I find them, I will become a living haunting."

Her hand trembles as she lifts the edge of the sheet to glimpse Ghita's face one last time, her keen eyes permanently closed, nimble body forever stilled. She presses a kiss against the cool purpling skin of her forehead. Not drying her cheeks, Shay staggers to the salon, her world painted black. Deebi helps her to sit on the seddari as the other brothers stand around her.

"Are you sure about this, Lalla?" Aidi asks.

"Yes, Sidi." Shay stares ahead into the shadows of the empty hearth. The weather has warmed to the point where it seldom needs lighting. A single lantern stands alone on the center table, shedding a thin globe of light to hold back the darkness.

She hears the shuffle of feet as the brothers migrate from the salon to the dining room. She listens to every crunch of bone that follows. Each slurp and swallow of flesh. The squelch and splatter of limbs ripped asunder.

She pretends the noises belong to something else.

Just her stray cats devouring their daily scraps. Only the market butcher at his stall, trimming fat and hacking meat into thick cubes for stew.

When the illusions crumble, Shay bolts to the washroom. Bile ravages her throat, splashing up the sides of the shiny basin. But this time, an empty stomach brings no relief. Her eye sockets ache, nearly swollen closed from crying. She washes her face and locks her mind against the rising memory of the mysterious red stain on Ghita's wall. She tells herself she's made the right choice.

She must face what happened, even if that means accepting it was her fault.

At last, the awful noises cease. Shay returns to the salon, as ready as she'll ever be to hear what the brothers will reveal. She wishes Khawla were holding her hand, imagines she feels the subtle squeeze of it, as though their friendship could circumvent such trivialities as time and space.

She sits opposite the brothers. The cadaverous creases of their faces are drawn more deeply than usual, their gaunt lips pulled in grim lines.

"Ready?" Aidi takes off his pom-pom hat and sets it on the low table between them.

Shay grips the cushions beneath her, the tips of her nails lacerating the fabric. A thought starts to form, something about how she will need to sew them later—but she stops herself, seized by the desire to rip holes in the world if that's what it takes to get justice for Ghita. "What happened to her?"

"It started with a knock at the door," Dasri begins. "In the middle of the night. An urgent pounding that could have indicated the arrival of a pregnant woman or the family member of one, but the midwife's senses weren't detecting any need for her services. It was another sense, a profound foreboding, that led her to wrap Sami in blankets to protect him from the cold and hide him in the cellar nook beneath the floorboards.

"When she opened the door," Kabeer continues, "she wasn't entirely surprised by the four-armed Moulays who pushed their way inside the dwelling. They instructed her to sit and stood over her as Mukhtar Jawad entered the dwelling last. Jawad questioned the midwife about the baby's whereabouts, which she stoutly denied any knowledge of."

"The Mukhtar stayed with the midwife while the Moulays searched the dwelling." Aidi takes over the story. "They discovered the bassinet. But even then, the midwife claimed she kept it around for emergency cases—the women who sometimes appeared at her door already deep in labor and stayed to rest following their births."

"All this time, the midwife marveled that Sami didn't make a peep," Hammu says. "She even worried he could have suffocated in his blanket. But she refused to admit to his presence. And then the mukhtar gave her an ultimatum. If she continued to withhold information, she'd be killed, but if she told him where the baby was, she'd be spared.

"*Why do you care about this particular baby?*" Beni says, his voice taking on a high, feminine quality as though the midwife is speaking through him. "*There are tons of orphans living in the squalor of the Bib who'd much appreciate your compassion.*"

"*His mother was a touched one*," Deebi answers gruffly, and Shay understands he has taken on the role of Jawad. "*It's rare for addicts to birth sons, you know? The child might be a hizoura.*"

"*Not unless he identifies differently when he is able to. Men don't have Shawafa, silly*," Beni says as Ghita, who seems to have then reconsidered whether adding *silly* to the statement was a step too far. "*Respectfully.*"

"*Just because something hasn't happened before, doesn't mean it can't happen*," Deebi says with an arrogant tone. "*The entire point of science is to expand the realm of what is possible.*"

"*You want to do experiments on a baby?*" Beni asks bluntly, this time without apology.

Shay sucks in a breath. Khawla was right. Al-Mukhtar really are jealous of women's magic, and for Mukhtar Jawad at least, his desire to harness it has led him to forsake all morality.

"*What I do with the child is none of your concern*," Deebi says dismissively. "*We are benevolent leaders, with abundant resources to care for the helpless orphaned and bereft children of our realm.*"

"*Ah. And seeing as you are so benevolent*," Beni says as Ghita, "*I suppose you plan on just letting me go once you have the child? Or maybe I should even get a reward.*"

"*I am certainly willing to offer you leniency for hiding the child.*" Deebi stands and begins to pace the room, clasping his hands behind his back. "*A chance to repay your debt to society. And yes, once that debt is repaid, you will be granted freedom. Just tell me where the child is.*"

"*Forgive me, Sidi*," Beni says, his sarcastic tone a rival to the one Ghita uses—used to use—when someone rubbed her wrong. "*I'm an old woman and feeble of mind. I need things explained to me in simple terms. What manner of repayment are you suggesting?"*

Deebi turns and faces Beni. *"A magical debt. We will provide the means for you to mine your Shawafa and wield it for the good of our beloved realm."*

Beni gasps, and so does Shay. Luring girls into using Snow and taking credit for the results of their magic is horrible enough, but forcing it upon women as some twisted form of remediation? It took a lot to surprise Ghita, but by the look on Beni's face, Jawad succeeded. *"Did you just offer to give me Snow? And suggest I use magic? I must have misheard you, since we both know those things are categorically illegal."*

Deebi smiles, and he looks more evil impersonating a human than he ever has as his bone-eating self. He shrugs. *"There are times, habibti, when the end justifies the means. It's a lot for your, as you called it, feeble mind to comprehend, I know. Which is why you should trust your leaders, whom God Himself has appointed."*

"Let's cut through the political jargon and see if I'm getting this right." Beni rubs his chin, the gesture chilling Shay with its familiarity. *"You want to arrest me and force me into drug-indentured servitude. Which leads me to believe the rumors are true. Instead of arresting the criminals who make Snow, you help them distribute it, and then coerce touched ones to use their Shawafa as it suits your purposes."*

"Close," Deebi says dryly. *"Except we're the ones who make Snow. Consider this: How do you think we ensure your crops are always plentiful and your medinas remain free of illness? We manipulate magic for the greater good, and by controlling it, we prevent its misuse.*

"Now, do think carefully about the generosity of my offer. Perhaps I can sway you with the knowledge that your midwifery skills are needed at the kasbah. A member of our entourage is with child. I believe you may have a history with her. Does the name Hind Hibachi ring a bell? Though you will find you are unable to run off with the child. This time."

Shay's mind churns, her thoughts bleeding together as she tries to make sense of the information it's receiving. She picks carefully through each word like a scavenger sifting for treasure among scraps. Hind is alive. And she's somehow *pregnant*. And she's at the kasbah.

If Ghita felt any surprise at these revelations, she hid it well. Beni only sneers. *"I'm supposed to overlook the fact that Snow kills women. Is that what you expect?"*

"'Kill' is such a harsh word." Deebi steps closer to Beni. *"You still have some good cycles left in you, so why not use them for the benefit of your realm? Besides, I'm told the high of Snow is pleasing. I'm positive the experience is better than swinging from the gallows, at any rate."*

Beni slowly shakes his head. *"You'll have to hang me."*

"Give me the child!" Deebi stomps his foot.

Shay's heart belts into her throat. The ripping sound as her fingernails claw over the seddari reminds her of where she is. It's all that keeps her from screaming.

Silently, Deebi sits back down.

Puzzled, Shay thinks the story may be over, but then Bono speaks. "The sound of the mukhtar stomping on the floorboards finally caused Sami to cry out. One of the Moulay fetched him, and another Moulay was ordered to take Ghita back to the kasbah."

Dasri speaks again. "Ghita knew she'd rather die than become a drugged slave. She fought the Moulays with vigor and even managed to wrangle one's musket away. She pointed it at Jawad, but hesitated. She'd spent her cycles bringing souls into the world and didn't welcome the notion of taking one out, even one so vile."

"The Moulays had no such qualms." Kabeer relays the story's conclusion in a rueful voice. "One of them shot the midwife in the heart. Bloody, God-awful invention, those muskets. Her last thoughts as she lay dying were that she hoped she'd done enough to protect the girl she considered her second daughter from the mother who refused to stay away, and that she looked forward to her soul's coming reunion with her first daughter, the one who was taken from her so young."

Shay cries out, straining every muscle in her throat. Deebi cuts Kabeer off with a harsh glare.

"Too much?" Kabeer asks innocently.

"Bono, go get the Lalla a mug of clean water," Deebi instructs. "She looks near to fainting."

The room blurs in and out of Shay's vision, everything warped like a mirage in the heat haze of tending season. She takes paltry sips of the water Bono brings as her thoughts unroll, stretching beyond what happened to Ghita to encompass the greater horror of what her leaders are capable of. Like a homing pigeon with a singular compulsion, they find their way to Hind.

A magical debt. What if the touched one wasn't to blame for her addiction? What if Al-Mukhtar manipulated her? Made her into a slave to serve them with her magic? They would use her until she died, an ending that could come about all too quickly, and then what would become of the child?

Shay's sibling.

✧ ✧ ✧

"Lalla." Aidi's voice draws her from the mire of her thoughts. "I didn't want to bring this up so soon, but something seems to be missing from my wardrobe. If it isn't with you, well, then . . ."

"Khawla is not a thief." Shay sets her glass of water down on the table. She's been dreading this confrontation, but if Aidi wanted the ring so badly, he could have asked her for it. Instead, he let her believe she could be *hanged*. "The ring was mine to decide what to do with. You told me you'd keep it safe, implying I would get it back. Here's my question: How did you know it was magic?"

"I already explained to you about the posters—"

"No, Sidi, I have reason to believe it was only the midwife who was looking for me." She folds her hands in her lap. The shame on his face reads like a handwritten confession. "Did you tell me I was a wanted criminal because you wanted the ring for yourself?"

"What? No. I only wanted to protect you, Lalla. Any embellishments or omissions were made only in service to that goal." Aidi strokes his clawed hand over the bald skull of his cane, its crown beaming brightly even in the dim glow of morning. "I don't care what the ring is as much as I care that someone tried using it to harm you."

When Shay nibbles her lip, unconvinced, he adds, "What need do monsters have of magic?"

He has a point.

Relief washes over her. Shay still wishes people wouldn't tell her lies so often, but she's finding herself more liable to forgive liars depending upon the exact reason why they lied. Yes, the bone-eaters manipulated her into staying with them. The saddest part is Shay is more moved than anything else. To think that they would go to such lengths, that her presence is *wanted*.

And Shay cannot find it in herself to sustain any anger while she feels such gratitude to the brothers for helping her. They have come through when she needed them to on more than one occasion now. They may not be perfect, but what family is?

Family. Shay never in her wildest dreams imagined she'd consider a bunch of bone-eaters to fall into that category. But then, she never thought she'd have one at all. But there's still the matter of her mother. Of her future *sibling* . . . The very idea strains the limits of her mind.

Shay understands from Ghita's memories that Mukhtar Jawad was not looking for her, but Sami. However, this revelation does little to assuage her guilt. She can't help thinking she could have done something to help if she hadn't left the way she did. She could have taken Sami with her to Kiddah. But she did, and she didn't, and thinking otherwise won't change a thing.

It's too late to save Ghita. But she can still save her mother. The fact that Hind now carries another life, another piece of their family, within her only solidifies her decision.

"Will you be honest with me going forward?" Shay asks Aidi, her gaze unflinching.

"You have my word. You are strong and capable." Aidi sighs deeply, as if admitting this is a grueling task. "I see that now."

"Good. Then no one will argue with the fact that I must go to the kasbah and help my mother get away from Al-Mukhtar."

"But she betrayed you," Bono protests.

"And she's an addict!" Kabeer bellows.

"All the more reason I must intervene," Shay says. "She cannot keep using Snow if she is with child. It's a wonder she didn't die when she had me. And now she is older and has been using longer. It's difficult to imagine luck will be so kind a second time. And yes, she betrayed me, but she is still my mother."

Shay looks down at her hands, wringing them. *Her mother. Her problem.* She doesn't need the bone-eaters' permission to go. She doesn't even want them to help her. She's not sure what she wants from them. Maybe just for them to understand. Is that even possible?

"Where are you going to take her?" Bono asks.

Her head jolts up, and everything inside her spirals toward her stomach, deflating. She . . . hadn't thought that far ahead. Her body sinks into the soft belly of the seddari's cushions. *No surprise there.*

"She's going to bring her here," Aidi says with a huff. "Of course."

Shay gapes at the elder in shock, but when she glances around, she finds agreement with the suggestion written on the faces of the other brothers.

"We should go with her," Dasri says. "It is too dangerous to send her alone."

"We cannot go to the kasbah," Aidi says firmly. "We do not directly involve ourselves in human affairs, and that would be crossing a line. We will, however, send for one of the rebels to help her navigate the forest."

"What about Khawla?" Shay says quickly, and wants to bite her tongue. They may be friends now, but Khawla has her own obligations to the Sisterhood. Shay can't expect her to neglect those duties to come to her aid. She wouldn't want to make the journey with a stranger, though, and considering that time is a luxury Hind can't afford, she needs someone who can make good time. No one can get her through the forest faster than Khawla. There will still be the matter of finding her way back to contend with, but Hind will be with her by then. The two of them can figure something out. Hind is the one who left her there in the first place.

"Fine," Aidi begrudges after a lengthy pause, the pom-poms on his hat jiggling as he shakes his head like he himself cannot believe what he is saying. "I will send for *Khawla*."

"No need," Shay says meekly. "She's coming here after you leave for the night."

Aidi grunts, but Shay swears she hears an undertone of affection in the sound.

"Don't worry, lallati," Hammu says softly, his spectral eyes full of faith in her. "This will be a good place for your mother to purge."

Shay nods, sniffling. The most she hoped was that the bone-eaters would listen to her and respect her choice. Support her a little, maybe. She didn't expect them to open their doors to someone else just because of what that person means to her. And Hammu is right. Ard Al-Ghul may not be a destination any human would visit on a holiday or dream of building their future home in. There may be bone-eaters, bloodsuckers, and—if Shay's memories of the tales she grew up on serve her correctly—creatures called night hags, though she has yet to run into one of those. But there's no Snow here. Which makes it the perfect place to bring Hind.

Shay just needs to sneak into the kasbah unnoticed and convince Hind to leave with her.

That should be easy enough, right?

22

Be sure to pay back all your debts before your final hour,
Or bone-eaters will raid your grave and grind your skeleton to flour!
Do not wear clothing stained in red or paint its shades upon your walls,
For bloodsuckers cannot resist the color, and one will surely come to call!
Always pray before you sleep, or a third fate will leave you in screams.
The night hags will hunch upon your chest, crushing your breath,
And peck away your dreams!

—a song often performed by traveling musicians and in storytelling circles

As night nears, a critical voice awakens in Shay's mind to taunt her, telling her that Khawla said they were friends only to make her feel good. That the rebel girl isn't really coming back. That she, like everyone else, will seize the first opportunity to be rid of her. But the brothers leave for the night, and true to her word, Khawla returns soon after.

Over tea, Shay recounts the dreadful scene the brothers reenacted, taking frequent deep breaths to keep herself afloat. It hurts to say the words, as if they're extracting little pieces of her as she speaks them, minute chips of bone and clumps of viscera. And yet, their passage loosens a burden in Shay's chest, allowing her to breathe, the way a mother must feel after expelling the child who has shifted all her organs around to accommodate their growth.

She expects Khawla to hug her again or offer words of consolation, but instead of filling with sympathy or compassion, Khawla's face tightens in resolve.

"So my guess is we'll be heading to the kasbah," she says decisively, proceeding to drain her tea glass and carry the tray to the kitchen as though the matter is settled.

Shay scrambles after her. "What do you mean?"

Khawla turns to her impatiently, clearly vexed. "Don't you want to rescue your mother?"

Shay nods slowly and gulps. She hasn't even asked Khawla to guide her through the forest yet, but it sounds like she's offering a lot more than that. And, while Shay can't deny she has no actual plan to speak of and could certainly use the assistance of someone more experienced in covert operations and clandestine activities, she understands that her endeavor is, in all likelihood, a fool's mission.

"I don't know if . . ." Shay flubs, then restarts. "You don't have to come with me, Khawla. This is my problem to solve."

"Don't be silly. I'm not letting you go alone." Khawla narrows her eyes, driving a slash between her eyebrows. "We can go to my parents' house tonight to gather the supplies we'll need and leave first thing in the morning."

Shay is still wary of getting involved with the Sisterhood, but she's admittedly curious about where Khawla lives, what her life beyond her arrangement with the bone-eaters is like, and whether Shay could be part of that life. The fact that Khawla is here at all, that she's insisting on helping Shay, makes her want—so badly—to believe she can. "And your parents will be agreeable with that?"

"Oh yes," Khawla says with bright enthusiasm. "They can't wait to meet you."

They can't wait to meet you implies that Khawla's family knows about her, that Khawla has *told them* about her. A warmth flutters in Shay's chest. It's a small, fragile thing that doesn't erase her doubts and apprehension, but it dulls the sharp edges of them. It doesn't fill the ache of what she's lost either, but it softens the raw sting of that, too.

To travel the streets of Ard Al-Ghul in safety, the girls slip some of the bone-eaters' unwashed clothing over their own, rolling up the long sleeves and using belts to keep the pants from falling. Shay gags on the rancid smell, but she supposes that's the point.

"Will this really be enough to keep the monsters away from us?" she asks Khawla.

"It will prevent them from being *drawn to* us," Khawla clarifies. "But don't worry. It's just an added precaution; I know what route to take and which to avoid to steer clear of trouble."

Khawla leads her into a place that turns out to be like a shadow version of her medina, deeper than she's ever been—or wanted to be. They weave past buildings constructed of cobbled bones, whose lawns boast gardens filled with spike-rimmed flowers, eyeballs blinking from their engorged centers. Plants with hinged lobes snap open and shut, revealing barbed teeth and forked tongues. Bare thujas twist like dancers, thick webs billowing from their branches like tattered grave sheets. Behind each glowing window and from every darkened alley, hosts of hungry eyes peer out. Giant rats the size of dogs scurry in and out of gutters. Shay hears what sounds for all the world like the cries of a baby from deep within the throat of a long drainage pipe. Khawla hurries her along, whispering assuredly that it isn't what she thinks.

On a street lined with businesses, strange, discordant music seeps through heavily-curtained window fronts. After making their way around an ornate marble fountain in the center square, flowing red with what Shay can only presume is blood, they make quick turns down a few alleys painted a color that glows muddy green in the pale of night.

The door Khawla finally stops in front of is the only blue one in a row of black. A yaz is carved into the wood, the same symbol from Khawla's marked trees. A circular hatch in the door snaps open, just big enough to accommodate the human eye that appears.

The knob jiggles. The door is flung open by an older woman with supple skin and crafty eyes. She tucks a lock of dark hair beneath her loose scarf and grins at them. "Labas, bnaati?"

Khawla has the kind of family Shay has always wished she had.

Every corner of their home exudes warmth. It's filled with plush cushions, silky drapes, and cozy wool rugs, all wrought in an earthy palette ranging from terra-cotta rust to golden saffron. Every aspect of their manner is affectionate and kind. The meal, a large clay tagine heaped with savory fish and vegetables, is placed in the middle of the table for everyone to share. Shay tastes their love for one another in every delicious bite.

After they pray together, Khawla shows Shay her quarters while her mother makes up an extra sleeping pallet. The contents of the room attest to a creative spark Shay has only briefly glimpsed in Khawla before now. Wall-mounted shelves and every inch of her dresser tops are filled with paints in every color and stacked papers of varying textures and lengths. Vases hold bouquets of pencils and brushes, all arranged so that their storage seems to be a work of art itself.

Khawla's sketches, no longer hidden in notebooks, are proudly displayed on the walls in testimony to her talent. But the paintings—*the paintings* are truly stunning. Hilly landscapes rendered in warm coppers and olive fields bursting with green.

Khawla exhibits unexpected shyness as she points out the newest addition. "I made this one last night."

Shay smiles, admiring the portrait of the cave ceiling from the forest shortcut, glittering with kindle worms. Their incandescence is captured so vividly, the paint seems to glow. It feels like her friend is sharing small pieces of her heart, tiny glimpses of her inner world. And when Khawla smiles back and stands a little taller, Shay feels that warm flutter grow stronger, like grasping tendrils spreading and taking root.

"Are you sure it's acceptable for me to spend the night?" Shay asks Khawla later, as they settle onto their respective pallets.

"Of course." Khawla drowsily finishes braiding her hair before letting her head drop to the pillow. "Thank you so much for indulging them. I know my mother can be a bit much."

"What do you mean?" Shay asks. "Your mother seems perfect." She hates how jealous she sounds. How jealous she *feels*.

"Yeah, that's the thing." Khawla smiles wistfully. "Things don't have to be perfect all the time, you know? But she tries really hard to make them that way. I sometimes wish she'd relax a little. I suppose she's overcompensating."

Shay was taught not to be nosy, but something in Khawla's voice makes her think she *wants* Shay to ask for elaboration. "Overcompensating for what?"

"I never told you this," Khawla says, and her voice sounds . . . not exactly softer, though smaller isn't the right word either. More vulnerable, Shay thinks. "But my mother was addicted to Snow for a short time. I was too young to remember much about it. I just know it was a difficult period, and my father almost left her. Then they joined the Sisterhood, and the sense of purpose that gave them was just the push she needed to get purged."

Shay likes that Khawla is opening up to her. That seems to be the sort of thing friends do. But at the same time, she's at a loss over how to respond. Is she supposed to say anything? Or does Khawla only want her to listen?

"The threat of relapse never completely goes away," Khawla continues. "But I'm grateful for my mother every day."

"I'm glad she got better," Shay finally says, her thoughts turning again to Hind. She hates how easily her grief over losing Ghita has been supplanted by worry for Hind, but after everything, she can't bear the thought of her ending up on a blood-wagon.

"Yours will too," Khawla says, her eyes shining, soft with sleepiness.

"And if women's magic is one day restored, what will happen to the bloodsuckers?" Shay asks, seeking reassurance that the blood-wagons will cease to exist—that things could actually be different, be better.

Khawla blinks, alert again. "The bloodsuckers are already on the verge of revolt. They're increasingly discontent with a food source they consider subpar. Many of them supply the rebellion with information in the hopes we'll eventually overthrow Al-Mukhtar, saving them the effort."

Shay gulps. She sits up, pushing down the blankets that suddenly feel too hot and suffocating. "But what about the truce? Would its dissolution give the bloodsuckers free rein to cross into our realm and prey on humans?"

"These are questions with no easy answers, Shay." Khawla rubs at a worried pinch on her forehead that refuses to be smoothed. "But at least if we have magic, we will not be defenseless. I prefer to seek an equitable solution between our kinds—to fight for it, if it comes to that—over the type of corruption that deems the blood of women a tolerable price for peace."

Shay agrees, in theory, but it sounds like a process that will take more time to work out than what Hind has left. In her mind she sees the touched ones Tarik fed upon, bound and shackled. Only, in this rendition, it's her mother's face superimposed over theirs, gaunt and fearful. Her haunted eyes reflecting her own death.

"Tell me more about them," she says, desperate to replace the image with something—anything—more pleasant. "The Lallat."

"Certainly," Khawla says, a smile curling through her drowsy voice. "On the cycle a girl turned three and ten, she would visit them, and they would perform a ceremony to reveal the girl's Shawafa. Those who chose to do so were then trained to develop their skills, since natural magic is not as potent as that induced by Snow."

Shay lies back down and draws her blankets over her. Her breaths soon fall into cadence with Khawla's, lulling her toward sleep. Maybe it's the simple warmth of this home, or the way Khawla's parents welcomed Shay with open arms, but something in her lets go. She allows herself, for just a moment, to release the terrible weight she's been carrying. She'll pick it up again tomorrow, but for now, she rests.

She dreams of four women.

She recognizes them, not from the waking world, not by name, but in spirit.

One is dressed in red and dances through a curtain of flames. Another, dressed in silver, floats on clouds as though they were travel carts. Another wears blue and rides waves like she's trained the sea to carry her. And the last wears green. Her face is smudged with dirt, her dark hair speckled with tiny white flowers. Her hands are crisscrossed with cuts the way Shay's used to be.

She's beautiful. They all are. They whisper to Shay of the way the world was before men stole women's magic. And they whisper, *It can be that way again.*

✧ ✧ ✧

Shay's first thought when she awakens is that Ghita is gone. Her chest feels both heavy and hollow. She hangs, like a dust mote trapped in moonlight, in a strange space where nothing is real and she feels everything.

By the pale twilight of dawn, Shay offers her prayers and supplications, reminded of Shadi's words about how worship is a conversation. Afterward, she's compelled to take the hjabat out of her pocket and cradle it in her palm. After much debate over the safest place to leave it, she decided to bring it with her. As much as she feared the talisman before, Khawla and Shadi's reactions to it have changed her feelings somehow—if only slightly. She still has no desire to put it on, but something about holding the ring seems to ground her as she listens in the early quiet, seeking answers in solitude.

She has yet to find any when the hearty punch of mint reaches her, carried on the air from other regions of the house where tea is being prepared. Instead of her thirst, Shay thinks of all the times she drank tea with Ghita. The fact that they will never be together again.

She cannot allow the same sadness that held her in its belly for the duration of resting season to swallow her again. Based on Ghita's final thoughts, she had a complicated history with Hind. But, surely, she would want Shay to help her—or at least the child she carries.

She hears muffled talking, a sound that strikes her as odd at this hour. There are at least three distinct voices: Khawla's mother, her father, and . . . a visitor? At the approach of footsteps, she quickly folds her prayer rug and pockets the hjabat. Softly, as though to avoid disturbing Khawla, who is still sleeping, the door creeps open and the silhouette of Khawla's mother appears.

"Shay," she says gently, stepping inside. "There is someone here who would be very pleased to meet you."

Shay nods, although the gesture is hidden by the dark, her throat suddenly incapable of producing sound. She's not sure at first why a dull dread drips over her, why her hand goes straight to her pocket, clutching the hjabat through the fabric. Then she knows with a sudden strike of certainly who the visitor is, and her dread sharpens to a cold knife's edge.

The Morchidat is every bit as formidable as Shay would expect the leader of the Sisterhood to be. Her face bears Hazmaggi tattoos. They're smaller in number than Hind's, and bolder, drawn in thicker, darker strokes. She wears a plain but elegant ruby-red robe, her hair wrapped in a high scarf of matching color. Her features are petite but strong, soft eyes offsetting a stern dusky-brown face.

She sits on one side of an L-shaped seddari, flanked by two young women. One of them smiles at Shay reassuringly, while the other either doesn't register her presence or willfully ignores her. Khawla's mother quickly joins her husband on the other side of the seddari.

"Sayeda." Shay bows her head, putting a hand to her chest.

"No need for that." The Morchidat waits for Shay to raise her eyes and then gestures toward the empty spot at the couch's corner. "Please, sit. I've heard so much about you."

"Tea?" Khawla's mother asks once Shay is seated, and Shay nods, grateful for something to soothe her dry throat.

"You must try one of the cookies we brought," the Morchidat says. "My daughter Yara baked them herself."

Yara, the smiling girl, hands Shay a kaab el ghazal—a thin pastry stuffed with almond and cinnamon and shaped in the curving crescent of a gazelle's horn—on a napkin. The girls, no more than a few cycles her junior, appear as if they could be twins, sharing the same creamy skin, dark eyes, and silky hair.

They must be Shadi's sisters. Although they look more robust and healthier than Shay would have expected, given what their brother told her about their need for moon pepper. She files this observation away to ask Shadi about later.

"Aren't you going to introduce yourself, Marjan?" Yara prompts her sister.

The other girl finally turns her attention to Shay, then grouses, "Are you going to eat that or just hold it like a piece of kaka?"

With horror, Shay realizes she's been staring at the scars on the Morchidat's arms, mapping their jagged path around her neck and collarbone to where they disappear beneath her robe. Her cheeks zing with heat.

"Don't be embarrassed," the Morchidat insists, briefly scowling toward Marjan before taking a cookie for herself. She winks at Shay. "You should have seen my opponent."

A squeal sounds from the salon entryway, and Khawla stumbles in with bleary eyes and unbrushed hair. "Khalti! Yar-yar! Marj-oon!" The surprise in her voice indicates she didn't know the Morchidat was coming, which gives Shay a sense of relief she can't quite explain.

Khawla bounces over and kisses first the Morchidat's cheeks and then her daughters' before turning to Shay. "Was she telling you about the ghoul clans?"

"I . . ." Shay stammers, and nibbles the cookie, which is remarkably good, out of nerves. "I think so?"

"It was a condition for members of the Sisterhood to be granted safe haven in Ard Al-Ghul," Khawla explains, squeezing in between her parents. "The Morchidat had to defeat the top fighter from each of the three ghoul clans."

Shay realizes she's absently added a few too many sugar cubes to her tea, but she stirs her spoon around the glass anyway. She gapes at the Morchidat. "Is Khawla saying you've fought a bone-eater? And a bloodsucker?"

The Morchidat nods, the gesture somehow equally humble and proud. "And a rather vicious night hag."

Shay shudders, then sips her tea, which is sweet enough to make her left eye twitch. "I should very much like to hear that story."

"Perhaps another time." The Morchidat sips her own tea. "Today, I'm here to personally thank you, Shuika Fulan. I hear you have obtained a most valuable object for us."

"Sayeda," Shay says, her throat going dry again. What exactly did Shadi tell his mother? "I believe there may be some misunderstanding."

The Morchidat arches an elegant eyebrow. "About?"

Shay flounders, but Khawla intervenes: "Khalti, Shay has merely agreed to show you the hjabat."

"Oh." Any warmth—and there had been little to begin with—leaves the Morchidat's face. She methodically sets her tea and cookies down on the low table. "So, you don't wish to join the Sisterhood?"

"No, I . . ." Shay finds herself unable to go on as she watches the Morchidat pull a rather large and sharp-looking knife from the belt at her waist and lay it on the table as well.

"Are you in opposition to our cause?"

"It's not that at all," Khawla says lightly, sipping tea and chomping cookies as if the tension in the room isn't growing palpable. "I told her you were the best person to ask about what the ring actually does. That's all."

"I think she can speak for herself." The Morchidat turns to Shay while pulling *another*, somehow *larger* and *sharper* knife from a thigh strap hidden beneath her robe and setting it next to the first.

"I'm not opposed to anything." Shay tries to keep her voice level while glancing at Khawla's parents. They appear unalarmed, and she wonders if they would intervene should the Morchidat decide to give Shay a personal demonstration of just what happened to her opponent. "I have some personal things I need to figure out."

Marjan snorts. "Lalla, don't we all?"

Yara elbows her sister in the side.

While Shay struggles to vocalize an answer, the Morchidat withdraws five more knives and knife-adjacent implements from various hiding places on her person and lines them up on the table. She smiles brightly. "Well, why didn't you just say so?"

"Shay!" Khawla laughs, spraying cookie crumbs down the front of her sleeping gown. "The look on your face!"

The Morchidat's eyes narrow slightly, then bolt wide. "Oh, did you think . . . Why, I wouldn't dare harm the girl my son is enamored with."

Shay works her jaw, these words nearly as frightening as the medley of weapons on display.

"Did Shadi say that?" Khawla boldly asks.

"He didn't have to." The Morchidat waves her hand and looks at Shay. "A mother knows these things. Just make sure you resolve these issues, whatever they are, before your relationship with Shadi goes any further. Now." The Morchidat slaps her hands on top of her thighs. "Let's see it, then."

Shay pulls the hjabat from her pocket and hesitates, but with a reassuring nod from Khawla, she deposits it in the Morchidat's palm.

The Morchidat inspects the ring, tilting her head first one way and then the other, her manner almost clinical. Her daughters lean in from either side for a better look.

"Which one is it, Mmi?" Yara asks, awe tinting her voice.

"This is the ring of Iman, blessings upon her name."

Unexpectedly, the proclamation causes a shiver to rush over Shay's arms, leaving goosebumps in its wake. "And can it help the Sisterhood restore women's magic?"

"It is only one hjabat," the Morchidat explains, showing no sign of handing the ring back to Shay. "There are four in existence, one belonging to each of our Lallat. We cannot restore magic without the other three. But having one would be a start—one that I'm happy to repay by gifting you any knife from my collection."

Shay stares at the row of knives, all cumbersome-looking and more suited to the infliction of gross harm than the precise harvesting of a delicate fiddlehead without damaging the plant.

Sensing her hesitation, the Morchidat holds one up, a menacing instrument with a handle in the middle and a wicked blade sprouting from each end. She closes her other hand over the hjabat, leaving one finger free, and strokes the blade in a manner that's almost tender. "Do you whittle? If so, may I suggest this one?"

Shay shakes her head wordlessly The knife in question looks entirely impractical for whittling, a point she thinks it wiser not to argue.

"Hmm, perhaps, something else, then?" She sets the hjabat on the table and asks Yara to hand her a paper bag from the floor beside the seddari. From the bag, she withdraws a pair of leather gauntlets and a leather vest and lays these out on the remaining table space. "Try them on."

For a moment, Shay can only stare. The garments are beautifully detailed, stitched with a level of workmanship not found in any market stall. No, she'd bet her last luneer that these were custom-made. The vest boasts a scalloped trim, is edged with rivet accents, and has buckle straps at the sides. The gloves have small steel plates sewn onto them and are bound by thick laces.

When Khawla clears her throat, Shay realizes everyone is looking at her and waiting for her to do something. Shakily, she stands and lifts the garments in her hands. They're even more beautiful up close. The leather holds a rich tapestry of browns within its sheen, and is as luxurious to the touch as a rare emollient.

"Let me help you." Khawla jumps up and buckles the vest over Shay's sleeping clothes while she laces the gauntlets.

Once fitted in the garments, Shay glances around to find everyone still staring at her, but now with expressions of approval. Even Marjan smiles appreciatively.

"Do you have a mirror, Widad?" the Morchidat asks Khawla's mother, who immediately races off in search of one.

"This is strong leather," Khawla gushes as she strokes her hand down Shay's back. "Strong enough to repel musket fire."

If the Morchidat finds this statement odd, she doesn't show any outward reaction. Though Marjan furrows her brow, as though pondering in what situation a girl like Shay would need to think about such protection.

Khawla is right, though. Shay feels it in the weight of the garment as she shifts her body side to side. And unlike metal armor, the vest allows for ample mobility. It covers her most vital organs, but there are still plenty of places she could be shot. Something she really should have considered before now.

Which only underlines the fact that she has no real plan. Did she think she would go knock on the prayer house door and question the Moulays who live there? Or write a letter of inquiry to the mukhtars to be delivered to the kasbah?

Khalti Widad comes back holding a long mirror. Shay keeps her eyes closed as she turns to behold herself. When she opens them, she expects to confront the image of a girl playing dress-up, but even in her sleeping gown, the garments afford her the fierceness of a warrior. They are sleek and practical, and they give edges to her softness, put a gleam into her eye. In them, she looks like someone who would know what to do with one of those weapons the Morchidat laid out before her like bridal gifts for an assassin. Like someone who could save another person.

Someone who could save her mother.

"What do you think?" the Morchidat asks, and in the reflection behind her, Shay sees the small smile teasing the woman's lips.

Shay nods. "They're perfect."

"Let's call it a fair trade, shall we?" the Morchidat asks, gathering her knives and replacing them in their various sheaths. "And you can let me know, after your affairs are settled, how you feel about joining the Sisterhood."

Shay notices that the hjabat has already been tucked away along with the weapons. She meets eyes with the Morchidat as she rises and grabs her cloak. "Agreed."

"*The way before will be once more!*" the Morchidat boisterously declares.

To which the others in the room chorus back, "*The way before will be once more!*"

The next twenty beakers pass in a cycle of goodbyes and well-wishes, at the end of which the Morchidat pauses and appraises Shay. She leaves her with these parting words: "I don't presume to know who it is you're trying to save, but remember that she is no less and no more than all the other women of our realm. The other mothers and sisters, the bakers and healers. Al-Mukhtar is a threat to all of us."

23

[this essay has been deemed a threat to the security of our realm and is no longer permitted to appear in print in full or in part]

—from "Prayer Houses and Other Places Where We Used to Exchange Ideas," an essay by an unnamed scholar later hanged for engaging in activities that support rebel entities

Khawla packs a handful of jinn sticks, some preserved meat and twice-baked biscuits, and a few other supplies, and later that morning, they plunge once more into the cool of the forest. As bright as the sun was outside, it makes a faint impression through the crooked umbrella shade of cedars. Their path is steeped with shadows, but a curious calm comes over Shay. The forest, for all its wither and decay, teems with life.

Shay can sense it now, like a multitude of flickering embers desperate to stay alight, organisms buried and trapped beneath suffocating moss and creatures rotting from within while somehow clinging to the bright kernel of what they were. Twisted, broken, and fused together wrong. Decomposing and regenerating and sucking the marrow of depleted earth. But alive.

Shay can't help but admire the persistence.

Khawla puts out a quick hand to stop her from stepping on a rogue tater sponge. "I know that was all a lot of excitement this morning. But how are you holding up?"

Shay considers her answer as they make their way around the dangerous pod. She appreciates that Khawla seems to understand that grief doesn't happen all at once. It has layers, and some of these are more hellish than others. On some level, she knows that this mission is partly a means of distracting herself from her woe, but that is not necessarily a bad thing.

"I just want to warn you," she says, deciding she doesn't really need to answer the question. It's enough that Khawla asked. "My mother is not anything like yours."

Khawla laughs. "Well, if the bone-eaters lied about the posters, at least that means she didn't falsely accuse you of stealing the ring." She cracks a jinn stick as they duck into one of the cave passages, swallowed up in a sea of darkness. "Though that by no means absolves her of abandoning you."

"I just can't imagine why she did it. I keep thinking about it over and over." Saying it reawakens all of Shay's loss and confusion. No matter what angle she turns it, it's like a shirt sewn without a neck: It makes no sense. "I know Snow makes people behave in strange ways, but even by the faultiest logic, I can only conclude she hates me."

"You deserved—and still deserve—better." A group of bats flutters over their heads, and Khawla waits for the chattering creatures to pass before she goes on. "You can ask her yourself, once we get her safely away from Al-Mukhtar. Just know, whatever her answer, it won't change that fact."

They emerge from the black womb of the cave into a liminal light, alternating in bands of bleak sage and cool jade, and walk in silence for a time.

"I think she took a liking to you," Khawla says after a while. "The Morchidat."

Shay frowns, unsure. She looks down at her new gauntlets, their leather shining in the soft gleam of the forest, almost as beautiful as the gloves gifted to her first by Ghita and then again by Tarik. The ones she doesn't think she'll ever bring herself to wear again.

"Khawla, didn't you say that bloodsuckers aren't allowed to prey on humans inside the boundaries of the human world?"

Khawla nods, curiosity flickering over her face.

Shay's fingers flex, anger flowing hot like lava to her extremities as her thoughts turn to the barkeep. The feeling is almost too much to be held inside one body. "And what would be the consequence if a bloodsucker broke that agreement?"

"It would be up to the Vampiiruh Presidium to decide." Khawla shrugs, then gives Shay a shrewd look. "Why?"

Shay sighs and tells Khawla about her encounter with Tarik, her suspicions regarding how he obtained the gloves.

Khawla's eyes grow wider and wider with every word. "That miserable leech! And you have the gloves? With the barkeep's blood on them?"

"Yes." Shay flinches, realizing she may have erred in judgement by giving Tarik the opportunity to erase the evidence. "Well, no . . . he cleaned them once he realized his mistake."

"Of course." Khawla's mouth tugs into a grim version of a grin. "It would have been hard to prove without a body, anyway. Lacking that, the best we could hope for is that they'd temporarily withhold Tarik's rations."

Rations. Shay cringes at the wording. Shay wishes she could live in a world where she didn't need to shrink in fear of untold dangers or to expand to bear the anger of every woman. Where she could grow as wildflowers do, in her own time and taking as much space as she needs. But that is not reality, and it will never be reality unless enough people are willing to fight to make it so.

Shay's heart is once again pulled in different directions. Is she wasting time on this mission when she could be joining the larger battle, as the Morchidat suggested? She bites down on her bottom lip. After everything, the longing for her mother's love still runs through her like a river, a craving as powerful as any addiction. Once more, she chooses Hind.

✧ ✧ ✧

Shoppers bustle along Sultan's Alley, haggling over choice cuts of meat and fine fabrics. It's a strange wonder to Shay, that the streets around her look and sound the same, that the world continues on like nothing's changed, when everything inside her has been uprooted and rearranged.

But something *smells* different.

Over heady wafts of cumin and whiffs of fresh orange juice, the smelly tang of sardines, hangs the scent of smoke. Shay sniffs, the heavy fumes in the air too thick to be attributed to a vendor's grill.

"Lalla." A young man with a basket of live chickens slung across his back appears next to Shay. "If I may interest you in purchasing a hen today, I am offering half off my regular price. No one wants to buy them due to the poor air quality, but I swear by God's greatness, their lungs are strong."

"Sorry, khoya, I don't need a hen today," Shay says politely, keeping her opinion about the hens' ruffled appearance to herself.

As the boy hurries off with his clucking cargo, Khawla comes to a sudden halt. Shay follows her stare to an empty lot where the ground bears wide scorch marks. It takes Shay a few beakers to discern the flash of sequins glittering among the scattered piles of ash and recognize the spot where Dounia's tent once stood.

"Excuse me, Sidi," Khawla calls out to a nearby garrab, a water porter with bells and hanging brass cups strapped over his colorful garments. "Do you know what happened here?"

"Many fires were set the night of the festival." The man frowns, adjusting the goat-leather waterskin at his hip. "Jou Boulka used to be about games for small children and neighbors coming together and sharing food, but the youth these days have gotten out of control. My sister and her children are staying with me now because their shelter in the Bib was destroyed. Thanks to God, they weren't home, but her husband was not so lucky."

"The Bib?" Shay's heart races until she reminds herself Hind is at the kasbah, and her imprisonment has likely spared her from the fire. Her next thought is of Badar, of Bushra, and of Muezza, and suddenly it's hard to breathe. "There was a fire in the Bib?"

The man nods, the bright tassels of his wide hat swaying. "The worst one of them all."

Thanking the man, Shay takes off in the direction of the Bib, while Khawla jogs beside her. She tugs Shay's arm gently and asks, "Where are we going?"

"I need to see it," Shay explains, unable to find the words to articulate the depth of this need. If she is not willing to stand and fight for her medina, the least she can do is bear witness to its suffering. Wordless understanding passes over Khawla's eyes, and she nods back.

They wind up steep slopes and down narrow stairwells, under covered breezeways and past decorative arched doors. Shay sprints the final stretch, greeted then by the stench of smoke, more caustic than before.

She stares, barely comprehending the destruction. This was a place where people lived whatever simple life they could grab hold of. There were animals here, livestock and pets. Newlyweds and families and babies. Elderly and infirm citizens.

Now the entire shantytown lies in cinders. No one and nothing is left, but the reek of charred wood in Shay's nose and the ghostly echo of screams gone quiet. Black shapes that may or may not be parts of bodies smolder from the wreckage. Whatever they are, they aren't moving.

But wait—someone with more substance than a ghost *is* out there. Shay hears them first, then sees them: men digging desperately through the rubble, some with tools and others with no more than their bare hands, searching for the missing, if only to bury them.

She turns to Khawla, her hands curling into impotent fists at her sides. "This wasn't out-of-control youth, was it?"

"This much damage could be inflicted only by a touched one with the Shawafa of Jinnamin." Khawla shakes her head, holding up the end of her light shawl to cover her nose and mouth. "No, make that multiple touched ones."

What she doesn't say, but they both nevertheless understand, is that even if touched ones were involved, they were only tools, living matches in the hands of those truly responsible.

"Shadi will probably be able to tell us more?" Khawla says, a question.

✧ ✧ ✧

Pink boughs of bougainvillea festoon the outer walls, stands of laden date palms rising behind them. Farther back, a building washed in ivory gleams, seeming to soar straight into the clouds. Shay recognizes the home of the sayeda from the birth she didn't know at the time would be the last she attended as Ghita's apprentice. That is, the last before Sami's, to which they arrived post-delivery.

Khawla makes a bleating sound that is a remarkable approximation of a goat. She repeats this every few beakers until Shadi appears at the gate.

The first thing he does is to hug Shay. It's only the second time their bodies have been in close contact, but it feels strangely natural, as if they are two parts of a matching set. As though he is perfect in the same places she is flawed, and she is whole where he is broken. Shay doesn't know about love at first sight, but she wonders if a body can recognize the sameness in another skin. Some of the despair Shay is holding on to seeps out of her, like Shadi is somehow absorbing it. Shay never knew physical touch could be so healing.

She can't fathom why Ghita, whose life's work was so intertwined with healing, never touched her. But maybe she was protecting herself, after the loss of her daughter, afraid of letting Shay get too close in case she lost her, too.

"Shay?" Shadi's worried voice breaches her thoughts. "Are you crying?"

"I'm sorry." Shay pulls away and wipes her cheeks, which are indeed damp with tears. "I'm fine."

"Hey." Khawla brings the edge of her shawl to Shay's face and gently dries it. "Never be sorry for feeling things strongly. That's what keeps us human despite the attempts of those in power to grind us down until we become numb and docile."

She's right about the *docile* part. How else can they get away with wiping out a whole neighborhood? Shay turns to Shadi. "What do you know about the fires?"

Shadi opens his mouth to speak, but his eyes wince closed instead. His lips curl inward as he struggles to collect the emotions on display across his face.

He exhales through his nose and, after recovering, beckons Shay and Khawla to follow him down the street to a door tucked between two shops. The door opens to a small room where passersby are free to stop and offer prayers throughout the day.

The room is divided by a curtain into two sides, for male and female worshippers. Since the female side is currently unoccupied, Shadi dons a prayer garment provided for women, and they all sit together at the back, where the quivers of sunlight from the small window carved into the ceiling can't reach.

"Nice garments." Shadi nods toward Shay's vest and gauntlets, looking at her admiringly in the hard-edged shadows. She hopes they're dark enough to hide her blushing.

"Did we come here to discuss serious matters or so you two could flirt?" Khawla asks teasingly.

"Oh, right. Uh, the fires . . . Skirmishes between Al-Mukhtar and Naturalists are intensifying," Shadi whispers, keeping a watchful eye on the entrance. "The raids are not as effective of a deterrent as they once were."

Khawla nods with understanding, but Shay is still confused.

"Why Dounia's? Why the Bib?"

"The Bib was something of a resistance stronghold," Shadi explains. "I believe the Naturalists felt safe hiding there, because they thought the touched ones would be something of a shield for them. Most of the addicts are still provided with Snow so long as they act as recruiters, racing to create the next crop of touched ones before the drugs kill them. As for Dounia's, I don't know, but the owners were not the pickiest about the clientele that frequented their establishment."

"It's more than that," Khawla says, and she looks angry enough to spit, but she swallows instead. "With the prayer house gone, the brewery was one of the last places where people could meet and engage in political debate, where perspectives could be shared and new ideas put forth."

Shay remembers passing Dounia's on the night of the festival, how packed it was with people. Not every customer was a rebel. Most were simply victims of circumstance. Shadi and Khawla have explained *why* Al-Mukhtar did it, but she still doesn't understand *how*. How could they treat innocent humans as collateral damage, not caring how many died or where the survivors would go? They were probably already making plans for what high-rent building or new training complex for Moulays they could build on top of the bones of the dead.

She smashes the heels of her hands into her eyes. She's tired of crying. She's tired of being tired.

A light rain patters on the glass above them, the subsequent dimming of the sun leaving them ensconced in shadows. She remembers the last time she saw her mother, how she found her that day in a darkened alley of the Bib. If Al-Mukhtar make and distribute Snow, then who was the man Shay saw threatening Hind?

"What do you know about the touched ones who live at the kasbah?"

"Technically nothing." Shadi frowns. He braids the tassels of the rug in front of him in a way that seems more efficient than a boy with short hair should be able to. Unless, of course, said boy grew up with two sisters. "The three mukhtar who currently reside in Nezjar—Jawad, Farouk, and Kamel—have invited prominent local businessmen and those of influence to the kasbah on several occasions to prove that the entourage of resident touched ones the Naturalists accuse them of keeping doesn't exist. These citizens were allowed to tour the entirety of the property and have reported in public statements that they found no evidence suggesting anyone other than the legally employed servants and guards reside there."

Shay holds back the scream that claws up her throat. "That's not true."

"I don't believe it is either," Shadi agrees.

"No," Shay clarifies. Either the mukhtars bribed their visitors into giving false testimony, or they're keeping the touched ones well-hidden and God knows under what conditions because whatever Shay thinks her leaders are capable of, they continue to prove they can do worse. "I know it isn't true."

"Oh?" Shadi stops styling the edges of the rug and lifts his eyebrows.

Shay fills him in about Ghita's last moments, how Mukhtar Jawad's words confirmed the existence of the entourage. She goes on to tell him about her future sibling and her decision to rescue Hind from the kasbah.

Shadi takes in the goriest of these details with minimal queasiness apparent on his face. He nods firmly. "Count me in."

Shay blinks a few times, confused, then flattered, then teetering, like she could fall right into that look of devotion she thinks she sees in his eyes. But the Morchidat's admonition about their "relationship" comes back to her like a cold splash of water. It's bad enough that she's already involving Khawla in her affairs; she can't entangle Shadi in them, too. "I'm sure you have more important things to do, like, you know, rebellion things."

"But this mission aligns with the Sisterhood's objectives," Khawla posits. "After all, if Hind was able to acquire one of the hjabats, it stands to reason that she may know where the other three are. If we can narrow them down to even a general location, I can use my affinity to home in on them."

"What she said." Shadi crosses his arms.

"More importantly, we're your friends now. Like it or not." Khawla grabs her hand. She stares at Shay, her brown eyes rich with light, the kind that can either make someone feel warm and cozy inside or set their soul on fire.

They emerge to find the cobblestoned streets glistening wetly, a coolness in the air that smells fresh. Everything looks softer in a way that makes Shay realize she really has missed her medina of blue-painted walls and steep, winding alleys. But does she love it enough to join the fight for its future? A fight that extends to the whole of Mekchaouen? She's not entirely convinced such a fight can be won, but she's starting to think that isn't a good enough reason not to try.

The kasbah lies at the heart of Nezjar, a short walk from the medina's square, and is fortified by high adobe walls topped with barbed crenellations. About a block out, Khawla hands Shadi a pair of field glasses from her hip bag, and he climbs to the highest branch of a twilight oak. The device is impressive. Such specialized equipment isn't easy to come by.

After shimmying back to the ground, he gives them the rundown of his observations. "Two Moulays pass the front gate every thirty beakers. The complex consists of four residential buildings, likely one for each mukhtar and the fourth used for staff, arranged around a central courtyard. There was also a slightly smaller building, not far from the back gate. Not sure what that one is for."

"The touched ones could be anywhere." Khawla nibbles her thumbnail, the stairwell they're hunkered behind swathing her face in shadow. "If we can get inside the central courtyard, I can use my affinity to create a mental map of the complex. Once I do that, I'll be able to sense irregularities, like the heat of human bodies, or the shimmer of Shawafa, in the vicinity and pinpoint their location. If there really is a whole entourage of touched ones in there, their combined Shawafa should be easy to pick up on."

"Really?" Shay asks, immediately thinking Khawla must have sensed where the monsters were in Ard Al-Ghul and thus avoided them. Khawla has downplayed her capabilities, much like she once kept her drawings tucked away. And Shay doesn't think it's because she's self-conscious or anything like that; it's more like she has little interest in showing off. "You're amazing, know that?"

"Thanks," Khawla says modestly. "But it requires us getting past the locked gate and armed guards first."

"Luckily, I have a plan," Shadi says. The afternoon lapsed while they waited in the prayer room for the rain to clear, snacking on the meat and biscuits Khawla had packed. Now his brown eyes shimmer with the pomegranate shades of dusk. He gingerly removes a bundle wrapped in clover bean leaves from a pouch tied around his waist. "Any guesses what this is?"

"Cookies?" Khawla raises a jaunty eyebrow. "Are we to bribe the soldiers?"

Shadi unfolds the leaves, revealing a tater sponge. Shay sucks in a breath. The trick worked when she tried it on a touched one who'd just given birth, but would it be effective on two healthy young men armed with deadly weapons? The same weapons that took Ghita's life?

Khawla's lips upturn, her smile growing wider as Shadi reveals his plan, a probable sign that her stomach, unlike Shay's, is not currently gnawing itself over the plethora of ways this could go wrong. Shay breathes like it's her new occupation, pushing air in and out to expel her nerves. She must either accept the risks, to herself, to the friends she has not had nearly enough time to enjoy the pleasure of knowing, or she can walk away and leave Hind's fate in the hands of Mukhtar Jawad.

She's not doing that. Not after that bastard turned his soldiers on Ghita and let them kill her.

The trio creeps up to the main gate, its solid wood doors carved with ornate and intricate designs, so beautiful that people often walk out of their way just to look upon them. Here, they wait quietly for the Moulays making their rounds to march by. After the metronome of their heavy boots first approaches and then passes the gate and continues on around the perimeter, Shadi employs a couple of special pins and a turning tool to pick the lock. The efficiency of his work, the speed with which the mechanism yields a satisfying *click*, speaks either to an issue of faulty hardware or of Shadi's hidden expertise in the art of burglary.

Thirty beakers later, the guards return. When the bobbing shaft of light from their lantern peeks over the edge of the high walls, Khawla hefts the tater sponge to the other side, where it hits the ground with, hopefully, enough force to burst on impact. The guards march forward, unaware they could be headed into an unseen curtain of poisonous fumes.

Two quick thuds. The lantern light swerves and stills, shining up from a crooked angle. Shadi slowly pushes the door open. Covering their mouths and noses with the leaves, they slip inside.

Khawla and Shay help Shadi drag the limp bodies behind a band of thick hedges to conceal them. Shay averts her eyes while he undresses one of the unconscious Moulays and switches the guard's clothing with his own. With a snarl of fabric, Khawla rips one shoulder of her tunic. She bends and digs her fingers into the earth, looking half-feral in the rising moonlight, and rubs soil in a cool, musty smear across Shay's cheek.

"Ready?" she asks.

Shay nods. After all, it's too late to do much else. She must hide what doubts fester inside her well enough, because Khawla nods back in satisfaction.

Khawla takes up the guards' lantern while Shadi holds a confiscated musket at their backs. He pretends to be marching the girls, who pretend to be his prisoners in an attempt to make it look like Khawla isn't the one they're following. She guides them toward the courtyard at the center of the complex.

Shay's heart pounds. With each pair of Moulays they pass, her fear surges. No one gives them a second look until they come to a garden with an extravagant fountain, one that could rightly be called a pond, burbling at its core. What appear to be lava rocks glow from the bottom and create a blue shimmer that reflects off the surrounding walls and tiles.

A Moulay, who seems to be taking a break from his duties, sits at the edge of the fountain with his back to them. He looks incredibly young, a boy who should be kicking balls with friends or catching salamanders in the creek. Khawla leads them past, quickening their pace to avoid his notice. As they're about to cut right around a screen of assorted shrubs, the boy calls out to them.

Shay isn't sure what he says because he says it in Waheeli, the language of the Hazmaggi tribe. Shadi must understand the words, though, because they bring him to a sudden stop. He doesn't turn around at first, not until the boy calls out again, this time a name: "Yassine?"

Shadi turns. The musket he's holding clatters to the tiles below. "Walid?"

The boy and Shadi stare at each other, both their faces sliding from shock to a much deeper emotion. Then, to Shay's confusion, the boy leaps up and runs toward Shadi at the same time Shadi runs toward him. They meet, or more accurately crash into each other, and cling in a tight embrace.

Shay doesn't know who Yassine is, but it's clear the two know each other in some meaningful way. If she had to guess, she'd say they're family. The boy wriggles from Shadi's arms and looks around furtively. When he speaks again, it is in Mekanch. "What are you doing here?"

Shadi lays his hands on the boy's shoulders and drops his voice to a hush. "We need to find someone in the entourage, someone who may be key to the Sisterhood's success. Can you help us?"

"The entourage is kept in a secret chamber of Mukhtar Jawad's residence," the boy says, speaking quickly. The look of concern on his face edges toward terror with each passing moment. "But you should leave while you can. The chamber is inaccessible to all but the mukhtars and the Snow Queen."

Shadi frowns. "Who is the Snow Queen?"

Khawla, who has picked the musket up from the ground, steps closer. "You've gotten bigger, Walood." She smiles and reaches to tousle the boy's hair, but he ducks back shyly

Shay joins them, sure to keep a watchful eye, scanning not only the lower courtyard, but the upper terrace that frames it. Though distant footsteps and voices echo, no one comes near enough to notice them.

"She grooms the young women who are brought into the entourage," the boy explains to Shadi, his mouth twisting in distaste. "But it's like Mukhtar Jawad did something to her. Her powers are . . . extreme."

"Yes." Khawla gasps. Her eyes begin to flutter rapidly, opening and closing. "I can feel her. She gives off a strange energy. I've never felt another Shawafa like it."

"Can you find her?" Shadi asks.

Khawla nods, blinking slowly as her eyes refocus. "I think so."

"You're not listening." Walid steps back, away from Shadi, shaking his head.

"Come with us," Shadi says with an ache in his voice. "We will help you escape, too."

"I can't," Walid says with a melancholy unbefitting his tender age. "We must find a system we can use to communicate. People often talk in front of me, and because I'm young, they think I'm not listening or don't understand. I can be an informant."

"It is dangerous," Shadi argues, but the struggle in his eyes says he knows Walid's suggestion is not without merit. "Mmi misses you."

"Yas . . ." Walid looks at the ground. He makes a sound like choking. "You don't understand the things they've made me do. I could never look her in the eyes again. You know her. The way she *sees* everything your soul tries to hide."

A flash of red fabric alerts Shay to the approach of two Moulays. She elbow nudges Khawla, who quickly passes the weapon back to Shadi.

Shay hangs her head as the guards come closer, her hair falling over her face. Khawla picks at her arms and tugs strands of her hair, mimicking the behaviors Snow predisposes touched ones to.

"Salaams." One of the Moulays steps forward and peers closely into Shadi's eyes. "Are you new to the kasbah, khoya? I have not seen you around."

Shadi swallows, then lifts his chin. "It's my first day."

The Moulay stares at Shadi for a moment longer before glancing at Walid, who nods in confirmation of Shadi's claim.

"They buddied you up with the tadpole? That figures." The Moulay chuckles, slapping a hand to Shadi's chest. "Well, if you've brought these two in to join the entourage, you better get them to the Snow Queen promptly. And don't be tempted to have a little fun with them before delivery. The Queen doesn't take kindly to that. The last Moulay who tried it lost his manhood."

"Frostbite." His companion grabs his crotch, wincing in sympathy for the plight of the Moulay in question.

The first Moulay's eyes roam over Shay, lingering at her forearms and torso. He dusts the front of Shadi's uniform before dropping his hand and stepping aside. "No one would blame you if you wanted to swipe those leathers, though. They'd fetch a comely coin."

"I—um—I'll be careful. Thanks." Shadi prods Shay and Khawla forward with the musket barrel, and Khawla subtly guides them toward the residential building on the right side of the courtyard, presumably where Mukhtar Jawad resides.

The door to the building is locked, but Walid has a key, which is fortunate because it would be difficult for Shadi to pick the lock with the two Moulays they left in the courtyard boring holes into their backs. Inside, a long hallway stretches out, the length of it dim despite the combined effort of glittering sconces spaced along the wall and a large punched-brass lantern roped from the ceiling.

As they proceed toward a set of stairs at the end of the hall, the rooms they pass appear to be used for storing food, goods, and animals. They ascend to the second floor, dominated by a kitchen too large and too busy, even this late in the evening, to have been designed for the dietary needs of one man, however holy he claims to be.

Continuing to the third floor, they embark down another hallway. The rooms here are painted ochre and white, with sections open to the terrace through a series of arches, revealing patches of starlight. They hold a mismatch of furnishings that could be arranged and rearranged to suit different purposes.

It is into one of these rooms that Khawla directs them.

The room contains several floor cushions, small shelves that hold books of scripture, and a chest of folded prayer rugs—and it is not empty. A mukhtar stands perfectly still in the corner, a viper in white robes and a red felt hat, poised to strike. Heart racing, Shay spins to escape, when Khawla places a staying hand on her shoulder.

Shadi struts up to the figure and angles the lantern inches from its face. That's when Shay understands what she's looking at. A statue. Mukhtar Jawad has had a life-size statue made of himself and placed it in a prayer room, of all places. Its marble eyes flip heavenward, a stone replica of the thick Book of Lineage clasped to its sculpted chest. The mockery is an insult to the Creator.

"They should be here." Khawla peers around the indeed-empty room, distraught.

"Are you sure?" Shadi asks.

"Mukhtar Jawad does spend a lot of time in here with the door locked," Walid offers. "I highly doubt he's performing extra prayers or reciting scriptures."

"Then there must be a secret passage," Shadi says, proving he's a hundred times more brilliant than Shay gives him credit for.

The four spring into action, scouring the room for a hidden door. They overturn cushions, pull out shelves, and tap their palms along the walls. As the limited possibilities dwindle, Shay turns in frustration toward the ridiculous statue.

"Where are you hiding them, Sidi?" She smacks the flat of her hand against the stone iteration of the book her name was never written in.

A loud, grinding screech brings the room to a standstill. The square tile the statue is standing upon lifts and rotates. The entire stone figure shifts aside, revealing a small room, no larger than a broom closet, hidden beneath.

Giving Shay an awed smile, Khawla immediately crouches to climb down into the vestibule.

"Khawla," Shay says, her voice keying shrilly. "What are you doing?"

"I can feel them," Khawla says with a confidence born of certainty. "The one they call the Snow Queen is sleeping, very deeply, as though recovering from heavy exertion."

"That makes sense," Walid says. "Jawad spent an extra-long time in here the last few days."

"Where is he now?" Shay asks, a chill pinging her spine.

"I don't know exactly, but he left the kasbah not long before your arrival."

Once Khawla maneuvers herself inside the opening, Walid follows, then Shadi, leaving Shay to make the descent last. There's a brief moment as she shimmies on her belly when her legs dangle loosely. She hangs by her knuckles and kicks around, scrambling for a solid surface. Firm hands grasp her waist, and she's momentarily airborne. Then her feet meet the ground.

She turns to face Shadi, their eyes locking, and in that moment, all Shay sees is him. His hands rest at her hips, his touch too light to burn the way it does, and his face is so close that, even in the eerie lighting, she can count the copper swirls like threads of saffron floating in his brown irises.

Walid clears his throat, reminding them that they are not, in fact, alone, but squeezed in an extraordinarily tight space with two other people. Shadi and Shay whip around in tandem to see Walid and Khawla studying the anomaly they were too distracted to notice.

Attached to the wall at the rear of the vestibule is a round wooden disk. Some type of glowing crystal is embedded in its center, the source of the eerie light, and a handle protrudes from the side.

"I think we're supposed to crank it?" Shadi suggests.

Each one in turn responds with a nod, approving this course of action. Shadi grabs the handle and rotates it in a full circle. A low humming vibrates in the walls, a grinding pulse that rises before it putters out and stops.

"I think you need to keep turning it," Khawla says encouragingly.

Shadi winds the wheel a few more times. The humming grows louder, and the room begins to drop. Lower and lower. Slowly at first and then faster. The square above them shows the distance between them and the prayer room growing longer and longer, until finally, the handle hits a stopping point.

The humming dies down. The wall opposite of the wooden wheel slides to the side, introducing a doorway. A new room has opened before them, and instead of the dank, cave-like dwelling Shay would expect from the underground dungeon she assumes they've been transported to, they step out onto a floor that flows like a spotless river of marble.

Walid lifts the lantern high, its light spilling across smooth walls that appear freshly painted. The living space is lush. Abundant seddaris abound, expansive enough for either sitting or sleeping on. Chairs are arranged in a series of spaces, each creating a sense of privacy while flowing together without feeling cluttered. Pillar candles in glass boxes sit on the floor around the room's perimeter, each positioned next to a door embedded with a small rectangular window that hangs at eye level.

The touched ones, and there are many, seem out of place in these comfortable surroundings. Most are sleeping. Others are too blitzed out to notice their dwelling has been intruded upon. Some, Shay realizes with slow-dawning horror, look young, and more than a few are riddled with bruises and other injuries.

Only one is visibly pregnant. Shay's eyes are drawn to her immediately, like mindless moths enchanted by the lure of a deadly flame.

24

Dearest Brethren,

By God's might, we have discovered the location of the raw material the enemy is sourcing to produce Snow. The next phase of our mission is to find all four of the magical talismans our informant from the bloodsucker clan told us about. According to intel he received directly from the Sisterhood, these talismans can be used to either reawaken or to destroy all magic forever. Any Naturalist who obtains one of these talismans will be accorded a position of highest rank and prestige in the New Dalwa.

A COMMON GOAL FOR A COMMON PEOPLE!

—an encrypted memo distributed to all known members of the CNM

Khawla stops at one of the doors and peers through the rectangular window. As eager as Shay is to cross the room to Hind, something on Khawla's face convinces her she needs to have a look for herself. All four of them end up taking turns peeking in on the first three rooms, the scene in each one stranger than the last.

The first has a padded floor and walls. Two women are inside. One picks the other up as though she weighs less than a loaf of bread and hurls her from one end of the room and into the opposite wall. She repeats this over and over, and the other woman bounces up as if unaffected every time.

The next room contains a large pool in which a handful of women swim. Sharing the water with them are a couple of octopuses. One crawls along the bottom floor, and the other shoots across the pool and back like an arrow sprung from its bow. At least one woman, her bottom half submerged in the water and her top half reclined on the stone stairs, looks to be in mid-transformation between octopus and human form.

In the third room, a group of women stands gathered around a long table. In the center, what looks like a three-dimensional map of Nezjar floats at eye level above the polished surface. Using precision focus, the touched ones direct the glowing vapor from their hands toward raised areas of the map that seem to represent things such as crop fields and major businesses.

As puzzling and intriguing as these spectacles are, the risk of being discovered is too high for them to look in on every room. Hind is already sitting up by the time they reach her. The lantern, now held by Khawla, paints her groggy face in a spectral light. Her eyes are so deeply hollowed, they might as well be holes. She grunts—annoyed, but proving she's not yet the ghost she looks to be.

Relief unfurls in Shay's chest. She's not too late.

"Too bright," Hind screeches slinging her arm across her eyes.

Khawla lowers the lantern. "Sorry."

Hind rubs her cheeks before focusing on Shay. "Shuika? What are you doing here?" Her gaze swings from Shadi back to Shay with growing fright. "How were you captured?"

"It's not what you think." Shay shakes her head. "We're helping you escape."

Hind points a thin finger first at Shadi and then at Walid. "Aren't they Moulays?"

Shay wants to explain that Shadi and Khawla are her friends. That they belong to a faction of the resistance movement. But her words get stuck as she stares at the shape of Hind's body up close. Knowing she was with child was one thing, but seeing the domed cup of her swollen belly makes it much more real.

"How is it possible?" she whispers.

Hind sighs, her hands instinctively cradling her womb. "It was foolish to come here. You should have stayed where you were safe."

Safe? It's a small word. Like a pebble that starts an avalanche of remembered hurt and betrayal. The last time she felt truly safe was with Ghita. "In Al-Ghaba Mayita, you mean?"

"You had a better chance of surviving there than here, especially if your father finds you."

"My what?" Shay retreats a step, and the backs of her legs bump the side of a body, another touched one sleeping on a low seddari. "You said you didn't know who my father is."

The woman Shay has inadvertently disturbed moans. "What's going on?"

"Nothing, go back to sleep," Hind mutters. "Just a pair of newcomers. I'll help them settle in."

Hind attempts getting to her feet in a series of unsteady wobbles. Khawla jumps in and helps her, allowing Shay a better look at her mother once she's upright. Any questions about her paternity slip away. Hind's arms have grown thinner, and they were not substantial to begin with. Her legs look liable to snap under the weight of her protruding belly.

She tugs Shay close by the elbow, swaying with the effort. "You need to get out of here, quickly."

"I'm not leaving without you," Shay huffs.

"I'll only slow you down." Hind's voice rises, high and tight, igniting a string of grumbles as more touched ones are jarred from their sleep. "Just go."

"I have a safe place we can stay," Shay insists, more gently. "If you don't care about saving yourself, do it for the child that grows inside you."

Hind pouts, but doesn't argue, seemingly stymied by this.

"Khalti, we must hurry." Khawla beckons them back toward the transportation box. Shay breathes a little easier when Hind allows herself to be shuffled along into the vestibule, where Shadi again turns the wheel that closes the sliding door. At the last moment, when only a slit remains, Shay thinks she glimpses a woman who rises to her feet and stares at them, a woman so pale that she radiates a faint shade of blue.

The opening seals, and with a noisy shudder, the box begins its upward return. Upon arriving back at their starting point below the prayer room, Shadi discovers that the handle of the wheel, when in a locked position, can be used as a lift to assist with climbing out of the vestibule.

All seems calm as the group emerges and makes their way downstairs, but back in the courtyard, it becomes evident an alarm has been raised. Moulays scramble in all directions, orders and replies shouted back and forth across the distance. The unconscious Moulays must have awoken or been discovered.

"Come, you should leave by the back gate, where deliveries are made," Walid says, gesturing for them to follow. "There are no incoming shipments on the schedule at this hour."

"Good thinking," Khawla says, "But maybe we should create a distraction, try to get everyone heading in the other direction."

"The ammunition building is nearby." Walid nods. "I know just the thing."

They use the abundant plants and trees throughout the courtyard gardens as positions of cover and make their way to the ammunition room, the small building Shadi noted when surveying the complex. *Small* being a subjective term.

"I'll be quick," Walid promises.

No sooner does he unlock the door and slip inside than two guards approach.

"Where are you taking these women?" the taller one barks.

"Mukhtar Jawad has requested us to be transferred," Hind says.

The second guard chuffs, narrowing eyes that look almost as cold and dead as a bloodsucker's at Shadi. "Do you need a touched one to speak for you?"

Big brass buttons wink in the dusty starlight, a vertical line down the front of the Moulay's pressed coat. Seeing his weapon pointed at Shadi the way it is, Shay wonders for the first time if that's why their uniforms are red. To camouflage the blood.

Shadi rolls his shoulders and widens his stance. "I was given instructions from the Snow Queen. The pregnant touched one needs to be evaluated by a midwife."

"Mezyan." The guard nods. "And what about the other two?"

"Can't you tell? Have a closer look, khoya," Khawla says, putting a hand to her very unpregnant belly. She steps forward, and faster than Shay can believe, Khawla rips the weapon straight from the hands of one Moulay and bashes the other in his face with the butt of it. Blood gushes from his nose.

Shay gasps, a sound she feels rather than hears, like her soul is shivering out of her body. Had she been exposed to Khawla's apparent combat skills sooner, she might have asked for a few lessons.

Khawla cocks the snagged weapon and points it at the unarmed Moulay. Shadi turns his weapon on the bleeding Moulay, who gathers himself enough to lift his own weapon in a standoff. Hind backs away, waving at Shay to do the same. Someone whistles loudly, and two new Moulays appear from around the corner of the nearest residence.

One steps toward Shay, the other toward Hind.

"Stay back!" The blast seems to come from everywhere when Khawla pulls the trigger. A warning shot, aimed at the ground near the guard's feet, sends him into a body swerve that defies gravity. Shock, hot and metal, reverberates in Shay's teeth.

Walid bursts from the building and hurls a small gray canister away from the courtyard. A smoke bomb. It hisses as it sails over their heads and lands out of sight, where it releases a loud *whoosh*. The air crackles and fizzes as it fills with reams of dark smoke.

"Fire!" Walid yells, his voice surer and more commanding than Shay imagined possible. "Fire in the rear quadrant. Remain calm and proceed to the front gate!"

While the guards are distracted, Khawla and Shadi lay down their weapons, allowing them to all join hands. Walid, who's on the end of the chain and has a free hand, keeps his. Ducking, they dive into the thick of the smoke and make toward the back gate.

The smoke stings Shay's eyes and lungs, burns sharp through the pores of her skin. Mucus runs backward from her nose down her throat, clogging her airway. She hears Hind coughing beside her and squeezes her frail hand.

Blearily, they power through, emerging with ragged gasps and sputters on the other side of the billowing cloud.

Shay catches sight of the gate first and then, with a sinking sense of disbelief, sees the large camel-drawn cart piled high with bags of salt that effectively blocks it.

"Devil be damned!" Walid exclaims. "The earlier delivery must have been delayed by the rain."

"Don't worry," Shadi tells him. "We'll find a way through the front gate."

Hind looks even paler now. Her eyes are red and tearing. She keeps holding tightly to Shay's hand, even when everyone else has let go.

"I don't think my mother can make it back through the smoke again." Shay eyes the lingering fumes. They're dissipating, but not quickly enough. "Let's keep to the walls? Make our way around the perimeter?"

"Good thinking," Khawla says.

They're on the move again, going a little more slowly now to accommodate Hind. But it's alright, because the Moulays seem to be looking for them everywhere but along the perimeter wall. That is until they're in the final stretch, the front gates visible in the distance.

A lone Moulay appears in their path.

Hind and Shay take cover behind Walid because he's the only one still holding a weapon.

The new Moulay turns his musket on the boy, nostrils flaring when he snarls, "Drop the weapon, traitor!"

Shay nearly drowns in the booming of her heart. Shaking, Walid slowly lowers his weapon to the ground, and Shay couldn't be angry at him if she tried.

She should be protecting *him*.

Not only is she old enough to be, well, if not his mother, his teacher or governess, but she's the one wearing armor. Shame flashes through her, and everything inside her wants to hug the boy to her chest, to reassure him all will be well.

A sudden crack like a split down a frozen lake captures everyone's attention. The woman who storms toward them with a guard on each side is tall. She wears a crown of twisted branches and white feathers. A light-blue gown cascades around her, layered with lace and fur. Her skin glistens, as if every part of her is covered by a thin sheet of ice. Her eyes are twin pits as dark as open graves, her lips like blue leeches clinging to a pale-white face.

"Lower your weapon, fool." Her words flourish the air with delicate puffs of mist. "I won't have the precious cargo Sayeda Hibachi carries exposed to harm."

The Moulay immediately complies.

"Take her inside." The Snow Queen addresses the two Moulays who accompany her, stout-looking brutes with hateful eyes who have somehow already secured Khawla's arms behind her back. The Queen turns to the original guard. "Round up the others."

Khawla struggles, fearless as ever, refusing to be dragged inside. The Snow Queen casually lifts her hand, now glowing with blue light. She brings it to her mouth as though blowing a kiss. Sudden wind whips Khawla's hair back from her face and leaves her eyebrows crusted in frost. A seam of ice glues her eyelids closed, depriving her of sight and allowing the guards to overtake her.

Shadi yells wildly, running forward. The guard leaps in his path, and Shadi punches him squarely in the face. The guard turns instead toward Hind, perhaps judging her a more manageable target, and brandishes the butt of his weapon threateningly.

The air itself has turned sharp with violence, nails springing out like a cat. A desperate clawing Shay can feel across her skin, inside her chest. None of this was part of the plan. But birthing has taught Shay that when things take an unexpected turn, you improvise.

She reaches for the musket Walid laid on the ground. Her heartbeat echoes like a chanted blessing inside her head as she cocks the hammer the way she watched Khawla do it and aims the barrel at the Snow Queen.

The queen simply laughs. "Go ahead."

Shay must act before the guards get Khawla inside the building. Hesitation builds in her chest, but then she remembers that hesitation got Ghita killed. She jerks the trigger. The ball releases with a bruising kick to her shoulder, filling the air with the rotten stench of gunpowder.

Her ears clang.

Through the smoke, a flick of the Snow Queen's hand creates a shield. Floating ice shimmers, hanging in midair long enough for the ball to ricochet off on a new path. It strikes the Moulay who called Walid a traitor, felling him in an instant.

"You'll need to reload if you want to try shooting at me again." She smiles mockingly at Shay, who keeps glancing at the Moulay's still body, expecting him to get up. But the Moulay is not screaming, no one is going over to help him, and Shay thinks, with a sick twist in her gut, that she was right. *Red is good camouflage*. "Not that it will do you any good."

She looks around in panic. Khawla and the guards are already gone. Walid is nowhere in sight. Shadi is carefully regarding the Snow Queen, shielding Hind behind him.

The Snow Queen watches, still smiling, as a new batch of Moulays approaches. Leisurely, she lifts her hand. Her palm swells like the touched one with the Shawafa of Hadiqmin back at the farmhouse and releases not a thorn but a long, pointed icicle, sending it spearing into Shadi's thigh.

He crumples. Shay cries out, anguish washing over her. While scanning the scene for some last-beaker way to turn things around, her sight snags on the exact moment Hind pulls a small glass bottle from her pocket.

"No!" Shay pushes her way toward her as she lifts it to her lips, but the distance is too far, Shay's feet too slow.

Hind tosses back the Snow. Not only is she endangering the child she carries, but Shay can't understand how the Shawafa of Shifamin will help them. Hind raises her fingers. Green smoke billows from them, a rippling wave suspended in the air as though coiling to strike. All at once, it writhes a serpentine trail through the melee and plumes into the Snow Queen's face.

The queen doubles over, spontaneously stricken with an uncontrollable fit of coughing.

"Run," Hind cries.

They make for the gate, Shay lifting the loose fabric of her skirt to grant her legs greater range, Shadi limping at a stilted sprint. A trumpet blasts, its peal echoing from a high tower. The feet pounding behind them swell in number.

Another blast. Shay stumbles as a ball whizzes past them. A near miss, this time, but proof that someone either missed the Snow Queen's directive against gunfire or has decided to ignore it.

With Shay's arm around Shadi's back to support him, they reach the gate, which is blessedly still unlocked. The bloody stain on his pant leg is growing, the icicle jutting out like protruding bone.

Shadi pauses for the briefest moment, looking back, whether searching for Khawla or Walid, Shay isn't sure. Then they're back out on the cobblestoned streets. He quickly ushers them down a dark alley and stops in front of a circular sewage port, where he squats and shifts aside the heavy lid.

"You're jesting, right?" Hind backs away from the hole. She looks over her shoulder in the direction of the kasbah as the sounds of shouting and footfalls grow closer, seeming to weigh her options between imprisonment and contact with human excrement.

Shay, a veteran of the messiest of life's biological processes, has no qualms. Besides, she's starting to trust that Shadi really knows what he's doing.

"Please." She squeezes Hind's hand, making her eyes soft and pleading, not sure in this moment if she feels more like a child begging an adult or the other way around. "It's our best hope to conceal ourselves."

Hind nods reluctantly. Despite his injury, Shadi refuses to go first. Shay knows she doesn't have time to argue with him. She descends the ladder, followed by Hind. Shadi clings to the ladder rungs last, handing down the stolen musket and sliding the cover into place, like closing the lid on a coffin. He hobbles down by feel alone. Shay waits at the bottom with her arms outstretched, meeting him in the dark as he maneuvers the last few steps.

They huddle in the darkness, shoulder to shoulder, their heavy breaths bouncing off damp stone walls. Stomps and commands fly back and forth overhead.

Shay realizes the jinn sticks were in Khawla's bag, but she pushes the thought away before it sets in, the shape of it too jagged to hold, too blistering to touch. Seeming to intuit her need, Hind raises her hands, and they glow.

Shay quickly examines Shadi's thigh. "Is it melting?

"Not fast enough."

"I can help him," Hind says, the green of her Shawafa reflecting in her white-cast eyes. "You pull it out. I'll close the wound."

"Just do it quickly," Shadi groans, his lips drawn thin and beaded by sweat.

Shay cuts the material away from the leg of his trousers with her pocketknife, both to see the wound better and for staunching the initial gush of blood. It takes more force to remove the icicle than she's prepared for.

She feels the tearing of flesh and muscle, as though the spear causes as much damage coming out as it did going in. Shadi doesn't scream, not out loud. His face contorts in a silent agony that rivals any laboring mother's expression Shay has ever witnessed.

What small relief she feels as Hind takes over is short-lived.

The world above them has gone silent, indicating they are no longer being hunted, at least not in the immediate vicinity. They are safe for the moment. She hopes Walid will be spared, since the Moulay who saw him with them is dead. She wonders what that young man was like before he enlisted. Of the friends and family who will mourn him. His parents.

And then there's Khawla.

All Shay can see are Khawla's eyes frosted shut. All she can think about is the terror Khawla must have felt, being sightless, not knowing where they were taking her. She imagines the moment Khawla's finally able to pry her eyes open again and finds herself alone.

That's the thought that breaks her.

25

Looking for a way to help your son develop vital skills? Our program offers:

STRENGTH & ENDURANCE

FLEXIBILITY & REFLEXES

FOCUS & CONCENTRATION

CONFIDENCE & RESPECT

SELF-ESTEEM & PERSONAL GROWTH

Contact your local recruiter today to learn how to sign him up for a term of two solar cycles in voluntary service as a Moulay! Your son could grow up to be a mukhtar himself!

THE ARM OF GOD HAS MIRACLES IN ITS FIST!!

—recruitment ad posted in the medina square of all four regions

Hind is not well. Her tolerance to Snow has become so high, she's rebounding faster. They make their way through the damp and putrid tunnels below the medina. Every step feels like a betrayal of Khawla.

"Walid will help her," Shadi says, as they slosh through ankle-deep murk.

Shay can't tell how much of the conviction in his voice is real and how much is him trying to convince himself. Him wanting to believe Walid himself is not in any immediate danger. That they haven't made things worse for him. "Is he your brother?"

"Yes." Shadi sighs, and the sound is layered with grief. "They've made him a Moulay. I mean, thank God he's alive, and we can certainly use information from someone inside, but I would have rather he had chosen to come home."

Shay palms the center of his back. "May God protect him."

"He'll be well," Shadi says, less certainly this time. "As long as Al-Mukhtar doesn't realize exactly who his mother is. Then they might . . ."

Use him to get at her, she thinks, and she understands too well the confusing mix of joy and pain that comes with finding out your loved one is alive but trapped, whether that be in a physical location or a prison of their own making.

"So, who's Yassine?" Shay asks, as much out of curiosity as to nudge the conversation in another direction.

Shadi nods, as if expecting this question. "*Shadi* is an alias. Anyone in the Sisterhood who lives in Nezjar has to have a false identity and backstory."

Shay thinks about the words Walid spoke in Waheeli, the tattoos on the Morchidat's face. "You're not from Umm Chanala, are you?"

"I'm from everywhere." He grins with a sense of pride. "I'm Hazmaggi."

"Well, it's nice to meet you, Yassine." Shay understands the necessity of being undercover. His name may not be what she thought it was, but in all the ways the matter, he's still the same. There's just one thing she doesn't understand. "I'm curious, if your tribe governs themselves, why is your mother a resistance leader?"

"Al-Mukhtar may officially recognize us as separate, but in reality, they steal our children all the same." His eyes flick to Hind, walking forlornly beside them and making a meal of her thumbnail. "When one group is oppressed, we all suffer. Evil is only be defeated when all good people band together as one."

"Good luck with that," Hind mumbles morosely. "The Sisterhood, the Naturalists, Al-Mukhtar, they all think their way is the only way and refuse to see past their own narrow views. Then you've got the clans of Ard Al-Ghul, who change their allegiances as it suits them. The solidarity you speak of is a childish illusion that doesn't exist."

Shay is taken aback by her mother's skepticism. She would have guessed someone with the ability to heal might be more amenable to restoring magic. For a moment, the ensuing quiet highlights the squeak and scuffle of unseen rodents. Shay declines to contemplate their numbers, pushing the word *horde* from her mind.

"Do you have an opinion?" Shay asks Hind. "Or would you rather we resign ourselves to defeat?"

"An opinion?" Hind harumphs. "Exploit magic or eradicate magic or use it, but only ever *for good*: The problem with all these paths is that no one is trying to understand magic, and you can't harness what you don't understand."

The answer surprises Shay. She realizes this is actually another tool Al-Mukhtar uses to reinforce oppression: keeping people ignorant.

"What did you do to the Snow Queen exactly?" Shay replays the scene in her mind. Whatever Hind did seemed to be the opposite of healing.

"Shawafa can be used in reverse," Hind explains. "It's a neat trick not everyone is skilled enough to pull off. Instead of healing, I was able to inflict a bit of respiratory distress."

"Walid told us he thought Muktar Jawad had done something to her," Shay recalls aloud. Despite the power Snow lends them, most touched ones appear fragile, but that's not a word she would use to describe the Snow Queen. "Do you know anything about that?"

"Zubeda? Or 'the Snow Queen,' as you call her? She's just another victim of Jawad's bizarre experiments. It can be challenging, keeping up with the miracles Al-Mukhtar needs performed to paint themselves as the saviors of the realm. Jawad figured why not make a few touched ones even more powerful. Instead of diluting the crystal they mine to make Snow into a liquid, he forced her to smoke it in little chips out of a pipe."

Shay wants to ask more questions, the most important one being where the other hjabats are, but Hind is suddenly out of breath. She grimaces, doubling over in pain. It takes both Shay and Shadi to help her walk, and they're practically carrying her when they reach the port that brings them to the ground near the forest.

It's only as they stand at the tree line that Shadi turns to her, with moonlight on his face and uncertainty in his eyes, and asks, "Do you remember the shortcuts Khawla takes?"

"I don't even think they're always the same. The forest . . . it changes. Khawla is only able to make sense of it because of her affinity."

Whatever discomfort Hind is feeling, it doesn't stop her from glaring incredulously first at Shadi, then at Shay. "Are you saying neither one of you knows the way through the forest?"

"I know *a* way," Shadi clarifies, unhelpfully. "But in your condition, khalti, it would be preferable to know the shortest way."

Hind sighs with an air of long-suffering. Then her eyes brighten. She pins Shay under her eerie white gaze. A gaze that is altogether too knowing. "What was your hizoura gift again? Something to do with animals, right? You can use that."

Shay pinches the bridge of her nose, heaving a sigh of her own. She's barely practiced communicating with the smallest of creatures and reserved her requests to the simplest of tasks. Half the time, she's not even sure if it's real or if she only imagines she can sense such things as the sadness of a bird who has lost a life partner or the determined will of an ant digging under a mound destroyed by rain, searching for a buried nest mate.

If she's really able to do anything at all, she's still not sure how it works. "It's not that easy."

A twig snaps. Two glowing lights pierce through the brush. A small smile tweaks the corner of Hind's mouth in a way that says, *I told you so*. The lights float closer, and the figure of a deer takes shape. Most of its body looks normal, except the way its eyes shine like white lanterns and its neck seems to be broken.

It walks right up to them. Right up to Shay. *Where do you wish to go, Lalla?*

The words are a whisper inside Shay's head. Even still, she glances at Shadi and Hind to see if they heard. They both stare at her as if waiting for her to *do something*.

"Uh, A-Ard Al-Ghul," Shay stutters, feeling self-conscious to have other people hear her talking to a deer, a slightly dead deer at that. "We need to travel the shortest route possible. Because my . . ." Shay grapples for the right word: *My female parent? My heart's wish? My ill-fated disaster?* "My *mother* is pregnant, and she's crashing hard from Snow. We need to get her to a safe place where she can rest—and quickly."

Follow me. I will guide you.

The deer turns and takes a few steps away before stopping and looking back at Shay.

"It would appear the deer knows the shortcut," Shay explains to Shadi and Hind, who both nod like this is a normal development.

The creature's glowing eyes blaze a path ahead. Despite its physical abnormalities, it bounds through the forest in graceful steps, adjusting its gait to match what Hind can manage. They fall into a rhythm of sorts. For a while, anyway.

By the time they reach the first cave passage, Hind's pace has slowed to a crawl. It's clear she needs to recoup. They stop, and Shay takes measure of Hind's bulging belly, calculating how many moons have passed since she last saw her.

Not long enough for her to be as far along as she looks. "Are you in your third trimester yet?"

"No," Hind says, a little too quickly. "It's early."

Shay doesn't believe that. She fears even the shortcut may be too much for Hind to withstand. It appears whatever Hind did to reverse the way she used her Shawafa had a draining effect. She barely had enough power left to heal Shadi. Shay can tell, despite his efforts to conceal it, he too is still in pain.

Shall I bring someone to assist you, Lalla?

Shay is so entrenched in thought, she startles at the deer's query. "I . . . Do you know of the seven bone-eater brothers?"

The deer tells her it does. Shay cuts a scrap of cloth from her djellaba for the deer to bring them, that they might surmise she needs their help. Then they wait. Hind and Shadi quickly fall asleep, one leaning against either of Shay's shoulders as they sit together on the floor of the cave. Shay can't say she blames them.

But she's too busy thinking about Khawla to find such rest. She sees the two of them on Jou Boulka, the memory as clear as an open window, running on the streets of Ard Al-Ghul like they owned them. How Khawla's face looked tilted back, long hair spread behind her like dark wings. Shay hears the sounds they made, wild howls offered to the moon.

Then she thinks about the entourage of women beneath the kasbah, how strange it was that some of them bore injuries when there were healers like Hind among them. Almost like someone ordered them *not* to be healed.

That could be Khawla, Shay thinks.

Before her mind can add imagery to the thought, she remembers everything Shadi said about evil being defeated when good people band together. She clings to the words until they seep into her veins, pour into her heart, and start filling all the cracks where it's broken.

No matter what Hind says, Shay knows what she must do.

Hind and Shadi awaken at the approach of yipping and barking. Shay stumbles out of the cave, with Shadi not far behind, to see what's happening. The bone-eaters have arrived in the form of seven hyenas. They weave through pines and cedars toward the cave, pulling a sled, each with one of seven long straps held tightly between their strong jaws. Hind's protests seem mostly perfunctory, and she ultimately allows herself to be strapped to the sled and carried the remainder of the way to Ard Al-Ghul.

Shay and Shadi jog to keep up with the creatures as the trees blur into blue and black stripes at their sides. They emerge upon the clay road that leads into Ard Al-Ghul, the pounding of their slippers making eddies of red dust around their ankles. Leaving them in front of the cottage, the hyenas trot, tongues lolling out and panting, back to the forest—where Shay presumes they will transform back into their primary form.

"I'm going to talk to Khawla's parents," Shadi says, and Shay's heart aches at the thought of their happy little family, the one she was so jealous of, torn apart because of her. "Then I'll report to the Morchidat, bring her word that Walid is well."

Shay stops herself from reaching out and squeezing his hand, not sure whether she'd be doing so to comfort him or herself. "Tell Khawla's parents I'm sorry."

"We'll figure this out." He reaches for her hand instead, his thumb soothing a circle inside her wrist. She thinks then that maybe there's no difference, only the mutual solace to be found in comforting each other.

"Tell the Morchidat I'm ready. I'll talk to Hind when she's rested, find out all I can about the hjabats and anything about the kasbah's layout and activities that might assist with Khawla's rescue. I want to officially join the Sisterhood."

"What about your mother's care?" he asks, his face gentle.

"She is my priority. But I'll find a way to make it work. Balancing multiple roles is what women have always done. If there is anything I can do to help Khawla, I must."

"I'll talk to her if you're sure, but you must not take the decision lightly." He tenderly releases her hand, glancing up at the moon as though in search of divine counsel. "My mother . . . she will ask for proof of your loyalty. Some sort of test or sacrifice. Whatever it is, it won't be an easy thing."

"I understand." Shay's gaze drops to his lips. She has the strangest impulse to seal her decision, to kiss away the uncertainty that lingers on his face.

"Hello!" Hind moans loudly from the sled. "Do you intend to leave me strapped here all night?"

"I'll return soon." As if he read her intention, Shadi leans toward her, his warm lips brushing her cheek, exquisitely soft, and all too brief. But enough for now.

Shay half carries Hind down the path to the brothers' door, where she stops and faces her mother. Fading moonlight strikes silver in her hair. But at least the sled ride doesn't seem to have made her condition any worse. "I want you to empty your pockets."

Hind shakes her head wearily. "I took the last of my Snow back at the kasbah."

Shay hardens her voice. "I don't believe you."

"Search me, then." The touched one tips her chin, a dare that Shay obliges.

She pats her palms over Hind's clothes, feeling for bumps or bulges, and reaches into her pockets. There, she finds a string of wooden remembrance beads, a few luneers, and bits of lint. "Unlace your boots."

"Seriously?" Hind groans, putting a hand to the doorframe for support. "I'm weak, bnti. It's been a long journey. I need to lie down."

"Unlace your boots," Shay repeats.

Pouting, Hind undoes the laces. Shay slips her fingers inside and digs around until she finds the vial. Wordlessly, she pours the amber liquid out into the tangled grass while Hind hovers nearby, making soft sobbing sounds that arouse little sympathy.

If Hind doesn't care enough, isn't strong enough, to make good decisions, Shay will do the caring. Shay can be strong. Ghita taught her many useful things, but the lesson she liked least may prove most useful now. Love isn't necessarily kind and soft. Sometimes, love is firm and unsympathetic.

Maybe that's the kind of love that can save her mother.

The sky beyond the lopsided cottage has gone from black to blue, starlight fading like melting snow. Morning draws near, bringing no warmth with it, only the cold wash of clarity. No bright spread of buttery hope. Only hard-boiled conviction.

For now, this too must be enough.

26

Still uncertain whether the Moulay Training Program is right for your son? Consider these testimonials from our young men and their parents:

"I sincerely couldn't be more thankful for the level of support and quality of training I've received from the Upper-Level Cadets. I'm very appreciative to have worked with men of such faith and integrity, and I honestly cannot recall a time when I obtained this kind of one-on-one personalized attention from an instructor at any institution I've attended. I honestly couldn't be more thankful."

—Majd, a recent graduate

"Our son was lacking direction in life. We didn't know where to turn. A friend recommended the Moulay Training Program. After he completed his two-solar-cycle term, we were amazed at his transformation mentally, physically, and spiritually. His potential has skyrocketed, and the skills he's gained will open many new doors of possibility in his future!"

—parents of Khalid

THE ARM OF GOD HAS MIRACLES IN ITS FIST!

—advertisement run in the quarterly tribunes of all four regions

Shay carries a tray upstairs, heaped with crisp toast and an array of fresh fruit cut into bite-sized pieces. She hesitates at the door with a murmured blessing.

For days Shay has found Hind either convulsing with chills or delirious with fever. She has been met with sweat-soaked sheets in need of endless washing and bout after bout of vomiting or diarrhea or worse—both. But Hind is finally awake and sitting up.

Shay approaches her with a tender smile.

She takes one look at the tray and blanches, her lip curling in disgust. "I can't eat anything."

"The tea will help you feel better," Shay insists gently. She foraged the herbs herself: sour terraparam for lowering temperature and golden hyssop for pain relief. She sets the tray on a wooden stand and cracks the window to air the room. "You must try to eat something. For the baby."

"Keep that shut. It's freezing in here." Hind rubs her thin arms roughly and rolls her eyes with disdain. "And don't start on me about the baby. You know what? If you care so much, cut the thing out of me and leave me to die."

Shay flinches. She sighs and closes the window, despite the room being uncomfortably warm and so stale that the walls are beginning to peel. Her voice is soft when she speaks: "You don't mean that."

"I would rather die than feel this way." Hind moans, flopping back against her pillows. She flails from side to side. "It hurts. Everywhere. Everything. My skin is on fire. My bones are melting. My organs are shriveled. I need one sip. Please. Just to take the edge off."

"That's not an option." Shay creeps closer. Hind has torn a hole in one of the socks Shay tied over her hands the last time she clipped her nails. A new batch of thin red ribbons have joined the older scratches on her arms. "Look what you've done to yourself. At least let me put some nigella nettle on your wounds."

Hind grunts, which Shay takes as compliance. She retrieves a bottle from a nearby drawer. Sitting on a leather starmia next to the pallet, she uses a clover bean leaf to dab the juice generously over Hind's skin. "Is that better?"

"It is nice and cool," Hind says reluctantly. She rubs her nose and snuffles.

"Mezyan." Shay smiles as brightly as she can, imagining Hind as a cat gone feral whom she's been tasked to tame. She readily remembers the resting season she spent in this same room, hiding under layers of blankets, sinking through levels of despair. Then Khawla came. Hind is going through a hard thing, but she doesn't have to go through it alone. "How about just a sip of tea?"

Hind nods and props herself up on one arm. Shay pours a glass, filling it only halfway. Given her recent fits of shaking, Hind is liable to burn herself. On second thought, Shay brings the glass to her mouth, to be safe.

The moment the liquid meets her dry, cracked lips, Hind shoves Shay's hand away. Tea splatters in an arc, spraying Shay's skin in a hot flare. The glass sails from her fingers and shatters against the wall. Long wet streaks trickle down in trails and run together, making it look like the cottage is weeping.

Muted light hits the glass lying scattered on the floor, the way the sun must glitter off ocean waves even when someone is drowning.

"Are you trying to poison me?" Hind scowls. "What did you put in that concoction?"

"Nothing bad." Shay's voice trembles. She fetches a clover bean leaf and wipes her arm, her skin puffing in pink splotches when she lifts the leaf. "Ghita taught me well about herbal remedies. The tea is perfectly safe, and beneficial."

Hind blinks. Her face softens, looking almost contrite, which makes her next words all the more shocking. "The midwife? Have you spoken to her lately?"

A lump of emotion lodges in Shay's throat and prevents her from speaking. She rises and takes a moment to gather herself, drying the wall and sweeping the glass. Her hands shake. She clenches them. Splays them open. Tries to shake the feeling that she's standing high on the edge of a cliff, water rushing so far beneath her, it sounds less like a roar and more like a purr.

Finally, she sits back down and says the words she still finds hard to believe. "She's gone."

Not missing a beat, Hind smiles cruelly. "Traveling?"

"No." Shay searches Hind's face, trying to glean where these questions are coming from. Her stomach twines around a pit of unease. "Mukhtar Jawad raided her dwelling, and—"

"Oh," Hind says with fake sympathy. "Someone must have turned her in for stealing that baby. But who would do such a thing?"

Horror seeps over Shay, the unapologetic look on Hind's face saying everything she isn't. Then Hind has the gall to laugh.

"Why? Do you understand that they killed her?"

Hind lowers her head. She shrugs one bony shoulder. "Sometimes the best way to get yourself out of trouble is to get someone else in it."

"Do you have any idea how heartless you sound?" Shay wishes Hind could only see herself, that she had some kind of magic mirror that shows people the magnitude of their own cruelty.

"Don't judge me." Hind jerks her head up, eyes wild. "I could have killed you before you were born. Your precious midwife would have given me the right herbs, had I asked. Would have saved us both some grief, don't you think?"

Shay leans back so far, her balance tips. She finds herself on the floor, gasping for a breath that doesn't come. She understands now, why Ghita wanted to send her to Kiddah. She must have known that had Shay stayed, she and her mother would have connected, sometime, somehow, and that Shay would only suffer as a result.

"Look how weak you are," Hind goads. "How can you even be my daughter?"

Shay snaps.

She springs to her feet and paces the length of the room. "All I ever wanted was for you to love me. I've seen countless children born and watched women from all manner of backgrounds and circumstances bond with their babies. It's a love that comes naturally to any woman.

"Except you," she spits. "You failed to do that one, most basic thing. And then you take away only woman who has ever come close to loving me the way you should have." Shay comes to a stop, her fists vibrating. "I swear by the One, I don't know why I keep choosing you. You're never, ever going to choose me back, are you?"

"If I'm so horrible, leave me to my suffering," Hind says, her voice brittle. She leans back on her pillows with one arm thrown across her face, hiding any expression she may wear. "I'm too tired to deal with you."

"You're too tired?" Shay sputters. "I haven't slept in days because I've been so worried about you. I lost my dearest friend helping you escape!"

"Did I ask you to rescue me?" the touched one whispers, barely audible.

"So what?" Shay stomps her foot. "You're going to confess this terrible thing and then roll over and go to sleep?"

"Shhh," Hind murmurs groggily. "Emotional strain is bad for the baby. Or didn't Ghita teach you that?"

How dare she utter the midwife's name? Even the truth of her words isn't enough to stop Shay from screaming in frustration. Feet pound up the stairs. Deebi bursts in. "Lallati, are you well?"

Shay shakes her head, trying not to cry. Trying not to scream again. Trying not to bang her head repeatedly against the wall.

Deebi approaches her slowly, scanning for any sign of injury. "Just take a deep breath, and tell me what's wrong."

All Shay can do is point a finger toward her mother, curled on the pallet and already—unbelievably—snoring.

Deebi nods as if that's a perfectly comprehensive explanation. "Whatever she did, whatever she said, she doesn't mean it. She's overwhelmed by the pain of the cravings, that's all."

"It's no excuse." Shay sighs. She'd rather conclude Snow altered her mother's decision-making ability than that she's just devoid of morals. But Hind isn't making it easy to be so generous, not when her hands are dripping with Ghita's blood.

"You haven't stopped working all day," he says. "Go relax for a while. I'll watch over her."

Shay hugs herself, exhaustion humming through her body. "Are you sure?"

"I've got this."

Shay smooths her hands down her kaftan and over her hair. "I guess I could start lunch."

"No need," Deebi reassures her. "Dasri is cooking today. He loves your couscous so much, he watched you make it and memorized the ingredients and steps. It should be ready soon."

"What about you?"

"Put some aside for me." He places a gnarled hand on her shoulder before she speaks. "Yes, lallati. I'm sure."

✧ ✧ ✧

Shay places the last cleaned plate on the drying rack and dries her hands on her apron. She leans against the counter, listening to the clamor of snores rumble through the walls. Unlike Ghita, the brothers revel unapologetically in their afternoon naps. They're not opposed to morning or evening naps, for that matter.

Shay always thought a mother's love was the ultimate expression of affection, a mirror of God's care and mercy toward his creation. How was she blind for so long to love's other forms?

The love of companions who appear in your life when you need help most, and perhaps because they need you just as much. The love of a mentor who shapes and teaches. The love of a friend who feels like a sister, like two patterns cut from one cloth. And the budding potential of romantic love, the kind that feels both like flying and like falling.

Unfortunately, she's learning that any love, even the most sacred, can be twisted into something that feels more like a disease, where every interaction leaves you battered and bruised. A love that consumes and consumes and consumes you.

And loving someone means that when the unimaginable happens, when you don't know what is happening to them and are helpless to intervene, it feels like your heart is being snapped in two, over and over and over again.

Shay doesn't hear Kabeer silently enter the kitchen until the swish of his long cape gives him away. She turns to find him peering out from his hood, his ghoulish features molded into a stern expression.

"That boy is at the door for you," he says, wrinkling his nostril slits in contempt.

While Shay has been nursing Hind, she's heard no news of Khawla, but now hope rears in her chest. "Shadi?"

Kabeer grunts in affirmation, then clears his throat. "Do I need to have a discussion with him about his intentions?"

"That's very sweet of you, but no." Shay can't help but chuckle at his almost-brotherly concern. "I shall remind you that I can take care of myself. Besides, you don't have anything to worry about. He's the last person who would ever harm me."

"All I'm saying is, a little threatening goes a long way." Kabeer cracks his bulbous knuckles with menace.

"Please don't." Shay throws him a pleading look before she hurries to the front door.

✧ ✧ ✧

Shadi has arrived with a riding cart and a donkey, a petite creature with delicate hooves the size of saltshakers and strong, steadfast eyes fringed in long lashes. Shay goes straight to the animal and pets the coarse fur between its shoulder blades.

"I see you've met Mufeed." Shadi's voice is light, but his face looks grim.

She has never seen him look so serious. Her heart drops, her fragile hope already waning. "Is it Khawla?"

"No, no news on that front." He tries to smile, but it's clearly an attempt to allay her fears, to ease the blow of whatever message he's been sent to deliver. "The Morchidat has summoned you. When someone requests to join the Sisterhood, there are certain initiation protocols. As a safety precaution, initiates aren't invited to the Sisterhood's main headquarters until the assessment phase is complete. This preliminary meeting will take place at a secret outpost."

"Wakha." Shay nods. That doesn't sound so bad . . .

He holds up a silken black cloth between his fingers, his smile turning apologetic. "It is procedure that you be blindfolded for the journey."

Shay stares at him for a moment. It's not that she doesn't trust him. It's just . . . if these procedures are meant to impress upon her the enormity of her decision, it's working. "How many initiates make it through this assessment phase?"

Shadi gulps so hard, his throat bobs. To his credit, he doesn't avert his gaze. "About half."

An uncomfortable itch spreads over her, like walking through the web of a king spider. She was so preoccupied with whether she felt ready to join the Sisterhood, she never considered the possibility they might reject her. Though she's sure a large number of those who go on to be rejected apply under false pretenses to start with. Hence, the need for precaution.

"What happens to the other half?"

He takes a moment to stare at her now. "I won't let anything happen to you."

Not an answer. But Shay is no longer sure she wants one.

She feels each slope and sway of the cart, the comforting squeeze of Shadi's hand, the press of his thigh against hers. He smells fresh and earthy, like apples and cardamon and rain. The daytime sounds of Ard Al-Ghul are more like her medina than she would have thought. Muted voices chatter. Feet thud in a heavy rhythm. Livestock squawk and bray.

In time these noises fade. The tenor of Mufeed's hooves changes, indicating they have traded the clay road for another surface. The clomps carry a hollow echo that sounds like wood. Below that, the faint ripple of water. A bridge?

Her legs are unsteady when Shadi finally guides her off the cart. Tall grass swallows her knees and clings damply. She hears the thrum of insects, feels them bump and bounce off and around her. Salt and mud scent the air. A door creaks, and Shadi instructs her to watch her step.

He guides her across a floor with wobbly boards and gently pushes down on her shoulders until her bottom meets the hard seat of a chair. Vague light flickers through the blindfold.

"I'm going to wait outside," Shadi whispers near her ear. "My mother will be with you soon."

Soon turns out to be long enough for Shay to perceive the temperature around her drop, an indication the sun is setting. A cool breeze brushes her skin, she assumes from an open window. It carries in the ongoing insect chorus, now swelling to a raucous volume.

"You can take the blindfold off," the Morchidat says. Shay heard no one enter the room.

She reaches behind her head and unties the fabric.

The only light is the soft glow of a candle, but even that leaves her blinking as her eyes readjust. The space is cramped and utilitarian, obviously designed for temporary accommodations. Opaque curtains cover a single window, but when the wind ruffles them, Shay glimpses dark stretches of greenish water, the gray bark of trees. Trees that appear to be growing *in* the water. A swampland?

"Tea?" The Morchidat sits opposite Shay across a square table.

It takes Shay a moment to decide which sister is which. Yara, sitting on her mother's right, isn't smiling the way she did at their first meeting. Her eyes are red and weary. Shay thinks she may have cried recently. Over Khawla, or Walid, or something else, Shay can only speculate. Marjan sits to her mother's left and glares at Shay accusingly.

She gratefully accepts the warm glass she's offered, letting the minty steam waft into her face. It soothes away some of her disorientation.

"What news do you have to report about the hjabats?" the Morchidat asks, getting right into it. "Has Hind provided useful information?"

"Not yet, Sayeda," Shay says meekly. "Her state is fragile. She is with child and deep in the throes of withdrawal."

"So you haven't asked," the Morchidat says flatly.

Shay sips her tea, thinking there's no good way for her to respond. The Morchidat certainly doesn't want to hear about her issues with Hind. And it's no excuse, is it? She should have been more direct instead of waiting for the right moment to broach the topic. Of course, it would have been difficult to ask her anything when she was at her most ill. But she was well enough to talk earlier today.

Well enough to pull the lynchpin of Shay's world with a few well-timed words.

The Morchidat sighs. "Yassine tells me you wish to join the Sisterhood."

It takes Shay a moment to remember she's referring to Shadi. She sets her tea glass down, nodding. "Yes. I want to do whatever I can to help bring Khawla back. I've already been inside the kasbah once; I can do it again."

The Morchidat is quiet, sipping her tea while regarding Shay over the rim of the glass. Lowering it, she says, "It's your fault she was taken. You owe me a fighter."

She states it without accusation, as though it is a point of data to be calculated.

Marjan crosses her arms over her chest. "Khawla is worth ten fighters."

Shay's throat burns, and not from the hot tea. She nods again, firmly. "I'll get her out of there."

"No." The Morchidat wags a finger. "Khawla can take care of herself. Yassine tells me we have someone on the inside who will assist her. You will take Khawla's place until she returns, and as a new recruit, you must perform a task to prove your worth."

"S-sayeda . . ." Shay stammers, confused. If not for Khawla, wouldn't the Morchidat want to send a team in to save her son? "I believe the women held in the kasbah are being abused. It is dangerous for Khawla to remain there."

Shay sees Yara biting down on her lip in a struggle to maintain her composure. Her eyes glisten, but no tears fall. If the Morchidat notices her daughter's distress, she ignores it.

"*Khawla* will have to wait." The Morchidat's tone brooks no argument. She flattens her hands on the table and takes an even breath. "Our astronomers have predicted that in one moon's time, there will be a portentous meteor shower, the likes of which have ushered in many historic events. They say the success of our mission hinges upon having all the hjabats in our possession at the time of this celestial occurrence."

Shay's body flashes with sudden cold—it tightens her chest and turns bitter in her stomach. She sips her tea, concentrating on the warmth as it glides over her tongue and down her throat. It seems like the Morchidat is saying all available teams are being directed to concentrate on their primary mission before this meteor shower. That doesn't mean *she* can't help Khawla on her own.

"You will bring me the other three hjabats," The Morchidat clarifies. She finishes her glass of tea and smacks her lips in satisfaction. "You have one moon to do so."

"I . . ." Shay can't believe her ears. She thought Shadi said his mother would ask her to do something hard, not something impossible. "Respectfully, we should rescue Khawla first; she has the affinity for finding things. Her gift as a hizoura is exactly what is needed for the mission you have proposed."

The Morchidat raises a sleek eyebrow. "Are you changing your mind about your allegiance already?"

"What?" Shay backpedals. "No, absolutely not. I don't take this decision lightly at all, Sayeda."

"Then I suggest you think about how the gift you possess may be of aid in your task." The Morchidat reaches into a satchel belted around her waist. Shay is relieved when she doesn't withdraw another blade, at least until she sees the hjabat sparkling on the flat of her palm. "Put this on."

All the fear of waking up in the forest alone and immobilized rushes back to Shay, but the memory pales in comparison to the dark future she envisions for Mekchaouen's women if the Sisterhood should fail.

If she should fail.

"Is it true that you saw them?" Yara asks. Though her voice is soft, Shay is startled she has spoken at all.

Reverence is thick in her voice, and Shay doesn't need to ask whom. "No," she corrects. "I heard them."

"They spoke to you? That is so amazing." Yara doesn't give Shay time to explain that it was more like they were talking to one another than to her. "Mmi had me try on the ring. Not just me. A few of us. All it did was make us pass out. Why do you think it was different for you?"

Shay thinks that is a very good question. One better answered by someone with greater knowledge of how magic operates. But then she remembers what Deebi said about bloodsucker venom affecting some people more than others.

"It may be all the births I've attended," she says, thinking out loud. Wishing she could ask Ghita. Wishing, with a new wave of self-recrimination, she'd asked Hind when she had the chance. "The time I've spent near the veil of life and death could have granted me a certain sensitivity. Or maybe it's some other reason Hind has knowledge of."

"We need to know where the other hjabats are, and we don't have time to ask your mother," the Morchidat says, still holding out the ring. "Besides, she's hardly a reliable source."

"Not like the Lallat," Yara adds, the shine in her eyes less sad, more hopeful.

Shay takes a trembling breath. "What if I don't wake up?"

That's when Shadi, who must have been right outside the door, listening, rushes in. The Morchidat narrows her eyes, but makes no outward remark.

"I'm here," he says to Shay, seeming to cross the room in a single bound to reach her. "I'll make sure you're safe and take the ring off if you're out for too long."

"I don't think the issue of your safety is in question," the Morchidat says with a cross between irritation and amusement. "Unless you decide *not* to put the ring on."

"Mmi . . ." Shadi says, somehow managing to make the word sound like both a warning and plea. A look passes between Yara and Marjan.

"Do not address me as your mother unless this is a situation where you are prepared for me to address you as my son," the Morchidat says. Her voice is calm, her face neutral as she stares at Shadi until his eyes dip, breaking contact.

"Of course I'm going to put it on," Shay says, louder than she means to. She gives Shadi a quick smile and takes the hjabat from the Morchidat, fighting the unsettling feeling of history repeating itself.

Shadi and Yara help her into a more comfortable position, sitting her on the floor and wadding towels and sweaters into makeshift pillows, as if she's readying to give birth. Marjan offers a reluctant chin lift in her direction, as close to a vote of confidence as Shay could ask for.

Shay would feel better about putting the ring on if doing so were helping Khawla in some way. But maybe if she can find out where the other hjabats are, it will earn her favor with the Morchidat and make her more receptive to Shay's suggestions. Nothing about her demeanor, especially with Shadi, gives Shay reason to think that would be the case, but it's the only thought that comforts her as she slips the ring on her finger and peers nervously into its crystal face.

She waits for the spinning to start, the intractable downward pull.

That seeping darkness.

"Just close your eyes," Shadi encourages. "Try to relax."

"I don't think it's working . . ." Shay mumbles, realizing her words are slurring right as she feels the off-kilter slope of her body, the makeshift bedding rising to greet her. Vertigo claims her, and her vision sparks—one bright burst of color before it all goes dim and a cloud of oblivion rolls over her.

27

My research indicates that when the Lallat ruled, the monsters of Ard Al-Ghul rarely crossed the boundary into the human world. They steered clear of the populated medinas, where the anxieties and fears they prey upon were in scarce supply because citizens felt safe and happy. This forced them to seek out those in vulnerable situations, hiding in abandoned, uninhabited places, where they would patiently lie in wait for the solitary traveler or explorers in search of a fear-inducing thrill.

My findings also show that the monsters were less organized then, less human in their attributes. More terrifying, existing in their most primitive and eldritch forms. Of the three ghoul clans, the night hags have changed the least over time and are said, by those who have survived an encounter with one, to have retained a most significant portion of their true nature.

—from the historical journals of the Morchidat

Shay floats in silver clouds. Tingles travel over her body. Odd, considering she isn't sure where her body is. Sparkles dance around her like a field of shimmering stars. She watches them glom together, the specks growing larger and more defined until four distinct shapes surround her.

One shines green, one silver, one blue, and one red. Four tall, glowing pillars that look more like the stalagmites in Shadi's cave than women.

"Lallat?" Shay tries to reach out and touch one, which proves impossible when she can't locate her hand.

A voice like crystal chimes flows from the silver pillar. "What do you need, kbida?"

"Who are you?" Shay asks uncertainly.

"My name is Iman," the silver pillar says.

"I'm Rasha," says the blue one.

"I'm Radia," says the green.

"And I'm Noor," says the red.

"We are the Lallat," they say in unison. "We are the past, and you, oh, bnt, are the heart and hands of the future. It is our pleasure to assist you."

"I . . ." Apprehension flashes through Shay's mind. Something about this feels too simple. Too easy to be true. But deep down, Shay knows she isn't going to be able to convince the Morchidat to rescue Khawla unless she first completes the task—the entire task—she's been given. Time is precious as gold, and every moment, as costly. "I need to know where the other hjabats are hidden."

"One, a necklace, is locked within a chest, deep inside the underwater cave of Chefrika, off the shores of Lahat," says Iman.

"Another, a pair of earrings, is hidden in a box under the bed of a Marabout who lives at the Holy Institute of Umm Chanala," says Rasha.

"And the last, a bracelet, is worn around the wrist of Muktar Asim, who currently resides at the Grand Palace in Kiddah," says Radia.

Shay's heart grows heavy. She has never been to any of those places, and none of them are less than a moon quarter's journey. It would be almost impossible to gather them all in time, even if Shay didn't have to care for Hind. "Wakha. Thank you. While I'm here, do you have any advice as to how I might travel to these places, collect all three pieces, and return before a moon cycle has passed?"

Noor says something, but her words are running together, distorting, becoming difficult to understand. The clouds begin to part, reality teasing at Shay's thoughts, the pillars drifting farther away. Shay focuses harder, holding tight to their image.

". . . keep chipping away at us, we'll soon be less rocks and more pebbles," Noor finishes, her voice resolving.

"Do you have to be so dramatic?" Rasha asks. "The kid is doing the best she can."

"Look, it's a new generation, sis. I hear they're pressure-motivated."

"Shuika, pay attention." Iman's voice again, commanding but kind. "The sleep spell on the hjabat is wearing off. Without it acting as a conduit, even your sensitivity will not be enough to breach the veil unless you come to us. To revive our spirits, you must bring all four hjabats and three other—"

The pillars rapidly blur together into a mass of colors. Iman's voice shrinks to a faint echo. Shay feels her consciousness being pulled along a steady track, like a fish hooked on an angler's line. The clear-gloss surface of reality looms ahead.

"Where do I bring them?" Shay asks, panicked, but her lashes are already flickering. The image of the pillars alternate with slices of Shadi hanging over her, his nostrils slightly flared at this angle.

"We're losing her."

Those are the last words Shay hears before her body springs into a sitting position of its own volition, her eyes wide open, the connection severed. *No, no, no.* Iman was telling her something important.

"Are you well?" Shadi looks pale.

"Yes. I learned where the hjabats are. I just . . ." Shay closes her eyes, trying to reestablish the connection, but it's to no avail. She reviews all that the Lallat told her, in case she missed something that will make her task easier than it appears, such as how to be in multiple places at once, for starters. One detail does stand out. She swallows and locks eyes excitedly with Shadi. "I think . . . I think the Lallat want us to reawaken them. If we can gather all the hjabats, they'll come back and fight Al-Mukhtar with us."

"That's incredible news." Shadi smiles, his color returning. "Mmi will be pleased when I report back to her."

"What?" Shay looks around the outpost, realizing they are there alone. She blinks a few times and rubs her eyes to test what she's seeing. "They left?"

"Um, yeah." Shadi scratches the back of his neck. "She's . . . a busy woman. Always attending meetings and studying old scrolls, and fighting—mostly practice, but you get the point," he says, and Shay wonders if she imagines that hint of sadness in his voice. "But she instructed me to give her the rundown of what you learned at her earliest availability."

Shay pulls the hjabat off her finger. "What about this?"

"She said for you to hold on to it, for now."

Disappointment deflates her. Shay realizes she was eager to see the Morchidat's reaction. Proud to have discovered something of use. And more hopeful than she had any right to be that providing the hjabat's locations might convince the Morchidat to help her with obtaining them.

"The hjabats are scattered far and wide, Shadi." She locks eyes with him again, this time in desperation. "Surely, she has the resources to send multiple retrieval teams at once. I'm just one girl."

He tilts his head, a slight curl playing at the corner of his lips that she might imagine kissing if she weren't so distraught. "She wouldn't have asked you to do it if she didn't think you could. She may be callous at times, but never careless."

Shay shakes her head slowly, still *not daydreaming* about his lips. *Not* admiring their shape. And definitely *not* wondering how they would fit against hers. How the feel of them might smooth away her ever-growing number of problems, if only for a moment in time.

She clears her throat. "Do you? Think I can do this? Honestly?"

"No." His eyes flick over her face, pausing at her lips, as if he's possessed by the same distractions as she. "I know you can."

He's sitting near enough that she feels the heat of his body. His breath stirs her hair, a soft flutter against her cheek that sends a delectable chill down her spine. Silver moonbeams reflect in his eyes.

Moonbeams? Shay straightens, snapping to her senses. She has left Hind unattended for far too long. What if she needs something and the brothers don't know what to do? What if she takes a turn for the worse? "I must get back."

"Of course." Shadi gives his cheeks a brisk rub. He stands and offers his hand. "By the way, Yara wanted you to know she thinks it's brave, how you're helping your mother."

Shay gets to her feet, forcing a smile. She wishes she had a mother whose love didn't require bravery. A relationship that came easy instead of leaving scars. "At least one of the twins doesn't hate me, then."

"First, no one hates you." He squeezes her hand before letting it go. "And my sisters look alike, but ironically, they aren't twins. They were born to separate families in different regions of the realm. Mmi adopted them after their parents and other family members were martyred."

"Oh." Shay's struck by the notion that there's something she meant to ask him, but she can't remember what it was. "I still think Marjan takes after your mother. In personality, at least."

"I'm sure she'd take that as a compliment." Shadi chuckles, his eyes soft with fondness. He uses the candle to light a lantern before snuffing it, shadows dancing to life around them. "I know she has a tough exterior, but there's a heart of gold underneath it all. You'll see when you get to know her."

They make their way to the door and step into the night air, which has cooled considerably. Mufeed brays softly, as if to say, *It's about time.*

A faintly sour smell on the air nudges Shay's memory into place. "The moon pepper! I've been meaning to ask you about it. Do your sisters still take it?"

"Funny you should ask," Shadi says, but he looks more perplexed than amused. "It was Mmi who told me to harvest it. But then Marjan refused to take it. Which I get. She's immensely proud of being a hizoura. It's validating to her as a mutahawil."

Shay nods in understanding. Shawafa belongs to all women, regardless of what body part she has between her legs.

"And then Yara also refused, more in solidarity than anything."

Shay finds it hard to imagine anyone going against the Morchidat's directives, especially after putting Shadi through the trouble of harvesting it. But more than that, it doesn't make sense that the leader of the Sisterhood, a group that advocates for the return of magic, would desire to suppress it in her daughters. "Why did she want them to take it in the first place?"

"That's what I wondered, too," he admits, gazing up as if the stars might string themselves together to spell out the answer. "All I know is, Mmi never does anything without a reason. Sometimes, I think we're all just pieces on a Parchis board to her, and she's always strategizing six moves ahead."

✧ ✧ ✧

Deebi has somehow persuaded Hind to eat a small amount of couscous by the time Shay returns. She hugs him before he leaves the room, barely registering the rotten-egg scent that perpetually lingers on his skin. *It's not that bad once you're used to it.*

"I need to check on the baby's development." Shay turns to find Hind quietly watching her. She braces for more arguments. "Are you feeling up to it?"

Hind nods compliantly. "What do I need to do?"

Shay lets out a long thankful breath. The glass from earlier may have been swept away, the wall wiped new, but her mother's volatile words still soil the room, as glaring as any stain. Her throat aches with the effort it takes to keep her voice calm and measured.

"Lie back and lift your clothing, please." She kneels next to the pallet and palpates Hind's engorged belly. "How far along are you?"

"I don't know, honestly." Hind stares expressionlessly up at the thatched ceiling. "The days tend to blur together when you're blitzed out."

Shay pauses. "But you said it was early."

Hind puffs out a short breath, then gives a meek shrug. "I didn't want you to worry."

How thoughtful.

"Plus, you have to consider the effect of my Shawafa on the child. Its development could be accelerated."

Shay crosses the room to her dresser and grabs a streamer of parchment she had the brothers procure from the medina, one she's marked with increments to replicate the strips Ghita used for measurement. She stretches the strip from the top of Hind's pubic bone to the peak of her uterus. Nibbling her lip, she holds the strip up to the lantern light to be sure the number she thinks she sees is correct. "One more thing."

Next, she retrieves a small horn she petitioned Dasri to fashion for her. Despite Shay's suggestion that he use a hollow piece of wood, the off-white color of its surface suggests he went with a different—more readily available—material. *As long as it works.*

She presses the cone-shaped end of the horn to Hind's mounded belly and moves it around in a slow circular pattern—then she hears it. Strong and steady. The sound of tiny galloping horses. The sound of new life. Her future sibling's heartbeat.

Her mind conjures images of a bunya-shaped head and tiny bean-like toes. A feeling unfolds inside her like rose petals softening to the sun. This baby will be loved from the day they enter the world. If not by Hind, then by Shay.

"Is something wrong?" Hind searches Shay's face.

"No." Shay forces a smile, declining to mention the possibility that Snow has caused some defect she can't yet perceive. No point in worrying Hind, which would only make things worse in any case. "Your baby is healthy and growing well. Also, you should go into labor before the next moon."

Hind frowns, pulling wrinkles around her mouth like a fruit left out too long. "Is there a midwife in Ard Al-Ghul?"

"I don't think so." Shay busies herself packing her equipment away, pushing down her hurt at the question. "Your body is amazing, though. It already knows what to do. You'll be the one doing most of the work, and I have the skills and experience to monitor and support the process." She steels herself for an insult.

"Oh yes, I forgot Ghita was training you." Hind shifts her clothes back in place, covering herself. "I'm sure you're competent."

She forgot. Shay gave up her whole life the day she went looking for Hind, but she forgot? The oversight feels like the blade of a dull knife, something that looks less dangerous, but inflicts much more pain than the clean cut of an actual insult would.

"I'm sorry, about earlier," Hind continues, her voice low and repentant. "I shouldn't have been so cruel."

"I'm glad you're feeling better." Shay smooths the fabric of her kaftan. Anger is still a smoldering heap in her chest, waiting to crackle to life, to enflame her throat and set her tongue afire. "But I still don't understand why you turned Ghita in."

"She was putting those posters of you all over the place! I could hardly take them down as fast as she'd put more up again!" Hind hangs her head, peeking sheepishly between fallen fluffs of hair. "I did it to protect you. Same reason I snuck you onto that blood-wagon."

The words are so unexpected, Shay's sure she misunderstood. She shudders. Then she shudders again. "You did what?"

"I know how it sounds," Hind concedes. "But I was in a panic, and I told the touched ones to push you off before you ever reached Ard Al-Ghul. I thought you could live there in the forest, like the legends of Mama Ghoula. Especially given your affinity to communicate with animals."

"Mama Ghoula?" Shay gapes incredulously. Snow is known to leave its users' minds in an addled state, but this is beyond ridiculous.

"The woman they say went into the woods on a dare and decided to never come back. She supposedly survived two hundred solar cycles living in a moss-covered hut and eating mushrooms."

"I know who Mama Ghoula *is*. They also say she has the legs of a mule, the tongue of a lizard, and a colony of frogs living in her hair. Does that sound like a real person to you?" Shay shakes her head. At some point, Hind has to take responsibility for the things she's done. And even if Hind thought she was protecting Shay, it begs the question: *From what?* "That whole story about a magical favor was made up, wasn't it? What did that man in the alley really want from you?"

"I told you I owed him a debt—"

"Enough lies," Shay says firmly. "We're beyond that. I want the truth."

"He wanted *you*." Hind lowers her voice to a wisp. "Admittedly, it's my fault that he knows who you are now. I messed up, but at least I tried to fix it."

"What are you talking about?"

"He's . . . your father."

"My father?" Shay swallows, then keeps swallowing, but something besides saliva seems to coat her throat. Something that taste like dirt and won't slide down. Hind lying about the man in the alley's identity is no surprise, but Shay recalls him having facial scars on half his face, the other half being attractive and young. Too young to have fathered her.

"His name is Jawad." Hind rubs slow circles over the expanse of her belly. "Since you were born, I've known he'd only hurt you. That's why I gave you to the midwife. I told Jawad I'd delivered a puppy. He was skeptical, but unable to deny such a clear and shameful curse from God. Till now, he's never told me what became of the poor puppy."

"Jawad?" Shay has only met one person with that name. Though she's positive it's not uncommon. A coincidence, surely. After all, Mukhtar Jawad, like all the other mukhtars, is old and gray and bearded, and the man in the alley was none of those things. "Like the mukhtar?"

"Same person," Hind explains. "In the alley, you saw his true face. It was scarred by a Shawafa so strong, no touched one can heal it. The entourage is able to keep him young or create a disguise that covers the scars, but it takes a lot of magic to do so.

"Jawad realizes that enslaving touched ones isn't sustainable in the long term. If more women die young and pregnancies drop, the population will be affected over time. So, years ago, he came up with the idea of creating hizoura children and raising them as magical slaves instead. The other mukhtars thought it would be dangerous, that the hizouras could rebel and bring about the return of natural magic. But Jawad went ahead and experimented by himself.

"He used other touched ones to keep me healthy during my pregnancy and ensure your survival. But when I failed to produce the child he wanted, he banished me from the kasbah. I was resigned to the filthy squalor of the Bib, and he still demanded that I assist him with luring young girls into the entourage."

Shay has the sensation of being inside a bubble. She can hear Hind still talking, but the words aren't quite penetrating. She remembers meeting Jawad in the hallway at that birth so long ago. Something seemed unsavory about him then, she realizes, but it wasn't obvious enough. It seems wrong somehow that someone so monstrous should be able to blend in with regular people.

"Then you came looking for me. I knew it was bound to happen sooner or later. Ghita couldn't have just killed you after you were born."

Shay gasps, horror sliding like the devil's finger down her spine. "First you said Ghita stole me, then you said you gave me to her. Now, you're saying you asked her to kill me?"

Hind grimaces, as though perhaps that was more than she intended to reveal. "I thought death was a better option than life as a slave. I'm glad now, of course, that she spared you. But when you showed up in the Bib, I was so desperate for Jawad to let me back into the kasbah, I admitted you were alive. He gave me the ring, spelled to render you unconscious so I could deliver you to him."

Shay barks a bitter laugh. She thinks back to the bone-eaters' retelling of Ghita's last thoughts, the hazy recollection of something about her mother not staying away. She wouldn't be surprised at this point if Hind said those things at the brewery on purpose, knowing the ensuing rumors would lure her into a trap. "What made you change your mind?"

"I'm ashamed to say I didn't until the last minute. Right when you called me 'Mmi.' That's when I panicked. I got you out of Nezjar and told Jawad you'd snuck off with the ring while I was blitzed. I told him the experiment didn't work on you anyway. That you didn't have magic, and you weren't worth looking for. He still wanted to search for you, until I told him about the other baby, the one Ghita had taken. It was the only thing I could do to distract him."

"Glory to heaven." Shay isn't sure which revelation is more gutting: that she was fathered by someone so evil or that her mother actually wanted her killed. Lies upon lies, tangled with half-truths. Shay can hardly keep it all straight. She massages her aching temples.

"If you failed to do what Jawad asked of you, how did you end up back in the kasbah?"

"Isn't it obvious?" Hind's shoulders slump. "This was his idea of revenge." She indicates her swollen belly, signifying the pregnancy was some twisted form of punishment.

Any anger at her mother's multiple betrayals is lost in the anguish Shay feels knowing she was forced to conceive against her will. That the beauty of bearing a child will be tarred by the trauma of rape. That she has been violated in just about every way possible.

She tries to absorb it, the atrocity of it all. Like pouring the entirety of the Cerabbi Sea into a tea glass. The Morchidat was right. The women of Mekchaouen are in danger. All of them. Jawad may be the worst of Al-Mukhtar, but how long before he convinces the others his "experiments" are worth pursuing?

"Is there anything else you haven't told me?"

"Nothing, habibti." The kindness in Hind's voice is almost jarring after her earlier vitriol. "But you should also know that Al-Mukhtar never plan to be replaced by younger Moulays. They make touched ones perform spells to extend their life. Spells that can transform their faces so it appears they've been replaced by a successor. They take credit for all the prosperity Mekchaouen enjoys, when the whole realm is held together by women's Shawafa."

"They use your addiction to enslave you," Shay says quietly.

She blinks into the purpled shadows of twilight. Numbness buzzes through her limbs. Hind obviously never knew anything about the other hjabats; even Jawad seems to have been more concerned with Sami than with Shay having possession of the ring. If Al-Mukhtar are using the hjabats for things like simple sleep spells, they probably don't know how important they are or that the resistance is looking for them. That's at least one thing potentially working in their favor.

Shay has never felt so tired or more awake.

Hind lets out a plaintive yawn. It straightens Shay to attention.

"I should let you rest."

"Wait." Hind grabs Shay's hand and presses the palm of it flat against her side. "Feel this before you go."

A series of small thumps brings a smile to Shay's lips despite everything. "She's strong."

"How do you know it's a girl?"

"I just do." Shay stands and shuffles in place, working feeling back into her arms and legs. "Do you need me to bring you anything else?"

"See if the bone-eaters can procure a bundle of fabric and sewing needles. Keeping my hands busy may be a useful distraction while I purge. Maybe I can make something for your sister."

The touched one lies on her side, her hands cradling the top and bottom of her pregnant belly. She looks, framed in the forgiving glow of lantern light, like any other expectant woman. Any loving mother.

"And please, open the window before you go? It's stuffier than the seven hells in here."

28

Shay's Rfissa Recipe

Ingredients

4 tablespoons olive oil
3 large onions
3 garlic cloves
1 teaspoon ground ginger
3/4 teaspoon salt, or more to taste
1 pinch saffron threads
cooked green lentils
4 large chicken legs
fresh coriander
1 teaspoon ground turmeric
1 teaspoon ras el hanout
1/4 teaspoon ground black pepper
vegetable or chicken stock
msmen, for serving

Steps

Heat 2 tablespoons of the olive oil in a large saucepan over a medium-high heat. Sear chicken legs until golden brown. Transfer the seared chicken to a dish and set aside. Heat the remaining 2 tablespoons of olive oil. Slice and add the onions, cover the pan, and cook until soft. Add coriander, garlic, turmeric, ginger, ras el hanout, salt, pepper, and saffron and cook for 5 beakers. Return all the chicken legs to the pan and cover with stock. Bring to a boil, then reduce the heat to medium low, cover the pan, and leave to simmer for about 45 beakers, stirring occasionally. In a separate small saucepan, add in the lentils along with a ladle of the onion sauce and warm up over medium-low heat. Taste the sauce and adjust the seasoning with salt if necessary. Serve chicken with lentils on top over a bed of shredded msmen.

Something is wrong. The thought wakes Shay like a pebble pinging against glass. Sunlight hits her eyelids in washes of red until she squints them open, and then it streams through the salon window, reassuring in its golden hues. She swallows, her throat a little dry. In the moon quarter since they put the past to rest, Hind has been steadily improving, she reminds herself, repeating it a few times.

She sits up on the couch. Judging by the leaves scattered over the table in front of her and the candle nub that has burned itself out, she must have fallen asleep while picking a bundle of fenugreek stems the evening before. After her morning prayers, she stores the herbs in a jar and goes upstairs to check on Hind.

Hearty rumbles greet her as she ascends the stairs. They can't be coming from Hind, because in Shay's experience, Hind doesn't snore louder than a Chanalan bear. Inside her sleeping quarters, Hammu slumps on Shay's pallet, his swerving antlers splayed across her pillow. She assumes he saw her dozing downstairs and, not wishing to wake her, decided to take over her nightly post in case Hind had need of something. Which would be sweet of him, if not for the alarming fact that the other pallet—the one Hind should occupy—is empty.

After a quick and fruitless look around the cottage, she circles back and shakes Hammu awake.

"Huh?" He blinks slowly, wiping a rope of drool from his chin with the back of his hairy hand. "Oh, I must have fallen asleep."

"Where's Hind?"

"I was keeping an eye on her in your place. I had a hunch that was the first sleep you'd had in days, so I couldn't bear to disturb you." Hammu heaves himself into an upright position and scans the room. "Did you check the washroom?"

"Of course I did!" Shay's voice rises. *Something's wrong, something's wrong, something's wrong*, her mind shouts over and over like an insistent street merchant.

Hammu leaps to his feet. "I'll help you look."

Soon, all the brothers have joined the hunt, rambling up and down the stairs, in and out of rooms, flinging open closets and shouting Hind's name in a frantic chorus. Shay is headed toward the front door to extend the search outside when there's a knock. She pulls the door open at the same time Aidi appears at her shoulder.

Hind is standing outside, unharmed, which is not the relief it should be, given the creature standing beside her, his gloved fingers folded over her frail shoulder.

"Hello, neighbors," Tarik says amicably. "I found this lost kitten wandering the streets. I believe she's yours, yes? I thought the neighborly thing would be to return her."

Shay tugs her mother inside firmly by the wrist and nudges her behind her own body, next to Aidi. She glares at Tarik. "Stay away from her."

Tarik frowns, making the gesture almost elegant. "*Thank you* would suffice."

Aidi steps around Shay and strikes his heavy cane against the door with a thud. "You'd better hope our guest reports that you were an honorable escort."

The bloodsucker staggers back a step. "I would never harm a pregnant human. Well, alright, that's a lie. Fetuses and newborns are an exquisite delicacy. But that's all the more reason why I expect a modicum of appreciation for my restraint."

"Get off my property now," Aidi seethes through gritted teeth.

Tarik doesn't acknowledge him. He keeps his dark eyes trained on Shay as he slowly backs to the edge of the lawn, a greasy smile smeared across his pale face. Just before he turns toward his imposing dwelling, he frowns. "I noticed you have new gauntlets, little dove. I hope they fit you well."

As soon as he's out of sight and Aidi closes the door, Shay rounds on Hind.

"What were you doing outside?" She scans her mother carefully for any injury she may have initially overlooked. "I was so worried about you."

"I'm sorry." Hind draws her eyebrows together and pouts. If she's pretending to be confused, she's doing an admirable job. "I wanted fresh air. I didn't think it would be an issue. Walking is beneficial for early labor, isn't it?"

Shay opens her mouth to continue chiding, but stops short. "Early labor? Have you had any contractions?"

"Only mild belly hugs," Hind replies cheerily.

Shay lays a hand on her mother's shoulder, squeezing gently. "Any bleeding?"

"A faint pink drizzle."

At that, the brothers all turn their faces away in various degrees. Shay's chest tightens, zinging between anxiety and excitement. Labor poses serious risks for Hind, but its occurrence is inevitable, and Shay can't wait to meet her sister.

"Let's go upstairs and prepare the room."

"Actually, I have a request." Hind smiles timidly. "I was hoping you could make me rfissa. I have a strong craving for the dish, and fenugreek is known to push labor along. See, I also know a thing or two about birthing."

"That's a lovely idea," Shay says, pleased she already had the foresight to forage a hefty bouquet of the herb. "I'll send one of the brothers up with you."

"No need." Hind waves her thin hand in the air dismissively. "I'm just going to finish up that blanket while I have the chance."

"You shouldn't be alone," Shay insists, looking around at the brothers, not one of who meets her eye. "Really? Are you all that embarrassed about female bodily processes?"

"I'll go," Deebi says, his expression he'd making it clear rather do anything else. He smooths a hand over his curving horn like it's a strength-giving talisman.

Shay peers intently into Hind's eyes and says, "Send Deebi down if there's any change in the frequency or intensity of your contractions. Understand?"

If she's excited about the birth, or afraid, or anxious at all, it doesn't show. Her face is serene, almost stoic. "Yes, I promise."

Shay fends off a shiver as Deebi follows her mother upstairs. Experience has taught her nothing good comes of promises.

✧ ✧ ✧

While the chicken-and-lentil stew simmers, Shay rolls out the dough to make the flaky squares of msmen traditionally served with rfissa. The give of soft dough beneath her fingers and the fragrant steam of spices swirling in the air have a calming effect on her.

Shay whispers blessings for a successful birth outcome. She never got to prove herself to Ghita while her foster mother was alive, but she hopes she honors her memory. That somewhere in the life that follows, the midwife's soul will guide her. That she'll be proud.

She leaves the dough to rest, empties the crumbs collected at the bottom of yesterday's khobz basket into her hand, and scatters the grains on the windowsill. Several midnight irises soon arrive to hungrily peck at them. The dark-brown birds have yellow beaks and a crest of shiny feathers down the middle of their heads.

Propping her elbows on the window, Shay watches them. "I wish I could fly like you; it would certainly make the mission I've been tasked with easier."

The biggest of the birds hops closer to her and lowers its head. *Our recent journey has been long, Lalla. Your offerings are much appreciated.* A ruffle passes through its glossy feathers, showering the windowsill in tiny white specks.

Shay catches a speck on her fingertip, and the cold crystal melts on contact with her warm skin. "Is this snow?"

The bird bobs its tufted head. *We've just migrated from the mountains of Umm Chanala, where the weather is not quite so warm as it is here.*

The weather is another factor she didn't consider that will increase the hardships of any potential travel. Even if she and Shadi make plans to leave right after Hind delivers, it will be next to impossible to cover such distances in so a short time while navigating diverse terrains like snow-flooded mountains and underwater seascapes. Even Khawla's gift may not have been enough to guarantee them success.

Think about how the gift you possess may aid you in your task, the Morchidat said.

Do you really want to feel what it's like? The bird interrupts Shay's thoughts.

"What's that?"

Flying? Do you want to feel what it's like?

She thinks the bird must have meant to say *know* not *feel*. Or perhaps it did say that—or think it—and her magic missed the correct translation by a degree. "Are you going to describe it to me?"

No, I'm going to show you. If you want me to.

Shay isn't sure if the bird is saying what she thinks or if such a thing is possible, but . . . sometimes in her dreams, she doesn't just talk to animals. Sometimes, she dreams that she becomes *one* with them. It's not something she ever imagined attempting while awake . . .

Regardless, it's not an offer one receives every day.

Shay nods, and the bird instructs her to close her eyes. First, she hears the flutter and sweep of the iris spreading its wings, and then she feels the whoosh of air as it takes off from the windowsill in flight.

A vision blooms in Shay's mind, like wearing optical lenses that magnify color and scope. She sees the horizon cast wide, a sky drenched in violet hues. Her heart thumps like a sandrabbit sewn up inside her chest. Tunneled air whooshes past her ears. In her new range of view, the world below looks reborn, the treetops of Al-Ghaba Mayita shifting and swaying like a great viridescent ocean.

By the time the bird flies a circle over Ard Al-Ghul and bids Shay to reopen her eyes back in the bone-eaters' kitchen, the seeds of a plan have rooted in her mind.

✧ ✧ ✧

Shay smiles. Rfissa is customarily served to Mekchaouen's women when labor is imminent, a part of their birth traditions that always took place before the midwife's arrival. Shay never imagined sharing her first experience of this special time, the calm before the storm, with her own mother.

She's adding the final touches to the tray when the echo comes—a reverberation that lights every nerve inside her. Her teeth hum with the strength of it, her field of vision swirling like the stroke of a paintbrush.

The baby is coming now.

Deebi freezes mid-pacing as Shay bursts through the door. "Thank goodness you're here."

She scans the small room, Hind nowhere in sight. Her heart plummets. "What is going on *now*?"

"She was fine when she asked to go to the washroom." Deebi glances in that direction and back to Shay several times, swallowing harder with each subsequent shift of his eyes. "But she's been in there for over thirty beakers, and last time I knocked, she didn't answer."

Shay grunts in exasperation. "And you didn't think to come downstairs and tell me?"

Deebi winces, pinching the tip of one horn in two fingers. "I didn't want to upset you."

Swallowing further remonstration, Shay rushes to the door with Deebi on her heels and frantically twists the rigid knob. "Hind? Are you well? . . . Mmi?" She pounds until she hears the faintest moan from within. "Deebi, I need you to break this door down. *Now!*"

Deebi nods and backs up several paces. He barrels forward and batters his shoulder against the door. Once, twice, three times. Concerned voices buzz below. Inquiring feet clomp up the stairs. On the fourth try, the door yields with a *crack*, like lightning splitting an ancient cedar.

Shay ducks under Deebi's beefy arm and into the washroom. Hind lies on the floor, her limbs akimbo like a carelessly tossed doll. Bloody fluid spreads beneath her, flowing down the cracks between the tiles. A reddish handprint smears the wall.

"Mmi!" Shay shrieks. She slides to her knees in the slick pool and cups her mother's face in her hands.

Hind's delicately veined eyes flutter open.

Her eyes are scrubbed white as pearls.

"There you are, zine diali. Kbida," Hind slurs, smiling softly. The entirety of Shay's stomach does a flip. Her mother is high as the moon. Disbelief springs in her throat like a trap, nearly snatching her voice altogether.

"How did you hide it?" she croaks. "Where did you get it from?"

"It doesn't matter where." Hind sticks out her lower lip and shakes her head in small rapid movements. "It matters why."

"Then tell me why!" Shay screams, her hands dropping to her lap. "Do you want to kill this baby? The way you said you wished you'd killed me? You could have stayed purged for one more day, just long enough to deliver her. So yes, tell me why!"

"I need my Shawafa to heal her in case she's born weak," the touched one mutters, her eyes drifting closed again. "I took the Snow to give her the best chance. Because I know how much she means to you. And I know I've been selfish and you have no reason to believe me when I say this, but Shuika, I do love you. I always have. Every day we were apart, no matter how low I was, or how high, I got down on my knees without fail and begged God to protect you. I never meant to harm you."

"You foolish woman." Shay sobs, a sound that scrapes her throat. Even if it's likely the drugs doing the talking, the hungry void inside her gobbles up her mother's words. She spent most of her life thinking she had no mother, when all along she had two, each only able to love in her own limited way despite good intentions.

"That's a terrible excuse. Your body is already working hard to deliver the baby, and you've added another stressor. It's a dangerous combination, for both of you." She hooks her hands under Hind's arms. "Help me, Deebi."

The bone-eater lifts her mother's limp legs. Together, they carry her out of the washroom and ease her onto the sleeping pallet.

"Don't just stand there!" Shay addresses the other brothers hovering worriedly at the edges of the room. "Fetch me three buckets of warm water and all the clean cloths we have."

The brothers nod and scurry from the room. Shay carefully peels Hind's clothes back, exposing her round belly. As she turns to grab her makeshift midwife's horn from the nearby shelf, Hind moans. The sound draws out, filling the room with its urgency. Her mother's eyes wince shut, her thin hands fisting into the sheets beneath her.

It's the kind of cry Shay thought she was used to. But hearing it now knocks fear into her bones.

29

May the story you tell yourself be true enough to endure.

—a blessing

As a child, Shay kept a "lucky" luneer under her pillow, believing it was imbued with the power to ward away monsters. When the luneer vanished after Ghita cleaned the linens, she dared not sleep for three nights straight, convinced if she nodded off, even for a single moment, a mob of hungry monsters would swoop in.

As she faces her first birth without the midwife, a different vigilance comes over her. She has the sense of entering a battlefield that stretches to the end of the earth, a fight for her sister that's only beginning, where every choice matters. And she's ready.

She releases a calm breath and sets down the midwife's horn. "She's well."

Hind gives Shay a small smile before groaning into the next contraction. They're coming closer together. It won't be long now. She checks her mother's pulse. It's more rapid than Shay would like; she'll need to keep an eye on that.

"Remember to breathe the way we practiced." Shay settles between her mother's thighs, her heart beating as steadily as the forward march of time. No midwife delivers babies. Mothers do that. The midwife's main function is simply to catch the precious cargo when it arrives.

Dasri, whom Hind has taken a liking to, sits beside her mother and wipes her forehead. A familiar euphoria surges over Shay with her first glimpse of the cresting infant, tufts of black hair glistening between swollen folds. It's gone in a blink. But each time Hind pushes with a contraction, the crown becomes more visible, slips back less.

Between contractions, Shay massages Hind's perineum with olive oil, stretching the delicate skin to minimize tears. She murmurs a string of earnest encouragements, and while Hind doesn't exactly acknowledge them, Shay still suspects they're helping.

"Ah, my hand," Dasri squeals with the next contraction.

Shay smirks. She peeks her head up to wink at Hind, who winks back, never pausing her continuous bellows. The other brothers are gathered around. They aren't a congeries of women from her medina, but they bring Hind pillows and help her to change positions like any good khalat would.

"I've had enough," Hind announces with sudden conviction.

"Just a little more," Shay encourages. "You're doing great!"

"No, I'm serious," Hind insists, her voice spiking, high and panicked. Sweat beads across her hairline faster than Dasri can mop it away. "I can't do this. I really can't."

"Give me your hand." Shay guides Hind's hand between her legs, helping her touch the baby's emerging head. She smiles widely. "See that, she's right there."

With the next contraction, Hind pushes harder than ever, releasing Shawafa from her fingertips in glowing green streams. The head of the baby pops out. Firmly and gently, Shay guides the small shoulders around the pelvic bone and lifts the slippery infant into her arms.

Shay chokes on the wonder of it. Her baby sister is perfectly formed, her dewy eyes staring into Shay's. But she's too quiet. Too still.

Shay can handle this.

"Why isn't she crying?" Hind screams. "Give her to me right now."

"I know what to do, Mmi," Shay says, a picture of composure. "Dasri, bring me the clover bean leaves."

Shay lays the docile baby on a sheepskin, willing the massage to do the trick with every vestige of hope inside her.

"No, no, no." Hind's fingers pulse green with each outcry. "Let me help her. Hurry, there's no time." She shoves herself off the sleeping pallet and lunges for the baby.

Shay reluctantly stands by while Hind lays her skeletal hands on the infant's chest. Green light races across her sister's purple skin until she glows like a jinn stick. Still, she doesn't stir. Still, she doesn't cry.

"Breathe. C'mon, breathe," Hind murmurs weakly as the light oozing from her fingers flickers and dims. The glowing streams wane thin, their brightness receding. She snatches up the baby, crushing her small body to her bony chest.

"She can't breathe if you're smothering her," Shay yells in frustration. She gingerly extricates the baby from Hind, who puts up minimal struggle before slumping back on the pillowed pallet, emitting a final disheartened cry.

Ignoring her, Shay works quickly to clear the mucus from the baby's nose and mouth. She delivers thumb compressions followed up with gentle breaths. There's a moment when her hope wavers. Ghita materializes in her imagination then, that same old look of disappointment in her eyes. Telling Shay in her grim, no-nonsense tone, *It's over now. Time to let go.*

The baby's leg gives a kick. Her tiny fingers twitch. She coughs, softly at first before her mouth stretches wide. Her beautiful, enormous cry echoes through the room like a trumpet. Shay laughs, a sound verging on hysteria. Around the room, the bone-eaters clap their hands and whoop with glee.

Aidi hands Shay a newly made blanket. Her eyes fill with happy tears as she appraises her mother's handiwork. The brightly colored threads are stitched in imperfect but painstakingly rendered strokes. She runs her fingers over the jagged swirls of embroidered letters.

Najla.

Her sister has a name.

"I told you I knew what to do." She swaddles the squirming, squalling infant in the soft blanket, whispers a blessing in her ear, and turns to Hind, who's curled on the pallet, knees folded to her chest. "Mmi?"

Her mother isn't moving. Her eyes are closed, face relaxed in the most serene expression. Shay could almost, almost believe she's sleeping, that it's only drool dribbling from the corner of her lips. But it's not drool. It's blood, a thin line stopping at her chin, red and glaring against her too-pale skin.

Shay passes Najla off to the nearest brother and slams to her knees beside the pallet. She shakes her mother's shoulders, chanting her name like a sacred verse she has to memorize, like it's a profession of faith. She feels for a pulse that no longer throbs. Listens for breaths that have ceased to flow.

She thrusts and thrusts and thrusts at her mother's chest, pushing her palms deep and hard. She streams breaths into her mother's mouth, forcing air into her stagnant lungs. She doesn't stop until her arms are limp. Until her throat is hollowed from the keening sounds she doesn't hear herself making.

Until a brother pries her from Hind's cold body and tells her what she already knows. What she knew the moment she turned around.

Her mother is dead.

30

Pregnancy myths in Mekchaouen:

If a woman eats too many red foods during pregnancy, the baby will have a birthmark.

If a woman is not given the foods she craves in pregnancy, the child will be a picky eater.

If the mother has a lot heartburn, the child will be a warrior.

If the woman is ugly during pregnancy, it's a girl. If she's pretty, it's a boy. The girl steals beauty from the mother.

Shay had it all planned. The henna was ready for painting Hind's hands and feet to celebrate the arrival of her second child. The heavy cloths were cut so Shay could swaddle her mother head to toe, settling her bones and speeding her recovery. Little did she know she'd instead be washing her mother's body in preparation for the grave. That she'd be wrapping her corpse in long white burial sheets.

Three days pass before she has the strength to venture outside. With less than three moon quarters to work with, she puts her idea for obtaining the hjabats to the test, but makes little headway. Instead, she spends most of the morning nursing Najla. As it turns out, she also has the echo to make milk for the orphaned child, same as Ghita.

Maybe she really was meant to be a midwife.

But that is not how things have turned out.

In these three days, Shay has not cried.

Three days of unshed tears are trapped inside her. Bottled up in her throat and sealed within her chest. Bloating behind her eyes and under her skin. She's waterlogged. Her every move is cumbersome. Her heartbeat sloshes in her chest. Her breaths rattle, slow and damp.

Every moment, she feels the flood level rise a little higher.

If she doesn't release them, she will begin to mold. Rotting at the seams.

But if she lets herself to cry . . . *forhindghitakhawlawalidbushrabadarmuezzathebarkeep.* For the girl she used to be. The child who believed in wishes. Believed that a mother's love was a magic potion that could fix any problem and heal any wound.

If she starts, she may never stop.

She can't afford that. Najla can't afford that. Or Khawla. Or all the other women, their power taken by men who simply couldn't stand the idea of not being superior. Not being the ones in control of the world.

So, when Najla is fed and changed and burped, Shay lays her in a basket under the shade of a stone pine tree, keeping her close by. The baby makes faces in her sleep, alternately grimacing and smiling. She's strong, healthy, and the most beautiful child who has ever existed as far as Shay is concerned.

Najla deserves a world that is just as beautiful.

31

If you would understand human nature, look no further than the ghouls that haunt us. The bone-eater and the bloodsucker, who bring the all-too-human fear of letting go to its worst conclusions. And the night hags, who reflect back to us our paralyzing fear of holding on.

—the poet Rimkin

Shay resumes her task. She nudges with her mind, trying to persuade a friendly, but easily distracted, raccoon to fetch the hjabat from where it is hidden beneath a large rock across the lawn.

The raccoon approaches the rock once more. Shay concentrates on sending it a message to lift and move the rock to the side. The raccoon stops, even looking back at her as though seeking confirmation. She nods encouragingly. The raccoon trots right past the rock, retrieves a gray feather that has fallen on the ground, and brings it to her.

Shay sighs and places the feather next to the raccoon's previous deliveries: an assortment of leaves, stones, shards of pottery, and one small animal skull. If this exercise is any indication, her plan is never going to work.

Shouts ring out, coming from the front of the house. Shay wraps Najla in a blanket and quickly ties the baby to her back. As she rounds the corner of the cottage, the brothers come into view. They're crowded around a body slumped on the ground.

She jogs up to them, panting. Hunched shoulders shift aside, giving Shay the sense of reliving a memory. Tarik lies sprawled on the ground as the brothers take turns kicking him.

"What is going on here?" The infant squirms against her back, and Shay sways side to side in a soothing motion. "Someone, please explain."

Aidi plucks his reed hat from the ground and smashes it over his balding skull. He flings his arm out, pointing a gnarled finger at Tarik. "He's the one who gave Snow to your mother."

Shay gasps, the words cracking in her ears, spreading like a fissure over ice through her mind as she slowly comprehends their meaning. She looks from one brother to another and finds confirmation on each face. "How do you know?"

"He admitted it," Bono growls.

Shay raises an eyebrow, needing to be certain. "Was that before or after you knocked him senseless?"

"What did you think?" Tarik strains to lift his head. He coughs, pinpoints of some blue-black substance flecking his chin. "There would be no consequence for your ill manners?"

"My what?" Shay sputters.

"You could have accepted my gift," Tarik moans hoarsely. "But no, you thought you were too good for me."

Shay shakes her head in disbelief. "Are you telling me my mother, my baby sister's mother, is gone because I didn't want a pair of gloves that were literally stained with the blood of a dead woman?"

Tarik coughs again, spewing more gunk. "She was a terrible mother anyway."

A metal *clank* rings out. Kabeer brandishes a dagger, the long steel blade glinting in the afternoon sun. Shay's belly tightens, everything soft inside her turning hard.

"Brothers, hold him down so I may pierce his heart." Kabeer shakes the dagger. "Let's see how immortal he really is."

"Wait!" Shay holds her arms out and turns to Aidi. "Will that actually kill him?"

Aidi nods solemnly, the wide brim of his hat layering his face in shadow. "It is one of the only things that will. Even sunlight and starvation do little more than weaken them."

For a fleeting moment, Shay imagines the life that could have been if Hind stayed purged. Perhaps, once the Lallat reawakened, Shay would have moved to the Cerabbi region and returned to midwifing. They could have raised Najla near the sea, playing with sand between her toes and salt tangled in her hair. It would have been a simple life, but a good one.

Or maybe it would never have happened that way. Maybe Hind didn't have what it took to give up Snow, to put in the necessary work to build a better life like Khawla's mother had. Maybe Tarik was right, and she was a terrible mother.

Shay will never know.

This vile, heartless creature robbed them of any possible future. Anger uncoils inside her like a poisonous snake. Staring at Tarik, she unfastens the blanket and carefully passes the baby to Dasri.

She strides to Kabeer and stops in front of him. "Give me the knife."

Kabeer hands her the dagger without a word, his face unreadable. With a nod, the other brothers understand her intention and leap to restrain the bloodsucker before he skitters away. Shay stands over him, straddling his body. She shoves back the stray hairs stuck to her sweaty face. Heat beats down on her head like a molten crown. She squeezes the dagger in two hands, her arms held straight and stiff in front of her.

Tarik stares up at her. Something in his black eyes quivers, but his voice is smooth as honey. "You're no killer."

Najla begins fussing, and Dasri coos to her in an adorably exaggerated voice that would make Shay smile under less severe circumstances.

"I wasn't before," she says, her voice a calm match to Tarik's, gentle as a cooling breeze. "But that's the thing about people, Sidi—they can change. If given the chance, or the right reason."

"If you kill me, you'll regret it," the bloodsucker blurts, speaking so quickly that his words run together. "I have information that will help the Sisterhood in their mission."

Despite Dasri's earnest efforts, Najla's fussing progresses to low, drawn-out cries. Without turning her head to see, Shay hears the increasingly familiar sound of the baby sucking hungrily on her own hand.

"Do you think I'd believe anything you say at this point?" she snarls. "Or that I would allow you to live, knowing you could come after my baby sister next?"

"I—I would never," the bloodsucker stammers, now plainly afraid.

The baby is full-on wailing. *Hungry.* Shay knows from experience that if she puts off the inevitable, she'll be rewarded with the appearance of two dripping wet circles on the front of her tunic. Her tears may be impounded, but leaking milk does not seem to be an issue.

She releases all the air in her lungs in one gush and turns to Aidi, handing him the knife with shaking hands. "I have to breastfeed her. But no one kills him until I return, understand?"

"As you wish, Lalla," the elder brother concedes.

Shay takes the afternoon to think over Tarik's words. The truth is, she could use help with her mission. As little as she trusts the bloodsucker, she hasn't seen Shadi since before Najla was born, and she's desperate to make some sort of progress.

The bone-eaters have brought the bloodsucker inside and tied him to a chair. His head hangs down, so all Shay sees is the domed top of his black turban. Darkness is gathering. The walls glow orange from the lanterns set into each corner of the dining room. The brothers, who would normally be preparing to go out around now, sit or stand against the walls as though waiting for a show to begin—Kabeer even made snacks.

Shay walks over and stands in front of Tarik with her arms crossed. "Still alive there, Sidi?" She delivers a kick to his shin.

The creature yelps, his eyes flying open. "Oh good, you're back. Is your miniature bloodsucker satiated?"

Shay holds out her hand for the blade, and Aidi obligingly places its handle in her palm.

"I've been thinking," Tarik continues unabated. "If you must kill me, you should at least allow me to request a last meal, shouldn't you?"

"Be quiet and listen," Shay spits out, flicking the tip of the dagger beneath Tarik's pointy chin. "I might not kill you. Provided you give me the information you mentioned."

The bloodsucker smiles uncertainly, treating Shay to a glimpse of fang. "How do I know you won't kill me anyway?"

Shay shrugs. "How do I know you won't give me false information?"

Tarik bristles. "I've been around a long time, little dove. Long before Al-Mukhtar, and if we can come to an agreement, I plan to be here a long time after. Such an interminable lifespan does incline one to developing some sort of standard."

"That's it. That's supposed to convince me you'll tell the truth?"

"I may not always be straightforward, but I'm not a liar," the bloodsucker puts forth indignantly. "I know what this information is worth. It will change everything, little dove. And I'm not uttering a word of it until you untie me."

Shay pulls back the dagger and taps the blade against her palm. "You said you wanted a last meal, right?"

Stillness takes over Tarik's face. "I may have mentioned that."

Shay draws the blade across her forearm in one swift motion, hissing against the violent sting.

"Shay!" Deebi cries out. "Are you sure about this?"

Aidi steps forward, but Shay waves him back with her unwounded arm.

"I know what I'm doing," she says calmly. Blood ribbons to her fingertips, where it hangs, suspended in a beaded drop. Tarik strains his neck forward, fangs fully extended, drool dripping from his lips. "Here, I'll let you have a taste."

She lifts her arm over his gaping mouth. Her blood splashes his lips and chin. His eyes roll back, and his tongue darts out, lapping every drop. "Ah, as delicious as I remember."

"You're only going to make him more obsessed with you than he already is," Deebi warns. "Lallati, please think before you take this any further. You are clearly in grief."

"Shhh." Shay steps back from Tarik, splattering the blue-tiled floor in red.

He rocks the chair, edging it toward her. "It isn't good to waste."

She plants her foot on the seat to still it, right between his parted legs, and leans over, keeping her bleeding arm behind her. "If you want more, tell me how to destroy Al-Mukhtar."

"Wakha, anything." Tarik nods eagerly. "The most important things to know: Al-Mukhtar used bloodsuckers' blood to vanquish the Lallat. When ingested by men, our blood makes new bloodsuckers, but if ingested by people who have Shawafa, our magic doesn't mix well with theirs. It has some unfortunate effects."

"What happens?" Shay dangles her arm a little closer.

Tarik snaps his teeth.

"Uh-uh-uh," Shay chides, snatching her arm away again. "Continue."

"It turns them into crystal pillars. That's what happened to the Lallat. If the resistance were to gather all four of the talismans the Lallat left behind and take them to where the pillars stand, the spirits of the Lallat could be released from their stony prison."

Shay's mind backtracks to the night of Jou Boulka. Shadi's secret cave materializes in her memory. The stalagmites. The way one of them exploded with light when she held up the hjabat. "By chance are these pillars in a hidden cavern in Nezjar?"

"Just another sip, little dove; I'm begging," Tarik pleads. "I'm so very thirsty."

"Tell me *everything*," Shay demands.

"Yes, the last battle of the Time of Women happened in Nezjar. Toward the end, the Lallat hid themselves in a cave, but Al-Mukhtar found them. If their spirits were to be reawakened, natural magic could be returned to all women. In such an event, Al-Mukhtar would no longer stand a chance."

Shay's spine tingles. She imagines a world where women have magic and don't need Snow to activate it. It would be a boundless resource. And a heavy responsibility.

"And where would your alliance be, if there were another war?"

"With whoever offers a more viable food source." Tarik shrugs as though the answer couldn't be more obvious. "Imagine, subsisting off table scraps; it takes a toll over time. Forget the sun, I can hardly bear to stand in direct moonlight anymore. Look at me, tied by mere ropes that I should be able to snap with ease. I'm a shell of what I was, what I could be. There is no creature as glorious as a well-fed bloodsucker. Quench my thirst, and you'll see the difference for yourself." Tarik licks his lips eagerly.

"Well, thank you. But no thank you." Shay turns to Deebi, half-sick and half-giddy for what comes next. "Could you bring me some clover bean leaves? I need to bandage up this wound."

"What's this?" Tarik frowns. "I've given you all the information you required."

Shay ignores him until Deebi returns and her wound is covered.

"What are you doing?" Tarik whines. "*Little dove?*"

Due to Mukhtar Jawad's inaccessibility, she may not get an opportunity to avenge Ghita right away, but the creature who essentially took her mother's life to make a point—that point being that he *felt slighted*—is right here. Right now. And the Vampiiruh Presidium won't do anything. They basically give bloodsuckers free rein as long as they stick to their side of the forest.

"Kill him," she says to Kabeer, holding out the knife for him to take.

Kabeer sets aside a sandwich and grins merrily. "As you wish, lallati."

"No, don't turn around, little dove. Don't walk away," Tarik calls after her. "It's not me you want. It's not me who's truly responsible for all your sorrow. I can help you get to him. You want my allegiance? I'll do better than that. If you let me live, I'll help you get your revenge. I promise. Do you hear me, Shuika? ARE YOU LISTENING?"

She pauses. It's almost as if he read her mind. Shaking, Shay whirls back, interrupting Kabeer seconds before the blade takes its deadly plunge into Tarik's chest.

She leans over him, her hands clamped to his shoulders, her face in his, as if by getting as close as possible, she'll be able to assess his true intentions. "Who are you talking about?"

He swallows, trying, she can tell, not to stare at the vein that throbs along the side of her throat. "I know everything you have lost now, Shay. Glory to heaven, *you feel things so strongly*."

It takes her a moment to realize the extent of her mistake. *Memories.* She got the information she wanted from Tarik, but she gave him information about herself in return. "And?"

"Ghita, Khawla, Hind." Tarik recites their names slowly, and Shay almost imagines she sees her own unshed tears glistening in the dark pools of his eyes. "There is one man responsible for all this. Who kept your mother addicted to drugs all these cycles? Broke into Ghita's home with his armed soldiers? And if he finds out Khawla is a hizoura . . ." He makes a sad click in the back of his throat. "Well, you can imagine what he might do."

Jawad. Shay's fingers fist in Tarik's shirt. She squeezes her eyes closed. Inhales.

"I can take care of my father myself," Shay whispers, but the words are altogether weightless.

And Tarik *knows it*. He chuckles. "Listen, you're smart. The Sisterhood has their own agenda. They may be able to get you close to Mukhtar Jawad. Or they may not. You will be obliged to follow *their* orders. Me? I don't follow anyone's orders. Except yours, now. If you allow me."

Shay pictures Najla sleeping upstairs. Tarik poses a threat to her, but what about their father? Is he not the bigger threat here? "And how will you get to him?"

"I may need time to come up with a plan, but I have great sway with the Vampiiruh Presidium. I can start by making things . . . disruptive."

"I never want to see you within touching distance of my sister. In fact, I don't want you to look at her. Know what? Don't even think about her. Ever." Shay sighs, glancing over to find Kabeer sulking. She doesn't turn far enough to see the incredulity on the other brothers' faces, but she feels it all the same. "Do you understand?"

"Yes." Tarik nods emphatically. "Now, for the love of all that bleeds, please, untie me. My wrists are one of my most attractive features."

✧ ✧ ✧

Shay stares down at her nursing sister. Moonlight pours over her angelic face. Staring right into her eyes, Najla reaches up and curls her tiny fingers into the hanging threads of Shay's hair. Her heart swells until she thinks it could burst. This is it. The feeling she's been looking for all her life. The unconditional love she never thought she'd experience. The funny part is, she didn't have to do anything to earn it.

There's a soft tap at the door.

"Is it alright to come in?" Shadi's voice drifts through a slight crack.

"Hold on." Shay shifts the blanket covering her sister to hide her exposed breast. She resists the urge to jump up and greet him, not wishing to startle the baby after spending twenty beakers getting her to calm down.

Shadi sits on the floor next to her sleeping pallet. He stares quietly through the window, his eyes reflecting prisms in the starlight. Shay withholds the questions that bubble inside her, momentarily content to take in the contours and shadows of his profile. The slope of his nose. The strength of his jawline. The sweep of his brow. Even in the dark, he's as dazzling as any constellation could be.

"I'm deeply sorry about your mother," he says softly. "I wish I had been here."

Shay waits, wondering if the tears will come now. The force of a tidal wave bears down on her. But nothing falls. Maybe she's in shock. Maybe she cried too much while her mother was alive. Maybe she already spent every day of her life in mourning.

"Where have you been?" she asks, suddenly hit with the delayed sadness of his absence, this loss she's had to grapple with alone.

"Did Kabeer tell you I've been stopping by?" Shadi asks, a trace of annoyance making its way into his voice despite the measured expression on his face.

"No." Shay makes a mental note that it's perhaps time for another "family" talk with the brothers, one hood-wearing brother in particular. "What did he say to you?"

"He told me you were resting, and to come back later." His lips twitch as he fights to keep a straight face. "And when I came back, he told me you were still resting."

Shay lowers her head, shaking it, her lips sliding toward a grin. "How did you get by him this time?"

"This time I went to the back door," Shadi explains, and winks. "I bribed Hammu with a bag of shiny baubles."

"Well, I'm glad you're here now."

She adjusts her tunic under the blanket and tucks the edges of it around her sister's sleeping body, soaking in her dimples and pudge, imprinting this moment in her mind so she'll always remember why she must fight.

Why the Sisterhood must win.

Shadi leans forward, his eyes wide with awe. He smiles up at Shay. "She's beautiful."

"Do you want to hold her?"

Before he can protest, Shay leans forward and takes his arm in her hand, guiding it around until the bundled infant is nestled in his elbow. He stares tensely at the baby for a few beakers before his shoulders relax.

"See?" Shay says approvingly. "It's not so hard."

Shadi continues gazing at the baby for a while longer. Then he looks up at Shay with a new hesitation in his eyes. "You're beautiful."

Heat fans up Shay's neck, and she's grateful for the cover of night. She's heard the words before, but those other times were unmemorable. This is the first time it's mattered. "I wish I saw what you see."

"Shuika." Shadi looks at her the way an astronomer might behold the mysteries of the heavens. "You're always thinking about other people, but I hope you know you're allowed to think about yourself sometimes."

His words ring true, as if he can see into her soul, all the insecurities she clings to, the pieces of herself she gives away. As if he sees the parts of her even she doesn't fully know yet—not only who she is, but who she could become.

He lays Najla gently on Shay's sleeping pallet and takes both her hands in his. "What do you want?"

His fingers twined with hers are warm and firm in the darkness, their breaths mingling in the air between them. Shay doesn't have an ultimate answer to his question, but she has an immediate one.

If she cannot release her sorrow by crying, she'd like to feel something good, at least.

"This," she whispers, and closes the gap. Their lips meet, merging like two candle flames in a surge of heat and radiance. Despite the certainty of danger and the uncertainty of everything else, Shadi's touch, his kiss, feels like safety. It's a feeling Shay wouldn't mind getting used to.

A sudden scratching at the window breaks their fledgling kiss, striking a cold spear down Shay's spine. She tenses and slowly pulls back from the sweet cocoon of Shadi's arms.

Tarik? No, the bloodsucker isn't going to bother her. For now, they have an alliance. And Shay has to admit, she's relieved. Whether or not he deserves to live is debatable, but that wasn't her decision to make. She was lashing out, wanting to hurt someone else the way she was hurting. Wanting to take back a little of the power that had been taken away from her. And Tarik was . . . there. That wasn't justice, and she would have come to regret her rashness.

The bloodsucker was right. Shay isn't a killer.

But *something* is scratching at the window. And it doesn't sound like a tree branch shaken by the wind. The noises are too organized, purposeful, as if whatever is out there is desperately prying their nails under the pane, straining to lift it. Her heart balloons into her throat, but as Shay inches toward the window and draws the curtains, she realizes she can sense the friendly, if annoyed, nature of her visitor.

Hellooo! Let me in!!

A face stares back at her, two black beady eyes like olive pits set inside a rind of dark fur. A glossy nose presses against the glass at the tip of a very recognizable white muzzle. The raccoon has somehow scaled the side of the cottage. Shay lifts the window.

The raccoon scrambles through and drops a shimmering object from its mouth onto the floor with a small *clunk*. The animal chitters, as if berating Shay for her delay in opening the window. When it has chastised her sufficiently, it sits back on its haunches.

Perplexed, Shay picks up the object—the *hjabat*!

Glory to heaven! Between caring for Najla and the situation with Tarik, she forgot it outside after hiding it beneath a rock. It was absolutely careless of her. Perhaps understandable, considering she has to wake up a hundred times a night to feed a newborn now and can hardly be expected to function at a normal level of awareness, but *still*. Imagine if she'd lost it. Good thing the raccoon brought it to her—

Wait . . .

The racoon brought it to her.

Judging by the mischievous sparkle of its eyes, Shay would have to guess it could have done that from the start if it *wanted* to. The tricky bandit was probably playing games with her all morning for the sheer enjoyment of prolonging their exercise.

She turns her gaze from the animal to Shadi, who has been watching all this unfold with a look of intense curiosity and some amusement.

"I had an idea the other day, of how we can get the remaining hjabats," Shay explains. "It seemed like a long shot, but . . . I'm beginning to think it could actually work."

32

The Lost Treasures of Moonsin Maroof

Once, a very rich man named Moonsin Maroof wanted to marry, but he did not want his wife to know how rich he was. He hid his treasure in caves and near wells and asked the spirits of these locations to watch over it for him. He had such an excess of wealth, he couldn't keep track of all the exact locations, so he arranged a password with the spirits. If he ever got turned around, he only had to utter the word, and the spirits would guide him to his fortune.

He would often go to visit his treasure, only to remind himself how rich he was, and did this at the neglect of his new bride. Assuming he was having an affair, she followed him one night. She began to allay her loneliness by using the password she overheard and helping herself to his treasure. First small amounts, then eventually enough that Moonsin noticed.

He accused the spirits of stealing from him, and as they had only helped him and asked for nothing in return, they were understandably upset. They buried Moonsin's treasure deep in the earth, at new locations, scattered far and wide. The spirits then took the ungrateful Moonsin's wife for themselves, leaving him alone with nothing. The wife bore children, and the descendants of these children, known by the strange marks they bear on their body, are able to locate the hidden treasures, many of which are still out there. Waiting to be found.

It takes a large part of the little time they have, but Shay begins to learn the capabilities of different types of animals, which ones are less cooperative due to their disinterest in pleasing humans—cats and reptiles—and which are most educable—rats and, surprisingly, pigs. She practices joining consciousness with them and trains herself to maintain that connection across progressively wider distances.

By the time she feels ready—relatively speaking—to attempt obtaining the first of the three missing hjabats, there is only one moon quarter remaining before the meteor shower occurs.

Shay rides the skies behind the eyes of a midnight iris. When they clear a massive cliff that appears to float on the horizon, she gets her first glimpse of water. The glittering waves appear all at once, blue suddenly stretching in every direction. As impressive as that is, it doesn't prepare her for what comes next: a plunge into the depths of the Cerrabi.

Underwater, Shay inhabits an octopus. There's a heart-stopping moment where she is uncertain whether she can breathe. Then she remembers that her body is still in Ard Al-Ghul at the brothers' cottage. She's in an altered state, but able to take in and expel all the air her land-dwelling lungs require.

She skims along the watery floor, past intricate shelves of coral reef and scintillating schools of silver fish, toward the submerged caves. The octopus's panoramic vision is not unlike that of the bird, but where the bird's vision encompassed a wider range of colors than Shay is used to perceiving, octopus vision consists of fewer colors. Extraordinarily, the creature is able to adjust the focus of its eyes when traveling from well-lit environments to darker ones, like the cave of Chefrika. It's as though the octopus has field glasses and light beams built right into its eyeballs and the muscles around them.

Her vision changes again when they locate the chest hidden deep within the cave. As she persuades a wrench crab to help pick the heavy lock that seals it, the world becomes a mosaic of overlapping images. The creature employs the extra pincers its species is known for with a deftness that puts even Shadi's burglary skills to shame.

It's a dizzying ride as she transfers her consciousness back to the octopus again. The necklace, a baroque red crystal girdled in brass prongs and strung upon an antiquated chain, is ferried across the ocean floor in the bowl of an abandoned coconut shell until they reach the shore.

Shay prepares to head home with the iris, amazed at how successful this first leg of her mission has been. She almost doesn't notice the boat.

It's the B'hamu divers among the crew that first catch her attention, identifiable by the sleek one-piece garments that cling to their forms. The sight of them here on the coast of Lahat would not be alarming in itself. But peppered among the crew are other men wearing the checkered scarves that denote an affiliation with the Naturalists.

Shay's excitement stalls. She may be tired from her new mother-adjacent role, but it doesn't take a brain functioning on a full night's sleep to reach the conclusion that the CNM is here for the same reason she is.

✧ ✧ ✧

Shay opens her eyes. She's sitting in the grass outside the cottage, right where she's been all along. If she feels a little off-balance, it's a small price for such an amazing experience. The day is sunny and fair, the kind where clouds take on familiar shapes that change if you keep watching them, the sky putting on a grand show of metamorphosis.

"You did it," Shadi gasps, smiling as his gaze swings from Shay to the iris.

The bird perches on a tree stump, the necklace sprawled at its clawed feet. The prized jewel embodies every shade of red, all bedazzled by the sun. Najla gurgles in her basket nearby.

"I had some help." Shay bows her head toward the bird in deep gratitude. "I hate to ask for more from you so soon, my friend, but I fear our window of time grows narrow. How quickly can one of your brethren be available for the next journey?"

My successor will arrive tomorrow, the bird reassures her before taking off.

"Shay?" Shadi lays a warm, worried hand on her arm. "Don't you need to rest?"

Her body answers for her with an irrepressible yawn. In the quarters since her arrival, the baby has brought Shay much joy and little sleep. She's drained, both from the frequent breastfeeding and from expending her Shawafa. Magic turns out to be a lot like physical training—one must build up their endurance.

Shay feels it, deep in her bones and in the very fibers of her brain: She's pushing herself too hard. But what choice does she have? Besides, when she does manage to fall asleep, she sees her mother as she last did, face masked in death, like the image has been engraved inside the lids of her eyes.

"We can't wait." Shay picks up the necklace. She cradles the crystal, as if it could impart the strength she needs, and it does, to an extent. The heavy weight in her palm is evidence that she's already accomplished more than she thought she could. Its smooth contours and sharp-edged facets remind her that Khawla, Najla, and all woman who hope for a future of dignity and self-actualization are bound to the same pulsing red heart of a common destiny. "I saw a ship. There were CNM members diving near the caves. I think they may be looking for the hjabats, just like we are."

Shadi receives this news with an anxious intake of breath, his shoulders rising and falling like a crashing wave. If anyone besides Al-Mukhtar would want to prevent the return of women's magic, it's the Naturalists. "That means there's a good chance they also know where the other two are located."

"Exactly." Shay moves toward Najla, who has begun to suck on her balled fist, an early indicator that she needs to be fed. "We aren't just racing against the clock anymore. We're racing against opponents whose skills and resources I can only imagine must be superior."

"Don't underestimate yourself." Shadi's lips hook in a half grin, a breeze tugging errant curls across his forehead. "We have to take this one step at a time. We can't control what the Naturalists know or what they're doing. But we can make sure you're as strong as possible, which means eating, drinking fluids, and sleeping. I can't do what you do with animals, but I can lighten your load by helping care for Najla, by caring for you, so just show me what you need me to do."

A sense of wonder washes over Shay as she settles back on the grass, Najla now cradled in her arms. She stares into Shadi's warm brown eyes. She thought she was beginning to understand what love is, but the way he seems to understand her needs without her saying a word leads her to believe she has only scratched the outermost surface.

Another iris "carries" Shay over the towering peaks and deep gorges of Umm Chanala to the lush oasis of the holy institute. The complex is built abreast of a cliff face with a waterfall cascading next to it. The air in the mountains smells like damp moss, dry bark, and wild roses. The sun seems to shine not down, but suffusing in a golden aura that radiates from every direction. Here, her avian friend has arranged for another helper to take over: a monkey with ginger-colored fur and shy, contemplative eyes.

The institute's entry lies at the end of a cobblestoned bridge that crosses the polished-mirror waters of Tafi Tafi Springs. The group of pilgrims departing with several Marabouts pays no mind to the monkey as they pass it along the bridge. The long sticks they carry and the broad hats they wear suggest they're heading out for a hike.

The entry is unguarded. The benevolent Marabouts fear no intruder, placing their safety in the remoteness of their location, their trust in the Creator, and their lack of any known enemy. The monkey creeps into the complex as if it's used to doing so, moving quickly between objects, sticking close to corners, finding cover when a human happens to be near, and avoiding what few busy areas there are.

The afternoon is quiet. The trill of warblers drifts in from the bushes outside. Though it's bigger than the kasbah, the institute is designed and decorated with an eye toward simplicity. Many of the rooms hold no furniture, sometimes no more than a prayer rug, a framed scripture tacked to the wall, and windows that draw the eye outward to the breathtaking views. The hazy glow of sunlight reaches every nook, illuminates each dust mote. A mellow infusion of rose petal and musk perfumes the air.

The monkey, to Shay's chagrin, makes an impromptu excursion to the kitchens. It pilfers a handful of berries and a half round of khobz before making its way to the wing that houses the Marabouts' sleeping quarters. Here, rather than pallets arranged low to the floor, the beds are raised on wooden frames. But even these are plainly made, chosen not for luxury or aesthetics. Their function is practical, making it harder for insects to reach the mattresses, and necessary, given the multitude of open doors and windows and the proximity of the surrounding nature.

The sleeping quarters consist of long areas, containing beds arranged six to a room, an identical box sitting under each bed. While the boxes, carved of beautiful and fragrant thuja wood, are no more locked than the doors, there is no way to tell which holds the hjabat.

Though Shay is reticent to comb through the Marabouts' personal belongings, the monkey holds no such compunction. It empties each box, one by one, spilling its contents onto the bed above it. Among these are functional items like brushes, soap, and tooth sticks, along with spiritual artifacts like remembrance beads, wooden incense chips, and small, pocket-sized books of scripture.

They are three beds into their search, halfway through the first room, when a Marabout clears his throat.

Shay never heard him enter the room.

He sits cross-legged in the middle of the floor, wearing the traditional garments of his vocation: a long robe sewn of mismatched patches from used and discarded clothing, turmeric-yellow slippers, and a white knitted cap. Seeing him, the monkey drops the stack of letters it is holding and hastens toward the door.

"Wait," the Marabout calls, firm but commanding. "Come here, monkey. Come, come."

Shay isn't sure whether it's she or the monkey who decides to obey, but they trot up to the Marabout all the same. He has leathery skin, bright eyes, and a paltry mustache. His face lends itself to the illusion of being both young and old at the same time. Shay assumes he's older. It seems more logical for an old man to appear young than for a young man to appear old. He stares into the monkey's eyes for a long time, his expression inscrutable.

"Greetings of peace to you," he says finally. The monkey smacks its lips loudly, which the Marabout seems to accept as an appropriate response. He leans forward, and the monkey leans back to a matching degree. "Please, sit still."

He leans forward again. This time the monkey tolerates his closeness. As he peers deep into its eyes, fragrant oil wafts from his skin. "Is there someone . . . *Lalla*?"

A jolt of shock reverberates through Shay's body, or her mind, or *something*. He can't know she's there—well, not there *there*, but observing what's happening there from where she is. And yet, the man is nodding profusely as if agreeing with himself.

"Oh good," he declares cheerily, covering his mouth with his hand in surprise. "I've been expecting you. Well, I wasn't sure, but I certainly hoped." He rubs his hands together. "Hold on."

The Marabout rises and dashes over to the last bed at the end of the room. He kneels to open the box underneath, shuffles through it momentarily, and returns with the earrings. They're made of green crystals, two halves of a teardrop-shaped whole, dangling from silver filagree hooks. He places them into one of the monkey's rather grubby-looking hands, folding its other hand over them.

Still looking into the monkey's eyes, which feels very much like he's looking into Shay's eyes, the Marabout recites in a reverent hush, "Our Lallat are waiting to be restored. The keepers of treasures, the fairest four."

Shay tries to thank him, but the monkey only chatters its teeth, which ends up sounding vaguely threatening. At that moment, another Marabout enters the room. Beholding the mess on the beds, the newcomer gently scolds and shoos the monkey away.

If the Cerrabi Sea and Umm Chanala Mountains were wonders to behold, the colossal extravagance of the Grand Palace is astounding.

Shay's helper for the third and final day of her mission is a common rat, a creature of higher intelligence than most people perceive. Its strong memory and ability to navigate complex environments make it perfectly suited for the task at hand.

In the stillness of night, they infiltrate the shimmering palace, so tall that its gleaming dome is visible from almost every point in Kiddah. They enter from the south side, near the stables, and traverse a series of gardens and courtyards en route to Mukhtar Asim's private chambers. Moonlight adds a layer of opulence to the stucco walls carved with swirling arabesques, the cedarwood ceilings painted in languid florals, and the floors paved with marble and zellij tiles.

There's a fountain built into one wall of the sleeping chamber and a blazing hearth set at the opposite end, an extravagance during such a warm season. A folding doorway stands half-open, revealing a balcony with a quaint breakfast table, and across the room, the mukhtar's bed is nestled into an alcove. A dark-stained wooden frame lifts a mattress piled with rich textiles, all ensconced by a sheer canopy suspended from the ceiling.

Mukhtar Asim is a heavy sleeper. Unfortunately, the hjabat is not around the man's wrist, where the Lallat said it would be. Though the rat proves adept at turning things over and squeezing into tight spaces while making minimal noise or disturbance, their long and thorough room search turns up nothing. Aside from the discovery that Muktar Asim has a fondness for women's lingerie, a fact Shay could, frankly, have lived without knowing.

It's only when she questions the rat, who has inhabited the walls of the palace along with its small colony since resting season, that she learns two unfamiliar humans were sneaking around a few nights prior. The rat is, however, unable to describe the intruders beyond the details of their footwear.

Both trespassers allegedly wore midsized boots caked with fine silvery dust the rat described as *carried in from a far-off region.*

33

"Our son did not return from volunteer service better. Quite the opposite. I fear for his mental health and future relationships. He behaves reasonably enough with his father and brothers, but he has started treating me like I'm his inferior. And his sisters, they refuse to be alone in the same room with him now."

—the testimony of a mother choosing to speak anonymously to the Nezjar Gazette *about her son's experience in the Moulay Training Program*

Shay is starting to doze off when the image materializes. The same, always the same. Her mother's face, pale and drained of life. The trickle of blood from the corner of her mouth, like a careless smear of lip paint. She looks almost restful, but if Shay doesn't open her eyes fast enough, those still lips will snap into a rictus of rotting teeth. Her white eyes will pop open, glowing with something not quite there, but not quite gone.

"Are you well?"

Shay gasps awake. Shadi sits beside her on the pallet with Najla cradled in his arms.

"I'm . . ." She blinks a few times to clear the clinging remnants of horror. "I'm fine."

"Did you have a bad dream?"

Shay wishes she slept long enough to have one of those. "Yeah."

He glances around the room, probably realizing for the first time that her mother died there. "Maybe we need to move things around. Put your bedding in a different position and change out the décor. At least until we can find a new place for you and Najla."

He doesn't say *with me*. But Shay wonders if he's thinking it. She nods.

"Noojla is freshy changed and swaddled. I think she's ready to eat." He hands Shay the clean and bundled baby and looks away as she lifts her shirt.

Shay kisses the top of the baby's head, smelling her new-baby smell, like fresh khobz. It washes away more of the dream that was too short to be a dream.

By the time Shay nurses the baby and puts her to sleep, Shadi has gone downstairs and returned again with a tray of tea and snacks. He peels an orange and hands her a slice.

"Thanks," Shay says, licking the sweetness from her lips. "I really appreciate this. You. That you're here. That you kept coming back even when Kabeer turned you away."

He laughs. "You can't get rid of me that easy, Shay."

"Seriously," she says, accepting another slice when he offers it. "You're spoiling me."

"Just wait until we go to the Island." His eyes get a far-off look. "I'll serve you fruits you've never even laid eyes on before."

"Where?"

"Oh." His face stills. He seems to consider that he has slipped up in some way and then decide it doesn't matter. "The Sisterhood headquarters are on an island. We call it the Island, which isn't very original, but don't let that fool you into thinking it's not amazing. Because it is. And I can't wait for you and Noojla to see it."

Shay thinks this over quietly for a moment. It does sound nice. But he seems to be forgetting what happened yesterday—or, more accurately, what didn't. Even with Shadi lending a helpful hand, it took Shay a day each to retrieve the necklace and the earrings, and another day to fail to do the same with the bracelet.

"Unfortunately, my task is incomplete, remember? Four days from now, I'm supposed to deliver four hjabats to the Morchidat, and I have only three, because someone—the Naturalists, I'm assuming—got to the fourth one before I did."

Khawla is still in enemy hands. The window to return women's magic and defeat Al-Mukhtar is closing. Shay suddenly feels a lot less hungry. Well, that's not entirely true, but she's a breastfeeding woman now. She *would* feel less hungry if that weren't the case.

"I'll leave this afternoon and talk to her," Shadi says decisively.

Shay chews her bottom lip. "Do you think you can get her to meet with me again?"

"If it's fine with you, I'll just take her the hjabats we have." Shadi sips his tea thoughtfully. "They have to count for something."

A knock sounds at the door. It isn't a loud knock per se, but it's a bone-eater knock, so yeah, it's loud. Shay freezes, looking over at her sleeping sister to make sure she hasn't been disturbed. Then she tiptoes as fast as she can to the door.

"Kabeer!" she whisper-shouts through the wood, not wanting to risk the baby-rousing creaks it will produce if she opens it. "I told you a hundred times not to knock like that. And before you ask, yes, I feel safe with *that boy* in my room."

"There are visitors for you downstairs, lallati," says Deebi, this time.

Visitors? Shay's first thought is the Morchidat, but Deebi said *visitors*, as in more than one person. Her second thought is Khawla's parents, which at first terrifies her, but then she thinks . . . *What if there's good news about her rescue? Or maybe she escaped?*

Shay rushes downstairs, but it is neither the Morchidat nor Khawla's parents she finds chatting with Bono and Beni about the widespread news of a recently discovered dragon fossil.

"Shoodi!" Yara squeals when she sees her brother, running to tackle him in a hug.

When Yara releases him, he hugs Marjan, who returns his embrace with no less exuberance.

Soon, they are all sitting at the dining table having tea, because if Mekchaouenians have one motto, it's *anytime is teatime*. Yara and Marjan both fawn over Najla, who, of course, woke up at the sound of new voices. Despite the tea being the best she has ever tasted—Yara made it—and the pleasant flow of their conversation, unease simmers in Shay's stomach.

Absurdly, she wonders if the Morchidat somehow already knows about her failure and has sent the sisters to assist her. She can't help noticing that their travel bags are large enough to carry overnight bedding, indicating that they have either traveled a far distance to get here or plan to travel somewhere else when they depart. And Marjan carries a lacquered wood bow and a quiver of feather-fletched arrows on her person, further indicating that their journey has been—or is expected to be—beset with danger.

"We are so deeply sorry about your mother." Yara lays her hand gently on top of Shay's. "Surely from God we come, and to Him we shall return."

"Is that why you're here?" Shadi asks, as if it has only just occurred to him that there may be a reason for their unannounced arrival. "Did Mmi send you to give her condolences?"

"Well, no." Marjan fiddles with the string of the bow she placed on the table in front of her when she sat. She glances at Yara. "But she has sent us with a message."

Shay tenses. Her breath tumbles through her lungs, hard as rocks.

"The astronomers have adjusted their original prediction," Yara says, and pauses for a well-timed sip of tea. "The meteor shower is now coming in two days."

"Can they do that?" Shay asks. "Just change their minds?"

"It happens." Marjan shrugs. "Although I do believe our head astronomer is growing a bit senile."

Yara looks at her sister aghast.

"What?" Marjan frowns. "I'm just saying I wouldn't mind seeing a bit more of that cute young apprentice of his."

This earns her a second look, this time from Shadi.

"Oh, don't you start."

"This isn't good," Shay says, trying to rope everyone back to more important matters. "I've been able to recover only three of the hjabats, and I have reason to believe that CNM members have taken the fourth."

Marjan and Yara both stare at Shay with the same blank looks.

"We should all go to the Island," Shadi says.

"What?" Shay turns to him, not sure she heard him right.

"We should pack up Najla and go with my sisters. If we all talk to Mmi, we can present a united front. Shay has more than earned admittance to the Sisterhood by obtaining two hjabats completely unassisted. She's also learned the location of where the Lallat's spirits are trapped, in a crystal cave in Nezjar, where we are to take the hjabats during the meteor shower. There is too much at stake to put this all on her shoulders when the Sisterhood has other resources we could utilize."

"United front?" Marjan shakes her head, wheezing. "Have you met our mother?"

"Mmi left the Island before we did," Yara says, somewhat apologetically. "She seems to think this new archeological discovery is in some way connected to the Lallat. She's probably somewhere in the middle of desert by now."

How could an ancient dragon skeleton possibly be more important than this?

Shay's mind hearkens back to Shadi's words about the Morchidat having a reason for everything she does. She wants to believe that is true in this case, but a small voice in the back of her mind warns that even if the Morchidat is somehow doing what is best for everyone, it is not the same as what is best for *Shay*.

"We will simply have to find a way to recover the last hjabat from the CNM ourselves." Shadi says, but his words don't thrum with the same conviction as the ones he spoke moments ago. "Surely, between the four of us, we can think of something. I'll gather a pen and parchment, and we can map out the known CNM bases. See which is closest to the caves."

"There is another option," Marjan says quietly. "One that offers a more precise direction, but also carries greater risk."

Shadi, already half out of his chair, sits back down. "I'm not sure I like the sound of that. But do tell us, khti."

"The night hags."

Shay murmurs a blessing of protection. She's still not exactly sure what a night hag is, but that may not be the most pressing question. She winces before she asks, preemptively disliking the answer, "And how will they help us, exactly?"

"The night hags have the ability to inhabit the human dreamscape," Marjan explains, staring at her tea as if talking to someone located at the bottom of her glass. "This allows them to scry the collective subconscious of humans for information."

"Dreams are where we process memories of experiences that took place while we were awake." Yara picks up the thread, her eyes flicking once to Shay before settling in front of her. "So, if anyone is thinking about the hjabat while they sleep, the night hags will be able to tune in to that."

"Which makes them the perfect spies," Marjan concludes, ending with a smile that looks more like a muscle spasm.

It gives Shay the distinct feeling that there's something Shadi's sisters aren't saying. Something they don't want to say. "Do these night hags usually grant their assistance to humans who request it?"

"She's smarter than she looks." Marjan smirks.

Yara blanches. "Why are you this way, Marj?"

"It was a compliment," her sister insists.

"They usually take something in return . . ." Shadi says, a crease rearranging his brow.

Of course they do. Despite feeling like she might throw up, Shay nods, encouraging any one of them to explain in further detail.

"To enter the dreamscape, the night hags need a conduit," Marjan says. She slides a hesitant eye first toward Yara, then Shadi.

"One human must volunteer to be their entry point," Yara adds, "through which they can access the wider dreamscape."

It doesn't take a scholar to deduce that since Shay is the one who has been tasked with gathering the hjabats, she'll be the one doing the "volunteering." A chill roots into her bones.

Shay sips her tea—which really is *remarkably* good. "What will they do to me?"

"We haven't decided who—" Yara is cut off by Marjan's lethal stare.

"They take a little piece of you while they're in there." Marjan taps a finger to her temple. "They could choose anything. A talent. A specific memory. A person. The ability to feel a certain emotion. It'll be gone, just like that." She splays the fingers of her hands like exploding bamboo bangers. "Poof."

Shay immediately thinks of how awful it felt when Tarik tethered himself to her mind, but this sounds worse. What's worse than losing a piece of yourself? Not even being aware it's gone.

Yara releases a worried breath, seeming attuned to Shay's distress. "We could draw straws or—"

"I'll do it," Shadi says. "Shay has done enough already. She's lost enough. Already."

"No," Marjan says, her voice a whisper that carries the strength of a shout. "It can't be one of us. Not after what happened to Mmi."

Shay gulps. "The Morchidat has done this before?"

"Yes," Yara says timidly. "A long time ago, and whatever happened, she's never done it again. We don't know for sure what they took, but Marjan, Shadi, and I . . . we have a theory that it was her fear."

Shay can see how that might be true. It also doesn't seem like the worst possible outcome. "Is that so bad?"

Marjan narrows her eyes to withering slits. "Fear is pretty essential to survival, Shay."

"What Marj is trying to say," Yara amends, "is that we worry about her constantly now."

Shay understands. They love their mother and don't want to lose her, and if the configurations of scars the Morchidat wears with pride are any indication, she may have had more than a few close calls with mortality. Shay thinks, one by one, of all the feelings, all the memories, all the people she doesn't want to lose.

She hits a sore spot when she comes to Khawla. She imagines them then, the thoughts she's held back all this time on the thinnest of leashes, thoughts of Khawla being abused, being forced to use Snow, becoming an unwilling tool in the hands of the enemy. Being made into an addict.

Shay can't let that happen.

She has to do something.

She extends her spine, like an animal trying to make itself look bigger. It can't be all that bad. Maybe the hags will feel generous and take some of her pain. She certainly has enough of that to spare. "Where do we go to find these night hags?"

"Shay—" Shadi starts to protest, but Shay turns to him, planting a finger firmly to his lips.

"It's fine." She quickly peeks into Najla's basket on the table, then leans over, removes her finger, and kisses him. Suddenly. Urgently. Pulling back when they both are breathless, and his sisters have had a thorough inspection of the floorboards. "It's fine."

She knows she should come up with a better argument than those two woefully inadequate words, but he seems to understand what she isn't saying. That she needs to do this. Because while Jawad may ultimately be responsible for what happened to Hind, and Ghita, and Khawla, Shay still blames herself. Still feels like she needs to atone. And maybe if she does this one big thing, she will be able to finally forgive herself for every costly mistake she's made along the way.

"We can go to the dream caves tonight," Marjan says, regarding Shay with a glint of newfound respect. "They're just inside the boundary of the forest."

Shay nods. "I'll pack up Najla's things."

Yara gasps, then sputters, "Y-you can't take a *baby* there."

"It's too dangerous," Marjan agrees.

"But I'm breastfeeding her," Shay argues, assuming that will settle the matter.

"Can't you squeeze out some milk or something?" Marjan asks.

"She's not a cow!" Yara argues.

"Marjan's not wrong," Shay says thoughtfully. "I could express milk and leave Najla with Shadi. He's so good with her. I just worry I won't be able to express enough. Or that she won't take it from a glass or spoon."

"I can help with part of that," Yara says. "My affinity as a hizoura revolves around remedies. Teas mostly, but everything from tinctures to soups. I could make a fortifying drink that will increase your milk flow, and you'll be able to leave enough to last Najla until your return."

"I can help as well," Marjan says, more quietly.

Shay turns toward the other sister, waiting for her to explain.

She clears her throat. "I, um, have some experience with sewing prosthetic breasts. If you have a bit of goat skin and a few other materials available, I can make a feeder that Shadi could strap onto his chest. It would simulate a real nipple. At least, I think it will be close enough to work in your absence."

Shay sees it now. What Shadi was saying about Marjan having a golden heart. She smiles. "Thank you. I love that idea." Then she turns to Shadi. "And will you fare well alone with the baby?"

"Of course," he says, without hesitation. "Will you? Fare well leaving her?"

Shay turns to the wide-eyed infant. So small. So helpless. So utterly dependent.

Part of her is saddened by the thought of being away from her.

But part of her is relieved.

And Shay hates *how much*.

She's also wise enough to know her relief is simply a feeling. A symptom of being overwhelmed, saddled with a new responsibility she was unprepared for.

It does not mean she loves her sister any less. Or that she won't continue to take good care of her. It will just be good to get away, only for one night—or maybe two if they succeed in locating the last hjabat. Even if she is going to the dream caves to open her mind to the mercy of creatures who scry dreams and steal fear.

She has to assume they won't be cute and cuddly to look upon either.

✧ ✧ ✧

"I have to sleep in there?" Shay stares down the dark gullet of the dream caves, the lantern she holds up of little avail. Instead of casting a forward glow, the light seems to cringe away. The shadows are so deep and still and solid, they've grown a skim of dust.

Her mother's face flashes in her mind. There's a feeling in the air here or, more accurately, an absence of feeling. A void. A heaviness that isn't heavy and a coldness that isn't cold. A feeling Shay is starting to recognize as death.

"We'll be with you," Yara says empathetically.

"And don't worry about not being able to fall asleep." Marjan's voice is calm, but the deep caves give it a distorted ring. The lantern makes her eyes flicker and flash. "They aren't called the dream caves for nothing."

"Is there anything I have to do?" Shay asks warily.

"They won't force their way into your mind," Yara says. "You have to accept them in."

Marjan visibly shivers. "No matter how terrifying they appear."

The opening here is much larger than Shadi's cave. Nothing about this place is hidden or secret or hard to find. The broadness itself feels like a trap. But as they make their way inside, multiple paths branch off, winding and narrowing. The sisters tell Shay there is no wrong choice. In the dream caves, all paths lead to the central cavern, the dreamer's sanctum.

"What is your affinity?" Shay asks Marjan, to make conversation.

The drink Yara prepared for Shay worked as she promised, allowing her to leave Shadi enough milk for a couple of days. Enough time for them to secure the last hjabat and take it along with the others to Shadi's cave before the meteor shower. Marjan's feeding device came out perfectly, too, though that was more ingenuity, less magic.

"I have really good aim." Marjan mimes pulling an arrow from the quiver at her shoulder, drawing the string of an air bow, and releasing it.

"I think you meant to say *unerring marksmanship*. Don't be so modest, Marj," Yara says. "Tell her about the time you shot an arrow through that apple on Mmi's head at fifty paces when you were three cycles old!"

Shay marvels at the fact she's met not one but three other hizouras now. She used to think she was alone. That magic was something to be subdued at any cost, even her health. She marvels, too, that Najla won't have to feel that way in the likely case she's also a hizoura. She'll have Shay and two khalat to guide her. Three if Khawla comes back.

When Khawla comes back.

As they walk, a calm falls over her. A not-unpleasant sense of tiredness. She hears a sound. Not water, not wind, but something in between. A low, soothing hum that gets louder as they go along. The tunnel ends, opening to an expansive circular space.

The cave walls in the dreamer's sanctum have eroded, forming shelves of identically-sized alcoves, like cells in a honeycomb. Many of these are etched with crude drawings, symbols marked in overlapping layers, newer scribblings covering older ones until it's hard to make sense of either.

Some cells are littered with scattered bones.

Shay chokes on a dry cough. "Anything anyone wants to tell me?"

Marjan frowns. "Did I not mention that sometimes the thing the night hags take is the dreamer's life?"

"You most certainly did not."

"That won't happen," Yara quickly interjects. "It only happens to, like, evil people."

"That's a theory," Marjan corrects.

"No," Yara argues. "Mmi has researched the ghoul clans extensively. If you read her journals, you'd know it's a reasonable assumption based on known facts."

"That's exactly what a theory *is*," Marjan insists.

Shay strongly thinks someone should have mentioned this before they left from the bone-eaters' cottage, but there's no point debating it now, when they're already here. When that sound has gotten, not louder, exactly . . . but stronger?

It's almost like a vibration, so, yes, she thinks *stronger* is the right word. It's relaxing. Shay can tell Yara and Marjan feel it, too. They've stopped arguing and started swaying their bodies back and forth, back and forth, to the calming rhythm.

Without much by way of further conversation, they set up camp. Each girl chooses a cell to sleep in and rolls out their cushions and blankets for the night.

When Shay closes her eyes, her mother's face is not there. Her mind is blessedly blank.

It's a relief she doesn't enjoy for long, because the next thing she's aware of is heaviness, a bearing down in the middle of her chest. She struggles to breathe, to roll over and change position. She can't move.

Her eyes flick open and go wide, beholding the creature perched on her body.

Night hag.

Shay tries to swallow her panic, but it goes only halfway down her throat before coming back up kicking and screaming.

Though the hag is crouched over her, Shay can tell she's tall. Long, straight dark hair falls over her shoulders like a veil. Her skin is alabaster white. Her eyes sockets are gouged, empty black pits from which some dark substance leaks, spilling down her pale cheeks in jagged smears. Her mouth hinges open as though eternally frozen in a muted scream.

From shoulder to elbow, her arms appear normal, but from the elbow down, the skin melds into thick black scales that end at her sharp-taloned fingertips. Her chest is covered by glossy black feathers that tip silver in the strange glow Shay realizes is coming from the cave drawings.

Clicking sounds, like nails scrabbling over stone. The whispery rustle of feathers. Shay lifts her eyes, searching the far reaches of the cell. More creatures crowd around her. She tries to count them, but the effort makes her dizzy.

The hag slowly extends a taloned finger and presses its pointed hook to Shay's temple. She scratches lightly. Shay would not be able to stay still if she had any choice. Every muscle in her body screams at her to thrash, resist, flee. The hag makes a moaning sound, and though whatever she's saying is unintelligible, Shay understands her request.

Her tongue loosens. Despite the burning desire to scream for help, she instead rasps out, "Yes, you can come in."

The sides of the hag's mouth twitch into a grotesque mimicry of a smile. The talon digs into Shay's temple, drilling deep into her skull. Pain eats through every thought until there's only the whoosh of flapping wings. Then she's airborne.

She looks down from the night sky upon the realm of Mekchaouen from the perspective of a crow, but it's not like when she joined minds with the irises.

This view is impossible.

It appears as though she's flying at such a height that the entire realm unfolds below her, every region visible at once. From the wind-furrowed sands of the Mourian Desert to the moon-crusted waves of the Cerabbi Sea. With each flap of the giant crow wings stretched out to either side of her, her vision is spliced by unbidden images. Images that feel like memories. Memories belonging to someone else. *Dreams!*

Dreams of falling, of being chased, of bloodied teeth that clatter against the porcelain sides of washroom basins. Of dying, dying, dying again. Over and over. A hundred different ways.

No, not dreams.

These are nightmares.

The hags wheel across moonlit clouds, sifting through dream after dream, jumping from nightmare to nightmare, in search of a clue to the hjabat's whereabouts. They drag Shay along through a disjointed parade of humanity's most ardent wishes and basest desires.

A surprising number of dreams feature jewelry of some sort, and a fair portion of these involve engagement rings, specifically. Finally, Shay glimpses the bracelet. Where the other crystals are set into a metal or wooden base, the bracelet is a thick band made of blue crystal in its entirety.

The hag dips low in the sky. The streets of Nezjar spring up around them. They glide past the darkened square, the abandoned market, through slumbering neighborhoods. With each successive wing flap, the image of the hjabat grows clearer.

The night hag's clawed feet touch down upon the dry earth of a bramble-filled clearing beyond the medina. Shay recognizes the rocky hillside. The familiar cave opening wrought into its side.

She doesn't walk necessarily, but her consciousness glides toward the lights flickering at the end of that long tunnel. Those streaming ripples of red, blue, silver, and green. She floats past the ledge where she sat with Khawla and Shadi on Jou Boulka. Down past the glowing pillars and deeper into the twisting innards of the cavern. Through tunnels where tracks have been laid and strange equipment has been left behind. Tools of the like used for quarrying and mining.

In a hidden cubicle, not unlike the cell where Shay's sleeping body now lies, she comes upon two sleeping figures. The hjabat glowing from the wrist of one is so brilliant, its aura casts a flare that obscures the face—and other identifying features—of both sleepers. All Shay gets a clear look at is their boots.

Boots caked in a fine sheen of silvery dust.

Caw. Caw. Caw. The crows' calls fill her ears, each cry growing louder and brasher, overlapping. Amplifying. She winces her eyes closed, and when she opens them, she's back in the dream caves. The night hag pants, her feathered breast fluttering. She still perches on Shay's chest, her talon embedded in Shay's temple.

The hag jerks her clawed hand back. Pain sizzles in a white-hot burst. Shay's vision sears and blurs before slowly shifting back into focus. Something pale and wormlike hangs limply off the night hag's talon.

Shay instinctively recognizes it as a piece of herself that has been plucked from her mind like an apple off a tree. She knows not what piece, won't know until one day when she'll be straightening her thoughts like books on a shelf and come across an untouched hollow in the dust where *something* is missing.

Shay's heart lurches beneath her sternum, already missing the ineffable. The hag lowers the clinging morsel toward her wide-stretched mouth. *No*, Shay wants to whisper. Wants to shout. *It's mine*. But whatever it is the hag has chosen to take, she swallows it down whole with a wet gurgle.

34

Breaking announcement:

Researchers have discovered a new thousand-cycle-old dragon skeleton! The green-hued fire-breather was found in a riverbed in the Valley of Muttaharoun and is believed to belong to a new species, possibly a gandawar. "Aisha" will be displayed this tending season at the Natural History Museum of Kiddah. Get your tickets early!

Come morning, Shay's throat is thick with sleep. The cave drawings no longer glow. Her right temple throbs. The hag's assault has left no outward mark upon her, but the ghost of something lost hovers just behind her shoulder. A smudge, at the edge of her periphery. And the thought of turning her head to behold its full form strikes her with dread.

The girls pack up camp, stopping to regroup once they've put some distance between themselves and the dream caves. Only then, over an outdoor breakfast, does Shay relax enough to tell her companions about her encounter with the night hags.

"If the rebels who took the bracelet are at the crystal cave, we must depart at once." Marjan glances up from her plate of khlea and boiled eggs as if she expects an argument.

Shay nods. The motion sends a ripple of pain through her forehead. She chews a bite of jam-smeared khobz, which makes it worse. Though the forest shade blocks all but the faintest trickles of light, the day feels too bright and glaring. She wonders how Najla is getting along.

Yara lays a cool hand on her arm. "Have you figured out what they stole away?"

"Marjan is right." Shay ignores the question. She doesn't want to tell Yara that it hurts to think about it. Literally. Each time she makes a conscious effort to take stock of her mental landscape, it feels like she's stabbing herself in the eye with a fork. "The meteor shower is when? Tomorrow night?"

Yara sips her cold tea and sighs. "I hate to poke holes in this plan, but have we considered that if the rebels are at the caves, that probably means they know we need to take the hjabats there? We could be walking into a trap."

"You think they know about the meteor shower? I didn't get the impression that the CNM put stock in things like signs and omens," Marjan says, and something in her tone makes Shay wonder whether she puts stock in them herself. "All the more reason to get there early, though, and during the day, so we can surprise them. And Shay said she only saw two of them. We already outnumber them by one. Sounds like good odds if you ask me."

Shay looks at Yara, expecting her to issue a rebuttal. To point out that Shay *seeing* two rebels is not the same as there *being* two rebels. But she seems to restrain herself, perhaps concluding, as Shay has, that they don't have to rush in blindly. They can do a little surveillance once they're in the vicinity. Assess the situation. Because while Marjan may be wrong, she may also be right. And there's only one way to know.

Shay just keeps thinking about the boots, how they reminded her of the boots *Moulays* wear. About how, while it makes sense that Naturalists on a mission would wear the same style of boots as another type of soldier, Shay has not been around many Naturalists. Not enough to pay attention to their footwear. Would they wear the same boots worn by Moulays? Or would theirs be different?

As they finish eating and clean up, Shay's breasts begin to ache. She wonders again how Najla is. How the brothers are coping with caring for a newborn. As much as she has come to think of the bone-eaters as an oddly wholesome sort of family, she can't help questioning her own judgement in leaving a newborn human under their supervision.

The wave of pain that rips through her head with that last thought is the worst one yet. It's enough to make her forget what she was wondering about at all.

✧ ✧ ✧

Shay summons the crooked-necked deer, who again agrees to be their forest guide.

While it's obvious the animals are able to exert some amount of autonomy, Shay is unsure how much of their compliance comes down to her hizoura magic being persuasive. She resolves to only ask for things that are necessary, until she can figure out something more conclusive.

More than once along the journey, Marjan orders them to stop. She peers into the forest at their backs and asserts that they are being followed. After a few rounds of this, with Yara dismissing whatever Marjan heard as just *an animal, the wind, a falling branch*, Marjan lapses into quiet. But her manner remains tense. Watchful. Her body language picking up where her words left off.

Upon arriving at their destination, the team decides to monitor the entrance of the cave. They find an abandoned barn nearby with a loft that offers an aerial view. Half the afternoon creeps by; no one comes or goes. Then Marjan suggests they enter the cave after sunset, while the rebels sleep.

"Or, hear me out," Yara says, "we could go in now, because if they're using the cave as a base, they could be out scouting or gathering supplies during the daylight hours."

Marjan looks at Shay. "What do you think?"

"I don't think we should go in without knowing what's waiting for us." Shay peers at the cave below. Next to the entrance, there's a flash of white fur. The shaggy leaves of a clutch of blackberry bushes stir. "Can I see the field glasses?"

Shay stretches on her belly to get closer to the small window. She presses the cool brass of the eye cups to her face. The view from the device is clear and crisp, though incomparable to sharing vision with a bird. A goat emerges from the bushes and slips inside the cave, seeking shade from burgeoning sun of late sowing season.

Shay lowers the field glasses and looks at Marjan and Yara. She momentarily debates with herself the necessity of what she has in mind and decides the current mission requires using every available resource. "I have an idea."

The goat is able to take Shay only as far as the ledge that overlooks the pillars. From this vantage point, she detects no sign of the rebels. Courtesy of an obliging spider, she scales the side of the rock face in a dizzying descent, gliding in leaps and bounds down a silk thread dragline. The spider turns out to have relatively poor eyesight, but its elongated legs can navigate tight spaces, and their vibration-sensitive touch aids in her tedious search around the base of the pillars and the floor and wall areas of the surrounding cavern.

Shay returns to herself once she has something to report. One second, she's inside a diminutive creature in a dark environment, and the next she's back in her fleshy body, the day around her deliriously bright. She flops back on a bale of brittle hay.

"What are you doing?" Marjan asks.

"Acclimating?"

"Did you see any sign of the Naturalists?" Yara asks.

Shay pushes herself up, smiling despite her disorientation. "No, but I found the bracelet. They must have assumed the cave was a safe place to leave it hidden."

"We have to go now," Marjan says urgently, grabbing her bow. "The Naturalists may return when the sun sets."

She insists on one last perimeter check, again making sure no one has followed them, before they head into the caves.

For Yara and Marjan, it's their first time seeing the crystal stalagmites. They bask in the awe of them. While Shay is not immune to their splendor, she's quickly realizing that getting to the bottom of the cavern is not going to be such an easy feat in their human bodies.

She studies the steep drop, her stomach quivering. Footholds are scarce, the distances between them wide. Slick dampness coats every crevice. It would be a treacherous endeavor for even the most skilled of non-arachnids who had the forethought to bring along equipment suited to the task.

"Shay?" Marjan whispers, an uncharacteristic touch of wonder in her voice. "You're . . . glowing."

Shay nods absently, assuming she's referring to the general radiance the pillars cast. Then she follows the path of Marjan's astonished gaze to where the hjabats are secured beneath her tunic. The pouch holding them glows with silver, red, and green light through the thin fabric. "Oh."

She feels it then, a vibration over her skin, like the hjabats are humming with energy. Like they're *waking up*. "*Oh*."

The two girls huddle close to Shay as she discreetly reaches beneath her tunic, something she's gotten proficient with thanks to Najla's lack of regard for time or place concerning her food supply. She unties the pouch and hands the necklace to Marjan, the earrings to Yara. She cradles the ring in her cupped hands. The pillars below flare brighter, as though fluorescent lava flows beneath their stony surface. Yara gasps as every crack and crevice of the cavern illuminates.

Then something more remarkable happens.

The face of a different woman appears in the crystal of each jewelry piece.

From the planes of the ring, Iman blinks at Shay, the silver streaks in her hair a match to the color of her gleaming eyes. From the surface of the necklace, Noor smirks, her lips ruby red against dark skin. Rabia smiles, her face split between the two earrings, green leaves tangling in the thick coils of her hair.

"Well, isn't this a precarious situation?" Noor's buoyant voice startles Shay, almost causing her to lose her footing. "You might even say you've found yourselves 'out on a ledge.'"

Shay's gaze darts from the necklace back to Iman's countenance in the ring. She wonders why the Lallat haven't used this form of communication sooner. "You can appear in the talismans?"

"Not usually," Iman clarifies. "Only when the hjabats are all in close proximity to the pillars we're trapped inside."

"This is amazing." Yara titters, also looking quickly from the earrings to Shay and Marjan and back down again, her grin growing wider and wider. "Isn't this amazing?"

Marjan, who seemed as amazed as her sister a moment before, now shrugs dispassionately. "It's a neat trick for sure, but we kind of need to get the bracelet before the Naturalists show up, so . . ."

"About that . . ." Shay ducks into her shoulders. "The bracelet was tucked away in one of those tunnels at the bottom of the cavern," she explains, to which Marjan frowns.

"Do we have enough energy to help them out, Sisters?" Rabia asks, her voice melodious and serene. "Since they've gotten this far?"

"I believe so," Iman confirms. "Put the hjabats on, and we'll see what we can do."

Glancing at one another, the girls each slip the piece of jewelry in their grasp onto their respective finger, neck, and ears. Instantly, both the jewels and the pillars blaze so bright, Shay clamps her eyes shut and throws her arm across her face, ducking to better shield herself. The blinding glare recedes, and when the glow dims enough for Shay to rub the fractured stars from her eyes, she peeks around.

She and her companions are no longer standing on the ledge. They've been transported to the cave floor, and the brilliant stalagmites now tower over them. All three seem to have the same thought at once, peering down at their hjabat for further guidance, but the faces of the Lallat have vanished.

"Figures," Marjan grumbles.

"Shhh . . ." Yara tilts her head, her face intently focused. "Listen."

Voices. Though the conversation is muffled, Shay thinks she hears one male and one female.

"I thought you said the Naturalists weren't here?" Marjan whispers-shouts.

"I didn't see them," Shay says. Then she thinks of the strange tracks that ran through the deeper tunnels of her dream vision. "Unless there's another entrance . . ."

Without further discussion, the girls move together to the outer wall of the cavern. They mold their backs against it and inch their way toward the mysterious murmurs. At a tunnel opening, a distinct blue light glows, coming from further down the narrow passage. The voices seem to have faded.

Yara's gaze travels from the blue glow inside the tunnel to the similar green, red, and silver glow from the other pieces of jewelry. She whispers, "Rasha's hjabat. It has to be."

Tingles course over Shay's skin in scintillating bursts. She and Marjan both nod. The tightness of the passage allows them to enter the tunnel only in single file. Shay goes first, nauseous excitement frothing in her belly. She's followed by Marjan, then Yara.

The clotted shadows of the tunnel are skewered by blue beams of light. Closer, Shay traces the telltale glow to where the bracelet dangles from a fist-sized protrusion of rock along the side of the wall, just high enough to be out of reach.

She looks back to check on her companions, reassured to see the red glow of Marjan's necklace and the twin green lights of Yara's earrings. Closer still, she makes out the shape of a shallow alcove that shoulders the spot where the last hjabat rests.

But it isn't resting at all, is it? That would imply the bracelet came to be in this most alluring position all on its own rather than being planted here, like cheese wedged on a mousetrap. Shay's excited tingles turn to spikes of alarm, needling across the back of her neck and down her arms.

The cave tunnel is silent but for the soft thread of Shay's breath interweaving with Yara's and Marjan's. Where did the voices go? She runs her palms along the back of the alcove, the light of her ring illuminating the stones in silver splashes. There's a small shelf at the back. Just high enough that if she steps upon it, she'll be able to reach the hjabat.

If it is a mousetrap, she can't find the hidden springs. She glances back at Marjan.

"Go ahead." Marjan nods. "I'll keep watch ahead, and Yara can look out from behind."

Shay takes a deep breath and steps upon the jutting rock lip. She stretches her arms upward, lifting on her toes. Rocks rumble and groan. The solid wall behind her shifts, a hidden passage yawning open. Her fingertips have barely grazed the hjabat when she's seized by phantom arms from behind. The cold blade of a knife angles against the bow of her neck.

"No one moves, or she dies."

The words are a sure threat, but the voice who spoke them calls tears of joy to Shay's eyes. She chokes out, "Khawla?"

Marjan and Yara turn around at the same time. They step forward, one's face lit in red, the other green.

The arms tighten, the steel kiss deepening to a bite. "I'm not joking."

"Khawla, lower the knife," cries a young boy's voice from deeper down the newly open tunnel. "Those aren't Naturalists, and if I'm not mistaken, two of them are my sisters!"

For a moment the world holds its breath, and then the arms around Shay loosen, and the knife withdraws. Shay can't turn around fast enough. She hugs Khawla fiercely, but her friend's body remains stiff in her arms.

Shay pulls back. She gently cups Khawla's face and peers into the brown eyes she knows so well. But as blue-silver light plays over them, she realizes how haunted they look now. How distant and almost cold. Her friend is thinner. And her thick hair has lost much of its luster.

Khawla squints, and then her eyes widen. A flicker of recognition. Her guarded mask splits. "Shay? Is it really you?"

Khawla embraces her, the knife dropping from her hand, her body going soft.

When she leans back and tries to smile at Shay, it is an echo of the carefree smile she once wore. It's as if her lips can't quite uphold it, a foal on new feet. "It's good to see you, sahbti."

"Good?" Shay's voice cracks. "It is not good to see you, Khawla El Fessi—it is all the joy in the world rolled together." She hugs her friend once more, burying the tears she wasn't sure she could cry anymore in Khawla's nest of curls. "I couldn't bear to lose you. Thank God. Thank God. And thank God again for bringing you back to me."

"How did you escape?" Yara asks, stepping close to Khawla. "Why did you come here instead of going home?"

"Where did you come *from*?" Marjan asks at the same time, peering down the passage. "And how did you get the last hjabat?"

"We came through the tunnel system," Khawla explains, as she and Shay release each other. "Would you believe Al-Mukhtar uses these passages to mine crystal from the pillars? Turns out, that's the main ingredient in Snow."

Walid emerges through the alcove then, only to be tackled by Yara and Marjan. They tightly embrace their brother, still dressed in a Moulay's uniform. Khawla is dressed in the plain shift of a prisoner, but on her feet are boots that Walid must have given her. Boots that match his own.

"Where is Mmi?" Walid asks, when his sisters let him come up for air.

"Don't worry, Walood," Yara says tenderly. "She will be so happy to see you when we get back. Thanks to our merciful God, what a blessed surprise it will be."

Confusion passes over the boy's face. He glances at Khawla.

"She already knows we were coming." Khawla eyes them uncertainly. "The team told us to meet her here to give her the hjabat."

"What team?" Shay asks, her voice merging with Yara's and Marjan's in an eerie unison.

"The team that rescued me from the kasbah. They escorted us to Kiddah, where Walid and I retrieved the hjabat. We were warned to watch out for Naturalists, so when we heard your voices in the cave, we didn't know what to expect."

Shay remembers learning the hjabats' locations from the Lallat at the swamp outpost when the Morchidat asked her to wear the ring. So why wouldn't she have told them she was sending Khawla to retrieve one? Or that she'd been rescued, for that matter?

While everyone else tries to process all this, Khawla climbs up and grabs the bracelet. Her gaze flits from Shay's ring to the hjabats the other two girls are wearing, understanding sinking in. "Do we really have them all?"

35

Today marks the twentieth anniversary of the Great Rescue in the rural area of Rifchat. For years, the surrounding villages suffered at the hands of a cult that stole their children and kept them captive for nefarious purposes. On this date, an unidentified vigilante slew the cult leaders and left the missing children safe in a local prayer house. Two and ten out of the three and ten children who had been reported missing were returned to their families. The children were targeted for their physical differences, but none of those rescued showed signs of being true hizouras, authorities say. One girl was never found. According to a statement from her parents, she would be ten and six today. This event mirrors a similar event called the Little Rescue that occurred in Tiglah one year later, where again, all the missing children but one were safely returned.

—*the* Chanala Chatpaper

Khawla loops the heavy bracelet onto her slim wrist. The four girls stand before the glowing pillars expectantly.

"Were we supposed to wait for the meteor shower?" Yara asks when nothing happens.

Shay realizes Tarik never said anything about the meteor shower, even though he knew about the cave. "I'm not sure it works that way."

"Me neither," Marjan agrees. "It's more about the window closing after the shower, so as long as it hasn't happened yet, the stars should still be in alignment for this to work." She shrugs one shoulder. "If you give credence to that sort of thing, like Mmi does."

That makes sense, in a way. Perhaps the true urgency had less to do with the meteor shower, and more to do with Al-Mukhtar mining the crystal pillars and weakening the Lallat. But if that's the case, what are they supposed to do that they haven't yet?

Shay pinches the bridge of her nose. Maybe they should say something. Some kind of chant or blessing. She finds herself repeating the words she remembers the Marabout saying at the holy institute.

"Our Lallat are waiting to be restored," she says, hoping she's remembering correctly. "The keepers of treasures, the fairest four."

"Oh, I know that rhyme from childhood!" Yara exclaims.

"Me too," Marjan says, nodding together with Khawla.

Even Walid joins in as the girls recite the rest: "Rabia tends the earth, and Rasha draws the tide. With the sun, Noor dances, and on the wind, Iman rides. Earth, flame, water, air. We remember their names, our Lallat fair."

Shay waits for the pillars to blaze again with light. To explode or disintegrate, revealing the women trapped inside, their bodies preserved from the ravages of time. Instead, they slowly go dim. Within beakers, the entire cavern is doused in black pitch, broken only by the lesser glow of the hjabats. The sound of their worried breaths mixes with the plaintive *plunk* of waterdrops.

In the absence of their glow, the markings along the bases of the crystals become apparent. Long strips have been crudely shaved off. Chunks have been gouged out, leaving behind round divots like a wounded tree trunk.

Shay recognizes the dizziness early this time. She looks down at the ring, the black spot spreading from its center like rot across the rind of a fruit.

"We should all sit down," she tells the other girls. She thinks it better to avoid falling around so many sharp rocks.

The leaching darkness grabs hold.

✧ ✧ ✧

The Lallat sought shelter in the cave, not from Al-Mukhtar, but from the citizens of Mekchaouen. The men seeking to overthrow the sister-rulers had poisoned the public against them. They invented chemicals and toxins and used these to manufacture illnesses, destroy crops, and even induce destructive weather patterns. They falsely blamed these ailments on the Lallat, telling the citizens it was proof the women had fallen from His grace.

That He had appointed the men as His new leadership.

They'd incited a mob. The Lallat needed a safe place to strategize how they should respond—how might they convince people of the truth. But it wasn't long before their secret meeting place was discovered, and they found themselves face-to-face with twelve men.

"Alright." Noor glared hotly at her three sister-rulers. "Which one of you didn't understand the part where we weren't supposed to tell anyone our secret meeting location?"

"Lallat." Jawad Lazar stepped forward as the men's spokesman, while the other eleven watched the proceedings from an elevated ledge far up the cavern wall. "It is our hope that we can convince you to resign from your posts without struggle. Let us show the citizens of Mekchaouen that we can broach a new age in peace, leaving behind the dark days of magic and superstition."

Iman stepped forward, meeting him, her chin upturned. "You call anything you don't understand, anything you can't control, superstition. Anyone with the capacity to reason will see through your deception."

"You don't seem to understand," Jawad said, his calm tone at odds with the rictus smile strapped to his face. "People have enough to contend with trying to survive. They don't want to reason, not if they don't have to. They need only the assurance of food and shelter, the safety of their family. To believe they are righteous, that they have chosen the side that opposes evil. At the end of the day, most will not let something as indulgent as reasoning prevent them from a good night's sleep."

"You assume people are lazy," Iman replied with disgust. "That is a dangerous assumption."

"Not at all." Jawad waved his hands dismissively, making ripples in his long white robe. "I think most people are willing to work very hard to avoid this exercise you call 'reason.'"

While the two exchanged words, the temperature in the cave was rapidly dropping. Iman realized she was shivering, despite the thick wool of her djellaba. She glanced back at her sister-rulers, the fog of their breaths clinging on the air.

She turned back to Jawad. "What's going on?"

"This is exactly why reasoning is dangerous," Jawad jeered, his smile becoming narrower, meaner, like his mouth was squinting. "While you are busy reasoning, someone else is acting."

The hair on the back of Iman's neck teased to attention. A familiar figure materialized from the shadows.

Zubeda. Her closest friend. Someone with the potential to be more than a friend, she'd sometimes thought. Had she read those signs all wrong?

"I knew it!" Noor exclaimed, pointing a finger at Iman. "You told her!"

Iman gasped around the painful clenching in her throat. "I didn't want her to worry. I thought . . ."

"We were friends?" Zubeda finished, blue ribbons of Shawafa streaming from her fingertips. "Where was your friendship when my husband was engaging in dalliances and you could have read his thoughts but said it was an invasion of his privacy? When he left me, and you could have changed his heart to love me again, but you said it infringed on his free will? What good is magic if it has so many restrictions?"

While Zubeda spoke, a layer of ice formed along the inner walls of the cave. It became cold enough that soon, the Lallat would have to funnel all their available energy to staying physically alive. Accessing their Shawafas would be increasingly difficult. With twelve men and four women, their magic was the only thing keeping them from being overpowered.

The men on the ledge made no move to apprehend them. If they had weapons, they kept them hidden.

"We must drive them away while we can," Rasha said, as though Iman had telegraphed her thoughts. Maybe she had? Her mind was already feeling wobbly.

Zubeda raised her hands. There was an unnatural tinge to the vapors pouring off her fingers, the blue casting a darker pall. Iman's first thought was that the woman had imbibed. Strong drink was known to make a woman's Shawafa both more powerful and erratic. But her speech didn't slur. Her eyes weren't bloodshot.

Her pupils, however, were abnormally dilated.

"Zubie," Iman said, concerned when perhaps she should have been fearful. She found it hard to believe the nights she'd provided her shoulder to be cried upon, the hours of listening over tea, always assuring her friend she deserved better, had meant nothing. Hadn't they baked until they ran out of sugar? Hadn't they laughed until they wept? Hadn't they danced under the stars for the pure joy of being alive? "Did you partake of some elixir?"

"Just a special powder Jawad is testing out," Zubeda said. There was almost a hum beneath her voice, as if her vocal cords, as if all the muscles in her body, were strung a bit too tight. "It gives your Shawafa a boost."

Iman glared at Jawad, raising her eyebrows, quite certain this powder would prove to be as risky as the other formulas he'd come up with. Didn't Zubeda understand she was being used as a human experiment? "I thought you wanted magic to go the way of dragons?"

Jawad shrugged. "Sometimes, you have to use a bit of venom to create a cure."

Rabia eyed Zubeda's glowing hands with growing apprehension, her own fingers barely producing the smallest filaments of green. "You understand that the punishment for using your Shawafa to harm another woman is having it rescinded, don't you?"

"Those are your rules." Zubeda laughed haughtily, gesturing to all four sister-rulers. "They won't matter if you step down."

Iman felt the very blood inside her body begin to freeze, slowing to a slog through her veins. Rasha, who had spurred them to action moments ago, now sat on the cave floor as though too weak to stand. Whatever Zubeda was doing, she seemed to direct it with precision so it only affected the Lallat in front of her, not the men above, or Jawad, who stood behind her.

Iman touched the Shawafa inside her lightly. She drew on Waswasmin, the spirit speaker aspect of her silver pantheon. It allowed her to sense the exhaustion rolling off her sister rulers. Rabia's aspects of healing and plant magic were particularly affected by the sudden brumal temperature. Rasha's attempts to draw water from the cave walls only made it colder.

It would have made sense for Noor to call on her fire powers to warm them, but she had enough strength to focus upon only a single aspect. She chose Hamsamin, shield power, but not for herself. She passed the protection to Iman, while her own energy dipped lower.

At the time, Iman puzzled over this choice. She concluded that Noor wanted her to take responsibility for her mistake in revealing their location by being the one to fight back. Later, when she would ask, Noor would say it was because she herself was so enraged, she feared she would burn every one of the twelve men to cinders. That would have made them martyrs and endeared them to the hearts of the people. It would have led to more men rising in their place.

She'd trusted Iman to be more judicious.

It was a mistaken call.

Renewed by Noor's immunity, Iman tapped into her Shawafa again, this time feeling for any creatures in the cave who had not yet fled the bitter chill. Some ally of the animal variety. She found only the lingering spirit of a species long extinct. Somehow, its ghostly residue was enough for her to draw upon.

She transformed only partially. Just enough to taste the release of acrid chemicals from her digestive tract as they spewed into her throat, feel the sharp spark as they mixed with an enzyme secreted from her teeth. Enough for her breath to turn to dragon's fire when it left her mouth.

Iman didn't aim this fire at her sweet Zubeda. She couldn't. Not when she'd been manipulated, led astray. She directed this torrent of flame straight at Jawad's smug countenance. It melted half his face before Zubeda could pivot and send a cooling spray of ice to douse the fire. Jawad howled and writhed in torment.

The men who had been watching jumped into action, drawing bows and arrows that dripped viscous black with an unknown substance.

"Wait!" Zubeda screeched. The light in her hands blinked out all at once as she retracted her Shawafa. "Jawad said we would only apprehend them. They might yet willingly comply."

But whatever Jawad had said no longer mattered. He was passed out from the shock and pain. The stench of his crackling flesh slathered the air in putrid musk. The men had received prior instructions of what to do if things escalated.

The arrows found their targets, delivering the tainted blood to the Lallat's vital organs, where it swiftly took effect.

Did Zubeda come to regret her betrayal? Iman would never know. Surely, her friend was long released unto death by now, granted a closure to this cycle of life and admittance to whatever punishment or reward awaited her. Meanwhile, Iman's spirit stayed trapped in the cave with her sister-rulers. Their only hope was that one day the people would realize they had been lied to, that someone would remember them.

That someone would come back.

✧ ✧ ✧

A beam of moonlight shines down where a section of the roof has collapsed. The pillars have vanished. The floor is strewn with rocks and scattered with ashes like petals on a grave. Walid drifts about the cavern like a ghost, his arms heaped with the bones he keeps finding everywhere.

The girls sit up. They blink haze from their eyes and rub the various aches that plague them. They brush their sleeves. The hjabats have gone dim. The Lallat have not awakened.

Unless they left. Departed to attend such important business as confronting the rulers who trapped them and committed unspeakable atrocities in their absence. Shay gazes hopefully at the hole in the ceiling. But then, whose bones are those Walid is collecting?

No, the Lallat have not returned, at least not in the way Shay expected. She examines her companions more closely as she whispers to them and they to her about their shared vision. Or was it a memory? They all experienced it. *The Last Battle*. It was like they'd been there.

No one wants to be the first to mention the changes.

Small vines grow from Yara's scalp and twine through her dark hair like braids. A red stain darkens Marjan's lips, a crop of freckles sprinkling across the apples of her cheeks. Khawla's eyes have completely switched color, from mellow brown to eggshell blue.

Shay sees herself, too. In the sly glances of her companions, their rapid flashes of disbelief. She knows it without a mirror, how silver threads her hair like streaking stardust.

A clattering. Walid stands frozen in place, staring at them with wide eyes. His mouth opens and closes in soundless shock. The girls stand to help him pick up the bones he has dropped in a jumbled scatter.

He bows and lowers his head in reverence. He whispers hoarsely, speaking into existence the words the girls are not yet prepared to hear: "I, Walid Jelassi, am honored to be the first to pledge my fealty to the new Lallat."

36

A Hazmaggi elder has put forth the claim that her daughter-in-law is the infamous Morchidat. The woman reports that the resistance leader's real name is Jumana Rajja, and that she is responsible for the death of her son and keeping her two grandsons in secret locations where the family is unable to contact them.

—"Does the Leader of the Sisterhood Have a Sordid Past?" A special report

The new Lallat stumble into the night to find a crowd has gathered around the cave entrance. Some people are staring at the hole that seems to have opened up in the earth. Some are staring at the sky, which is abloom with shimmering arcs of light. The meteor shower has arrived, one night earlier than the last prediction.

Among the crowd are Naturalists wearing checkered scarves. Some of these begin to whisper, pointing at the girls.

"Is it them?"

"They wear the sacred jewelry."

"Should we apprehend them?"

"You girls must get out of here quickly."

Shay jolts at the voice. She turns and looks into the tattooed face of the Morchidat.

She notices several things at once. One, the suspicion with which Marjan regards her mother. It brings to mind all the moments Marjan stopped them on their journey, her nagging concerns that they were being followed. Another, the way Walid seems to wait for his mother's eyes to land his way, seeking some reaction he never gets. Lastly, she notices that the Morchidat shows no surprise about the changes in the girls' appearances.

"It's her. The one they call the Morchidat."

The Naturalists have increased in number. A group has separated from the peaceful onlookers and is forming a loose circle around them. Among these, men who brandish swords with blades too long and sharp-looking to be carried about so casually. The Morchidat draws her own double-bladed weapon. Flashes of steel shimmer in the blue-black darkness. Tension spikes through the crowd.

A deep rumbling draws everyone's attention to the line of trees that borders the nearby forest. A second later, all seven bone-eater brothers, plus some additional bone-eaters Shay has never met, burst from the timber at a running gait. They too carry weapons. Knives. Spiked Clubs. Chained balls. They head straight toward the encroaching Naturalists, who turn their blades away from the girls, toward them.

It would appear the brothers decided to break their rule about interfering in human affairs.

"Run!" the Morchidat shouts at Walid and the girls.

Shay runs.

She runs as if all their lives depend on it. As if the burning in the back of her calves, the deep ache in her heels, could bring back Ghita, bring back Hind. Bring back the unknown thing the night hags took from her.

Footsteps pound the earth as what sounds like a small group pursues them. In her periphery, Shay sees Marjan clutching a handful of arrows and firing them back in succession as they flee. Something tells her they all find their mark.

They run straight into the forest. The clash of swords and grunts of men ring in the distance behind them. Shay doesn't see or hear anyone pursuing them now. It would be hard if they did, for the forest seems to both open a clear path before them and close like a seam behind them. Branches bend. Trees collapse inward. Vines stitch themselves together.

Shay stops, gripped by panic.

"What's wrong?" Marjan glances around, assessing for threats, then into Shay's eyes.

"The brothers . . ." Shay turns back toward the medina, but she can't see the crowd anymore. She can't even see a path in that direction anymore. Panic eats the edges of her vision. Her throat is raw with it. "If the bone-eaters are there fighting alongside the Morchidat, who's with my sister? Who's taking care of Najla?"

Yara whispers something to Walid and Khawla, perhaps explaining that Hind died in childbirth. That Shay is now caretaker to a newborn.

"What do you mean?" Marjan says slowly. She shakes her head. Slowly. "Shadi is with Najla, Shay."

A bolt of pain blasts the base of Shay's skull, nearly knocking her off-balance. "Who is Shadi?" It hits her again when she repeats the name. She plants her hands on her knees and breathes deeply until it passes.

When she stands back up, Yara is giving her the saddest look.

"What is going on?" Shay doesn't like the way everyone is looking at her. The way they don't seem as worried about Najla as they should be. *She's a newborn!*

"Shay, we need to keep going," Marjan insists.

"What is going on?"

"The night hags took him from your memory," Yara says. "I'm so sorry, Shay."

Shay doubles over again. She can't think about the night hag. About the meaty thing that dangled from her talon, the thing that used to be a part of Shay. Doing so causes her unbearable pain.

Yara crouches next to her, telling her to breathe. Shay stands again. She shoves the heels of her hands into her eyes until her lids are painted with sparks, until she no longer feels like she is dying. Until she can focus on what Yara is trying to tell her.

"It's fine, Shay. Najla is well. I promise."

"How can you say that?" Shay screeches in frustration. "How can a newborn be well if no one is with her?"

"We have a brother," Marjan says carefully, watching Shay for any adverse reaction. "Our brother is with your sister."

"Walid is here with us!" Shay feels like she's losing her mind.

"Not Walid." Yara looks at Marjan, who nods. "A brother you haven't met yet. Let's go. You'll meet him when we get to Ard Al-Ghul."

"Another brother?" Shay doesn't understand why they never mentioned him before. "And does this other brother of yours know how to take care of a baby?"

"He's taking the best care of her," Yara says soothingly "I'm absolutely sure of it."

They continue on, moving at a quick clip, but no longer running.

"I don't understand," Khawla mutters softly, to no one in particular. "Why did you have to go to the night hags? The Morchidat should have told you where to meet us."

✧ ✧ ✧

As they approach the bone-eaters' yard, Tarik is outside, fussing over his shrubs, brandishing a shiny pair of oversized gardening sheers. He stares at the girls with unabashed awe. Wordlessly, he raises one hand in greeting, a gesture Shay returns.

Khawla does a double take, frowning. "Are you two friends now?"

"It's complicated," Shay hedges.

It is decided that Yara will go inside with Shay while Marjan takes Khawla home to her parents. Shay hugs Khawla once more, then watches her receding figure, seeing now what she didn't see inside the cave. What she didn't want to see.

The changes in Khawla are not just physical. The fearlessness she once wore like sparkling jewels has dimmed, and whatever mantle of leadership the Morchidat manipulated the four of them into inheriting is not enough to bring it back.

Shay finds this brother of Yara and Marjan's upstairs, sleeping on *her pallet*.

Najla is on her tummy, dozing on his chest, her little body rising and falling like a tiny ship with each breath he takes. The sight gives Shay a strange twinge in her chest she can't place. Part of her was worried she'd find the baby crying her lungs out in desperate hunger, and her relief that this is not the case acts as a balm.

She sets a lantern on the windowsill and clears her throat.

The boy opens his eyes. He sees her standing there, and a wide smile spreads slowly across his handsome face. Very carefully, and with the ease of someone who has practice handling an infant, he shifts the baby onto the pallet and rises.

He's walking toward Shay.

His arms are extended wide to his sides. His expression is joyful.

She's preparing to take about three steps backward to avoid what appears to be an incoming hug from a complete stranger, when he stops. Confusion flashes over his face.

"What happened to your hair?" he whispers. His eyes dip to the ring on her finger. "What happened to you, Shay? You don't look the same."

She flinches when she hears her name. Without thinking, her fingers glide through her hair, the soft strands glinting in the moonlight through the thatched roof. Feet pound up the stairs.

"Shhhh," she and the boy both say together when Yara appears at the top of them.

"Oh, sorry," she whispers. "I need to borrow my brother for a minute."

"But Shay just got back," he says. "And you have something weird in your hair, too, khti."

"I know. It won't take long." Yara gives Shay a lingering look before turning to her brother again. "I need your help with something important."

"Wakha," he says reluctantly to Yara. "Sorry," he says to Shay.

"No problem," Shay says. "I might go to sleep, honestly. But thank you. For taking over the care of my sister after the bone-eaters had to leave."

He looks more confused about this than he did about her silver hair. "Shay?"

He says her name like it's a question, and as little sense as it makes, she almost feels like she should know the answer. Like if she tilted her head just so, a different image would slide over the one she sees now. And this feeling that she is missing something would fade away.

But these are not rational thoughts. He must just be curious about what happened at the caves. Shay shakes her head, fighting a yawn. She should probably wait up for the Morchidat and the bone-eaters to return, but she doesn't know whether she could if she tried. Whatever she did last night in the dream caves, she doesn't think it counted as sleeping, not as far as her body is concerned.

Clearly, she's exhausted. "I'm sure Yara can fill you in. But, truly, I cannot understate my appreciation for the service you have provided. My sister is everything to me. From the bottom of my heart, I pray that God will reward you for this kindness you have extended to a stranger."

He doesn't look confused then. He looks hurt. Terribly, terribly hurt. Yara starts dragging him down the stairs, her hand gripping his upper arm so hard, her knuckles strain, but he keeps gazing up at Shay with wounded eyes.

She shakes her head again, turning toward her room. *Boys are strange creatures.*

She creeps into bed next to her sister and presses the softest kiss to the top of her head. It's silly, the urge Shay has to wake her up. She truly missed her. Also, her breasts are painfully full. But sleep falls over Shay like a quiet shadow.

She does not dream of her mother's face, not tonight. Not ever again. She dreams of another life. Battles she's never fought. Places she's never seen. Magic, love, and milestones that belong to someone else.

Someone whose spirit is now irrevocably tethered to her own.

37

A crystal mine in Nezjar has been destroyed in an act of terrorism by rebel forces. Four young women, suspected of using Shawafa as a means to work against our realm, are wanted for questioning. Please report any sighting of them to local authorities immediately so that peace may be quickly restored.

THE ARM OF GOD HAS MIRACLES IN ITS FIST!

—pamphlets dropped from hot-air balloons over all residential neighborhoods in Mekchaouen

The forest no longer frightens Shay. The places she once thought were inhabited by monsters have become her refuge, and the places where she most wanted to belong have been exposed as the seat of the truly monstrous.

There's dark beauty in the pathways between the giant trunks, beneath the sprawling shadows of twisted cedar branches. Unique plants wait to be discovered, and winding caves beg to be explored. Even the half dead creatures that call the heart of this slithering foliage home are growing on her.

It's here, in the quiet shade of a stand of twilight oaks, that the bone-eaters helped her dig her mother's grave. That was one moon cycle ago. She's come back today to pay her respects before she leaves for the Island. She does not know when she will return. Just that the Morchidat has told her the move is necessary, both for her safety and so that she, Khawla, Marjan, and Yara can be trained.

Laying her palm upon the flat stone that marks her mother's resting place, Shay closes her eyes. A soft breeze wafts over her, laced with the scents of burnt leaves and damp earth.

With the pillars gone, Al-Mukhtar will soon run out of Snow. Their web of lies will begin to unravel. The girls have scant time. They must harness their own powers so that when the women of Mekchaouen are ready, they can guide them in reclaiming theirs.

But they'll need more than power. They'll need strategy and negotiation skills. They can't defeat Al-Mukhtar without winning the support of the Naturalists and, though Shay may not like it, the bloodsuckers. At least the bone-eater clan has aligned themselves with the Sisterhood—or with Shay, as Aidi clarified when the brothers returned from their skirmish with the Naturalists.

"I'll take good care of her, God willing," she says, in case her mother's spirit lingers near the veil. She's let go of any bitterness she ever held against Hind. There's no use in wasting anger on people who are simply fallible when there is true evil in the world to contend with. "And I'll tell her that you loved her, when she's old enough to understand."

She looks down at her sister, tied to her chest with a sturdy cloth. The baby's eyes are wide and innocent. Shay makes two small balls out of plant wax and mud and fits them into Najla's ears.

She stands. She opens her mouth. She screams.

A scream to let it all out before she has to go pretend that a few silver streaks in her hair make her something better than she was before. That she would have accepted this responsibility if anyone had given her an actual choice in the matter.

A scream for all the women hurt by men with big egos and tiny hearts.

A scream for the women betrayed by other women who think it will gain them favor with such men.

A scream for the parts of herself she gave away before she knew their worth. For the part that the night hags stole. The something she cannot name but misses just the same.

A scream to remember that injustice is something no one should ever get used to.

Her wails echo through the treetops, quivering branch to branch, stirring throngs of birds to flight.

Quiet.

Then the forest screams back. A shrieking cacophony of hoots, chirps, yelps, caterwauls, and howls sets every leaf set to shaking with its collective power.

Power that belongs to her and always has.

Acknowledgments

My journey to publication has been a lengthy one, and many people have helped me in different capacities along the way. I wish I could thank each person individually, but in this limited space, I will mostly be including those whose support and care has impacted the creation of this specific work.

I first want to thank Allah, whose plans are always perfect. Whatever is good in what I have created, it is because He made it possible, and if there are any mistakes in what I have created, I take responsibility for those flaws.

The Lustrous Dark would not be the book it is, and may not exist at all, if I had not been blessed with incredible experience of being part of the Highlights Foundation's Muslim Storytellers Fellowship. Thank you to the Doris Duke Foundation for funding this one-of-a-kind program that has nurtured and uplifted so many Muslim creatives. George Brown, Alison Green Myers, Zaynah Qutubuddin, Jamilah Thompkins Bigelow, M.O. Yuksel, S.K. Ali, and Narmeen Lakhani, thank you for all you have done to usher this wonderful program into existence and foster its continued development and growth. You have given so many the gift of courage to tell their stories, and so many more will be gifted by those stories as they bloom and flourish. It is truly a sadaqah jariya—an act of giving that keeps on giving.

The Highlights Foundation does so much to give writers the tools to bring stories into the world that will impact children in positive ways, and their retreat center is my favorite place on earth to be. If you write for young people, please check out their courses, retreats, and scholarships!

A special thanks to the Storytellers in my YA fantasy peer group: Diana Ma, Heba Helmy, Zaynah Qutubuddin, Instisar Khanani, and Fatima Samatar. Jazak Allah Khair for your wisdom, friendship, inspiration, and the love you have shown to me and my work. You have made even the hard parts of writing and publishing brighter with your delightful humor and beautiful hearts.

I am so grateful to everyone at Peachtree Teen for being the fairy godparents that made my story a real book—a feat nothing less than magical. My deepest thanks goes to my editor, Ashley Hearn, who has been the greatest champion I could ask for and whose insight and vision has raised this story to new levels of potential. (Tarik also thanks you for convincing me to let him live to garden and be a menace another day!) Thank you to: copy editor Manuela Shadow Velasco, proofreader Stephanie Cohen Xu, associate managing editor Jamie Evans, the sales team at Candlewick Press, assistant director of publicity Sara DiSalvo and her team, and senior marketing manager Alison Tarnofsky and the rest of the marketing team. And a special thanks to editor Inès Ibanay for your warm words and help with Darija! As a debut author, it means so much to have such a remarkable team of passion and skill behind me.

Thank you to my agent, Lane Clarke, for believing in my writing and opening the door of opportunity for me after years of languishing in the query trenches! And many thanks to the entire Ultra Literary team!

My awe and eternal thanks to my immensely talented cover artist, Tom Roberts, and designer, Lily Steele, for giving me the dark, creepy, whimsical, epic cover of my dreams! It is so unique and eye-catching and more beautiful than I could have imagined.

As a writer of the introverted variety, I am so thankful to my writing bestie, Khadijah Van Brakle, for always having my back and being by my side.

Thank you so much to the early readers of *The Lustrous Dark*: Huda Al-Marashi, Diana Rodriguez Wallach, Melissa Kendall, Briana Garrett, Nadirah Ashim, and Sara Codair for your generous encouragement and valuable feedback.

I want to thank my family for all their antics and chaos! To my husband, Mohamed, and my sons, Zaid and Hakim, I love you and am so grateful for all the noise and color and joy you bring into my life. I wouldn't trade all our weirdness for the world! And a special shout-out to Hakim for your helpful suggestions when I was creating the night hags!

And lastly, thank YOU, dear reader. When I was young, books were an escape that got me through troubled times and bad experiences. If you find something in these words that touches you, something that speaks to your truth and makes you feel a little less alone, then I have done my job. Thank you for making my story part of your story.

A final note: It has been a challenge to edit and promote *The Lustrous Dark* while a genocide has been taking place. To try to enjoy seeing a long-held dream come to fruition while simultaneously bearing witness to the heartbreaking images of bombed and starving children.

But stories are one of the few things that give me hope for a better tomorrow. So, I continue to write, and read, and allow myself to feel the happiness alongside the grief. This story is a work of fiction, but the oppression it depicts is a very real reflection of our world, and so is the ability of good people to turn things around and fight together for a future that is fair and just.

Free Palestine! Free Congo! Free Sudan! And all oppressed people, everywhere.

About the Author

Loretta Chefchaouni is a former early childhood educator from Florida who writes for teens. Her fantastical tales turn grief and fear into myth and monsters and explore all the scary parts of being human within the safe space of stories. She is an alum of the Pitch Wars mentorship program and the Highlights Foundation's Muslim Storytellers Fellowship. *The Lustrous Dark* is her debut novel.

Instagram: @LoreChefWrites

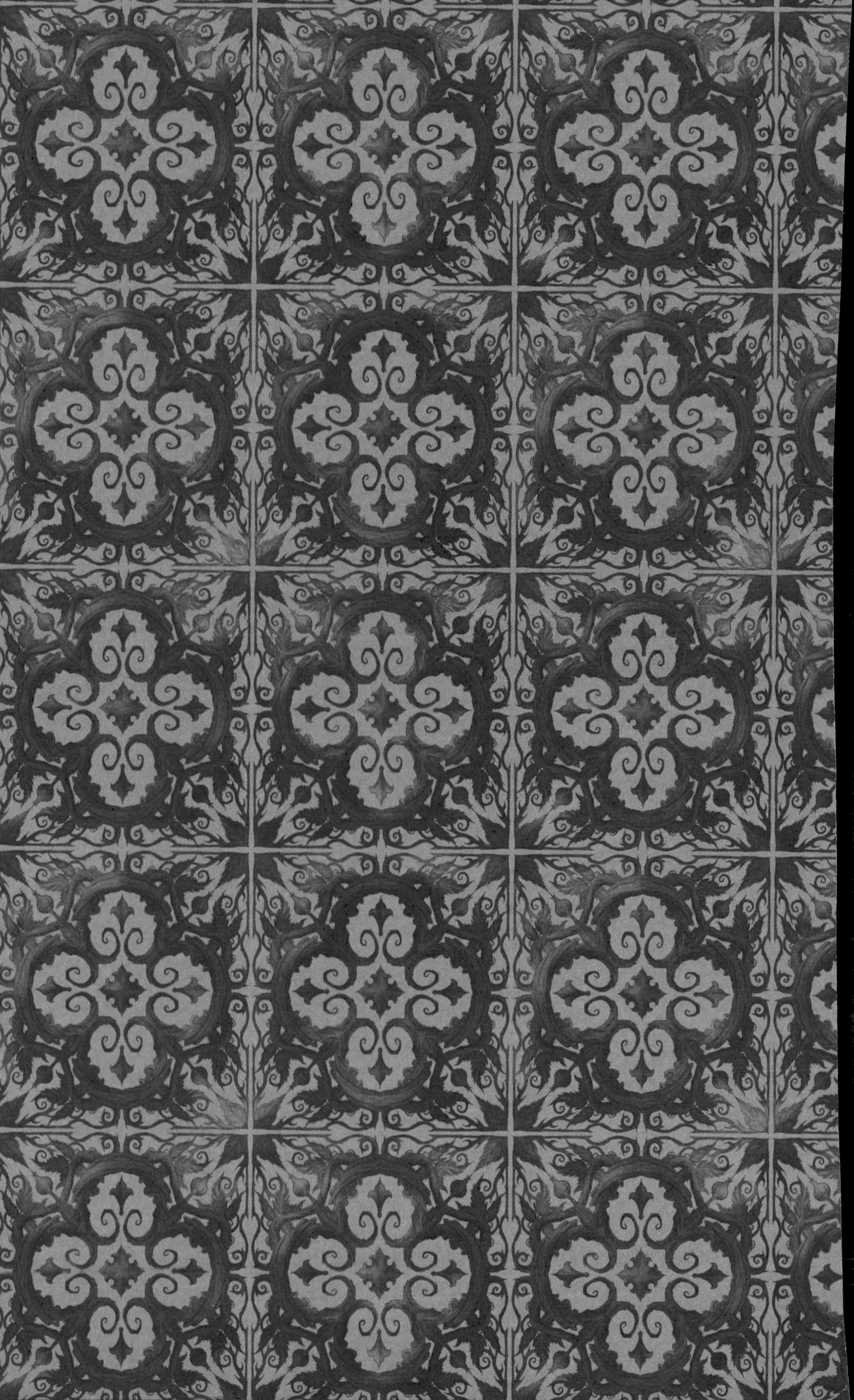